To Johnny Ashford

'Nijinsky'

Chapter 1
The Greatest Match Ever at the Manor

Oxford Utd v. Everton, 30th April 1986

Oxford United, at Wembley, April 1986. The Milk Cup final. 36,000 Oxford fans in a record OUFC crowd of 90,396. You could argue that this was the greatest match Oxford ever played, and anyone who has ever been to a football final will know that, despite the odds, it was still 11 v. 11 after all. Oxford had long been written off, but this team were skilful. They were battlers who had had their first season in the top flight and had been made to scrap for points and results every week.

They had easily swept through the leagues and into the 1st Division by winning the 3rd then the 2nd Division titles in consecutive seasons, both won handsomely and effortlessly. Life in the top division had proved more difficult – the legendary John Aldridge scoring 20 goals before the final, while his amazing striking partner, Billy Hamilton, had been injured and out nearly all season.

Of course, John had been at Wembley, travelling up with his Oxford buddies, the two Jimmies, Oram and Lorden, their mutual mate and United regular, Brian and John's father-in-law, Mick Hieatt. Ollie, his first son, was just a baby then. His headstrong daughter, Corine, still only three, had refused to wear the proudly-purchased new junior Wembley shirt, forcing John to return it to the Manor shop on the Osler Road.

The final had been an epic match. Oxford, with their star-studded mixture of youth and arguably 'ageing' experience, deserved to be treading the hallowed Wembley turf, after years as a fabulous lower League Cup team – a team that the legendary

Jim Smith had assembled following their resurrection under Ian Greaves.

In the final, Oxford started as complete underdogs. The punditry and media opinion was that they didn't stand a chance against the classy Queens Park Rangers. Bizarrely, Smith had moved on from Oxford and was the opposing manager in that final, the manager of QPR.

Trevor Hebberd, Ray Houghton and Jeremy Charles sealed a one-sided encounter in front of Oxford's delirious fans – on their first trip to Wembley – with a 3-0 win. The team had made its debut in the top league with some great football, amazing results and, in a relegation scrap since mid-March, taking a paltry total of just four points from eight games.

So, after the heady after-shock of the final and bringing home the trophy from Wembley, it was back to the reality of the fight for First Division survival. Incredibly, they still had four games left to play, due to the cup run and re-arranged fixtures.

Just six days after the epic lifting of the cup, Oxford narrowly lost away to relegation rivals Ipswich Town in a disappointing 2-3 reverse.

The remaining three games were all at home, against Everton, Nottingham Forest and, in the last game of the season, Arsenal.

The first of these was the midweek game under floodlights against Everton. Kick off; 7:30 pm.

Televised highlights of the match, pre-Sky Sports, would be shown later that night on the BBC, and it was a match that Oxford United simply had to win.

Don't argue. This was the best. Unmatched in atmosphere, importance, survival, guts and drama. Just ten days after their greatest win. Now, perhaps their greatest test?

From the outset, the atmosphere was electric. The London Road was full. In this season, most of the home matches had attracted around 10,000 fans, but on this night, there were 13,939 – the biggest crowd of the season. And a virtually full Manor.

The night was a deep cobalt blue, cold, clear and frosty. The lush and muddy green pitch was illuminated by the dazzling floodlights. The fans were jammed into the terraces, cramped and swaying, almost spilling over the white walls onto the pitch. This was intimidating and personal. The love and support for the team was palpable. The opposition, despite their lofty position in the league, must have been a little nervous.

In the London Road end, John, the Jimmies, Marc, John's mate from Grove and Tom (Tommy) Cannon, who worked with Marc, pushed their way upwards through the terraces towards the back of the stand. Many of the extra fans had chosen to stand, and the atmosphere in the stadium was super-charged, especially in the London Road.

The sea of yellow and blue moved and swayed and sang as one. The expectation fuelled the mood and the occasion.

Everton fans in blue and white had filled the Cuckoo Lane End. As title contenders, their team flew into Oxford in the early stages. They missed a handful of early chances. But on the counter-attack for Oxford, Billy Hamilton was unlucky when he hit the bar. Everyone knew what was at stake, and the Oxford fans were deafening in their raucous support. The atmosphere intensified.

The home team began to dominate in the second half, Hamilton again hitting the bar off an Everton defender, then Houghton being brilliantly denied by keeper Bobby Mimms after a great cross from John Aldridge. The crowd kept singing, a tumultuous chorus buzzing excitedly as the atmosphere became tense around the ground. Now Oxford attacks swept up the pitch time and again.

The Toffees were now battling flat out against the football and the noise, as every fan willed their team on to score. The crowd surged forward and spilled down the terracing with every near-miss. Everton couldn't get out of their own half, and Oxford kept sweeping forward. The cheers from the London Road reached fever pitch.

With just two minutes left on the clock, the Oxford players finally found a winning response.

A long ball was held up by Hamilton, and he turned in the area, laying the ball back to Les Phillips. The little midfielder struck the ball first-time, and his low shot flew into the net from the edge of the box.

It was as if the crowd had willed the ball into the net. The fans went into raptures at this reward for their vociferous support – such was the importance of the goal. Their relief *was* palpable. The team trooped off, knackered, after the final whistle. And the Oxford fans, still singing and on an incredible high, began to climb down the terraces to the exits.

Some of the players – tattered and scruffy after their exertions, and their socks hanging around their ankles – were grinning insanely, doing little jigs and applauding the crowd, thanking them for their terrific vocal support throughout the match.

The boys, applauding them back, filed down the emptying terraces as gaps appeared on the steps below, joining the jubilant throng that snaked past the London Road stand, ecstatic.

'Fucking hell!' exclaimed Tommy, as they waited for a space to clear below them.

'What a game! What an atmosphere!' cried John.

'Never experienced anything like it!' cried Marc shaking his head. 'Unbelievable!'

'Shall we go to The Butchers for a pint?' suggested Tommy, punching the air.

John looked at him quizzically. 'The Butchers? Where's that?' he asked, bemused. 'I've never heard of it!'

John and his mates usually went to the 'Britannia', the 'Black Boy' or the 'Quarry Gate', where they had been before tonight's game. It was easy to find a parking space, an easy walk in and an easy escape.

'The Butchers Arms in Headington, John!' retorted Cannon, with his lopsided grin.

Marc looked at John and raised an eyebrow. 'You up for a pint in The Butchers Arms then, chap?'

(He'd never heard of it either).

'Right, Tommy!' cried John, over the din of the escaping crowd, 'I'm not doubting your knowledge, but I've lived and worked in Oxford for ten years, and I have repped every pub, hotel, guest house and college for 30 miles; I don't believe I've ever come across a pub in Headington called The Butchers Arms!'

'You eedjut!' laughed Tom, grin widening. 'We always go there!'

'Whereabouts is it then?' John was still looking doubtful.

'Down the back of Lime Walk, past the "Brit".'

John thought for a moment. 'No way!' he declared. 'No fucking way! How much do you want to bet? A fiver?'

'Mate, I don't wanna take your money, but it is def-in-tely there, and I will bet you any money you like!'

'Come on then, my son, lead the way!'

As they stepped into the crowd now making its' way down the London Road exit, John said, shaking his head and smiling, 'There's no way, there's a pub down there, mate, that's a fucking easy fiver.' He winked at Marc.

'Well, he seems pretty confident, John, I dread to think where we're going if it's not there.'

'We might catch the late show at the Moulin Rouge!' suggested John.

Across the London Road in front of the Mirabelle Indian restaurant, the Jimmies turned left into the thinning crowd, saying their goodbyes.

'We'll soon see, mate,' said John, pushing ahead and waving a goodbye to the Jimmies and Brian.

They walked across the London Road, down past the 'Britannia' and onto Lime Walk. They turned left when they got to the crossroad, then took a sharp right down an alley for 50 yards and then took a left again.

One hundred yards along the road, a sign with 'The Butchers Arms' swung on the left, illuminated with yellow, red, and blue lights. Yellow light streamed from every window – The Butchers!

And that was it. John happily paid the fiver to Tom while buying the first round as the jubilant Oxford fans streamed into the pub, still singing. From that night on, The Butchers became their official meeting place and watering hole.

The Butchers was a Fuller's pub, so it always had *London Pride* by the pint and by the jug. Cheese and onion and ham and mustard rolls, football on the telly, convivial hosts – all spitting distance from the ground.

John could not believe he hadn't known of its existence. At least he knew now!

And Oxford were staying up. Hopefully! But this was a good first step! Just a matter of Forest and Arsenal next – should be no problem, right?

The crowd in the pub, already thick with yellow and blue, seemed to know the answer.

'U's are stay-ing up, I say U's are staying up!'

'U's are stay-ing up, I say U's are staying up!'

What a great night!

Chapter 2
Early Years

A stream of swooping starlings swept low over the trees, rising and falling as one, humming, whirling, tumbling and expanding, silvery wings dipping and glinting in the weak morning light. The distant hum of traffic infiltrated the early morning chirping and twilling of birds around the edge of the field where John walked with Sally, his border collie. The fields were blanketed in grey dew; the pitches, green and expansive, stretched into the distance, with sentinel-like rugby posts eerily looming through the mist, awaiting their next action. Dogs sniffled and rummaged in the hedgerows and on the banks of the nearby canal, and walkers mooched past, occasionally grunting a muted 'good morning' to each other.

Far-off barking and the occasional rumbling of an early morning train reached his ears as he exited through the canal gate back onto the Wasborough Fields. Apart from those noises in the early day, things were reasonably quiet. John loved it here for that reason, and he often brought the dog over early before too many people were about. But they also liked to come over in the late afternoons on the bikes with a ball, when the kids had finished at school. He loved to experience the noise and excitement of the junior teams while training with their over-enthusiastic coaches as they strove to make a team from a bunch of kids, raggedly running in all directions.

John and Lyn had moved into the country from Oxford in a bid to bring up their two children, Corine and Oliver, in a quiet and respectable area, just 15 miles from Oxford, but really in the very heart of the countryside. They had settled after Corine was born, and while Ollie was still in the making, in Sutton Courtenay, a beautiful little village outside Abingdon. Their life in

Oxford had consisted of John being a chef and Lyn a hairdresser. Both worked locally, Lyn close enough to walk up to the Slade, where she worked in a small, friendly salon. They had saved while John had worked split shifts, living in a flat donated by the company in exchange for John's promotion to Head Chef at 23.

A missed promotion where fifty percent of the board wanted his youthful experience, and the other fifty thought he lacked experience for the Head Chef's position at the Elms Hotel, in Iffley. The stick of disappointment was soon forgotten when they were presented with the golden carrot – the flat – a large, one-bedroom Victorian first storey, jutting out over the busy Iffley road, one of the main arteries into town. This came with a good pay raise, and more importantly, an ideal rent-free situation. The flat was comfortable and trendy, if a little draughty sometimes, but the utilities, including the rent, were part of his wages. So, after Lyn had moved in, the young couple put all their energy into saving every penny till they cobbled enough deposit to afford their own house.

On their pitiful wages, they were actually laughed at in an Estate Agency in Headington, before being shown the door. At the time, they were chasing a biggish semi in Blackbird Leys, but were told they would 'never be able to afford' the £13,500 asking price. So, they saved, lied about their income and intently watched the market before being tipped off about a house in Florence Park, which was coming up for sale without an agent. They met the vendors, a genial pair in their fifties, Daphne and Alec Bratton, got on handsomely with them, and secured the deal without any agent being involved, again £13,500.

So as not to lose the deal, the couple, at John's insistence, used to visit the Brattons regularly, ensuring that the house became theirs and didn't bring down the aesthetic of the street.

That first home was a comfortable mid-terrace in East Oxford, just off Cowley Road, being handy, local and cosmopolitan.

It was quiet and in a great position in East Oxford, a five-minute walk from Cowley Road and a really nice first place to live. They moved in and married six months later, lived and worked happily for a few years, John swapping chef-ing for wholesale catering from a local butcher's shop in Littlemore. Two years later, Corine was born. It was then that they started thinking about moving the family out to the country.

John had really always been the impatient, restless one and was constantly on the lookout for a business opportunity. Every Friday, he bought the *Oxford Times* and was always scouring the papers. One particular Friday evening, he was reading the *Oxford Times* and, in the *Central Business Agency* section, saw an advert – a hairdresser's shop for sale, with accommodation and freehold. After some discussion, the young couple both agreed this was something to be seriously considered. It was an opportunity to start their own business and move out into the country in one fell swoop!

They agreed to view it, taking baby Corine with them, on a spectacular September evening, with the sun setting through the trees, and the golden rays slanting through the hedges and spilling out through the slatted gate onto the gravel drive. The house itself was small, but was littered with climbing roses, a giant garden shed, a sprawling, gnarled apple tree, and enough room for a vegetable patch.

They fell in love with the house at first sight, and they both agreed – this was the place.

The shop had, until very recently, been a sweetshop. The previous vendors had quickly realised that there was very poor trade in a community with many other options. So, they had converted the sweetshop into a hairdresser's, although they had precious little experience, inevitably inviting the opportunity for a quick sale. The prospect of taking their young ones out of East Oxford and into a rural setting was a real tonic to the young couple, who sold their old house and moved in quite quickly.

They immediately realised that the house was not quite what it may have been on that sunny September evening. They discovered, upon moving in, their idyllic viewing turned out to be a cramped and freezing kitchen with flaking, damp walls, single-glazed and badly fitted windows and ancient and dangerous electric wiring. Despite all these issues, they loved the house, and they set about repairing and renovating it with gusto.

In the early eighties, when property was booming, the next steps were obvious. Ollie was born in the new house; the hairdresser's flourished, and before too long, John found another opportunity in Wantage. John was now working as a frozen food rep, having stepped out of the kitchen to take a role in sales. He was in his second year at VJG Polafreeze where he had had to follow up a lead at BNF Metals, Wantage. BNF were based on the old Air Force base and had down-sized their catering operations and were looking to provide the remaining staff with ready meals, having closed down their kitchens. He spotted the opportunity and set up a catering operation, providing lunches to two directors' rooms and workers' lunches, while starting up a new catering business.

The business proved successful enough for them to move into Grove, eventually sell the hairdresser's and buy a very nice three-bedroom in a peaceful cul-de-sac, basically occupied by other young couples with children, in the heart of the village. The children soon became fast friends, attending the same schools and meeting in the street after to play football, kerbie or tennis.

While Lyn brought up the kids and John the business, their life became relatively easy, and their friends and neighbours often met and socialised through clubs and social events. When John had lived in Oxford, he had mooched about local pubs and walked to parks to watch a bit of local sport, never really having had a satisfactory sporting youth. It had always 'nearly been', although he was a really skilled footballer. He often thought how unbelievably cruel his chances had been.

He bitterly remembered his first school trial at Church Cowley Infants School. At 10, he was already one of the most skilled players on the rec. But his parents did not put the kind of emphasis that modern parents now do into furnishing the 'kit', although they both worked – his dad at Morris', on the line, in the trim-shop (and, therefore, quite well paid for the sixties). His mum worked part-time for her father, an entrepreneurial, Irish-descended ex-black-marketeer, who had made his fortune on the back of the war, and who co-owned The Swan Garage in Cowley.

John had held his 'boots' in one hand, hating everything about them.

He grimaced at the thought of lacing on the old-fashioned 'boots'. They bore no relation to the slim-line trainer-style boots that modern players wear today.

Steel toe-capped, fully round-toed, they were the type of boots Stan Mortenson and Stanley Mathews might have worn twenty years earlier. His had been un-giving, bulky shoes with stiff, studded leather, more akin to deep-diving boots than to sport-wear. They were hand-me-down wrecks probably handed down two generations. They were the colour of faded sand, with a thick leather sole, which was beginning to curl upwards. The six studs were also of hardened leather, with the tacks visible on the ends.

These were the boots that John laced on behind classroom 8, while other more fortunate boys skipped out onto the field. When they were finally on, John was painfully aware that these were antiques, that the other boys had far superior footwear, that some of them thought his were hysterical, and that this was not something he had ever worn before in any shape or form. He sensed imminent disaster. Embarrassment and discomfort engulfed him.

Mr Griggs, the class 8 teacher, was the team coach and knew absolutely nothing about the boys' abilities – who played where, their strengths, their weaknesses. He was gangly and dark, with wrinkled black-grey hair and black-rimmed glasses. Although he was clueless about sports in general, he was usually fair, had a bit of a temper, and was never wrong.

The trial was on the pitch, a gently sloping field at the end of the school. Light rain had sprinkled the field for most of the day, so the goalmouths were muddy and slick.

John eventually joined the other trialists on the edge of the penalty area. Boys were passing and heading the ball to one another without much order. John joined in and watched as, whistle poised, Griggs scanned each name on his clipboard.

He put Tim Sherwood in goal (who was no good in goal, but was tall), and as he called each name, Barratt, or Coster or Earl, in alphabetical order, they would approach the half-way line. Mr Griggs was barking orders. 'Right. Each boy take a ball and place it on the half-way line. Then kick it as hard as you can at the goalkeeper, so we can see who can kick the farthest.'

On the rec, John could pick up the ball, feint and dribble with a drop of the shoulder, and leave five defenders sprawling in his wake as he slid the ball past a helpless keeper. He often beat them so badly he would stop and head the ball in off the floor. He had never played in football boots, let alone those clod-hopping monstrosities he had been forced to wear for the 'trial'.

Dribbling around the penalty area with as much control as he could muster, he heard Chris Farr's name being called and realised it would be him next. He rolled the ball to the half-way line, where the white lines had faded into the mottled, stud-marked mud. Now he stood up to the ball, and the bearded, bespectacled Griggs shouted, 'Gomm, your turn. Hit it as hard as you can towards Sherwood.'

This was the trial. No kick-ups, headings, turns, pace or skill. No overhead kicks, dummies, one-twos, back-heels. No defence v. attack, no corners, no goal-hanging, no three and in, no through-balls. Just one kick. At the goal. In a pair of diving boots. From the half-way line. John eased forward. The ball was more like a medicine ball than a football. It was tan with scuffed leather, laced and soggy. John started his run-up, drew his right foot back. He agonisingly watched the result – he completely scuffed the kick, 15 yards left. Nowhere near the goal. He looked at the teacher for a sign of help. Just one kick. And failure.

'Sorry, sir. Can I take it again?' John gasped, crestfallen.

His hands dropped to his side and his shoulders slumped.

Linton 'Edgy' Edgington strode over and shook John, his best mate. 'Come on, Gommy!'

He looked at Griggs, 'Sir? Please let Gomm take it again. Let him have another chance.'

John looked gratefully at his mate, then hopefully back at Mr Griggs.

Griggs, irritated, looked at his watch. 'No, you didn't reach the goal.' A blast on the whistle. 'Smith – next.'

Trial over. Failure.

'But sir, Gomm really is the best player we've got!' protested Edge.

'No. His kick didn't reach the goal – the trial is over. I'll let you know the team later.'

As each boy attempted to reach the goal, John looked on with biting worry. Even the worst plodders could whack the ball somewhere towards the goal, and one after another, they did. It looked like his was about the worst attempt so far. His heart sank as he realised that if he didn't make the team, there would be no reason for his parents to buy him new boots.

'Don't worry, Gommy.' Derek Newman wrapped his arm around his mate's shoulder. 'He can't be that stupid – we'll have a word with him. He'll want the best team.'

At the end of the session, Griggs called the boys over to the wall where they had changed, outside class 8.

'Right, boys. If I call your name, you are in the team, if not, you will all get another chance.' His eyes moved over the boys through steamy, rain-flecked specs. They fidgeted under his gaze, damp with the drizzle.

With a deep breath and without further ceremony, he crisply announced, 'Sherwood, Barratt, Giles, Hill, Edgington, Jeffries, Owen, Coster, Newman, Earl, Smith and sub – Webster. The rest, keep trying and prove to me that you are good enough to make the team next time.'

But there was never a next time. Those twelve played in the few games that Church Cowley played, never remembering how they ever got on because it was irrelevant. Playing in the rec, cruising past defenders, scoring 21 goals on a summer afternoon was great. But John never made the school team.

Thereafter came the 11 plus. John sailed through the exam. An incredibly annoyed older sister. A new but unbelievably ordinary bike – a bottle-green Raleigh with a three-speed Sturmey-Archer. And a grey saddle bag about as modern as the boots had been.

'John, you know at "Oxford Boys" they play rugby, not football.' Edgy had told him after a session with the 'Johnny Seven' one afternoon. 'I know, and I'm going to Cheney,' he'd replied.

'You know, that's miles further on. It'll take you ages to bike there.'

'But they play football, Edgy, and I en't playing rugby. I want to play football, and I can choose, so I am going to "Cheney".'

'I think you're making a mistake, you know, Johnny. We're all going on to "Oxford Boys", except for you and Hilly.'

'That's good for you then, Edgy. We'll still play in the rec. But I don't care how far I have to bike, I want to play football. We'll still all be mates.'

And that bike ride was a bitch. Through Cowley, down through the Marsh, then past the 'Regal' and up 'Southfield Hill', the final mile of three, culminating in a 45-degree incline right up at the top. But it was worth it. John wasn't going to have to play rugby. The chance to be at a grammar school with football and a chance to prove he could play with the best was all he wanted.

Chapter 3
House Football

After about five days, all the lads at Cheney Grammar School, by playing football before assembly, during lunch, and at both morning and afternoon breaks with a tennis ball, knew who the footballers were. They played in a main game, joining in as first years, or by the doorway of the woodwork shop, playing Wolves v. Coventry, or Leeds v. Man Utd. They met up at the 'Manor' to watch Oxford United. They talked, walked, ate, slept and dreamt football. They knew the nickname of Lincoln City (The Imps), the ground of Bury (Gigg Lane), and the founder members of the football league. The boys all fiercely supported a 'Big' team – Chelsea, Man. Utd, or Leeds. John and his mates even went to Stamford Bridge to watch Chelsea quite often.

Oxford United were on the rise, captained by big Ronnie Atkinson. They were in the third division (things were much simpler then), having won promotion from the fourth. They were a decent footballing side and were well supported by the factory lads and their kids.

The Manor was a ground built by the fans in Headington over time, so each part of it was unique. The London Road stand was where the lads all gathered, as near to being behind the goal as possible. The only seats were in the Beech Road (where the posh, older people sat). The rest of the ground was a mismatch of sheds and shelters with various types of terracing, and you could walk right round the ground and stand where you wanted.

The Cheney boys, and kids from Cowley, Headington, Marston, Littlemore and Blackbird Leys populated the main stand – the London Road end. On match days, they breezed through the turnstiles, clambered up the steps into the stand and squeezed and picked their way through to their positions, knocking waves of supporters down the terracing while trying to get a view. They tried to find a foothold where they could stand without being squashed against a crush barrier – where you could keep your feet on the step and get a glimpse of the pitch without breaking your neck!

They sung real football songs, with verses and words. They sweated, they surged, and they sang as the team toiled and shed honest sweat to give all they had. The Manor, in truth, was a bit of a shithole, but it was also a formidable – if ramshackle – fortress.

The fortress was breached of course, like any battleground. In the sixties, there was no segregation, so the away fans could also walk around the ground and stand where they liked.

Sometimes there was a jostle for territory, sometimes a battle. Sometimes, and unbelievably in today's world, the Oxford fans begrudgingly moved en-masse to the Cuckoo Lane end as Birmingham City and Aston Villa efficiently piled three thousand of their own fans into the London Road end.

The powerless Oxford fans scowled and chanted abuse, but they were simply outnumbered and outmuscled.

They would simply have to watch the game in their own 'away' end!

They would stand jostling and scrapping (or avoided scrapping, if possible) as Bristol Rovers, Millwall and other hostile fans, sometimes armed with darts and billiard balls, 'took' the London Road. Fighting, sparring and circling for position, precariously balanced and always liable to a surge from the back, where you could lose your place and be swept down, crazily trying to keep your balance as you were forced twenty or thirty steps down in a crush.

During one afternoon match, rammed half-way up the London Road terraces, Edgy got smacked by a copper right on his nose when a joker behind them in the crowd reached three rows forward to flip that constable's helmet spinning down towards the goal. The copper reacted instantly, turning swiftly and administering a sharp right jab to the unaware youngster. The astonished Edgy got a big, bloody nose and cursed him for a bit. Then they carried on watching the match. The poor police stood singly in the middle of all this with no back-up and were generally alright. But in those days, the police's presence was exciting. And the Manor, when full, was magical.

John's English project was on the team. It was a pink scrapbook featuring Ron Atkinson, Cyril Beavon, David Sloan, Ken Skeen and Colin Harrington. Autographs were taken, and glorious football prevailed. Oxford signed on an Irish whiz-kid goal-scorer, Ray Gaston. The boy hardly ever scored, about 3 goals in three months, and was soon sold on to another team. There were promotions, record crowds, where children were taken out and sat around the pitch so that everybody could get in. Floodlit games, great football, and a wonderful atmosphere.

And as all this football wonder grew, they were given their houses in the first few weeks of term.

Mr Mills, the squat, curly-haired and intense Games master was new to the school. And trying to please. His genial assistant 'Basher' Bates, who was also the Music and Geography teacher and a very fine man indeed, called the entire first years to order.

It was the first games session, and football was on the agenda. The footballers knew who they were, and most of them (the bigger, leaner, more athletic ones) were picked to join the 'A' group. John joined the 'B' group. 'A' went off across the field to a pitch with Mills. Bates took charge of 'B' and set them up on a pitch nearer to the cricket nets.

Having selected two teams, Mr Bates quietly instructed, 'Lads, organise yourselves, find a goalie, and a defence – don't all crowd around the ball, spread yourselves out and let's see what you can do!'

It was a mellow autumn day, with the conker trees' leaves spreading crispy and golden at the edge of the pitch.

The sun was up but not hot, the sky blue, and the underfoot slightly damp. John had his new Pumas with a slick red flash emblazoned on the side. He felt like Pele. Group 'B' was awful somehow, except for about four players. John intercepted a cross-field pass early on, feinted a square pass beating the last defender, drew the stodgy keeper and slid the ball home for 1-0. He chased and harassed, cajoled, tackled, set up number two with a back-heel. He headed the ball off his own goal line, organised his team, cut in from the right, and caressed the ball into the corner off the post with the outside of his right foot. He sprinted the length and breadth of the pitch.

He was in heaven. As he intercepted a dodgy clearance from a different goalie and was about to slot an eight-minute hat-trick, Bates blew the whistle in two curt, shrill blasts.

'Right. Gomm, off you come, over here with me.'

'Yes, sir.' He knew what was coming. Promotion! His eyes shone with delight.

They were escorted across to the main game, where a match of different proportions was running. Mills looked up at their approach.

'Gomm is to join you, Martin, a real livewire this one. Scored three already, running rings around them all.' Old Basher Bates loved John like he had 'discovered' him.

'Join in here then, lad. What's your name?'

'Gomm, sir.'

'Well, let's see what you can do, Gomm. Join the reds.' He looked sideways at Bates. 'Where does he play?'

'In attack – number 8, I'd say. Inside right.'

In!

***

Drake, Nelson, Brooks, Rhodes

These were the school 'houses', and they were announced after assembly in early September 1967. By now, all the boys knew the footballers. As names were called out, John tried to remember who was in *his* house, and eventually, his name was called and 'Gomm-Drake' didn't really mean anything at this stage. Afterwards, the lads were chirping excitedly about who was where, and he was here and so and so was there, and didn't Nelson look strong and Breakspear (the footballing genius) was in Rhodes, with Green, Woods, Bridge, and other really talented footballers. Bielec, 'Sid' Rogers and Harvey were in Brooks, along with Beesley, and so on.

When he looked at the full list the next day, John's heart sank.

John Ogg (*Oggy*), Martin Quartermain (*Morrocco Mole*), Paul Mankelow (*Manky*), *'Tiny'* Evans, Steven Jones – all really nice blokes (swats!), but not footballers. Drake was a pile of poo. They didn't have any footballers. Well, except for John, 'Billy' Wilkinson and Charlie Williamson, just the three then!

He couldn't believe it had happened. It was like a conspiracy. The other houses were really strong, well split and even. And even at that early stage, John realised that Drake were going to be the whipping boys.

John was voted Captain, in the absence of any other suitable applicants, with no problem. He had been Captain of the glorious athletics team in year 11 at Primary school, who had triumphed at Barton in the finals. But he had had talent then – Jeanette Webb, Susan Aldridge, Stephen Coster, Colin Earl and two brilliant relay teams. Not this bunch of misfits.

After the team meeting, he and Billy sat trying to arrange the names into some sense. But it was no use. His house was shit.

***

He had walked the fields around the pitches in Grove many times, with the kids and the dog. Many times, his thoughts wandered around reminding him of his early sporting life, a life still somewhat unfulfilled. He had played for the school team but had represented the school's cross-country team as many times as he had played football for the school, simply due to a lack of fixtures. And he'd hated cross-country. The house matches were great fun in the end, and in his time there, Drake always came last. But he never had any regrets about his decision to go to Cheney.

Not until years later when he realised what a fantastic game Rugby Union was that he wished differently…

But often, he encountered rugby and football training over on the Wasborough fields as he walked the dog. And now, he had a son of his own who was six-and-a-half-years old. He decided to find out how his son could join a little team. He had seen tiny kids over here, training. So, he was determined to find out who the manager was of the... what? The Under Sevens? And get Ollie in.

Shouldn't be too difficult, he mused as he approached the gate.

The stream of starlings, now a murmuration, swirled down again and fled off to the north.

He headed back to his car, whistling a random tune and ushering Sally along before him.

Chapter 4
Sunderland v. Swindon. Play off final. Wembley 1990

In 1990, Swindon Town beat Blackburn Rovers over two legs to qualify for the play off final against Sunderland. The Black Cats were in great form, having beaten their local rivals, Newcastle United 2-0 away at St James' park. So it looked like a great, odds-on bet that Sunderland would stuff Swindon in the final. John was pretty confident of this result – the winners of this match would be in the top-flight. A big match.

It is hard to explain to people who don't have local rivalries just how much you hate, loathe and despise some neighbours. But the Oxford–Swindon rivalry is just about as bad as it gets locally.

In the 60s, when Oxford, Swindon and Reading were in Division three, Reading were almost as hated. But somehow, they drifted off and left the Oxford and Wiltshire clubs to passionately feud and hate each other. Each faction referred to the other as 'scum', and the rivalry on the pitch was matched by the fans' ferocity and fervour. The matches, home and away, simply had to be won, and bragging rights could last for seasons!

So, as a staunch Oxford fan, John decided it would be great fun to have a day out watching their neighbours and bitter rivals get beat at Wembley. A bit of a different experience, but hey-ho!

No pressure. A nice day on the piss and the joy of watching the Swindon fans get devastated. So, after quick consultation, he bought four tickets for himself, two mates, Marc and Boily, and a semi-dubious football fan and 'friend' who was a driver for *Weddell-Swift*, (a wholesale Butcher) and also bit of an animal – Derby.

Saturday, 28th May, came around, and the guys were at the station waiting for the train to Paddington when Derby joined them at 10 am, swinging an ex-four pack of lager, judging by the two missing cans. They were dressed casually, though Derby was wearing his England t-shirt, plastic Union Jack bowler hat and calf-length cherry-red Dr Martens with turned up jeans. He looked like a relic of the 60s, with his shaven head, scarred face and missing front tooth.

'Fuck me, Derby!' said Boily, as he swung into the vacant seat. 'You look like a fucking hooligan, yer fat git!'

'Talk about pot, kettle black! You ain't much different Stevie!' retorted Derby.

Boily (Steve Westwood – John's butchery manager at work) was nearly as bulky, dishevelled, scruffy and careless. Today, in jeans and a t-shirt, he was just somewhat better dressed than Derby.

'Just me football gear, Steve,' he grinned back.

'What's the plan?' asked Marc.

'No concrete plans really.' said John, watching the approaching Paddington train roll to a stop.

'Let's get into London, find a pub, sink a few, grab a burger, and then hit Wembley!' grinned John.

'Will we be looking for Swindon fans?' Derby's eyes lit up, backed up by his giant, one-tooth grin.

'Course we fucking won't, you moron.' snorted John. 'We just want to see them get beat, have a few beers and then home!'

Derby looked inconsolable. 'Just wanted to meet a few,' he

scowled.

'Hey Derby, you should be wearing yer fucking trainers then, you hard bastard.' 'So's you could run away from them!' laughed Boily.

'Fucking in-breds. I wouldn't mind a word or two.' Derby screwed his right fist into his left palm.

As he sat down on the platform bench, Boily spotted the tattoo on the top of his t-shirt. 'What does that say, Derby?'

'All Coppers are Bastards, mate,' he grinned.

Boily jumped from his seat and pulled down the top of Derby's t-shirt to reveal the full legend, *All Coppers are Bastards* written in a haphazard arc across his shoulders in two-inch black ink.

'Fuck me, Derby! Did you do that yourself?' Boily was wide-eyed in amazement.

'Course I did, Boily. I did it in the mirror!' Derby grinned with his one toothed grin. 'No, I got it done after I got out of the borstal.'

'Fuck me! I really hope we don't get arrested,' grimaced Marc, looking at the work of art. 'We'll be fucked!'

'For fuck's sake! Put it away boys, here's the train,' clipped John, moving up the platform.

Derby pulled his t-shirt up, swung onto the train and jumped into a vacant block of four seats, flopping down and cracking open his third can of *Stella*.

They got the underground from Paddington to the West End.

On Moorgate station, as the three lads sprinted down the steps out of the sunshine, Derby loitered at the top of the stairs, looking around for something.

Whilst distracted, Boily thought it would be a good idea to lose him.

'Run!' shouted Boily, and they pissed it down to the trains, leaving the poor old sod wondering where they had gone.

'Fucking retard.' said Marc as they caught their breath. 'Hope he can find his own way!'

'Jesus, how childish are we?' laughed John, out of breath and looking over his shoulder for Derby.

The pub was somewhere near the West End, cavernous and sprawling. The bar was on the basement level, with carpeted steps up to two nice seating areas with plush red velvet, booths, brass and mirrors.

It was absolutely crammed with Sunderland fans.

The atmosphere was electric, pulsing. Geordie songs, guttural banter and laughter filled the air. Red and white scarves and shirts were everywhere.

The guys gathered at a booth near the back and surveyed the scene.

'Awesome,' said Marc 'there are thousands of them.'

At the bar they were serving, amongst other ales *'Younger's Scotch IPA.'*

'Fuck me!' shouted John, eyes gleaming. *'Younger's IPA.'*

'Just like the old days in the Prince of Wales, Iffley.' He pointed to the IPA pump to the barman.

It was a stunning pint. But in those days, in the 70s, drinking this at lunchtime was not the smartest move, and he was often on the wrong side of sober after a couple.

But there it was for the taking.

Marc and John were real bitter fans, and it went down like nectar.

'You can always tell a perfect pint of bitter (as opposed to any other drink), 'cos when it's good, it just goes, and you don't know you're drinking it.'

'What d'ya think chap?' John asked Marc, smacking his lips.

'Stunning, mate. Stunning! Do you fancy another?' Marc was just as impressed.

They got another round and sat at the table overlooking the Sunderland hoards, joining in with their songs and getting in the mood.

'Geez, these bastards are really enjoying themselves.' laughed John.

'Mate, this is a good pint of ale.' Marc emptied his glass.

'Yeah, we used to drink this down at the Prince, bit heady though. But what a pint!' quipped John.

They moved up from the bar to a booth near the back of the pub, overlooking the whole scene.

'Pretty strong though.' shouted Marc above the din.

'Fucking shut up about the beer, you twats! It's only fucking beer,' yelled Boily over the din.

'Steve, this is much better than beer, or that lager shite that you're drinking!' Marc jested. 'That's only piss mate!'

Marc put his pint down and skipped down the steps to the loo.

As soon as he was gone, Boily grabbed Marc's glass, quickly looked around the room, unzipped his fly, got his old man out and pissed half a pint of his own urine into Marc's third-full glass.

John looked at him in amazement.

'Sshhh!' Boily shut him up with a glance and a wink. 'I'll show him who's drinking piss!'

The Sunderland fans were going through their repertoire. Their songs filled the pub, and the lads joined the chorus.

Marc returned to the table.

'Awright, Marc? Fuckin' weak bladder! Ha Ha!' Boily laughed, pulling Marc's stool out for him to sit.

'Fuck off, Boily. Who was it who had five pisses at the Villa before half-time last week?'

'Cheers!' said Boily, 'Only kiddin' mate.'

'Cheers,' John raised his pint, eyes wide and full of laughter.

'Salute,' said Marc, downing a quarter pint of select *Younger's IPA* and Boily's piss, and then smacking his lips.

'Fuck me,' thought John, 'I'm keeping my fucking glass

empty.'

John didn't visit the bogs except when his glass was empty and couldn't be 'tampered with'. But every time poor Marc got up, he got the same piss-pour treatment and ended up quaffing a couple of pints of Boily piss!

Boily was up at the bar getting the drinks with alarming regularity.

'My round, mate,' John remarked a couple of times.

'You're all right Johnnie, I'll get 'em in.'

Good old boy, a really generous mate.

Beer, more beer. The round table was full of empty pint glasses.

Round after round came and went.

Sunderland songs filled the air as the Black Cats filled themselves with beer. Little surges and knots of red and white fans swept up and down as the bar staff bustled to keep up with the flow.

Lads were swaying and shouting and starting songs in small groups until the chorus or second verse was embraced by the whole pub joining in with raucous appreciation.

The music swirled, and the banter increased, amid the shrieking laughter of the three friends as they got more and more drunk. Marc oblivious, John on guard and Boily conducting operations. Beer and piss flowed, and they were having a real good laugh and were totally happy.

John suddenly felt really pissed.

'Fuck me, I am *really* pissed!' he said, looking around. 'Jesus, where's everybody gone?'

The whole pub was empty.

They'd been so caught up in the drinking that they hadn't noticed that every Sunderland fan had left. Vacated. They didn't notice anyone trickling out, hadn't realised they had been left behind!

'Jesus, they've gone to Wembley! What time is it?'

'Twenty to two! Jesus, we're late – gotta get to Wembley, come on!'

John got up and walked through the glass doors into the fresh air.

Jesus-pished! Fucking hell.

He didn't remember getting on the tube, or where they were or where they were going. He vaguely remembered rolling around on the floor of the train later, not really knowing how he had got there; he wasn't really bothered. How had he got so rat-arsed?

They got off the train near Wembley, and Boily decided he was hungry, so they stopped at a burger joint.

John was totally out of it and didn't remember any of the conversation.

He drunkenly and greedily devoured the burger. Then, unbelievably, he realised he was on his own again.

Jesus, they had done another runner!

Boily?

Marc?

Fuck…

He made his drunken way to the counter, and the waiter was looking the other way.

'Oh, fuck it!'

He ducked out following his 'mates' and then sprinted out into the high street with a little Asian guy in hot pursuit…*run like hell.*

'You must pay, you must pay…!'

John lost him from his trail as he was never that game for the chase. But he never saw where Boily and Marc went, so he just kept on running. And then he found himself hitchhiking down towards Wembley Way, thumb stuck out (despite the fact he had never hitchhiked before in his life)! He innocently looked into cars of families passing by, like a true lush.

'Giy us a lif…?'

Why am I so pissed?

The hitching was shite. He was still so pissed that only eventually did he realise he had walked right past Wembley which was now behind him.

He staggered round, checked and re-traced his steps.

All the fans were inside and the game was underway.

He searched for his ticket, intently scrutinised it for a couple of minutes, and found his gate. A bunch of coppers stood in front of the gate. It was completely surrounded by police. And by continuing up the steps, so was he.

Composure…composure…

As he approached the gate, he reached the first policeman and said, 'Ve got tickets fr the game,' noticeably and horribly slurring every syllable.

He was about to offer his wrists for hand-cuffing when, amazingly, the police opened up and let him into the ground!

Amazing!

Wembley!

He stumbled in, eventually found his seat and looked at his watch – 3:40 pm.

The stadium was awash with red and white (both teams' colours). The Swindon fans were singing and making more noise, so it looked like they were winning. The Sunderland section was a little quieter.

John looked around him. Derby was already in his seat a couple of rows behind.

He gave a curt, sarcastic nod when John caught his eye and gave him a thumbs up.

The other two jokers weren't there yet.

'What's the score, mate?' he asked a Sunderland fan sitting next to him.

The Geordie replied wearily, '1-0 to them – A bloody deflection!'

Already a goal down.

Shite! And his drunken pre-hangover was already starting to

form as his temple throbbed.

Boily and Marc rocked up during half-time. In the second half, Sunderland were looking like they would almost score, but never managed to get the equaliser.

Finished 1-0 to the scum, and their promotion from the fourth to the first division was complete. Fucking Argie Ardiles.

They trooped out of the stadium, John inconsolable on seeing the Swindon fans in delirium.

The happiest result for John was that, just ten days later, Swindon were demoted by two whole divisions for illegal payments to players! No promotion to the top flight!

All right, it was reduced, under review to just one division, but their plea of 'punish the guilty, not the fans' was not accepted, and they languished, quite rightly, where they belonged for the foreseeable future! Some things just aren't meant to be.

John crept onto the train, so fucking glad for a seat, and nuzzled into the patterned, smoky smelling velour, trying to coax away the already nagging headache at the nape of his neck.

On the way home, Derby did meet some Swindon fans on the train, but he actually got on with them really well, and unbelievably, after a bit of banter, they actually seemed to like him! Loving, not scrapping. And for the time being, they believed they were up!

Morons!

Marc filled John in with the turn of events in the Bay Tree on Monday night. With great delight!

It turned out that every time Boily had got a round in, John had received a complimentary double vodka in his pint! No piss – just eight double vodkas! No wonder he had been so out of his head.

A real day 'on the piss' had just ended!

Marc didn't believe the piss in his beer story. Well, there was bugger-all he could do about it!

That fucking Boily!

Chapter 5
Under-7s

After asking a few questions around Grove regarding Ollie potentially joining a team, John was eventually directed to the vice chairman of the Challenger's club, Joe Moreland – a genial young Northern Irelander with a quick wit, a lopsided smile and a shaggy black fringe.

'Yeah, John. As a matter of fact, we are looking for a manager for the under 7s.' He drawled on, 'The job's yours if you want it. All you need is enthusiasm-and a sense of humour!'

'What? That's it?' asked John. 'Don't I have to do a test or something?'

'Yeah, round up a team – you'll get plenty of response at that age; they're as keen as mustard. Pop into the next meeting, and I'll give you some gear, balls and all that. Good luck, John!'

Dumbfounded by the simplicity of it all and still bemused, he unfolded his plans to Marc in the pub.

'I got Ollie into the under-7s after all.'

'How'd you manage that then?'

'I'm the new manager.'

'Ha! Ha! You know bugger all about managing a football team.'

'What about our five-a-side team?' retorted John. 'Who'd you think made all the arrangements for that?'

But Marc thought it was quite funny. 'What about Ollie? He's hardly kicked a ball.'

'Well, we'll train him. What you doing Saturday?'

They took Ollie into town and bought him a new pair of *New Balance* football boots – really trendy and highly recommended by the salesman. Then they took him to Wantage rec and set up camp around the miniature, rusty goal set in a patch of mud on a 30-degree slope. Ollie wasn't very good. At all.

'Ha! Ha! Corrie's better than him, John. He can't kick! Bloody hell, look at him trying to head!' Marc scoffed. 'He's going to take a lot of work chap!'

Bless him, Ollie did try hard, but his co-ordination was iffy, technique non-existent and skill level negligible. But try he did, and the three of them had a right old funny training session. Funny in that they were rolling around at some of the air-shots, trips and hashes from temporarily having two left feet. Still, Ollie realised that he had got a smart new pair of boots and that he had had a little private tuition from two decent footballers – the attention didn't go unnoticed. But he didn't seem overly interested.

Corine *was* actually better than him, because John had trained her on the patio for a couple of years. Her speciality was the volley, and John went in goal and defended the patio doors (the perfect size for a kiddie goal), lobbing ball after ball to her. She could slam that ball back with glass-shattering power, on the volley and the half-volley, until one day, after a dazzling hat trick against the glass, father and daughter were banned from playing. She could play a bit of football but wasn't really that interested. She liked horse riding, and she was committed and good at it. She shared a pony that was based in the country at Goosey. She was the oldest, and Ollie was still only six. He had a lot to learn.

As they walked down the hill, Marc turned to John and

chuckled, 'Not being funny, chap, he's shit!'

John, undaunted, got back to the house and started wording ads for players, placing them in the four shops and post offices around the village that Saturday afternoon. By Wednesday, he was picking up the phone and speaking to parents who had seen the advert.

He arranged the first training session before the start of the season on a misty September morning, and was rewarded when 14 youngsters turned up, dropped off by their parents. To be fair, some of them really looked to be no more than infants, but there were also some obvious footballers. John had picked up two leather footballs from Joe, and he bought another two, along with a pump, adaptor, a set of coloured stacking cones and a whistle. The whistle was slightly faulty; the pea didn't vibrate properly or something, but this wasn't a huge initial problem.

He introduced himself to the parents, ticked the boys' names against the register that he had prepared from the phone calls, and lined the boys up, telling the parents they could stay and watch, or return in an hour. The boys were already running about with the footballs, mixing and having a good old kick around together.

John had met Karen Brind, Sparkie's mum, who was a personal friend of the Gomms and knew from the Brinds' time keeping 'The Volunteer' pub at Grove Bridge. Karen offered to help register the players and collect the 50p per week, which they had decided to take for funds.

There was a great big lad amongst the milling players – about a foot and a half taller than any of the others. This tall lad was a great gangly seven-year-old named Oliver Dimblow. He came with his dad, Peter, and for a big lad, was actually making quite a fuss, because he had turned up in huge black plimsolls.

'You'll be alright,' his dad was reassuring him.

'Oh Dad, they're no good. I can't play football in these,' he moaned, all soppy looking.

'They are fine, Olly. Stop making a fuss.'

'They're rotten. I can't play in these.'

'Right, come on. Get on with it, join in or we'll go home.'

Well, he had to be a goalie. He was massive. What a result. John raised his eyebrows at Karen, and she rolled her eyes as Olly joined the rest.

John ushered them into a line and regarded his ragtag troop.

'Right, my name's John. I'm your coach. We're gonna have a lot of fun and make you into a decent football team. I'm gonna set these cones up, and I want you to get a ball and dribble between them and then shoot the ball at me when you pass the last one.'

The boys' abilities were clearly mixed; his Ollie was about average. There were some who couldn't really even kick a ball, but that would come. Some were tiny and frail. And there were two kids who were out of this world. John couldn't believe it. These two kids – both six years old – jinked through the cones, using both feet, and one placed the ball into the corner of the goal; the other stung John's hands when he went in goal with a rasping drive! John was amazed. These two were already footballers.

He had the beginnings of a team. As he worked them through some easy training routines. He introduced them to corners, heading, trapping and the usual stuff. He began to enjoy it and was quietly impressed.

There were five primary schools in the immediate area, so some of the boys knew each other.

A few knew Ollie, but only one or two.

They had a little practice match for the last fifteen minutes. Everything went well until the ball went out for a throw-in. His son Ollie took it, and John nearly died of horror as Ollie ran up to the line and threw the ball back into play. He threw it forward – underarm! The boys in the know all laughed, but it did highlight the age of the players. Clearly lots of work to be done. Ollie nearly died as a result of the laughter!

Olly Dimblow had got on quite well, and John stuck him in goal for the practice match. He had had a couple of mishaps, even though he had been sliding about a bit. A loose ball rolled back to him, and as he went to clear it, he took an almighty swing with his right leg. His smooth-soled plimsolls offered no grip on the damp grass, the combination of which was akin to the results from an ice rink!

His left leg slid murderously underneath him, and completing a full air-shot, he lumbered in the air before crash landing on his back, flustered and dazed, as the ball rolled into the net. Winded and embarrassed by the hoots of laughter, he burst into a flood of tears and loped off to the car park, screaming.

'I told you so! I told you so!' he wailed to his dad.

'Come back, Oli-Vaa!' Peter pleaded, but the boy was already lolloping off back towards the car.

'I told you I needed proper boots,' he sobbed.

'And the kid is obviously right. He does need more than plimsolls.' agreed John to the grinning Karen.

Karen looked wide-eyed at John for a reaction.

'Bloody hell, I hope he comes back – he does look like a proper keeper.'

'Oh, I don't know,' she laughed, still shaking with laughter, 'he might make a better netball player.'

Dunno about that but the size of him will at least give him a chance as a goalie!'

The subsequent training sessions went well, and another couple of gifted boys joined, notably Sean Revell, who was as skilful as any of the best boys. He actually nutmegged John in his first practice game. Sean's brother Liam also came to training and turned out to be a brave, if diminutive, stand-in keeper in the absence of a proper one, (Olly Dimblow hadn't returned to training) although he was a year younger – barely six and really tiny.

A couple of inter-club friendlies were arranged, using some of the younger players, a few from the older age groups, and a couple of the parents helped out. John arranged a full-sized training match on the main pitch. It was massive.

He had talked to Tony Keen, who marked up the pitch, as he was white-lining one Friday night.

'Hi, Tony! Which pitch will we be on for our training game on Sunday?'

'This is it, mate. Billy's under-8s are playing at home tomorrow.'

'So, this is our pitch too?'

'Yep, this is the main pitch.'

'Tony, are you certain this is the right sized pitch? It's immense!'

'Yeah, John. This is a regulation pitch for up to under-15 age groups.'

'But under-15s are massive, surely this pitch should be half the size?' He countered. 'Under-15s are like full-grown men!'

'Well, this is regulation.' said Tony, brushing a chunk of chalk off the wheel of the white lining machine.

'What about the goals, Tony? They're enormous!'

Tony had shown him which frames to drag from the enclosure, marked with red tape for their size. They may have been smaller, but they were as big as the world to the team's tiny keepers.

Liam Revell would be absolutely dwarfed by the goal frame – you would hardly see him. So much for the description 'goalkeeper'.

'No, those are definitely the right ones, mate.' said Tony, looking quizzically at John.

'Sorry, but that's them, and them's what we got!'

John mused, scratching his chin and looking intently at the size of the pitch versus the size of his little players. He couldn't imagine it.

'Tony, haven't I seen men playing on this pitch?'

'You have, John. But they uses the bigger goals,' Tony said, trying to reassure him.

Looking at the varieties of goalposts, crossbars and stanchions, John could clearly not see anything in the compound that was of any different size!

'Tell you what,' began Tony. 'Why don't you come along tomorrow and have a look at the under-8s playing?

'Chalgrove, I believe.' He grinned as he looked over his shoulder on his way down the line.

Kick-off at 10:30. I know 'cause I'm reffing it!'

John considered this. 'You know, I think I probably will,' he said, turning towards the shed.

The next morning, as the Grove under-8s kicked off against Chalgrove, John winced on the touchline as the older age group tried to play football on this huge pitch.

It was the same dimensions he had seen under-14s and under-15s playing on. The goals still looked enormous, and despite the players being a year older than John's boys, they were dwarfed against the pitch's length and width.

The boys took ages to get the ball near the goal from one end to the other, there were acres of space in the midfield area and between the half-way line and the goals.

Billy's boys had been given some football coaching, but still, both teams mainly ran around in a big huddle chasing after the ball. It was not a pleasant sight. John left with the definite view that these small age groups should be playing on scaled-down, six-a-side style pitches to encourage their ball touches and awareness, alongside the fact that they would get far more enjoyment out of the games, and their development as footballers would surely be accelerated.

As a manager, he would have to bring this up at his upcoming first football meeting in the rugby club.

Anyway, when Sunday came, as arranged, the boys took to the pitch in their hand-me-down, black and white striped (Newcastle United) colours. Joe Moreland had brought the kit around to John's during the week. It was literally a black bin-liner full of a mismatch of previous small Grove team uniforms – frayed, faded and sometimes holed.

John and Lyn had picked through and found the best of the worst, sorting 16 shirts, 16 pairs of shorts and (nearly) 16 pairs of socks. Lyn washed them and here was the under-7s first kit.

The boys were glad to receive their new kit in the changing rooms, smiling with happiness whilst pulling their new colours on.

Most of the boys were very small and looked comical with skinny legs and huge baggy shorts. But they were happy, chuckling little fellows and very keen to get on with the match. They looked proud as they trickled out onto the front pitch. Liam had to go in one goal, despite being easily the smallest.

The training match featured opposition from some of Billy's players who had played against Chalgrove, one or two Grove under-9s plus a few younger boys; so, this was a pretty casual affair as an exercise.

The size of the pitch though, yet again, meant that the match was a bit of a joke. Some parents came to watch and were keen to see their sons playing. The better players' dads stood together, sternly looking on, watching out for a moment of skill. There were some good moments too. Once, the ball went up near the goal, and the footballers in the team easily took on the novices and scored freely.

Young Billy and Liam, the keepers, made valiant efforts to keep goal. Ritchie, Dwight and Sean controlled much of the match and everyone ran around a lot again, mainly in one mass after the ball. As a training match, it did give John an inkling of how difficult it would be to arrange a formation, or any semblance of an organised team performance. Still, it was only a friendly!

As training continued through the summer, more boys drifted in, and the team were able to stage more mock matches against each other, helped by the over-enthusiastic parents making up the numbers. It was a great atmosphere, and the parents were as keen as the boys (keener in some cases)! They trained on ball skills and keeping shape, along with all the basics. John just made it up as he went along, not really knowing the first thing about training. There was just no need to work on the physical side, because although the boys were by and large still quite small, they were as fit as fleas – the only thing they did all day was race around.

The practice matches became marginally better, although John kept them on half-sized pitches marked up with cones, while trying to find smaller goals. The boys enjoyed this immensely, although the full-sized pitches would be the norm when they started their new season as under-7s proper.

So, with 20 or so players, albeit an absolute assortment of shapes, sizes and abilities, they trooped off – prepared for their first proper match.

***

Under-7s Friendly League

At this time, teams were unable to join proper leagues, so there was a 'friendly' casual league for the under-7s, where managers contacted other known clubs and arranged friendlies. John had lists of contacts, along with his players' parents' phone numbers. It was pleasant to arrange games with likeminded local people, and easy to inform parents about who was selected, and what time and where to meet.

The Grove parents were largely working middle-class folks and very amenable, just wanting the best for their kids and happy to be involved.

The First Game Ever – Didcot Away

The Grove parents met at the Gomm-by (the lay-by near their house), appropriately dubbed by the Gomm family, on the A338. It was the perfect place to meet, with easy access to the neighbouring towns. The cars straggled in with mums and dads, brothers, sisters, pets, grandparents and babies. They filed over to Didcot in convoy, finding their way to the recreation ground. There was a good parking area, and a walk to the changing rooms, which were tidy enough.

The place was overrun with small boys scraping footballs around, boisterous and excited. This was the first match. Didcot Casual Boys – away. The match had been arranged between John and Fred Johnstone, who had been running the Didcot boys teams for forty odd years. Fred was a lovely, old, wizened grey-haired pensioner, with a passion for boys football. As they shook hands and chatted, John began to understand his simple philosophies. He just wanted to give these young lads the chance to play football. Simple.

He also appreciated the Didcot attitude. They were in it for fun. The boys were there to play football, but they were just little kids, and they were there to enjoy it. This was Didcot's third match, but canny old Fred had done all this several times and for many years.

'Fuck, me. Look at the size of the pitch, Marc.' John winced. 'Bloody bigger than ours.'

'Yep, and the goals are full size,' noted Marc.

'Ridiculous!' sighed John.

'Gonna be a long match, chap,' laughed Marc. 'Are you sure that's our pitch? It's bloody massive.'

'Mate, don't even go there.

The match kicked off and, from the outset, it was a pack affair. The boys mainly swooped around the ball with a mass instinct to get there first and run the ball into the net. It wasn't pretty. Grove scored first and Didcot equalised thanks to a mistake by the full back. Stephen Edwards was at fault with the goal and let a shoddy half-hit shot squirm under his body. Goal kicks were like conceding penalties. Unless Sean came back and took them, nobody else could get the ball out of the area, so the offensive attack camped like vultures around the edge of the box!

John had put Stephen Edwards in goal because Liam was so small, and Billy was useful in midfield. He had played in goal for the second half of the training match and had made a couple of decent saves.

Dwight hit a cross into the box, and Richie's head met the ball full on to drive number two under the bar. Grove went three up when Shaun jinked into the box to set up Sparkie with a tap-in.

But Didcot came back to equalise when the pack surged towards the Grove goal. As the cross came over, Edwards was out of his area, swiping with his feet and miss-kicking, leaving the goal at Didcot's mercy, and they equalised softly. Half-time came and the score was 3-3.

The first half-time team talk. The boys were still officially under-7s, meaning that most were only about 6-7 years old. So, the team talk was mainly John trying to praise the boys without criticising them. He was also conscious of not picking on anyone in particular because: a) He didn't want his players bursting into tears on him and b) He also didn't want to make a dick of himself. After all, this was only small boys football!

At this time, the boys still had to play on these full-sized pitches and this had been the single biggest problem of the first-half. John had been thinking whilst watching the first-half and had formulated an idea that would combat the pack action – he would limit his back four.

'Right. Boys, listen up! Listen up, Colin! Right, we're doing ok, but we conceded goals because all our players were in the attack. So, defenders, once we clear an attack and send the ball forward, you guys are not allowed over the half-way line. Understand?'

Five pairs of eyes stared quizzically back at him.

'Yes?'

'What, we're not allowed over the half-way line at all?' questioned Colin.

They seemed to understand, but didn't look very happy about it. Still, it had to be tried!

'Okay! That's right. Hold your positions. Don't go over the

half-way line for any reason. Okay?'

'Okay,' they muttered, not convinced.

'Clear? You must not go over the half way line?' He motioned an imaginary line for effect.

Five bemused nods.

'John, are we allowed to go *back* into our own half? The forwards, I mean?' Sean Revell stared up earnestly. He had a big silly grin on his face and a twinkle in his eye.

Ritchie and Dwight were grinning from ear to ear.

'What d'you mean, Sean? Jesus, of course you're allowed to go back in your own half, you need to help defend.' He motioned them back for the second half.

'It's just the back four. Let's go!'

Marc burst out laughing – living up to his nickname, 'Giggly'.

Ollie, Andrew Dawson, Colin Mercer and the back four in general duly moved up to half-way after clearing an attack.

They resolutely remained there on defensive duty. Grove had a very good midfield and attack and would bombard Didcot at every opportunity. Meaning those rear-guard stalwarts would be on the half-way line with nothing to do. It worked quite well, but it didn't look great. The keeper stood dwarfed under the giant frame, and he was miles back from the back four, who were rooted like sentinels to the half-way line.

John wasn't sure this was quite what he wanted; Didcot certainly weren't playing like that. Time would tell. Grove scored twice early on and piled on the pressure. Didcot got one back following another disastrous goal-kick, which was ransacked on the edge of the Grove penalty area and slapped back into the net. But Grove had a lot of the second-half possession. All eyes were on the Didcot goal, and for 15 minutes that was where all the action was.

After this period of pressure, Marc poked John in the ribs.

'Chap, what's your old boy up to?' He pointed across to the right-back position, occupied by John's son, Ollie.

'Ha! Ha! What's he doing?'

Following Marc's finger, John was amazed to see his son and prodigy doing 'spins' on the half-way line. He looked again, and right at that moment, Ollie – with a determined look steeled onto his face – leapt into the air, spinning around twice or thrice. He was checking how many times he could spin in the air. He was bored! Obviously, the new defensive rules were boring for the defenders, who had started to amuse themselves while awaiting the next action.

Almost immediately, Didcot attacked through the middle while Andrew Dawson was looking the other way. He was staring at Ollie and counting his spins, silently waving his fingers in time with them.

'Wake up!' John screamed at them 'Wake up and look out! They're attacking!'

Ollie landed awkwardly from his triple axel and started off lamely in pursuit. Dawson was twenty yards behind. He ran, stumbled and fell clumsily out of embarrassment. Edwards came skidding out of his area again, completely isolated and missing the ball entirely, and Didcot were level once more!

As the match progressed, the pattern continued, and both sides laboured up and down the enormous pitch. It was end-to-end stuff, but it took all day to get there. Didcot had a smashing little left-winger, and he broke out late on chasing a hopeful punt out of defence. The Grove back four relaxed again, and John was mortified more than once to see his bored back four, some 40 yards ahead of the keeper, lined up in a row having a good old chat with each other.

'You lot!' John screamed, 'Get back into the match!'

Mercer was taken by surprise with the winger and the scream. He careered around in panic. But he was too late. The ball came across, Stephen Edwards dropped the cross right at the feet of the Didcot No.9 – it was 6-5. Dawson and Mercer had galloped back, also unaware of the swiftness of the attack – but too late – and could only watch, panting, as the ball hit the net. Of course, it didn't matter, because Ritchie grabbed a late equaliser in the last few, after a mazy dribble had left three defenders sprawling in his wake. It had been a great start, a real fun game and a good result. The boys had enjoyed it and came off buzzing at full time, half of them still too young to even get their muddy boots off themselves!

John shook hands with Fred and the ref, and they arranged to do it again sometime. There were a few baffled looks from some Grove parents. But, on the whole, everyone went home happy about the day, the performance and the result.

And it had been an immensely enjoyable experience! A real piece of theatre.

John did suffer his first player casualty though. Stephen Edwards's dad approached him after the match to tell him he didn't want Stephen playing matches anymore. He was a teacher, and he didn't want his son burning out! To be fair, the lad wasn't a goalie. For the time being, while they were playing friendlies, Liam would probably make a better fist of it in any case despite his size. The more likely reason was that poor old 'Eddie' had made a bit of a disaster out of his debut, despite being dead keen, and had embarrassed his dad full-time.

But…despite everything, the boys had not lost. Result!

The following Monday, Marc and John were having a laugh about the Didcot game over a beer in the Bay Tree.

'I reckon old "Eddie" has been watching match of the day, you know – the way he came for that first cross! Bloody hell, he was bloody miles out of his area!' Marc guffawed.

'Yeah, he was wandering about a bit – he was even facing the wrong way when the ball came in.'

'Well, never mind chap, it was a funny game. They were running around like a swarm.'

'Yeah, but what about the half-time innovation? The backs hardly moved over that half-way line!'

John nursed his *Old Speckled Hen*. 'The backs just haven't got a chance really, we'll have to work on that bloody gap.'

'They're about fifty yards from the keeper,' he continued, rubbing his chin in thought, 'and forty yards from the action when we're attacking!

'You're gonna have to stop young Ollie from doing them spins, mate. What with that and the rest of the back four counting on them, we got well turned over for a couple of goals. Ha! Ha! What a crack!'

'Well, for the next training session, we'll try to reduce the size of the pitch – get them closer together, and get the backs involved in the team.'

'Yeah, well, you could also do with them being about a foot taller per man, chap. They're so tiny!' Marc laughed.

'And you need to get Dimblow in goal!'

Cumnor Minors Away

A hastily arranged second game took the team away to Cumnor, a delightful little village about five miles north. The midweek training session had been a lot of fun, and John had tried to explain to the lads about the huge gulf between the attack and defence. The truth was that the most promising lads were in midfield and upfront, and it seemed that the small boys and the less talented were left in defence.

However, there was a great spirit among them, and after an initial scrap, Grove overwhelmed their opponents, eventually winning the game by seven goals to nil. The difference was in the quality of the front boys, who were outstanding, with a brace for Claydon and Brind, and a goal apiece for Ciampioli, Revell and Webb.

Fair play. Those boys had listened and did come back to assist the defenders. But the truth was, this was not Didcot. Grove dominated Cumnor and dealt with any threat they had to offer, usually on the half-way line. There was just the one embarrassing incident when Andrew Dawson, in a period of attacking activity miles away near the Cumnor goal, was seen to be stooped down on his haunches intently surveying something on the ground.

'What the fuck?'

'What…Andrew!' shouted John from the touchline.

Andrew looked up, surprised. He guiltily stood up, swaying like a baby horse standing for the first time.

'Picking daisies! He's picking fucking daisies!'

In his right hand he was clutching a nice little posy of daisies that were growing near the touchline from his left back position stationed at halfway.

'Can somebody stop Andrew picking daisies?' cried John desperately.

The watching parents were alerted, and thankfully someone pointed it out to his dad Frank, who was hovering nearby. Frank swiftly dealt with it with a cuss.

Mark was beside himself. John shook his head in disbelief.

The two friends shared the moment in amusement.

The pitch was smaller, but only just. But the midfielders and forwards, despite the pitch size, seized the game and flooded forward dangerously whenever they got the ball. Little Liam had replaced Edwards in goal and was awesome despite his size and age, coming out bravely to thwart attacks in the box and diving at the feet of his opponents with absolute bravery. But he was ridiculously small for the goal, so anything lofting over three feet had him beaten. He was only just six years old!

Still, for the time being, this was an improvement.

With the team shaping up, after another couple of friendlies and some more boys joining, a little team emerged – about 21 players with around 12 half decent players and a number of smaller, younger boys. Some were obviously not footballers, but they were all keen as mustard and turned up for the training sessions on Sunday mornings, or occasionally on Wednesday nights.

Training was a bit of a hit and miss, as John still really hadn't a clue about what he was doing. But training normally involved a bit of dribbling, passing, shooting and general football practice. At that age, the physical training wasn't really necessary, as the boys nearly all had energy to burn. There were boys – like Johnny Wells, Sean Webb, Billy McDonald, Colin Mercer and Jamie Wilkins – who had been there from the start but were improving. So a reasonable eleven was starting to form. In that first year, everyone just loved it, did their best and played football.

In the last quarter of an hour of training, John used to play a small-sided match, usually with himself and another helper on one side or another which, again, the boys loved and which also highlighted their abilities and brought them on more.

Marc often came to training, as did the dogs; his Oscar, more often than not, getting embarrassingly amorous on or off the pitch by chasing down some passing dog (it didn't need to be a bitch) or practising his speciality of pooping on a log or bag, but never on the grass.

The first home match was against Florence Park. John had called the parents for a Sunday morning kick-off at 10 am. About sixteen players were selected, and John had asked all their parents to come over at 9 am, giving them an hour to set up the pitch. The pitch was marked, having been lined in advance. The goals were amongst five sets of tubular iron, D-angled sides and male and female connections, painted white over red oxide and flecked with spots of rust. They were heavy, had to be found (there were two different sizes) and they had to be hauled from the compound to the pitch in four pieces, (two D-frames, a crossbar and a back, ground bar).

They were over-encrusted in white paint, having had a new coat of paint every year for the six-a-side tournament – Grove's primary fundraiser. This made them thick, cumbersome, unwieldly and very difficult to manoeuvre. This was a real effort. One man could not have managed this on his own.

The pieces had to be carried by two men over 100-200 meters, and assembled once carried to position. It was back-breaking and frustrating work. The frames often had to be carried back and replaced because the joints on the posts didn't marry up.

Once the correct frames had been matched (usually on the second or third attempt), and the ends had been forced together, the nets (also in two annoying sizes) were draped over. The nets were always holed, and there was never anything to fix the holes with. Sometimes John would take along some string or find a piece of twine. Then the holes had to be crudely stitched together, so that a perfectly good shot would not whip through any holes in the netting, causing arguments.

Sometimes the holes were so big that the net was all puckered up and gathered in places, making John wince in embarrassment. All this took some time, and John liked to delegate the work. As was normal in these circumstances, the few good parents were the same ones who put up the goals, ran the line, helped with the transport or generally assisted. In the early days, when the matches were novel, there was plenty of assistance, but now most of the parents' enthusiasm to help had fizzled away.

John insisted from the outset that the parents must arrive and at least get the goals up. His job was difficult enough without all the exertions that came with getting the goals for the match together!

As this activity progressed, the visitors arrived. John made sure that the changing rooms were fit and opened (sometimes they were not, and the caretaker had to be woken). He made sure that the ref was booked, although he used his mates at this level. He had a bucket and sponge, two good, size 12 match balls, and all the practice balls in the boot, a pump, a whistle, his book of contacts with emergency club numbers (including the caretaker's), six poles and flags for the corners and half way, his two linesmen's flags and a mobile phone – quite an innovation back then.

He wrote the opposition manager's name down somewhere convenient in case he forgot it.

Then he went amongst the dads to find a willing linesman. It was amazingly difficult – they mostly vanished into thin air when he started looking! He then gave a little team-talk to the boys and made sure the team were smart – shirts tucked in (a club rule). With their track-suit tops on, the boys ran around a bit, and took them off just before kick-off, and the game was about to begin.

There were no pre-match warming up to stretch their muscles. So, with the pitch being set, the coin tossed, and ends chosen, they were ready for kick off.

Florence Park were a little suburb of the Oxford town team, and John had the choice of Marc or Steve (Boily) to be referee. This was all very casual, so Marc agreed, without any training, just using his wits and guile. Unfortunately, he turned up in faded, grey, track-suit bottoms and a scraggy shirt, unshaven and looking like he didn't belong. Truthfully, he looked like he had just woken from a night on the beer. With the reluctant linesmen in place, Marc blew for kick off. The whistle didn't sound. He tried again and got a vague pea-rattle. Shaking his head, he waved play on, and the match was underway.

He gambolled after the play, wasn't forceful at all and had a real problem with the whistle – the pea somehow wouldn't work. So, there were many errors that went unpunished, causing lots of moaning and criticism from the parents.

This match was a much sterner test than either Didcot or Cumnor; these lads were townies, with a bigger attitude, and some were naturally skilled players, steeled by their environment. After a competitive goal-less first half – in which they had threatened poor Liam's goal half a dozen times – the Oxford team took the lead mid-way through the second when Wells missed a tackle on the half-way line. They flooded forward and the back four left a great gap. As the gap widened, their diminutive, raggedy centre forward – who was quick as lightning – nipped in and hoisted the ball over the hopelessly tiny Liam.

One-nil!

Dwight rallied his troops, and they now had to battle to get back in the match.

The boys worked hard, and Florence Park repelled them, almost catching Grove on the break.

With five minutes left, there was an incident where Ritchie had turned his marker inside out once too often, and the defender sliced him down from behind on the edge of the area. It was a bad foul, and a clear free kick. Marc was well behind the play, but still had a very good view. He blew for the foul – but there was no sound. He trudged after the play, but the ball went safely back to the Florence Park keeper. The Grove parents were all cursing Marc (not many of them knew who he was). Several of them were jumping up and down.

'Oy ref, are you blind? That was a penalty!'

'Look at him ambling about!'

'Blow your bloody whistle! What's wrong with you?'

John waved up two of the back four, Sean Webb and Andrew Dawson, to support the free kick. They were only too pleased to get over the half-way line. 'Webby, take Andy and get some pressure on. Ollie, Col – stay back!'

The remaining defenders shot him dark looks.

Marc was impervious to the insults in his own quiet way, and after losing the moment, waved to play on. Carlo screamed at his team who had all stood still – waiting for the free kick. The Florence Park keeper had the ball in his arms. But he was unsure of what to do. He looked around behind the goal, past his stationary defenders to his dad, a charming Iranian chap.

'Go on, Ali. Kick the ball! Kick it away! Kick it very hard!'

Marc looked over at John with a massive grin on his face.

'Kick the ball very hard, Ali!'

The diminutive keeper took three steps forward to the edge of the six-yard box and drop-kicked the ball out of his hands. Its flight was halted after four feet as it crashed into the face of the hapless Andrew, who was standing right in front of him.

Andrew was a lovely boy, quiet-spoken and polite, very keen and rather gangly.

His reaction however, was stunning; he looked shocked to the core, immediately turning scarlet and opening his mouth in a huge gaping bawl as he exploded into tears. 'Whaaaaaaghhh! Whaaaaaaghhh!' He bawled as he gasped for breath. His dad raced onto the pitch. Marc ignored him and waved to play on.

John raced onto the pitch full tilt with his sponge and bucket. Marc falteringly put the whistle to his lips to blow up for a goal-kick, but could still be discerned, refereeing duties aside, shaking with laughter.

No sound came from the whistle. He took the whistle from around his neck, peered down its barrel, shook it, and tried it. A feeble blow, barely audible.

He approached John grinning from ear to ear. 'Chap this whistle doesn't work. It's getting me into trouble.' Unfazed, he was still laughing.

John, calming Andrew down, said, 'Well, if you can't get a sound, shout "stop" or something. The game's nearly over!'

'Goal kick!' shouted Marc.

Justice was done for the missed free kick and the ball in the face. The ball had rebounded off Andrew Dawson's face and out for a goal-kick to Florence Park. Once again, the result was, at this level, virtually a corner!

The Grove team hurriedly assembled around the penalty area in gleeful anticipation. Could Ali even get the kick out of the box? Marc violently blew on the whistle, managing to only move the pea around, which quietly rattled away to itself. The Florence Park keeper had really struggled with his goal-kicks. He seemed to be the weak link in the team – perhaps the only player they had who would go in goal?

His dad was still stalking the goal area with advice, 'Kick the ball hard. Very, very hard.' The keeper shot a despairing look at his father, but the old man was adamant and becoming very insistent.

'Put the ball down and kick it very hard.'

Marc turned again to the half-way line to where John was standing.

This repeated urging from the dad creased Marc up, and he shook with laughter again. As he waved play-on, his kick had to be re-taken twice because the ball didn't go out of the area. On the third attempt, the ball hobbled out of the area to Dwight who lashed it back with venom on the half-volley. Ali, credit to him, dived to his right. The ball bounced off his shin and, as it bounced on the penalty spot, was lashed into the roof of the net by Mark Brind for a late equaliser. 1-1 – Job done.

Marc did shout 'stop' once when the whistle didn't work, but by then, most of the parents were also trying to stifle their own laughter.

'Who was that ref?' John was asked by several parents. 'Was that his whistle?'

'How much is it to hire a proper ref, John?'

Andrew Dawson and Marc both left red-faced for different reasons.

Every week, John bashed on and arranged – on the phone and through recommendations and mates of mates – a fixture for the next week.

The back-four rule was dropped, much to the relief of the Grove defenders.

The next under-7s fixture was a creditable 4-4 draw against an invigorated and improved Florence Park (away), which still included the diminutive Ali in goal! There followed another draw, this time a 3-3 in an end-to-end battle at home with Didcot with a Mark Brind hat trick.

Wins at Botley (4-0) and at home over St Edmunds (6-1) pushed up the boys' morale and reputation, who were now beginning to be more organised and disciplined.

Further run-outs were Launton away, a decisive 4-0 win, Garden City and Cholsey 2-0 and 7-1, followed by a hard-fought draw at Witney Vikings at 2-2, resulting in an unbeaten first season, and a very satisfying one, given the shambolic start, the size of the goals and the pitches.

Not a bad first season at all!

With training techniques improving, and the boys' abilities and ambitions coming together, the team was beginning to become a unit. The acid test came in the very last fixture of the season against who would become 'the old rivals' – Abingdon.

Chapter 6
Basketball Football
Liverpool v. Palace semi-final

Ian Mould, a general builder, had been in Bay Tree after work on a particular Friday and, after several pints and innumerable jokes, blurted, 'Did I hear you right, John? Did you say you wanted a patio built?'

'Mouldy' was a friend of Boily's – a stocky, well-built lad with a shock of curly-blond hair. He had a massive, animated head with mad green eyes and a constant grin. He was a brilliant laugh and a joke-machine, very funny and full-on.

He was looking quizzically and intently at John for his reply.

'Well, yeah. I've got a nice garden, but there's a grim grassy bit right outside the patio windows.'

John knew Mouldy was in the building trade.

'Oh, okay!' Mouldy replied, grinning madly 'Right, well, I can do that for ya! Let me come around and have a look and I'll price it for ya?'

Mouldy started the job two weeks later, on a Saturday morning. He had finished it the next night.

The result was a two-level patio with a ridge a brick high through the middle of the garden, right across from left to right.

It was uneven, poorly laid, and frankly, dangerous.

He'd also said, 'John, I've got enough bricks left to build you a brick barbeque. What d'ya fink?'

So, to the left of the two-tier, unsightly, uneven patio was built an even more unsightly solid brick barbeque which resembled a small brick shed, inconveniently and unsuitably situated more or less in the middle of the garden.

Mouldy was paid. The wife was unhappy. It was a disaster. The slabs had been laid shiny-side up; in other words, upside down, meaning they would be treacherous in the wet, with the children potentially slipping and breaking limbs. The whole thing sloped to the south.

The barbeque was in the wrong area, and it also leant like a mini leaning tower of Pisa. Fifty per cent of the slabs were uneven and rocked when you walked on them, and the sand that Mouldy had brushed into the cracks as a 'finish' was dirty and mixed with mud and cement. This meant that if it rained, there would be trails of cement and sandy footprints everywhere.

They lived with it for six months, until one day, Marc, who was round having a beer, sat on the patio door-jamb and said, 'Crikey, chap! That is a piss-poor job!' He laughed. 'Did he actually have the nerve to charge you for that?'

'Oh don't, mate. I'm not happy about it, and Lyn is furious!'

Lyn walked out at that moment with a tray of nachos and some salsa.

'Yes, I am bloody livid!' she fumed. 'I've told Johnny to get our bloody money back. We had a nice back garden till Mouldy got his pork sausage fingers on it. Just look!'

They all looked and laughed. 'Well, it was pretty cheap,' joked John, backing off defensively. 'And we did get a beautiful brick shithou–I mean barbeque, free of charge!' He winced with mock humour.

'John, you're a chef, right?' she asked testily. 'Can you ever see yourself actually cooking on that bloody monstrosity? Or even having the gall to invite guests round?'

Without giving John a chance to speak, Lyn continued, 'They would be dying of laughter! No, I've looked at this nightmare for six months now, and I want it gone. I don't know or care how or where. But it is not staying.' She gave her death-stare, to which there was no answer.

'Well, I'm not going back to Mouldy.'

'Are you having a laugh?' she snarled. 'I wouldn't have him build me a sandcastle.' With her hands on her hips and eyes flaring, Lyn looked deadly serious and quite frightening.

'What we need is a proper builder,' she further fumed. 'A craftsman.'

Marc had been quietly musing, watching and listening carefully.

'Let's rip it up,' he announced. 'I can build you a proper patio. You don't need a builder, we'll do it ourselves.'

'What? Have you ever built a patio before, chap?' John seemed astonished.

'Chap, I built a small one at our first house. And I'll tell you what, it was a damn sight better finished than this. Come on, what are we? February now? We've got the slabs and a start on the bricks – assuming you're going ahead with the demolishment of your barbeque? We'll be finished in a month.'

So, the whole thing was dug up, and under Marc's guidance, they ended up toiling for a few months, with Marc as the major architect. He was, John learnt, a bit of a stickler for perfection.

John was more of a bodge-it-and-see merchant. But Marc was around digging, then digging deeper. When they had finished digging, he would want it deeper again. They spent the evenings till it got dark, and much of the weekends till late. On and on they dug and trimmed and filled. They staked. John looked at the hole and couldn't believe how big and deep it was.

Virtually the whole garden, which had included three fishponds when they had moved in, had been utilised. They were to retain a raised flower bed to the left of the patio doors, a small flower bed in front of the rear of the garage (which faced the patio doors). Then there was the pathway from the gate up to the ornamental silver birch and another raised flowerbed, which produced the most amazing powder-blue and navy-blue Delphiniums annually.

Apart from those areas, the rest was to be laid to patio. Neither men had a problem with this. They could both envisage the end result, as could Lyn – who would have the final word. But when it was being dug out, it looked like a huge bombsite. The whole area was pure grey clay. This went on for weeks. They filled four full-sized skips with mud and clay and broke the rocks and bricks for hard-core. They broke down the garden fences at the rear and dug up the grass area.

Once the hole was deep enough, square and ready, which took them about three solid weeks of spare time hard labour, it was time to lay the stakes. Obviously, Marc had done this before, as he was so certain of what to do. They cut lengths of two-inch timber and drove them into the clay floor of the whole area, at regular intervals of about a meter square. Each stake was finished square and at an identical height. Once the first few stakes were in place, the bricks, rocks and assorted hard-core were added.

This was then pummelled down with lump hammers into

small pieces that would form the basis of the support.

It was back-breaking work. And it took longer on this part than it did on the digging, which now seemed easier in retrospect. But bit by back-numbing bit, the area began to fill. They had to get more bricks. Once again, Marc was a hard taskmaster. He wanted this bit to be perfect too. Several times, John thought they were broken up and deep enough, only to find Marc throwing in more bricks and leaping into the hole, smashing the bricks to smaller smithereens.

A week later, the concrete arrived. They had decided one lorry load was enough. As the cement mixer lorry spewed out its load of ready-mix onto the area that had once been the lawn, they filled barrows and shovelled the wet mix into the abyss.

When it arrived, the amount of concrete looked abnormally large. But as they threw it into the prepared pit, the rubble and then the stakes began to disappear. They filled the massive abyss right up to the top of the carefully measured stakes, so that the square end of the wood was all that was visible. There was surprisingly little cement left over. The concrete was smoothed over to form a proper flat surface. They let the cement go off a bit, then wetted down the slabs and laid them in random colour order (they were red and grey).

The two friends, cracking open a can of *Stella* each after their hard work, looked at the results of their labours.

'There, just a bit of tidying up, trimming and the grouting, chap,' said Marc, admiring his handiwork.

'Well, d'you know what, mate? That is a really good job. Thanks for all your efforts.'

'Shall we call that a day then?'

'Yeah, we'll finish it off tomorrow.'

On viewing the result the following Sunday morning, they agreed that their efforts had produced a substantial, flat, safe area that was converted into a patio, or something resembling a small basketball court. Marc's attention to detail throughout the entire construction process meant the whole thing rested unerringly in a mixture of concrete and hard-core about two–three feet deep. This patio was here to stay.

On that last Sunday, as they finished the job – tidying up and finishing touches – it was the FA Cup semi-final day. Man. United v. Oldham later, but first–Liverpool v. Crystal Palace.

At first, they had it on the radio. Palace was still in danger of being relegated, and Liverpool was cruising through the Cup and on for another league title. The teams had already met twice in the league – the second occasion bringing an embarrassing 9-0 thrashing for Palace. The lads laid the last couple of slabs, viewing the game through the open patio doors. It was no surprise that having had all the possession, Liverpool took the lead after fifteen minutes.

With Steve McMahon, Ronnie Whelan, Houghton, Beardsley and John Barnes in the side, they dominated proceedings, and Ian Rush latched onto a through-ball from McMahon giving the Reds an expected early lead.

At half-time, with the patio almost finished, Liverpool had finished strongly and were still one-nil up. The lads cracked open cans of *Stella* and, as they finished in-filling and tidying up, listened to the commentary filtering into the yard. John, and Marc, joined by young Ollie started to watch the match in earnest. As the second-half started, Ollie watched the match lazily slumped over an armchair and the boys watched from the open patio door.

Whatever had been said in the Palace changing-room at half-time was having an immediate effect. Crystal Palace came out of the blocks flying at Liverpool. They had decided to have a real go and were, from the kick-off, really on the front foot

Not long into the second-half, John Pemberton raced down the right wing, flying past stunned defenders. His deep cross was met by Barber at the far post and headed back across the goal to John Salako. Without hesitation, Salako smashed a stunning volley into a hapless defender. The ball cannoned back to a grateful Mark Bright, who joyfully smacked it past Grobbelaar for the equaliser.

The two workers were now sitting half-way in the lounge and were amazed at the comeback.

The recovery was against all odds without Ian Wright, Bright's usual partner! And this proved to be just the start. Palace continued to attack, piling men and balls into the area on every possible occasion. Villa Park was humming, and there was the chance of a big upset. The game had turned full circle, and the atmosphere was crackling.

As Geoff Thomas began to get an iron grip on the game, feeding the influential Salako, Bright and Andy Gray, Liverpool began to wilt. Gary Gillespie was taken out of the defence injured and neither his replacements, Barry Venison or Glynn Hysen, or even the experienced Alan Hansen, looked at ease with the ferocity of the relentless Palace bombardment. This seemed to affect Liverpool as a team, and suddenly they were looking shaky. Palace rained crosses, corners, throw-ins and set pieces at the weakened defence. In the 69th minute, that defence was breached again. A free kick from Andy Gray was well met by

Bright, and O'Reilly came crashing in to force the ball over the line.

'Jesus,' said Marc, 'what a game – amazing! Palace are going to do 'em.'

'Well, lunch is ready, so turn the TV around, and you can carry on watching it from the table, if it's that good,' said Lyn, as she started to carry the lunch in.

'Can I watch it, Mum? It's great!' But Ollie was by now prone in front of the TV.

'Look, here they come again!' screamed Marc in delight, as Palace launched another sweeping move.

'It's relentless!' John was awestruck. 'Awesome!'

It was true. The game was completely mesmerising!

Liverpool continued to repel the warlike Eagles and tried to fight their way back in. But in another twist, they lost Ian Rush to an injury, and their main striker was replaced by Steve Staunton. The game ebbed and flowed, never losing impetus or atmosphere.

With just eight minutes left, and this time from a Liverpool free kick, Palace failed to deal with the cross, and McMahon equalised with a crisp twenty-yard drive into the corner. The Reds now got their second wind. A minute later, substitute Staunton was upended in the area, and John Barnes converted the penalty. 3-2 to Liverpool with 5 minutes left.

From the table, the lads looked on in amazement as Palace, despite the reverse, crashed forward again and again, narrowly missing two chances and having defenders hacking clear at the last minute. What a game! When all seemed lost, and the valiant efforts were seemingly exhausted, once more the ball was floated into the far post to be met by a soaring Andy Gray, outjumping the defence to steer another header home for the equaliser.

The tools, spades and the last dusty slabs, the dishes, the cold roast potatoes and veggies in the kitchen; everything was forgotten and now they all gathered around the TV. With virtually no time left, another Palace attack ended with Andy Thorn smashing the ball against the bar leaving the Liverpool defence spectating.

There ended 90 minutes of one of the most amazing football games ever seen and surely, the greatest semi-final ever.

As the group enthused about the quality of the game and refreshed their beer, extra time started. The game's pace understandably cooled, but Palace were giving every bit as good as they got. Whether Liverpool at the outset had started complacently was now largely irrelevant. The fact that the Eagles had used the set-pieces to their advantage so well brought the ultimate reward from a corner. As the ball flew into the six-yard box, Thorn helped it on, and Alan Pardew headed the winning goal that would take Palace into the final with a 4-3 victory.

The Palace fans at Villa Park could hardly believe it. This had been a day out they had dared not dreamed of winning. The whole ground was in ferment, and what a great advertisement from the FA Cup across the TV networks.

Unbelievably, there followed the second semi-final soon after, which was also a high scoring affair between Manchester United and Oldham, another epic game that astonishingly finished 3-3.

The group watched that game too. The patio had been finished; thankfully, there hadn't been too much to do that last day, and Sunday, the 8th of April 1990 – the day of the epic Crystal Palace v. Liverpool game – lingered long in people's memories.

***

When the time came, a proper and professional basketball net was installed above the new patio. About eight feet off the floor, similar to regulation. Ollie had a Chicago Bulls basketball one Christmas, a grey ball with a bull's head on it, and they used to play a bit of basketball in the yard. But John remembered that when he was a kid in Cowley, the kids used to play a little football game between four semi-detached garages off Barns Road.

Together, these garages were the size of a good-sized goal; they had natural posts and a bar, as in the garage construction. And a regular half-way line in the concrete ran across. He and his mates didn't have a name for the game, but it was like playing football tennis. The garage doors were made only from plywood, so if you really whacked the ball, you could bust right through. This was disallowed. It was known as a 'slam', and if you hit the ball too hard – no matter what the position – it would be a 'No Goal'.

In the sixties, young boys, young men and football fans in general were simply amazed by the infinite and unbelievable skill that George Best possessed in his peak, as a young man at Manchester United.

In those days of George Best, his astonishing, indescribable skills were on display week after week. With George Best on *Match of the Day* every Saturday, along with other similar talents like Charlie Cooke and Jimmy Greaves, football in this era was great. The boys watched in awe every week as Best set off on mazy dribbles, beating man after man, riding lashing, scything tackles, waltzing across the breadth of the pitch and back, the ball seemingly glued to his feet.

His audacious, cheeky lob against Tottenham, scoring delectably under the crossbar was and still is one of the greatest goals ever scored at the highest level.

It's all right displaying that sort of skill in the rec, but in a live top-flight game with the nation watching – it's mesmerising. If you watch any video of Best, the most amazing thing is the way he rides the ferocious tackles coming in from all angles from bomber Harris of Chelsea and Norman 'Bites yer Legs' Hunter of Leeds, and scores of others like them. They often caught him, but the way he rode those tackles was astonishing!

As a ball-carrier and dribbler, he is, to this day, unsurpassed. He would get the ball and take on any and every player with his feints, dummies and body-swerves, swathing towards the goal relentlessly, leaving defenders sprawling in his wake and watching from the floor in awe. In the modern game, no-one has that much skill and bottle. Plus, the very first of any of those ridden challenges today would see the attacker rolling around in 'agony' for five minutes, wasting time and trying to get the offender sent off.

So, having watched and adored Georgie Best, the boys wanted to be like him. Their game developed into a game of remarkable touch and skill, and John used to love to lob, feint and tease the ball into the goal, and they played it for hours. Sometimes, they would see one of the garage owners, and they were always up on the flat rooves retrieving the ball, but nobody really bothered them, and it almost became a cult game.

The thing about this game was the development of touch,

thought and vision. All the skills were there – both feet, heading, chipping, and it was a delight to play, as well as a great improver. Sometimes, John and his mates from Cowley would be there until dark, and they developed lots of football awareness skills in that man-made football/tennis cul-de sac.

In a similar vein, and as a natural successor to this game, John and Ollie's new patio game became 'Basketball Football'. It was just as simple. A football, two players, any size or age. The rules – score a basket without using your hands, only two touches per play, one point for a basket, two for a left-foot basket, two for a back-heel basket, and minus one for an own goal (up through the basket from the bottom). The first to nine wins.

John and Ollie played this very often ever since Ollie was about eight years old.

It honed his skills very quickly, so that by the time he was nine, the competition was fierce, and Ollie was hard to beat. His eye-to-ball coordination improved, he became as good with his left foot as he was with his right, and his heading, touch, control and vision came through to the fore.

Marc used to come around and give John or Ollie a game, and that newly laid patio in the garden actually became the 'basketball football' court.

The skill levels required were intense. Lobs, heading, control, first touch was everything. Skills developed with stature and awareness, and their skill levels, especially those of the young Ollie, reached another level. And the amazing thing about the game was, it was great. Ollie and John were out there playing for hours. Ollie soon became really difficult to beat, despite his size. His first touch became silky, his awareness superb and ability awesome.

It was such a brilliant game that Marc would often just wander round and play 'the winner', whoever was left on the court. Marc was a pretty good footballer, who still played Pub football for 'The Red Lion' in Brightwell, near Wallingford. The three of them played and fought hard – for hours sometimes. It used to drive Lyn mad, as the ball constantly bounced on the patio's concrete slabs. Worse, the net was very close to the kitchen window and the patio doors.

Father and son talked quite a lot about football as Ollie progressed. Ollie clearly loved it and was getting better at it, so John took an interest and tried everything to encourage him.

'Try and think of a footballer who you'd like to be.'

'Why, Dad?' Ollie looked at him curiously.

'Watch him, study him, see how he moves, what positions he gets into, how he controls the ball – watch Shearer.' John explained.

'Here, stand there – right, now throw the ball at my chest, softly.'

Ollie threw the ball.

'Now watch.' John cushioned the ball on his chest and let it drop to a volley, softly nurturing the ball back to his small son.

'You don't get time to stop, control the ball, wait for it to bounce, and then shoot. You've got to deal with it quick – before the defenders and goalie even know what you're up too – Bang! The ball's in the back of the net! Watch Shearer!' John volleyed the ball gently back in one move.

'I like Klinsmann, Dad. I'll watch him,' Ollie said. 'I want to be like Jurgen Klinsmann. I think he's amazing!'

'Okay, but no diving then, eh?'

'Okay!'

The two of them also used to go along to the training ground with their collie, Sally. Sally had grown up with both kids, so she was family.

They had a good little training routine that involved Sally, who used to be mad about playing with the ball. They would start passing the ball to feet, from close in. Then they would call Sally to join in. Sally would come and try to intercept the ball, and the distance between father and son would get bigger. Sally would literally hare after the ball, forcing them into quicker, accurate passes until she got it. So, it was good for everyone, including the dog.

John often happily took Ollie over to the field with Sally. Ollie was beginning to be a tidy little footballer.

***

A little team was shaping up by now, complete with some cracking characters.

Oliver Dimblow

An upcoming force who would, when established, hold the keepers' jersey throughout the age groups. Quick off his line, sturdy and sound as a shot-stopper, he could make himself massive in front of opposing forwards (he was also a really nice chap).

Liam Revell

As already discussed, he was too young to join the team in the first league but had the heart of a lion. He played in goal for two seasons despite his astonishingly small size. His speciality was rushing out from the goal to hack the ball away from danger. He could look after himself and was never phased by anything. He was also very cheeky and possessed a mature and funny turn of phrase with a cute delivery, which was always accompanied by a cheeky, dimply smile.

Andrew Dawson

Lovable Andrew. He was always first to training and was amazingly polite. Although brave, Andrew's speciality appeared, as mentioned earlier, to be getting struck full in the face with the ball and bursting into uncontrollable sobs with his amazing mouth taking in great gasps of air. Cruel as it sounds, this was a truly incredible sight and was unbelievably hysterical.

Colin Mercer

Of all the boys who joined the team, and there were an amazing number of characters in the team, little Colin Mercer was one of the biggest characters. He was normally left-back, absolutely tiny (only slightly bigger than Liam Revell, despite being eighteen months older) and had a cheeky, squeaky voice and without any malice, and he had an answer for everything. He was a real trier, always giving everything, and he never stopped smiling. His dad Alan was a reliable parent, always helping with putting up the goals, and often, far, far more often than most of the fathers, ran the line. Sometimes, little Col had worked so hard on the pitch, he came off exhausted, smiling, hands on hips, red-faced and panting. His squeaky laugh could always be heard in the dressing rooms, and he was a tiny bundle of happy energy.

Ollie Gomm

As he progressed from his early training, Ollie became a quiet, hard tackler with a great attitude, once he understood the game. Always on the small side and a latecomer. Blond-haired with a baby face and great skill to come. A ball-winner in the thick of things, his short-passing game and mobility made him a reliable team player. He was a fierce competitor with a rock-solid tackle and a great passion for the win. He was not prepared to head a long dipping ball though!

Billy McDonald

Billy was a true gem. Another blond, but craggy, taller and rangier, he was more like a rugby player in build. He was fearless, hard and hard-working, always getting stuck in, and he would run all day. Bill had a famous old blue anorak that actually managed to creep into more than one of the team photos. Not the most naturally gifted player, but he was always in the team for his guts and grit – he was a real grafter and somehow, he was nearly always covered in mud! And he was a truly delightful and honest guy!

Sean Webb

'Webby' was a stocky, freckled, serious lad and had been there from day one. He was neither flamboyant nor pacey, but he was solid, with a crunching tackle – a fearless header of the ball (not the favourite pastime at that age, lots of boys went out of their way to not use their head).

He was the natural choice for Captain, and John made him his skipper early on, and without many exceptions, so he remained while the team was together, through the various age groups. He did as he was told with quiet grace and was a rock for the team in defence. He was always a very good, honest and reliable footballer, and he contributed a good deal of goals whenever he joined the attack.

Sean Revell

Sean was Liam's older brother, slightly old for the group, at the top of the age limit. He was blessed with skill. In fact, as mentioned, he nutmegged John on the first day of training. He had a florid complexion, a stand-up hairstyle and was stocky and well built. His dribbling skills, dummies, and ferocious right foot were famed. He was also a real battler and a very cheeky young man – another one with a little answer for everything. Great out wide on the right. Opponents used to ask, 'Is Revell playing? Who's marking him?' He was reliable, dangerous, and quick with great vision. Sometimes he took on one defender too many, but he would often beat players on a mazy run to set up a teammate or score himself. Always grinning! Always!

Dwight Ciampioli

Always miles ahead of the game, he was making Cruyff turns at seven (during matches)! He had abundant talent that his dad helped along with a steel middle. A proper footballer with skill, brains and mettle. Simply head and shoulders above any player that age John had ever seen. He was three feet tall with a low centre of gravity and was a very special and lovely lad to boot. Dwight dominated simply every game he played at this level. Fiercely competitive with a huge desire to win, he was a lovely bloke.

Johnny Wells

Johnny was the team's madman right from the start. A big, gangly lad even at that age, he had a bit of skill, was quick and could hit the ball very hard. He was a strong character with a mop of blond hair. He was constantly joking or moaning. He had a shambling, dogged gait, and he stuck to opponents annoyingly and was hard to knock off the ball or beat. He was possessed by football at an early age, and had a rasping, right-foot shot from outside the box. He started in midfield and became the other central defender alongside Webby.

Mark Brind

Mark was big for his age; a likeable, bright-eyed kid who had good skills, a powerful shot and was quick off the mark. He started in defence and midfield, but soon became a regular up front, grabbing goals from tap-ins to long range efforts. Supported from an early age by a talent of midfield support, he was to become a regular scorer along with his partner, Ritchie. Quick, quick-thinking and direct, he was never afraid to take anyone on for pace and was always a handful. He scored goals for fun! The names 'Brind and Claydon' were later to feature in *The Oxford Mail* every week because the two forwards always scored. Prolific!

Richard Claydon

Absolutely cheeky, he was a slightly-built left winger with an abundance of skill. Quick, bright and capable of turning a game, he was a regular starter in attack, scoring goals and roasting opponents with ease. His skills were actually spotted and encouraged at Roma when he was five years old and living in Italy. A great header of the ball, good at dribbling and crossing, he was a constant danger down the left flank, and it was a great sight – even in the early days when the pitches were inordinately large – to see Ritchie bearing down on the goal. He was a prolific scorer who loved to take opponents on for skill and pace. But he was such a good footballer that he bought space and time for his teammates. He was our amazing outlet who scared defences to death.

As the teams and fixtures kept coming, John was approached

by Tim Butler at Abingdon, who had heard through Didcot that Grove had a reasonable side. Tim was a soft-spoken gut whose son was a useful footballer in defence and particularly in goal. Grove had Didcot at home, with another well fought draw (this time 3-3) with Dwight outstandingly controlling the midfield. Two weeks later, they made their first ever trip to Abingdon away.

The Team Sheet

Liam Revell

Ollie Gomm   Olly Dimblow   Sean Webb   Colin Mercer

Sean Revell Billy McDonald Dwight Ciampioli Johnny Wells

Mark Brind   Richard Claydon

Subs: Will Roberts, Nick Howe, Martin Rowlands, Andrew Dawson, Richard Maurice, Phillip Millsom

By now, they (and the opposition) had enough boys for a couple of teams. So, Grove took a second-string team to play Abingdon B. This gave the very youngest boys a chance to play in a match. One of the youngster's dads, Ian Clarke, had run the B-team, taking them over for an earlier kick-off. It wasn't very pretty, and Abingdon were stronger, running out 7-0 winners. The main team had the same fixture an hour later. John thought it may be quite a test. He had spoken to Fred at Didcot, who had played Abingdon twice and lost both times.

'Yes. They're very strong, they have some good footballers and are quick on the break and strong at the back,' noted Fred, astutely. 'You'll have to get close to them.'

'How did you get on then, Fred?' asked John, as they strolled down the line towards half-way.

'Well, our first game was close. They won 8-5. But a few weeks ago they beat us 10-1. They outmuscled us!'

John had warned the lads they would be in for a test.

When they arrived at Abingdon that first time, they parked up and watched the end of the B-match. The changing rooms were right by the small pitch, with an expanse of other sporting pitches stretching off into the distance on three sides.

The changing rooms were big, and they had the whole room to themselves.

John gave his first team talk, warning the boys to give as good as they got, win the tackles and attack them.

'Right, lads. Listen up!' John called, raising his voice over the changing-room cackle. He looked around at his little troop, who were eagerly awaiting instructions.

'Colin…' John rolled his eyes in mock exasperation before continuing. 'You will find this a little bit different from Didcot or Cumnor, right? These lads have been together for a while, and they will expect to beat us easy.' He jumped up onto the wall-seat for effect.

The boys looked up, now silent.

'Try and compete for every ball, and don't be put off or let them knock you about.' He went on, clenching his fist.

Dwight and Revell's eyes twinkled at the prospect of the challenge.

'I'll make sure they know we're out there, John,' piped

Dwight.

'Well, you might have to Dwight.' John winked.

'We'll give 'em a going over,' grinned Revell.

'Don't let them wind you up, Revs. Let's beat them by outplaying them. And,' John paused, wringing an imaginary tea towel, 'let's kick some Abingdon arse!'

The team whooped in delight.

'Let's go get 'em!'

John let the team roll over to the match pitch, two pitches distant, following behind with Marc, the bucket and sponge.

It was a damp autumnal morning, the dew still rich on the grass, and there were a lot more parents and spectators than usual. Several people were milling through, walking their dogs and hanging around the changing rooms, chatting. The wintry sun was up glinting on the fields that sloped down to the Marina. It was a clear and pleasant start to the day.

As they neared the pitch, Richard Claydon and Ollie came running up to them.

'Oy, John. We've just gone to kick the ball around in that end.' Ritchie pointed.

'Yeah! And they told us to fuck off, this is our fucking end!' shouted Revell, who had raced up behind, red-faced and grinning. He thought it was quite funny.

Charming!

The Abingdon boys had been together for a while and had some tough cookies on the team. They obviously wanted to beat

Grove badly and were starting, as they meant to go on, with a bit of verbal intimidation.

'Move down the other end, lads. Those guys don't know the way!' shouted John sarcastically, waving his players towards the right.

After giving them his usual run around, the Grove team watched as the Abingdon lads were put through their paces. Tim Butler and his 'assistant' ran them with their knees up, had them stretching both legs in many different ways, kicked their legs right back as they ran, and basically put them through a proper warm-up routine. They obviously did this pre-match routine, and John noted, with a little envy, how good and professional it looked.

They all wore the same track suit tops, hooded and black with 'Abingdon' emblazoned in gold on the back with a sponsor's name across the front. Their kits were new, yellow and green, and their set up, look and attitude actually made Grove look a bit like a poor 'village' team.

The Grove boys also noticed this and looked on expectantly, already in their team positions, not knowing how to react, as the Abingdon lads eventually erupted from their huddle. Daunting.

'Come on, Grove!' shouted John from the touchline.

'Yes, come on, Grove!' echoed the Grove parents.

Fair play to Grove. They physically gave a good show and put themselves about. But the Abingdon dad who ran the line was giving offside every time Grove went forward, and they began to be second best. After ten minutes, Sean Revell, back-tracking, chopped their left winger down as he steamed into the box. Liam stood no chance from the penalty. Then Grove lost a bit of discipline, and the game became scrappy.

It was a lesson. The Abingdon boys took control and went 2-0 up ten minutes later, after some desperate away defending.

They also had a few boys who could really belt the ball, so they were peppering Liam at every opportunity and from anywhere.

The team came off exhausted at half-time. They had been put through the mill.

John told them from the centre circle, 'Right, boys. I want to make a couple of changes to help you out.'

He looked at Liam. 'Liam, I'm going to sub you – don't worry, you're playing well, but with these kids and the size of the goals, you haven't got a chance.'

'Billy – sorry mate, I want you in goal,' said John apologetically, patting Billy's shoulder and looking for affirmation from his midfielder. 'Okay? We all know how good you are there in training.'

Billy nodded. 'Yeah, no problem, John.'

'Good lad,' said John, proudly.

'Johnny, you drop into the back four. Colin, you make way for Millsom, and Ollie – move in behind Dwight and get the tackles in early.'

'Okay?'

'Yes? All okay?' he repeated. 'Everyone know what you're doing?'

'Yes.' A good response.

'Keep doing what you have been, get your tackles in early, stop them playing. Johnny keep tight on that Richard Wilson, don't let him turn. Ollie – help him out. Ritchie start your runs from inside our area, and Dwight – keep your head and pick Ritchie out. Sparkie – keep working and battling hard. Let's get a goal!' John was pumped, and the boys were ready and re-charged.

'Come on, Grove!' was the collective shout as the team wheeled back into their positions.

'Come on, Grove!' shouted the parents in response.

The second-half reparations worked well, but Abingdon were still well up for it, and it was they who got niggly when things didn't go their way.

Grove had a cast-iron penalty denied when Ritchie was clean through in the box, and another appeal when the centre half pushed a shot from Ciampioli onto and around the post with his hand. No decisions were going Grove's way from the Abingdon ref or the linesman, but the changes to the defence and midfield worked well. Billy McDonald was superb in goal, and the Abingdon forwards stopped shooting on site because of his size compared to Liam.

The midfield tightened right up and although Grove never stood a chance of winning, they could and should have scored. When Mark Brind sped off down the right wing with the goal opening before him, the parents groaned as the flag went up for the twentieth time. He had run from his own half, and they had a defender five yards in front of him.

As the Grove players protested, Abingdon sent a ball down the line. Their little full back, Hayes, sent over a low cross, their centre forward held off Webby, and Wilson hammered it goalwards, where Billy could only palm it into the net.

After the first few friendlies, they had come up against an organised and committed opponent. John couldn't help but notice Tim's slight smugness as they shook hands after the match. Gary Revell, Sean's dad, had a little set too with the dubious Abingdon linesman.

'Yeah, great game, John. Cor! You've got some decent players out there,' said Tim, as they headed back to the changing rooms.

'Yeah, I think we need a little work though,' replied John.

'Christ, that Ciampioli is amazing, ain't he? And that little left winger? Caused us a few problems.'

'Well, Tim, we enjoyed it, mate. Let's get together and arrange a return at our place,' said John, offering his hand.

'Spot on, mate. Give us a call – and well done again,' replied Tim, returning the firm hand-shake.

The Abingdon boys, however, couldn't supress their delight, and they wound the Grove lads up all the way to the dressing rooms. Their team did possess some cocky little buggers.

In the changing room, John addressed his weary, still smiling troops.

'Right, lads, we've been given a lesson, and we may have been unprepared for that welcome.' John was back on the seat, waving for quiet.

'Bastards!' shouted Revell.

'Well, we've learnt a lesson,' John announced, wryly.

'They were up for it – nasty, cheating and dirty. They had a bent ref and linesman, and we lost 3-0 with two penalties disallowed. They can't do that every game – they won't get away with it!'

John held up his hand for quiet.

'We started with Liam in goal, who has been great, but we need someone bigger, and we'll have new players joining, which will help us compete with teams like this.' He surveyed the team scattered around the changing room.

'Okay?' John looked around the room again for agreement. 'And that second-half performance was one of your best displays so far.' He paused and noted the ripple of satisfaction from the team. 'Keep your heads up, be proud of what you have done – these were no mugs, and they were the hardest team we have met so far. Look, I'm not going to go on – you're only little kids, right?'

'Ye-eeesss!!' came the concerted reply.

'But we are getting better.' He laughed, jumping down from the seat.

'So, we've got to enjoy it, we've got to learn from it, and the next time we play them, we've got to kick their smug Abingdon asses! Right?'

'Right!'

'Man of the Match – Dwight Ciampioli!'

A big cheer, and then the boys drifted off to their parents.

Chapter 7
Meetings
Oxford United v. Aston Villa

The meetings were always on the first Monday evening of the month and held in the Rugby Club. The Challengers shared the Rugby Club, of course, and this was a 50/50 arrangement. But truthfully, the rugby and football clubs never got on – they never really had.

In the early days of the football club, the changing facilities for the early Challengers and rugby boys were in a shared hut.

The fact that the football side had helped raise the funds to elevate themselves and the rugby boys still used the broken-down, draughty tarpaulin hut was soon forgotten. And the alliance became known as 'The Rugby Club', whose members tolerated the football side – but only just.

Fair enough. The new building was comfortable, with changing rooms and a large bar with a decent kitchen. It imposed itself on the 7-acre site as the centre-piece, with steps up and a modern construction, facing out over the cricket area (in the summer), and the various rugby pitches to the rear.

To the front was a dedicated football pitch; it was too close to the road and, therefore, with housing on two sides, impossible to have a sensible rugby game. But the nature of the problem between the two clubs started with the changing rooms. The door to the changing rooms from this pitch led straight into six open-ended concrete cells, the seating arrangement being a basic wooden bench with rows of hooks above. The shower ran the whole wall side with high-up, frosted windows and the open corridor at the other end.

This meant a lot of through traffic, stagnant water and wet mud. There was a strange, lingering, damp concrete aura. The place was always dirty. Even after it had been cleaned, it looked and presented shabby at best. Every so often, on opening up before a game on a Sunday morning, the place was thick in mud from the previous days' sport, mud, water and mess —the dank hanging funk always prevailed. The rooms were no more than two meters wide and five meters long, so they were quite tiny anyway. And you couldn't afford to drop your best clothes on the floor for fear of ruining them.

On top of this, you needed two changing rooms per game, and often there were four or five games (football and rugby) – and up to under-16s, so sometimes it also had to accommodate men's changing needs – so they were often cramped as well as dirty.

John would often go in before his side kicked off and clean up his allocated changing rooms, as a courtesy gesture to his opponents, and this didn't help the relationship between the clubs either, despite repeated complaints.

The club beyond the changing rooms did get progressively cleaner. Down a corridor past the ref's changing rooms and the men's and women's toilets was a small entrance hallway and a functional office that comfortably seated about eight. Further down to the right was the fairly tidy and reasonably-equipped kitchen with a proper serving hatch, for rugby breakfasts of buffets, leading into the bar.

The bar was compact and staffed by volunteers on rotation, usually, to be fair, from the Rugby Club, with *Fosters*, *Morland's* and *Guinness* on draught (to name a few), and with a well-stocked bottle, can and snack section, all at reasonable club prices.

Yet again, the place – having seen a great deal of activity over the nine or so years of use – looked a little worn out; it was furnished with a large bulky TV overhanging the corner of the bar, two gaudy fruit machines and a pale green floor, which would need replacing in the not too distant future.

Around the edges were ageing, crushed velour bottle-green seating with standard oblong tables and small velour-topped, four-legged stools in the same green.

John stood at the bar at ten to seven and, being the first manager in to the meeting, ordered a pint of *Morlands Original.* Soon others started to arrive, and they drifted to the bar, some with notebooks, or battered folders.

'Hi, mate,' said the grinning Pete Whareham, tapping John on the shoulder.

'Hi, Pete,' replied John, happy to see his mucker at the meeting. 'How's it going?'

'Yeah alright, mate,' continued Pete, still happily grinning.

'Let me get you a pint, Pete.'

A couple of older ladies and an older gentleman came in together – secretary Brenda Evans and her husband Bill, the chairman, amongst them – as did Joe Moreland, who nodded in greeting, making his way over to Pete and John.

'Hi guys, you got a pint?' his Belfast brogue heavy in his speech.

'Thanks, Joe. How's it going? Let me get you one?'

'Guinness, mate. Cheers! Yeah! It's going well. We got a couple of new players this year, and they're good lads and all!'

Joe motioned to a vacant table under the trophy cabinet.

'Come on, let's take the weight off,' he said, settling his Guinness on a bar mat after taking a sip.

'They're all footballers,' he continued as they sat. 'We won the league last year and came runners up in the cup,' grinned Joe, proudly.

'Well done, mate. How long have you been at it?'

'Same as you, John, started at under-7s, bought my lad along.'

'John, let me introduce you – Billy Mulcock, under-8s and you know Pete, under-9s.'

John wasn't a good meetings man, having chaired in various degrees, meetings at work over strategy, sales plans, wages and staffing issues. He tended to want to cut to the chase and could use three words instead of expelling and wasting several hundred. Basically, he found that meetings were overlong, drawn out and laboured on points that only took seconds to evaluate.

He soon found that the football club meetings were just as bland.

Agenda.

Minutes.

Those present.

The changing rooms.

The Club's six-a-side tournament.

Managers' reports – This was the most tedious, as each manager was his own little powerhouse and the reports were often as such:

Dave Reed; (reading from script),

'A really promising October, when we actually managed to draw away at Highworth – who have six Swindon rep boys in their side. Played five, won two, drew one, (at Highworth), and lost two, the second 9-0 to Cholsey, because our keeper had to go to his sister's christening, and three of our regular back four were down with the flu. We are seventh in the league and are playing some attractive football. We could do with signing some more boys as cover, as we only have a bare 15, and this leaves us short, as in the Cholsey match.'

The managers and committee members would nod sagely in response, and then the next manager would get up, clear his throat and nervously start on the same tack. Of course, as with everything, some of the teams (like Joe's) were really successful, and, therefore, quietly resented for their success.

'Yeah, well, not a bad October. We played five, won four and drew one, scoring 26 goals and conceding 8. Two of our boys, Mathew Walley and Paul Gozzard, are in the Vale rep side and also up for County trials. Our goalkeeper has had a trial with Oxford United, and we are through to the semi-finals of the Sam Wallet cup. The boys are a credit to Grove, and their behaviour and bearing at all times is fantastic!' Joe stated in his soft, unassuming brogue.

After these managers' reports, John was officially introduced and made a little introductory speech.

He kept it brief, as he didn't have anything of any importance to say.

Following this was what John came to dread in the

subsequent meetings – 'Any Other Business'.

Amazingly, 'Any Other Business' nearly always made the meetings overrun and was nearly always held by the same people who spoke about the same topic. This time, it was the 're-siting of the goals shed'.

The goals shed was, as it sounded, a regular shed that you may have in your back garden. It was of stone-panelled construction with a pitched roof. The panels had begun to move away from the cast-stone beams holding it all together, several of which have given way slightly, allowing shafts of light to penetrate the interior. Its wooden door was kept locked, there was an old window aperture, coarsely boarded up with soggy chipboard and there was no light – it being situated roughly in the middle of the front and rear pitches, away from everything except the goals enclosure. To see inside, you had to keep the door open and use the natural light.

Inside, the shed was a real mess. White lime dust covered the rotting wooden floor, and the white-lining machine, rickety wheels encrusted with generations of chalk, sat in a corner. It was never cleaned out properly, so there was always a smelly grey-white liquid floating about inside, and the edges were also caked in coagulated ancient lime. Six sets of goal nets – orange or white nylon in various states of disrepair and knitted together with rudimentary patch-ups – were stuffed into black bin-liners for storage.

In another crevice sat three sets of corner flags, or rather corner poles, most missing the little plastic tip for inserting into the ground, some missing the black and white Grove flags (which could be found by rummaging through the morass, but on match days, you could only ever find five out of six)!

There were also dozens of off-shaped tent pegs for holding the nets down, and a number of variously shaped stakes to hold the goals. There were also two weighty iron mallets to drive the stakes and prevent them from toppling forward and causing grief.

In short, this was the shed where the managers had everything they needed to set up a pitch, albeit you could never find a matching net and struggled to find absolutely everything needed at the same time of a kick-off.

'Any other business?' winced Brenda Evans.

Tony Keen stormed straight in. A stalwart of the club – whose two boys were still playing at a good level – Tony was an ex-footballer and now a carpenter. But he was also Mr. Grove and had sat on various committees of leagues and referees (now being one himself). He was thick set with a large mane of white hair, a furrowed, weather-beaten brow and a steely blue stare. John was to find out that he was also very difficult to shake off, once he got his teeth in. He had already met Tony whilst he was white-lining.

'Yes, the re-siting of the goals shed.' Tony stared straight at the committee.

Visible shudders could be observed in some of them.

John had not yet heard of this, but it became a major issue in every meeting for the next few years.

He shifted position, taking a swig of his *Morland's*, and listening keenly.

'Ah, yes. We have been in touch with the Parish council…' said Bill Evans, with resignation.

He knew there would be a battle coming.

'As we were last month, Mr chairman?' leered Tony Keen, eyes gleaming.

'As we were last month, indeed, Tony.'

'The thing is, the shed is not technically ours. Half of it belongs to the Rugby club…'

'But the Rugby club don't use it,' Tony blurted. 'And they use the white-liner.'

'Yeah and our bloody mallets,' said John Peters, the under-12s manager.

'It took me 40 minutes to find a mallet on Sunday. I had to send Peter Richie home to get some in the end, or we wouldn't have kicked off in time.' Peters expostulated, looking around the assembled managers for support.

'Yes. Look, that's not the issue.' Bill was trying to remain calm.

'You try putting up them goals with no mallet, Bill. You don't want any accidents, they have to be secure,' continued Peters.

'We couldn't find matching goals on Saturday – one of 'em was a smaller one, so the whole thing was skew-whiff,' joined Pete. 'Then we couldn't get one of 'em apart! That took us twenty minutes.' he continued.

'One of them small goals is split on the join now. Someone's welted that this week,' pointed out Mulcock.

'Gentlemen, gentlemen! Please – order!' Bill had a prominent purple vein in his forehead that was beginning to visibly pulse.

'The issue is the siting of the shed, not the problems with the contents, now…'

'The issue is the attitude and the laziness of the Rugby Club, who think they bloody own everything – including the shed,' grimaced Tony.

'And it'll be them that's holding up the moving of the shed, because they don't want it moved.' Tony was on a roll.

'You tell me, Mr chairman,' he continued, apace, 'why it is that a simple garden shed on Parish Council land can't be moved 100 yards?'

'It's because we, the Grove Challengers Football club, have politely asked for it to be moved closer to our changing rooms, for our convenience.' Tony raised an eyebrow to the chairman.

He also searched the assembled faces for support.

'The Rugby Club have got the garage.' (There was a double-doored garage, used as a workshop, close to the shed). Tony waved in its general direction.

'Why don't the Rugby Club buy their own white-lining machine and some lime, and store it in there?' Tony raised his eyes and hands in exasperation.

'Because…' Bill was quickly drowned out.

'Because,' interrupted Tony, still pushing the pace, 'they want to keep the Football club in some crummy little shed, covered in shit and lime, until they are ready to kindly allow us the honour! That's why!'

Tony ended up dramatically coming down on the table with his fist, shaking and rattling the half-filled pint glasses.

'Tony, I really don't think they are the stumbling block,' said Bill, obviously ready to finish the argument.

John looked at his watch. Pete yawned. Joe gave John a quiet, knowing glance.

And the time went on.

The meeting started at 7:15 pm and should have been finished by 8:30, but Tony went on and on about the shed. The meeting finally came to a halt at ten past 9.

The siting of the goal-shed had not been resolved. Brenda was going to write to Clare Parry, who was at Grove Parish Council.

Gary Jenkins, Chairman of the Rugby Club, would be invited to the next meeting for his views.

The girls drifted off, and the guys stayed for another pint, talking football and getting to know one another a bit better.

Given the dreary hours and mundane fodder of the meeting, and dreading this could go on for hours, John decided to leave the matter of small-sided football and sensibly-sized pitches until the next one!

Further Training

As the boys started telling their mates about their weekend matches, others started to swell the ranks of training, and better boys also started to come along, egged on by their mates. Grove had two decent primary schools, and there were another three in Wantage, not to mention near outlying villages. One day, at an informal training session in the summer, when training was sparse due to the holidays, John was running a quiet session with just a few of the boys and two parents.

There were no more than nine boys, and they were split into two teams, having a little five-a-side game. Dwight was there, being carefully watched by his dad who had groomed and trained him from a very early age. Jeb Ciampioli was well known in local football circles, having played at a good level as the hard man in the centre of defence. He was not tall, maybe 5ft 9in, had a low centre of gravity and was as hard as iron. As a footballer, he liked to impose himself on the game as soon as he could, intimidating younger, leaner opponents.

At 35-ish, he was coming to the end of his career, but he was still a difficult man to play against. You wouldn't want to be marked by him. He was dark-haired, with a Mediterranean look and dark brown eyes, which were much too close together. A good word to describe him would be 'menacing'. He was taciturn, almost moody, but was actually a nice bloke.

He mostly kept to himself, preferring to keep company during training and games with Dave Claydon, Ritchie's dad, Ritchie being of a similar skill level. But Jeb would never join in with the boys' training. He was there to monitor his son's progress. Pure and simple. But he always watched.

As manager, John used to casually participate in the final training game, occasionally along with Marc. They would play and offer their assistance and guidance for each team, and the training 'game' was always the last (and often the best and most fun) part of the training session.

Richard Maurice's dad, William, was also at training. He wanted to join in, and as the numbers were low —and it wasn't unusual anyway – John said yes. It wasn't ideal to have the dads joining in, as the kids were still really small. But as long as the adults only played to 50%, John had no qualms about the occasional parent joining in. So long as they realised how big, bulky and heavy they were. If one of them landed on a child, they really would flatten them! He allowed the kids to play and encouraged any participating parents to assist and develop the players understanding, whilst helping the players with through-balls, etc. These training sessions were fun, one-touch for periods, concentrating on movement off the ball, sometimes only left footed, sometimes two-touch.

Richard was an only child with a bit of a vacant look. Nice enough, but never really one of the group. He wasn't the most gifted player but could really strike the ball well, so he was always at the edge of the team.

His dad, William, was more of a little kid than his son. A bit older than the group, probably nearing 40, but full of life and fun. But he wasn't a footballer. Richard had heard of the team's exploits from his school pals and had got his dad to bring him along to join in.

The five-a-side was always the best bit about training, and inevitably, in those early days, a couple of the parents did join in. On this day, John was on one side with Dwight in his team and Jeb observing from behind the goal. Richard Maurice and his dad, William, were on the other team. The boys could really express themselves during these games, and lesser players could thrive. It soon became obvious that William had not played much in his younger days. He dashed about as if his life depended upon it, John duly noted.

'William, calm down – remember, this is for the boys. You are only helping.' John patted him playfully on the back.

But with the score at 10-7 or so, and William getting more excited, John slid a pass into Dwight about half-way. As usual, Dwight noted everything around him, and as William bore down for the challenge, Dwight side-stepped and then dragged the ball back in a turn. Maurice, face contorted in total concentration, came flying forward, his 14-stone bulk racing wholeheartedly for the diminutive footballer.

His speed and bulk carried him forward, and as the ball eluded him, he came in with a two-footed sliding tackle that crashed into the area of Dwight's feet and ankles. Dwight anticipated the challenge but was caught by the big man's momentum and was sent flying over the onslaught, crashing down, unharmed but shaken, a few feet away.

John was horrified!

Time stood still.

It was as if Jeb came onto the pitch and towards John in slow motion, handing his Shih Tzu's lead without taking his eyes off Maurice. With a grim resolve etched onto his face, he walked up to him, staring daggers. With chest puffed out and fists clenched, he strode right into the terrified Maurice.

Jeb stuck his forehead right into Maurice's terrified face.

'What the fuck was that, you prat?'

Maurice shrunk back in terror.

John almost shat himself. It looked like Maurice was going to get his head kicked in.

'If-I-ever-see-you-do-that-again to my son or anybody else's, I will kick your bloody head in.' Jeb was fuming. 'Do you understand me?'

Richard Maurice, who had witnessed the entire scene from close quarters, now burst into tears.

John watched on as Jeb stood menacingly close to the now desperate William, wondering what may develop and hoping for the best.

'If you ever do that again,' Jeb spat, 'I will break both your arms and beat you with them.' His look could have killed you! 'What the bloody hell do you think you are doing?'

'Jeb, I'm sorry. Dwight, I'm so sorry – it was an accident.' William was looking to survive a beating.

Jeb's face reddened further. 'An accident?! A bloody accident?! You'll be the accident – Are you okay, son?' Dwight was getting up a little sore.

Jeb was no stranger to a bit of fisticuffs and stayed in William's face, ready to strike, looking evil.

It was all he could do to not head-butt William. He stood glaring with his forehead against Maurice's. Jeb face had reddened, and he had outstanding, pulsing veins showing in his neck.

For his part, William was by now so terrified, he was on the verge of tears.

'Come on, lads,' John stepped in. 'William, come on. That was way out of order, you could've hurt him bad.'

Jeb backed off slightly. 'Let me see you do that again,' he threatened, narrowing his eyes.

'I'll fuckin' kill you, you fat little bastard.' Jeb walked away slowly, scowling and muttering obscenities.

Maurice slunk off, trailing behind his son, and the training continued without them.

After this incident, John was reluctant to allow parents to be involved with the training. Obviously, the parents were so much bigger, and so tackles, long balls, etc. were absolutely of no relevance to what John was trying to achieve with the boys. When they were allowed, they were not allowed to tackle. So poor old William Maurice never played in the training sessions again.

***

In the Pub

By this time, John's business, Market Place Catering, had moved from the old BNF kitchens in Grove to Abingdon, where John had acquired a purpose-built and fitted catering unit with a large catering kitchen, adding to the butchery business at unit 1 on the same site.

The trip home from Abingdon was long enough to encourage a little pit-stop at the Bay Tree on a regular basis, especially on early Friday evenings.

'Alright, chap?' Marc got the phone to his ear.

'Not bad at all, mate,' John replied, sensing the end of the working week.

'What time you getting finished?' asked Marc. 'Pint?'

'Half past four. Boily coming?'

'Oh yes.'

The boys arranged to meet up at the Bay Tree on the way home.

The Bay Tree was a proper village local; Grove being a

sprawling, well-populated village with the pub smack in the middle of thousands of houses and cottages. This meant that you could meet, leave the car in the car park and stagger home, if necessary – which happened more often than not on a Friday night.

What was great about it was that everyone they knew, who was allowed, dropped in there between 4 and 7 on a Friday night. In those days, it had a spit-and-sawdust bar adjacent to a padded purple lounge, with booth type seating around the tables.

The *Morland's* bitter was acceptable, as was the *Speckled Hen*, although that was certainly not a 'Session bitter' back then – being 5.2 or so per cent!

The three blokes were mates, and they were all involved in the team in some way. Marc's nickname, 'Giggly', always applied on a Friday night, as he was always laughing.

'Well, what are you gonna do, Johnny? Now that you've played a real team?' laughed Marc. 'Abingdon were all over us! We could have lost 6-0!' he grinned.

'Yeah but we didn't, did we?' pointed out John, nursing his pint. 'We only lost the second half 1-0. They were good, and we made some necessary tactical changes to compensate.'

'Oh yeah, what did you do then?' asked Boily.

John explained what arrangements they had made against Abingdon for the second half.

Boily looked over his pint in thought. 'So, have you scrapped the back four ban from the half-way line?' He grinned.

'Well, you could still do with a couple of players,' continued Boily. 'Still too many, too young, and too small.'

'Yeah, he's right, John. Abingdon were much bigger, and even the smaller kids they had were stocky and hard to beat. We do seem to need a bit of muscle.' Marc nodded.

'We'll get the boys to ask around,' mused John, nursing his pint. 'There must be some decent footballers about in the area whom we don't know about yet.'

They went on talking and drank another couple of pints, making plans and talking rubbish, until someone decided it was time to make a move.

'Oh, by the way,' said Marc, on their way across the car park, 'did you get our away tickets for Oxford-Villa on Wednesday, Boily?'

'Yes, mate. Neil got them today. We need to meet them before the match to pick them up. Rob's coming down with Neil.' (Neil and Rob were brothers and mates, both mad Villa fans from Oxford and now living up in Liverpool).

'You got your ticket, John?'

'Yep. In the London Road, thanks. I've even got Pikey a ticket, so he can drive us there! We'll meet up for a pint before, shall we?'

'Absolutely. See you!'

Oxford United were in the First Division (the old Second Division), about mid-table. They were at home in the first leg of a league Cup round two, match to Premier League Aston Villa, Boily's love and passion. Old Boily did like a drink and was famous for getting hopelessly hammered and out of control. As Darren Pike (Pikey), one of John's trainee butchers, drove them to the ground after work, Marc was his giggly, animated self.

Pikey was quiet. He worked by and was dominated by Patrick Briggs. Pikey was Paddy's neighbour in Sutton Courtenay. He was short on confidence, had a mousey demeanour, and would not have said boo to a goose!

'Oy chap! Boily's in a right state! He's rung me three times to ask where we are. The last time, I could hardly understand what he was saying!'

'Where is he then?'

'He's in the White Horse.' (Headington – about half a mile from the Manor).

'How long's he been in there?'

'Well, he took the day off work, so probably since they opened?'

'Jesus, the game doesn't kick off till quarter to 8. He'll be slaughtered.'

'Ha, ha, can't wait to see him!'

They parked in a nearby street and walked up to the White Horse. It was then the unofficial 'away' pub. The whole front, side and garden was taken up with Villa fans, who were also crammed into the massive bar area inside. Plenty of drinking had been going on, but the boys weren't wearing Oxford colours. The place had a drunken, happy, boisterous feel, with an overtone of menace to the incoming and sober Oxford fans.

The Villa fans were in full voice inside, their songs, shouts and laughter splitting the smoky atmosphere. The bar was spacious, with comfortable furniture, coloured glass and subtle lighting. There were two barmen serving pints as quickly as they could pull them.

The Villa contingent were all through the pub, taking up the bar, the available seats and the standing area. The three men squinted as they acclimatised to the smoky gloom of the interior and went straight to the bar. They had no trouble finding Boily, who was precariously balanced on a tall barstool and slumped untidily across the front of the bar. As they got up to the bar, a Villa fan was trying to rouse Boily, whose head was lolling from side to side. He was dressed in jeans and an off-white cricket jumper, creased and beer-stained, over his Villa shirt. He had drooled on the shoulder of the jumper, which had a pale orange curry stain down the front. He looked like he had just woken up.

'Eyar, pal. Eh, Treacle, Treacle? Here's your pint.' A Villa fan they didn't know pushed a pint of bitter at the massive frame that took up the equivalent of at least two spaces at the bar. Boily resembled a big, old sleepy bear, but was a happy drunk, not a fighter.

Pikey, John and Marc watched Boily rouse himself. His eyes were heavy-lidded, bloodshot and glazed. He took the pint and sloshed half of it back carelessly.

'Treacle?' laughed Marc. 'Hey, Boily, what's going on? You alright?'

'Oh, oright boys,' he croaked as he began to recognise his mates. 'Where av' you bin? I thought you were coming over early?'

'Well, we're here now, mate. How's it going?'

'Eh! Treacle!' called another Villa fan nearby.

Why the fuck are they calling him fucking Treacle? Wondered John.

Poor old Pikey looked on, wide-eyed. It looked like he was

preparing himself for a long night.

The guys didn't recognise any of these Villa fans. They had obviously been drinking together all day. They were bound in the stupor of excessive alcohol consumption. They were gallivanting about the pub, talking too loudly, spilling beer, and hugging their new-found buddies.

'Here's your whisky, brother.' One of them smacked the slumped Boily on the back and set a large whiskey down on the bar in front of him.

'Whiskey!' Marc winced, laughing out loud. 'Brilliant! Hey Pikey, shout 'em up. Let's get a beer. We've got forty minutes to kick-off yet, this I have just got to see,' he said, shaking his head and laughing.

'Boily – drinking fucking whiskey! Never seen that before!' John shook his head in disbelief.

Boily was lolling about on his bar-stool. The smoke was thick, and the heaving mass of fans that clung about the bar seemed to be returning with even more regularity for refills. Pikey passed their pints over, and Marc gave him a tenner to pay.

Despite the hilarity, John was now a bit concerned.

'Boily?' he said. 'Steve?'

Boily swung his head lethargically and looked groggily around.

'I'm not being funny, mate, but you wanna get some coffee or some water. You'll never be allowed inside the stadium in this state. You wanna be trying to sober up a bit, mate. Yeah?'

'Oh, I'm oright, Johnny. It won't stop me getting in…'

'I dunno…' Boily seemed too drunk to even leave the pub, let alone get into the ground.

'What'd you reckon, Marc?' John asked.

Marc responded with a grin and a shrug of the shoulders.

'Treacle, did you want another short, mate?' A huge bloke in a short-sleeved Villa top bawled from the side. Another double whiskey arrived and Boily downed it in one gulp, hardly looking at it. He wiped his lips, lit another cigarette with great difficulty and swayed off the stool, landing stiffly on two legs.

'Bloody hell!' shouted Marc, roaring with laughter. 'Don't forget we've got to meet the guys to get our tickets, mate. We better get going. Where are we meeting them?'

'Neil's got 'em, and we're supposed to meet 'em in the Britannia,' drawled the drunken Boily.

'Well, drink up then, son, we should be on our way,' ordered Marc, with a wink at John and Pikey.

After fifteen minutes, the Villa fans had mainly filtered out, along the London Road, towards the Cuckoo Lane entrance right on the far side of the ground. Marc prised the empty whiskey glass from Boily and steered him out of the pub for their walk to the ground via the 'Britannia'.

John and Pikey walked with them and left them when they wheeled left into the London Road entrance towards the turnstiles.

'See you guys after the game?'

'Okay, good luck! Not!'

As John and Pikey joined the throng queuing for the turnstiles, Marc and his drunken mate crossed the London Road and walked into the 'Britannia'. Neil was holding their tickets, and they had two more for themselves. They had driven down from Liverpool earlier and had arranged to meet Boily in the 'Brit'. After exchanging greetings, Neil passed Boily the two tickets, and the two brothers finished their beers, walking out briskly, being now quite short on time and agreeing to meet up in the Cuckoo Lane.

'Shall we have (urp!) another pint, Marc?' asked Boily, as the brothers left.

'You're having a laugh, chap. Its half-seven now, come on. We've gotta go.'

As they stepped out into the night, looking at crossing the London Road, Boily staggered and lost his footing on the steps, haphazardly catapulting himself across the pavement and landing badly in the gutter.

He smashed down onto his elbow and cracked his knee with a thud. As he rolled to a stop, he cried, 'Ow, ow, bloody hell! I've broken me bloody leg! Ah Jesus! I think I've broken me arm!'

He had fallen clumsily, and he looked massive and unmoveable, lying winged in the road.

Marc, as usual, found it amazingly funny and tried hard, but without any luck, to get him up. Boily looked really glazed and dishevelled. His face was scarlet, and his hair was messy. He looked crazy-drunk. In truth, he was actually blind-drunk!

'Crikey, chap! Are you okay?' he laughed. 'Come on, get up. We've got to go. We'll be late for kick-off.' He consulted his watch – just five minutes to kick-off.

'No, no!' croaked Boily, looking up pitifully from the gutter. His jeans were ripped and soiled. His cricket jumper holed and filthy. He was laying in the gutter, propped up on his good elbow, his eyes were glazed over. A bloody graze showed through the hole in his jeans.

'Steve, get up, man. I mean it! Come on, I'm going,' Marc hissed, visibly irritated.

'Go on. You go and get seated up, mate,' cried Boily, wincing in pain and waving his mate away. 'Just give me a minute to recover, and I'll see you in there.'

'Well, let's have my ticket then, mate,' asked Marc, looking down. 'All right?'

Boily clumsily searched for the tickets, still lying on the wet ground.

Eventually he succeeded in extracting them from his jeans pocket, but his wallet flew out and landed at Marc's feet. Marc was in a hurry to get in by now and still had to get right around the ground. He was sure that his idiot mate would make a quick recovery and be joining him in a few minutes. He took one ticket, leaving Boily with his, and also took the wallet and mobile phone for safe-keeping.

'You sure you're all right, Steve? I've got your wallet,' said Marc, looking over his shoulder.

'Yeah, yeah, go and get seated up, mate' the big Villa fan croaked. 'I'll see you in a minute, I'll be fine.'

Marc strode off down the Osler Road, chuckling to himself. There were no seats in the Cuckoo Lane!

The match was an anti-climax for the Oxford fans. The 3000

Villa fans were the happier supporters, gaining revenge for their last cup game at the Manor, a semi-final in the Milk Cup (this competition, re-named), which they lost 2-1 in the second leg back in 1986, allowing Oxford the trip to Wembley and the subsequent lifting of that trophy!

This time, they scored early on, dominated possession and easily won a one-sided affair. What looked like a completely lost cause was given a lifeline, when Joey Beauchamp pulled one back for Oxford near the end. But all too late – the Villians' won 2-1.

They met at the car after the game.

'Where's Boily?' asked John in concern.

Pikey looked on, sober and wide-eyed.

'Dunno, chap. He fell over outside the Brit,' laughed Marc.

'When?'

'Before the match!'

'Jesus, what happened?'

Marc recited the events of before the match. Marc had found Rob and Neil behind the goal at the Cuckoo Lane end but had not seen a sign of his mate at all.

'Wonder what happened to him?' wondered John.

'Fuck knows, but I didn't see him at the match.' Marc shrugged.

'What a fucking twat!' cried John in exasperation? 'He's a total moron!'

'Where are we off for a beer then, boys?' asked Marc as they reached the car.

'Let's go off-piste, as Pikey's driving?' suggested John. 'Let's go up to "The Prince".' Okay, Pikey?' Pikey had no choice in the matter.

They all laughed and drove off down to John's old local, the Prince of Wales, Iffley.

Soon enough, they entered the warm, glowing interior of the lounge bar.

Marc addressed the group as they reached the bar. 'Right, lads, let's have a pint on our good mate, Steve!' suggested Marc, pulling out Boily's wallet from his inside pocket.

'Jesus, you nicked his wallet?' asked John incredulously.

Marc looked at John feigning immense disappointment.

'No, mate,' He gave a little look and smiled. 'he gave it me for safe keeping – What did you fancy?'

'Got to be the scotch then, seeing as Pikey's driving.'

Younger's Scotch IPA!

Boily's money paid for the drinks and then (obviously) another round.

They were sitting near the door, and still having a right laugh, when John announced, 'This is my old local – I used to work up the road. Uncle Andrew will be in in a minute.'

'You what?'

'Uncle Andrew,' said John, 'always comes in for a couple at last orders.'

'Mate, when were you last in here? Five years ago?'

'Creature of habit, Uncle Andrew!'

'He's probably dead!'

John knew Andrew, a mild eccentric who lived up Rose Hill, just a short walk up (or down) the lane away. He was actually the uncle of Jimmy Oram, one of the two Jimmies: an old acquaintance of John's and an Oxford fan.

If Uncle Andrew wasn't dead, he would be in any minute.

He always came in around ten-thirty for a couple of pints.

On cue, the door opened and there he stood, grinning.

A wizzled little man, tanned, wrinkled, and with a badly receding hairline; he was wearing old jeans and a tweed jacket, shaking the rain off his coat as he entered, blinking and smiling.

'Good evening, all.'

'Evening, Andrew' said Bridy, the barmaid, as Andrew reached the bar, tugging off his tweed cap.

Marc, already in high spirits, fuelled by the evening's events – the Boily situation and free drinks – thought this amazingly funny!

'Bloody hell! You were right. It is Uncle Andrew, ha!' He laughed as they stepped into the car park.

Pikey drove home with a big grin on his face as the others fell asleep in the car.

The next morning, when he got home at 12:45 am, Marc got a very irate phone call (they didn't use mobiles much at that time) from Nanette, Boily's girlfriend (she and Steve's mother had driven into Oxford to release Boily from the police cells). He had been arrested and taken in for drunk and disorderly and had had a couple of hours kip in the Cowley police station. She was really pissed off that Marc had left him (although Steve couldn't actually remember much about what had happened).

When he woke up, and when Nanette arrived, he couldn't find his wallet. He was still really pissed, still slurring his words. He accused the police of stealing his wallet and had to be restrained as he tried to recover it from them. She was really upset as there was a ruckus and a nearly full-blown fight!

'Cheating Oxford coppers, I know I had me wallet, and there was loads of money in it! Bastards! And me fucking mobile! – You won't fucking get away with it! I'll report every one of youse!'

Marc didn't have the bollocks to tell Nanette over the phone; she hated Marc and John anyway. Best let Boily know in the morning. He was sure Boily wouldn't be that bothered.

He'd also let him know he had his mobile. And that there was no money left!

A pretty good – no, bloody amazing! – Improvised football trip, right on the doorstep!

…And on a school night!

Chapter 8
Under-8s and Two New Full Backs

With new players still being attracted to the team, and the question of the continuing suitability of the 'B' team, the squad now began to become a stronger unit. With the luxury of warm summer training, when the under-8s season started, the ranks had swelled, and John counted sixteen good players at the final training session in August – just about the perfect number.

Olly Dimblow had returned to the training sessions one day with a brand new pair of *New Balance* boots and a very nice pair of yellow goalkeeping gloves.

The season commenced, albeit in a 'friendly' way, i.e. no structured league. The fixtures were arranged on the phone with some of the managers whom he already knew and had previously played. The 'A' team virtually picked itself and consisted mainly of the same characters who had played in the previous season, with Oliver Dimblow and occasionally Billy McDonald sharing the keepers' position. As the season wore on, Olly started to shine as the 'keeper', whilst Billy was becoming a robust midfielder, able to fiercely tackle and run all day. Liam Revell had dropped down to his correct age-group, this year's new under-7s.

So, this was the bedding of the team 'proper', and the boys – beginning to get used to each other – began to put some decent performances together, all being from Grove, all mates, and all playing for enjoyment with the bonus of some really good wins.

The first under-8s fixture was a hard-fought 1-1 draw against Littlemore at home. There followed another draw, this time 3-3 in an end-to-end battle at home to Cholsey with a Mark Brind hat trick.

There were good wins at Launton (4-0) and at home to Botley (6-1), giving the new under-8s unit a great unbeaten start to the new season.

A good show of improvement.

There was an early return by their neighbours, Abingdon, in September.

Abingdon (Home)

Marc refereed, which was a big mistake, and it was probably the last time he actually did it. Gary Revell ran the line (about the only time he ever volunteered – as probable retribution to the dodgy linesman-ship by Abingdon and their parents in the previous encounter). It was the team's biggest game so far, and they were up for it. It was on the front pitch, which happened to be the largest, on a Saturday in September, so the sky was balmy and clear.

The match was niggly and bad tempered (on the pitch and off of it – thanks to lots of verbals from the parents)! Abingdon eventually ran out as winners by 2-1.

The 'B' team played simultaneously on a back-pitch and were hammered 0-7.

In the 'A' game, the main chances and most of the possession fell to Grove.

Ciampioli, Ritchie, Revell and Johnny Wells all went close or missed good chances, and they should have won fairly comfortably.

With a little more luck, less dubious linesmanship (again) and a couple of converted gilt-edged missed chances – including a

Mark Brind lob, with two minutes left, that cannoned off and over the bar – they could and should have had the result.

The boys trooped off despondently; they had given a very good account of themselves but left with the grim realisation that whatever they tried hadn't come off, and they walked back to the changing rooms carrying the hollow weight of defeat.

Despite their best efforts and dominance, Grove had been exploited by Paul Hayes in midfield, who continued to feed the lively Richard Wilson and Andy Hough on the wings. These two, when Grove lost the ball and Abingdon counter-attacked, constantly exposed the Grove full backs and relentlessly punished their weaknesses down both flanks.

Poor Colin and Andrew were roasted for pace and guile, and the Abingdon goals came from these avenues, even though Grove held their own in every other department and position on the pitch. Still, the massive size of the pitch made it difficult for a cohesive game – the boys, especially the full backs, were made to look weak and exposed, even if they were giving the game their all.

Both full backs looked knackered after the game; Dawson was substituted after the second goal and Colin with ten minutes left. But this is where the game had been won and lost.

After the game, Tim Butler, the Abingdon manager, joined John in the Rugby Club for a pint. There were some football and rugby families relaxing with their muddied kids, who were drinking coke from cans and eating packets of Pickled Onion Monster Munch.

The two new friends settled in a corner, with a view out over the back pitches, whilst a rugby game flickered high up in the far corner on the telly.

Not many of the Grove parents had stayed, so they found seats opposite each other.

This time, Tim wasn't smug at all.

'Johnny, well done. You should have won!'

'No, mate, you deserved it. You took your chances and kept us out.'

'Yeah, but you were a different team than we played two months ago, mate. You've got some really good players, all over the park.' Tim smiled.

'*Nearly* all over the pitch. You got in behind us too much today.'

John was exasperated.

'You'll work it out, John. You've got a couple of contenders in the B team, haven't you?'

'We'll see. But the B team has nearly run its course, mate. It's all but finished.'

Tim raised an eyebrow.

'How do you mean?' he asked earnestly.

John looked him in the eye. 'It's just too much mate. I need to concentrate on the main team,' he paused, 'I can't run both. So, the B team really has to go.'

They reached the bar, and the smiling barman came over to them, waiting for their order.

'*Speckled Hen*?' asked John.

'Cheers – don't mind if I do!' replied Tim. 'Be rude not to.'

'You know,' he continued, 'there is a new Oxford League next season – as we've discussed – and it's official – the Vale league is in disarray.'

'It would be a big step up if you had one decent team that could compete.'

John was only too aware. He had heard the older age group managers talking about games being called off for lack of players, poor refs, leagues of six and teams so weak you could win 22-0.

'Yeah, I am desperate to join the Oxford League,' said John, who was hankering after playing some stronger teams.

'Well, that's what we are doing,' said Tim. 'No apologies. We are not going to Cumnor and Steventon. We want some real competition, and we want to play every week.'

'Well, I'm going to struggle, because the tradition here is that we are in the Vale league – and always have been,' squirmed John.

'But you want to join Oxford?' Now Tim looked into John's eyes.

John carefully placed his half-gone pint down onto a beer mat and looked back at Tim, straight in the eye.

'I will be joining Oxford, boy, even though I'll be the first. I don't know what my argument is going to be, but I'll see you there, cos I want to kick some Abingdon arse next season!'

'What about your B team?'

'Well, what about your B team?' countered John, finishing his pint.

'Got to go, mate!' cried Tim, handing John his glass.

'Brilliant! And mine. I can't give thirty boys a fucking game every week.' He took Tim's empty and frothy glass.

'It just can't be done!'

***

Sean Revell, Ritchie Claydon, and Dwight Ciampioli as outstanding talents were supported throughout the team by the improving Brind, Gomm, McDonald, Wells, Webb, and of course, the now established keeper, Olly Dimblow.

After a few games, Olly Dimblow grew to look like a goalkeeper. He was really tall by now – almost 5ft at seven and a half years old – was steady, imposing and quick, albeit slightly ungainly and looked the part in his goalies peaked cap. But he was now the first-choice keeper.

Andrew Dawson's family was moving away, and John and Marc would be truly sorry to see him go; his dad was one of the better parents too. Stephen Casey and John Monery stepped in, and both were competent enough players, who fitted in well with the team.

Amongst the improved training sessions, Ollie Gomm, who had now had six months of matches, training and daily Basketball Football, was also developing into a good footballer.

In the training sessions, backed up by a stronger back-four behind him, he suddenly began to command the ball, win the ball with strong, well-timed tackles and beat players with skill and pace. He looked every bit like a real transformation.

'John, Ollie ain't no full back any more,' Boily mused during an evening training session. 'He's becoming an attacking midfielder. Look!'

They watched as the improving youngster drifted past a defender to plant a crisp shot beyond Billy in the other goal. Time and again, he got the ball, played his way through, with one-twos with Ritchie to threaten the goal. Nobody could get the ball off him. And he was really enjoying it!

John thought back to the days when they first started, not so long ago, when Ollie wasn't even allowed over the half-way line!

Grove Challengers were starting to challenge!

There followed a run of four straight wins – a gritty 2-1 win at Witney Vikings at Carterton, (with the B team going down by 1-3) then a 3-0 home win against Cumnor Minors, a 7-2 demolition again against Witney Vikings, with braces for Ciampioli, Revell, and Gomm plus a Brind penalty, followed by another fine, hard-fought 2-1 win at Launton.

Another away return match against Abingdon netted a reverse – this time by two goals to one in a hard-fought and even match. That voodoo was one that was proving too difficult to crack!

The penultimate matches were an away win at their local mates Didcot, with another warm meeting with John's old mate Fred, and a commanding 3-2 win; followed by a cracking game in a first-time meeting with a lively and spirited Kidlington side, in their first encounter, finally ending all-square in an entertaining 4-4 draw.

The 'B' team, due to lack of 'B' opposition mainly only had run-outs at home to Vikings – going down 3-1 – and, on the last day of the season away at Kidlington, as a credit to their persistence, they had a cracking 4-0 win.

Unfortunately, this was to be the last of the 'B' team games; the boys had moved on and chosen other clubs or things to do. Officially.

John gave a sigh of relief.

As a matter of fact, this had become too cumbersome a vehicle to push.

He would now be able to concentrate on his 'A' team.

Two New Full Backs

'Jamie Skelton – "Skets".'

'Who?'

'Skelton. He is an amazing footballer; he's really skilful.'

They were in the kitchen, and Ollie was responding to John's question of whether there were any footballers amongst his mates who were good enough for the team.

'Right, I'll give his Mum and Dad a ring,' said John, looking up the surname in the telephone directory.

'Dad, don't. You'll embarrass him and me. I'll ask him if he's interested and if he can come to training,' said Ollie, looking worried.

'Right.'

'Alright, let's see if he's interested first.'

Jamie Skelton turned up at the next Saturday training, brought along by his mate, Johnny Wells. Jamie was tall for his age and well built; he was almost gangly.

He was a likeable lad right from the start, with a mop of fair hair and a cheeky lopsided smile.

John could see from the start that he was a footballer; he was skilful and wasn't afraid to use his left foot. He could head the ball, strike it well and was a good tackler.

Most of the boys knew him, he mixed well and was accepted straight away. And he seemed really keen.

The following Wednesday, John cycled down to Wasborough Field with the bag of balls over the handle bars. As he laid the cones for training, another lone boy picked his way up past the Rugby Club, sauntering along and swinging a boot-bag over his shoulder.

'Who's this then?' John asked Ollie.

'Trigger!' shouted Ollie. 'Dad, this is Trigger – Jamie Elliott,' he beamed. 'I asked him if he would like to play football with us.'

'Well, come on in, Trigger,' said John. 'Come and join in. Let's see what you've got.'

Dave Gomm

Again, he was quite well built, skinnier than the rest, and not as tall as Skelton, but solid. He was a good little footballer, with a bone-crunching tackle, who loved sliding tackles and getting stuck in. Although very one-footed, he was hard to knock off the ball from and had some good footballing skills. A perfect right back. With a perpetual grin!

In the last three matches of the season, John introduced the new players and line-up, moving players in and out while tweaking the defensive positions. Both Launton and Witney turned out to be well organised and hard to beat.

John used a combination of the new full backs, placing Johnny Wells into the back four, pushing Ollie into midfield with Dwight – the new team began to shape up.

Olly Dimblow

Jamie Elliott   Johnny Wells   Sean Webb   Jamie Skelton

Sean Revell   Ollie Gomm   Dwight Ciampioli   Billy McDonald

Mark Brind   Richard Claydon

Subs: Colin Mercer, Richard Maurice, John Monery and Stephen Casey

This was the team fielded for the last three games, and they did look much stronger and cohesive! They dominated the Didcot match again and were comfortable winners, by five goals to two, despite a last-minute second goal from Didcot.

The Kidlington match was a much different affair. They were a well-organised and skilful side put together by a couple of good footballing dads with a good catchment area to choose from. This match could have gone either way but was a good precursor of what might come in the new Oxford league next season. The Kidlington boys were very skilful lads, fit, competitive, well organised and with a never-say-die attitude! Quite formidable opponents.

Marc and John were happy as they walked back to the car. A late equaliser, this time for them, when Ritchie waltzed through the defence to curl one into the roof of the net. He sent them all home happy. It was a good result all round!

The football got better as the boys grew, both in stature and confidence, while their passing and running off the ball improved immensely. True, the pitches (still full-size with everything except the goals) were too big and much too difficult for them (or their opponents) to be able to induce sweeping, fluent football.

But nevertheless, the boys were now knocking the ball about a bit; plus, they were all decent players now, so the quality of play began to look attractive. Once they had cleared the half-way line, Brind and Claydon's pace – after being supported by a sound defence and a ball-winning and creative midfield – started to create panic amongst their opponents, who they were beginning to run ragged.

Bullingdon, Littlemore and Cholsey were unceremoniously despatched 8-0, 7-0 and 8-1 respectively, before a 1-2 reverse at Kidlington and, remarkably, a 0-0 draw at home to Garden City.

Following these results in this friendly league, Grove went on to win their next five games as the team began to emerge and unfurl. The last of these was a home match in which they had slaughtered a strong Kidlington side 5-1, with braces for Sean Revell and Oliver Gomm in a match that left their opponents deflated.

Revell, Gomm, Claydon, Wells, Webb, Ciampioli, Brind, Dimblow, McDonald and Elliott were the core of this success, playing with each other on a weekly basis. They were making quite a reputation for themselves along the way.

The football was a joy, the camaraderie was strong, the support and the parents were all good – John thought that perhaps they had made it.

He was still determined to be the first 'Vale' side to play in the Oxford League, and he knew that his old mate, Tim Butler of Abingdon, also wanted to go that way.

The under-8s season had been very reasonable and before their final game, the results were as follows, with the Littlemore game still left to play:

Seasons Results (Unofficial Friendly League)

Played	Won	Drawn	Lost	F	A	Pts
17	10	4	3	61	22	24

This final game was a trip to Littlemore, another one of the Oxford teams that were apparently becoming quite useful! It was another tricky city game in South Oxford. It was a sunny Sunday morning and the conditions were good. The pitch was on the heavy side, but not massive. After the Kidlington game, there was a feeling that the team had now arrived. The personnel had now sorted itself and was as organised and strong as many of their better opponents in every department.

Grove kicked off and thundered into their hosts, with Ritchie, Dwight and Revell dominating, whilst Webby and Wellsy, unbeatable at the back – now supported by the strong, footballing full backs – tackled and pushed forward.

Ollie Gomm and Billy McDonald scrapped and won every ball in midfield and overwhelmed the opposition in the 50-50's. Mark Brind benefitted – as the recipient of all this graft, skill and effort – to hit two belting goals, the second one an absolute screamer, before half time.

Ritchie was on fire on the left-wing, turning his defender inside and out as he raced towards the goal, time and again, causing panic and pandemonium.

The team continued to dominate after the break when Ciampioli robbed a midfielder on the edge of the Littlemore box and sent in a lob that nestled into the far corner, leaving the flat-footed keeper helpless.

The fairly large crowd of parents and onlookers enjoyed a great game of football, and the Grove parents were ecstatic about the display, as the team continued to delight, as they had done all season in this delightful little friendly league.

Littlemore were never giving up, and they rallied towards the end. Paul Miller tapped in after a superb save by Dimblow who parried into his path. But this was their only consolation as Grove saw out the game with a fine 3-1 win.

There was lots of back-slapping and cheering inside and outside the dressing rooms – it was perhaps Grove's best performance ever. Marc and John were grinning from ear to ear.

'Shall we go for a pint?'

'Well…'

As they were walking back to the car with a bag of netted footballs, a bucket and sponge, they spotted Dwight Ciampioli on the far side of the pitch, clutching the Man of the Match trophy for the umpteenth time that season. John noted with angst that Jeb was in earnest conversation with the Littlemore manager and another couple of guys, who were standing around with their kids. Dwight was looking up at the group deeply concentrating on every word his dad and the manager exchanged. John looked over and caught Jeb's eye, who looked away.

'Look at that.' He gestured to Marc, as they moved past the parents dismantling the nets off the goals. 'Lots of chatter over there, eh?'

Marc stopped and peered at the group.

'Mmm… No smoke without fire,' he mused, walking on to catch up with John.

As they walked down the path past the changing rooms, towards the road, Dave Claydon motioned John over.

The spring sun was in John's eyes as Claydon approached.

'Hey, mate, can I have a quick word?' asked Claydon, Ritchie tucking in behind.

'What's up, Dave?' John somewhat knew what was coming.

'Just thought I'd let you know, John, the Littlemore manager called us over.'

'Oh! Okay, what did he want?'

'Well, he wants Ritchie and Dwight to sign for them next season.' Dave Claydon looked apologetic.

'What?' sighed John. He hadn't contemplated anything of this sort happening!

'Well, he says it would be a quick line into Oxford United, as they are on the doorstep.'

'He's actually quite persuasive,' continued Claydon.

John took a moment to gather himself. After some thought, he said, 'Dave, Ritchie and Dwight will work their way to United or another club in good time. Jesus! He's dangling a carrot! They're just kids!'

John was somewhat annoyed. 'What an arsehole!'

Claydon stood in John's path, before replying.

'John, I know, and we don't need to think about it. Ritchie's not going. I want him to stay at Grove with his mates – and you.'

John sighed with relief. Jeb and Dwight were now walking back around the pitch with the Littlemore manager and parents.

'What about Dwight?' he asked Dave.

'Well, you need to speak to Jeb.' Claydon looked sideways forcing a smile. 'But I think that might be a different proposition.'

Chapter 9
Tranmere Rovers v. Oxford United
Football League Division Two – Relegation Decider

John woke up and languidly remained in bed early on the morning of Saturday May 2nd, 1992. Life was good; the sun was streaming through the bedroom windows and making vivid splashes on the floor. The lemon yellow and pale blue curtains played in the breeze. He was slightly muzzy after an average Friday night at the Bay Tree and a steak dinner with Lyn, which was washed down with a nice Merlot. He looked around the room and marvelled at how summery it looked. *She is a great decorator.* The wallpaper was also a washed-out pastel yellow, with small hints of pale-blue dashes. The carpet was new: a deep-pile cream that went all through the upstairs. The duvet was a darker blue, with yellow – it was all very luxurious.

I am a very lucky fellow, he smugly thought to himself, as he lay on the fluffy blue pillows. He could sense rather than hear Lyn downstairs making coffee. He turned over and stretched to turn on the radio for the 8 o'clock news. As usual, Lyn had the radio alarm set and tuned in to BBC Radio Oxford. *Bizarre,* he thought. She was the only person he knew who listened to that station. He couldn't stand it. Too much talking, too much arguing, too many (well one) do-gooders with bizarre American accents, always debating on fly-tippers, or gallstones, or other rubbish. Anyway, he couldn't be bothered to re-tune – he only wanted to listen to the news.

The kids weren't up yet. Here she came with the coffee.

Lyn talked about the kids and other matter-of-fact things she had been up to, while John half-listened to what was going on in the world.

John sipped at his coffee and became aware that he was listening to the sports news.

'And today, as the season comes to an end, Oxford United have a dramatic do-or-die battle away at Tranmere Rovers...'

'Ssh! Ssh!' he waved, putting his finger to his lips.

'...United must win and hope that other results go their way. Leicester, Newcastle, Plymouth and Blackburn all have a part to play – and the U's could still be relegated even if they take all 3 points.'

John and Marc had all but given up on Second Division survival. They had been in the London Road end at the Manor to witness a gutsy performance and an amazing sweet, dipping 30-yard thunderbolt from David Penney to beat Wolves 1-0 in early April. All the fans went home in raptures and full of hope that night. But the wheels had wobbled and then started bursting off as they took just 3 points from their next 5 games, plunging them deep into the relegation mix.

To be fair, United did have a difficult run-in, with games against the top three in the space of a hectic fortnight. A disappointing 3-1 reverse to struggling Plymouth Argyle at Home Park was sandwiched between an unconvincing home draw to Bristol Rovers and a solitary point against the eventual Champions, Ipswich town 1-1.

'Manager Brian Horton is very optimistic about United's chances. Here he is, talking to Gabriel Clarke.'

'Well, Brian, a real chance to stay up?' asked Gabriel.

'Look, of course we know what we've got to do,' said Horton, 'and I can assure you that we will give 110% effort today. We had over ten and a half thousand turn up for the Ipswich game, so we know the fans will be right behind us…'

'Yes!' shouted John at the radio.

'We know that we can only get out there, play some football, play our usual game, and we can beat anybody. We're under no illusions about the difficulty of the task today, and we are aware that we can go out and get a result today, but still get relegated. But we believe we can get out of it. There are many other teams playing today, and two or three that could still go down, including us.'

Brian continued, 'Let's hope that the results go our way, and that we all have a great day. Our fans will love it – it'll be like a cup-tie, and I urge all our fans to turn up in numbers and get behind the team.'

'And how safe is your job, should relegation be the result?' queried Gabriel, posing the age-old question.

'Look,' said Horton, 'we are not contemplating losing. We think we are too good to go down. We're playing good football, not relegation football, and we've had a really tough run in. I think today the boys will give everything. And as I've said before, we can and have beaten anyone in this league. We have some fantastic professionals and some fantastic skill in the side, right through. If we go down, then it's only been in our hands! We need to win today, and as manager of this football club, I will be doing everything in my power to keep us in this division.

'If I fail, then we have to ask ourselves "Was it because we weren't good enough? Or wasn't Brian Horton good enough?" And I think the answer to both is no. Will I get the bullet if we go down? Ask the board! I am going up to Tranmere today to keep us up! And that's what we all intend to do.'

'And what part can the fans play, Brian?' questioned Gabriel.

'The fans of this football club, as I have said, are behind us all the way. There's no sense of doom and gloom about them. Believe me, they want to stay up just as much as we do. They will play an essential part today, because they will turn up in massive numbers and be right there supporting the team. It should be a fantastic day!'

'So, there you have it,' purred Gabriel. 'Oxford United fans, get yourselves up to Prenton Park and get behind your team! Thanks, Brian. Good luck!'

'Pleasure.'

'We'll keep you updated with live commentary from Prenton Park from 3:00 pm,' said Gabriel. 'Back to the studio.'

John looked into space.

'What am I doing laying here?'

'What?'

'I'm fucking going!' he stated to Lyn.

'You what?'

'I'm going.'

'Oh, no you're not!'

'I've got to go, haven't I? What sort of Oxford United fan am I, who hasn't even thought about going up to support the lads in their hour of need? I've got to go, and I am going!' he cried, leaping out of bed.

'Well, what about the shopping? I need you to help me with the kids. And I haven't seen you all week.'

'I'll see you Sunday! We'll go out.' Pulling on his most faded *Levi's*

'Where's Tranmere?' she glowered.

'Liverpool somewhere, not too far.'

'How will you get there?'

'I'll bloody drive, I don't care,' he said, reaching for the phone.

'Well I'm not happy,' she scowled. 'Who are you ringing now?'

But he was already on the phone.

'Oright chap? What you doing today?'

An hour later, John and Marc were on the road. John had a very nice 5-series white BMW, and they made good time getting up to Liverpool.

'Let's do it a bit different this time,' suggested John.

'What d'you mean?'

Normally on a football trip they would find a shitty pub near the ground, or a second-rate Indian, and have a couple of pints and a pie, or a quick balti. This would often be what they could find near the ground. Even at Oxford, they would park up near the Quarry Gate or The Butchers Arms in Headington, down a few pints of *London Pride* and walk to the ground, maybe grabbing a pasty at half-time.

Today he didn't fancy trawling round Tranmere on the off chance of finding some pub crammed with football supporters that may be a mile from the ground. So, they drove to the ground, then kept driving. They drove out and on, leaving the ground behind. Out into the country. After fifteen minutes, they found a pretty little country pub – The Shrewsbury Arms at Claughton Firs – with a car-park almost completely devoid of cars and a sunny aspect overlooking rolling hills.

Here they ordered from the bar menu, a delicious home-made steak and ale pie, with chips, which they washed down with a couple of pints of *Theakston's Old Peculiar*. They had passed the ground at about 12:20 pm, so they still had plenty of time to enjoy this: a proper home-made meal, in convivial surroundings, with time to spare.

'Luxury, sheer luxury!' beamed John.

'Life doesn't get much better than this!' agreed Marc.

'I can't believe we hadn't even thought of coming. We never even mentioned it in the pub last night!'

'Well, we're here now, chap – loyal supporters through and through!' Marc replied sarcastically. 'How d'ya think we'll get on?'

'We're gonna do it, no question. Whatever happens, at least we're here. We've got Paul "Don" Key in goal and Joey Beauchamp on the wing, Johnny Lager (John Durnin) and Trevor Aylott up front and the greatest full back on earth!'

'Gary Smart?'

'The very same! And with "Mad Dog" snapping heels in the middle, we're sure to be victorious!'

They sauntered back down to Prenton Park and parked about

300 yards from the ground on the main road.

Prenton Park was a fairly ordinary old ground for the Second Division. But the atmosphere was fantastic. There were probably 3,000 Oxford fans packed into the away end in a crowd of just over 9,000. This end of the ground was a sea of yellow and blue, with scarves, shirts, banners and flags. And, as predicted, it was a cup-tie, carnival atmosphere. The Oxford fans were making a lot of noise. It was a beautiful, sunny spring day, and you could cut the tension with a knife. They started pushing their way up through the densely-packed Oxford fans, muscling their way through and upwards.

'So, what needs to happen?' shouted John, as they took their places behind the goal about three-quarters of the way up the concrete terracing.

'Well,' Marc cupped his hand over John's ear so he could be heard. 'Right, if we lose, we are down. If we draw, and Plymouth lose, we are down on goal-difference. It looks like Leicester need to beat Newcastle, or Plymouth need to lose against Blackburn. But we still need to win, whatever happens. If we win, and Newcastle lose, we stay up. If we win, and Plymouth win, they stay up. Even Grimsby could go down, I think!'

'Basically, we need to win, and one of them needs to lose,' he grinned, settling with his mate high up behind the goal. 'Simple really!'

'Amazing!'

'Come on, you Yellows!'

This was life and death as far as Oxford die-hards were concerned. Anyone who is fanatical about a team will understand. The thought of losing, of relegation, was just too much to contemplate. It made the fans sick to the stomach. It was inconceivable. It must not happen. It couldn't happen!

Brian Horton led the team out alongside Tranmere Rovers. Dreadfully ominous amongst the Rovers team was the former United legend, Johnny Aldridge – so often Oxford's match-winner and a 30-goal-a-season man back in the glory years of 1982–1986. How ironic would it be if he scored the winner to relegate his former club?

This was not a good omen. However, the Oxford end roared – a deafening, thunderous roar – as the teams emerged, drowning out their Tranmere counterparts. The team were very aware, applauding the fans as they made their way to the centre, then breaking off, the United team going straight to their fans, smiling and still clapping.

'Yellows, Yellows, Yellows!' came the guttural chant.

At kick off, with the atmosphere on the terraces pulsating, some of the Oxford players looked a little nervous. Trevor Aylott had scored when Oxford won their home fixture 1-0 back in October, and Tranmere had all but finished their season, comfortable in mid-table.

Still, Oxford fired into them from the start, creating some good early chances. Joey Beauchamp had one, two, three gilt-edged opportunities to score, driving the Oxford fans mad as his chances went begging. He fluffed one easy chance high into his own crowd when he got through, then miss-hit a weak shot when he looked certain to score. Surely, it wasn't going to be one of those days?

Beauchamp was having a cracking game, although, today he just didn't appear to have his finishing boots on.

He was still giving the full back no end of trouble and roasting him time and again for pace and skill. The fans still believed that Joey could be their match-winner.

Then, Paul Kee pulled off a magnificent save from Tranmere's Martindale to keep them in it, much to the relief of the Oxford fans, who had given him a torrid time for his inconsistency throughout the season. The game continued to ebb and flow, with Oxford having the majority of possession and still creating the better chances. Just before half-time, Joey Beauchamp left the fans holding their heads in amazement. Again, through on goal and certain to score, his shot ended up more like a pass-back. Joey sank to his knees. The Rovers' keeper, Eric Nixon, clutched the ball to his chest, smiling. The Oxford fans howled. Still goalless.

The transistor radios were out and about in the crowd and as the whistle blew for half-time, fans gathered around the people with radios to see how the other results were going.

'Grimsby are winning.' Groans rippled through the crowd.

'So are Newcastle'. Derision – this result, if it stood, could send Oxford down.

'What about Plymouth?' John was jittery now.

'Wait…beating Blackburn 1-0!' cried Marc, eavesdropping on a transistor report close by.

'Jesus, unbelievable,' shouted John. 'If it stays like this, we are going down.'

'Aw, come on! We've got to score in the second half; we were all over them,' bawled Marc.

'Bloody Beauchamp! He would have had a hat-trick in any

other game!'

'Ah, he could still get one yet!'

Out they came for the second half, but Tranmere started to take a grip on the game for the first time. They shackled Oxford, and Paul Kee had to be on his mettle to keep them from scoring. He kept out a Kenny Irons shot with a superb reaction save, then saved the U's again, pushing away a superb blockbuster from Thomas. The swing of the game had entirely reversed, and now Oxford were hanging on, with Tranmere dominant and threatening with every attack.

Midway through the second half, with the Oxford fans now nervous as kittens, a minor roar in the Oxford ranks rose to a crescendo, with fans jumping about and hugging each other.

'What's up?' shouted Marc to someone close.

'Blackburn have equalised!'

'Yes, come on!' The ripple went round the crowd. The players must have sensed it. The United bench and management became more animated.

Eric Nixon launched a huge kick from his area. The ball bounced dangerously clear of the Oxford defence. A Tranmere forward was through – John Aldridge.

The Oxford fans held their breath.

Aldridge controlled the ball, took a pace; he drew back his right leg to shoot. This was a potential disaster. Johnny! Johnny! No…

His shot flew wide. More jumping, more elation. Oxford were under the cosh and just barely hanging on.

By now the atmosphere was absolutely electric. Fans were screaming and jumping; tumbling down and up the terraces with every chance missed at either end.

Then, the turning point.

Against the run of play, in the 70th minute, United's Gary Bannister cleverly anticipated and intercepted a wayward Tranmere back-pass. He saw Johnny Durnin's run and slid the ball into his path. The fans held their breath as Durnin latched onto the ball, with a sweet first-touch, drawing Tranmere keeper Nixon; he slipped around him and fired the ball low into the empty net to gloriously open the scoring – 1-0!

Pandemonium. Delirium. The Oxford fans were now ecstatic!

Another rumble boiled and erupted through the crowd.

'Leicester have equalised!' Unbelievable!

'Game on! Come on! We can do it!'

The Oxford fans were jumping for joy, punching the air and running up and down the terraces.

'U's are stay-ing up, I say U's are staying up!'

'U's are stay-ing up, I say U's are staying up!'

Marc and John huddled and skipped on the away terrace.

However, this unconfined joy was shattered immediately.

Tranmere launched a swift and immediate response. Their next attack worked the ball into the box. The loose ball was missed by an Oxford defender, stretching to clear. The ball fell to Aldridge in the box, who, this time, slammed home a left-footed half-chance to equalise. His fortieth goal of the season. What a time to start breaking records! What a bastard!

Down came the gloom. The fans were shattered again. How cruel!

A minute later, another groan from the crowd.

'Christ – what now?'

'Newcastle have just scored again at Leicester,' a desperate Oxford fan announced, distraught.

The Oxford fans, with nerves shot between despair and elation, sensed that they were embroiled in drama of the highest order.

Without signal, the 'Come on, you Yellows' chant echoed through the stadium. The Oxford fans shouted until they were hoarse. The crowd became one throbbing, pulsating mass.

'Come on, you Yellows! Come on, you Yellows!'

This was beginning to be an epic encounter and series of events.

Around ten minutes later, the excellent Mickey Lewis – who had battled like a warrior in the middle – won the ball in midfield with a muscular tackle. Righting himself, he played a smart one-two with Bannister, taking the return and once again sending it away to Joey Beauchamp, clear.

The Oxford fans craned their necks, and this time they were unreservedly expectant. Joey Beauchamp took the pass, sped into the box, dropped his shoulder, committing Nixon and almost – it seemed to the maddened fans – pushed it too far ahead. But he steadied and took the ball to Nixon's right, sliding the ball with slide-rule precision into the corner of the net for a potential winning goal, causing an immediate and sensational effect amongst the now deafening away support.

Unbelievable! The uncertain script was nearing completion.

The whole of the seething mass of fans in the Oxford end were in ferment. The swings of the afternoon had been electrifying.

Another rumble in the crowd. 'David Speedie has just scored again for Blackburn!' came a cry from the terracing above.

At last, as the game ebbed away, it looked as if they may just get the wanted result.

But Tranmere did not lie down. They continued to push forward with relentless pressure. United hung on. Paul Kee made a fine save later on from Martindale. Then he had to race off his line to deny the alert Aldridge. Time slowly ticked away. The clock on the scoreboard went past 4:45.

The Oxford fans hung on too. And prayed. And prayed.

Three thousand fans watched as the referee put the whistle to his lips. Many times!

'Come on, you bastard, blow!' Whistles echoed from all angles.

He blew for full time. Now it was pure delirium. Relief, euphoria, exhaustion.

Now the wait, to make sure one of the teams around Oxford in the league had lost.

'Newcastle have won.' John wringed his programme 'Fuck!'

'Grimsby have won.'

'Shit!' cried Marc.

'What about Blackburn?' Now they could only wait in hope.

The management brought the players out and down to the Oxford fans, where they all celebrated madly nonetheless. It had been a fantastic performance and result. They couldn't have done any more, the players or the fans.

The exhausted players – in rolled up socks and grimy yellow tops – were embroiled in the drama as they all applauded each other.

The whole party was poised and together. Surely, we were safe?

Five minutes went by. Still waiting. The celebrations became unsure, a little muted.

'The Plymouth-Blackburn game has been delayed for fifteen minutes!' shouted a fan with a radio clamped to his ear.

The fans, caught up as they had been in the merry-go-round afternoon, stood and waited. Another few minutes crawled by.

Finally, with the players, managers, trainers, reserves, physios and anyone else there connected with the club all gathered on the pitch in front of their supporters, one final quiet rumble became a roaring, thundering maelstrom of madness, noise, gaiety, madness and delirium. Blackburn had won 3-1. Oxford were safe. They had done it. Breathtaking!

To round off the most astonishing, impromptu day, the two elated friends floated back to the car and, despite the fifteen-minute delay in the Plymouth game, started the engine and were driving past Prenton Park at 5:30 pm. Oxford had secured their status in the Second Division! Mission accomplished.

John was able to put his foot down on the accelerator as the BMW raced down the M6, M42, A34 and A338. They didn't bother stopping. They left Tranmere at 5:30 pm and pulled into the Bay Tree just before 8:30 pm. There were some people in there that they knew, a few old mates, and they continued their euphoric day, enlightening anybody who was prepared to listen.

They filled up on unbelievably beautiful *Morland's* bitter, left the car in the car park and walked home, still buzzing.

Chapter 10
Under-9s – Life Without Dwight

When Jamie Elliott showed up on the pitch the following week after his first Wednesday training session, he was not alone.

John looked up to see his mum accompanying him, with a determined stride – she definitely did not look happy.

Short, with black hair, quite pretty but fiery as hell, she went right up to John and confronted him head-on.

'Hi,' said John. 'Mrs Elliott?'

Ignoring the niceties, she demanded, 'Are you s'posed to be the manager?' in a very broad northern accent (Hull, as it turned out).

John thought the question to be somewhat obtuse.

'Yes. John. How do you do?' He offered his hand.

Another snub.

'What d'ya think you're doing letting eight-year-old boys walk home on their own? That is not responsible!' she glared at him.

Truthfully, John had never even considered it. In the early days when parents brought their boys the first few times, they drove them down and stayed to watch, or sometimes even joined in with the training practices.

Now the boys just rolled up on bikes, or boards, walking, or running from seven different directions. Karen Brind had even stopped taking monies for training, preferring to collect the unofficial fees on match days when nearly everyone turned up.

'Well, he walked here,' countered John. 'I saw him come in past the Rugby Club.'

'But there was no-one at home when he got back,' she snapped.

One of his pet peeves was the fact that some parents simply used clubs like it as a babysitting service.

'Mrs Elliott, it is not my responsibility to make sure your children get home. If you don't like it, bring him yourself and then pick him up afterwards.'

John wasn't afraid to tell it like it was.

'He turned up, I am assuming by his own volition, from somewhere close by, as he didn't even have a track suit with him!'

'You should stay here until they are all gone home!' she shouted. 'Anything could happen to them!'

'With all due respect, I am not a babysitting service,' said John calmly, although his hackles were beginning to rise. 'I train the boys twice a week – they turn up, they go home. If that's not good enough, as I said before, bring him down and pick him up yourself.'

Sharon Elliott stood her ground and glared at the coach.

John returned the vehement stare.

Sharon went to say something and then changed her mind.

By now, Jamie was dying of embarrassment, limply still attached to his mother as she seethed and searched for a better hold in the argument.

He looked up at her, imploring her to let go.

'Look, Jamie is new here,' John continued, 'but he's got loads of mates. Where do you live?'

'It's none of your business where I live,' she hissed.

Christ, talk about trying to be helpful!

'Well, if he registers, I'll know your address. But in the meantime, if it's down Tubbs Close way, I'll send one of the lads back with him – or we'll cycle him home ourselves. My Ollie is a good friend of his,' John continued, shrugging. 'We pass by that way going home. But if you're not in when he gets back – not being funny – that's your problem. Okay?'

She was fuming and still wanted the last word.

John didn't want to suggest his dad bring him down, if he came from that vicinity – she may have easily been a single mother.

As it turned out, his dad was away in the Navy, and they had recently moved to the area. Hence, the Newcastle United Shirt.

'It's not Tubbs Close, actually. It's Sharland Close. And I need to know the timings,' she fired.

'Weekends, normally an hour – 9:30 to 10:30. I let you know on a Wednesday. Wednesdays, 5 till about 6:15, depending on the light,' said John nonchalantly, with *almost* the last word.

She was still standing defiantly, legs apart and hands on hips, still glaring.

'And 50 pence a week,' he couldn't resist adding, with a wry grin.

Mrs Elliott looked like she might scream something at him. Then she looked like she might say thank you. But she simply pursed her lips, dropped Jamie's hand and spun on her heel. After a dozen steps or so, she shouted, 'Jamie, don't be late!' in her Hull accent, without looking back.

John was busy that summer. He bought 10 new regulation footballs, size 12, drove over to Haddenham and purchased Trevor Spindler's *Soccer Training Techniques*. He arranged a brand-new kit, including glossy black and gold tracksuit tops from Mike Bellinger at Bellinger's Vauxhall dealership in Grove, the new team sponsor.

He had the team picture taken, with the team posing in front of a four-by-four and a new Vectra and sent it to the *Wantage Herald* along with the *Oxford Mail* and *Times*. The headline read, 'Grove on the Right Road'. In the article, he stated he was still looking for players and gave his phone number for contacting.

He advertised by word of mouth and kept his ear to the ground, phoning parents of boys from other schools or clubs who sounded like they had some talent. More boys came through. Charlie Harris, Martin Rowlands and Danny O'Sullivan.

Now there were often eighteen boys at training, all of a pretty good standard; the training, now that John had something to work with, became much more organised and disciplined, but still great fun.

Jeb had turned up to the next training session after the Littlemore match to tell John that Dwight was signing for them. John wished them well, but told Jeb that he didn't want Dwight to train with them anymore as they had to stand in their own right as a team. He thought hard about this; half of him thought it was a petty, selfish reaction on his part. After all, Dwight had been there from day one, was one of the lads, a great asset plus a lovely kid, who got on well with everyone. But he couldn't help feeling betrayed, to lose their star player at such an early stage in the development of the team.

Was this selfish? Inevitable? After all, this was boys football, not the Premier League. Nevertheless, he thought the decision was the right one for the team. So, they parted amicably (as far as he could tell), and Dwight actually moved up an age-group at Littlemore.

John wished them both well and told them to stay in touch, which they did.

***

The first competitive game was held on the 21st of August, 1993. John had used his guile to attempt to steer the club away from the sinking Vale League. The Oxford League was in the process of being formed and was welcoming new teams. The Vale League sent out their invitations, but John chose Oxford, utilising his contacts, and his Grove Challengers team were accepted.

They were to be the first Grove team to compete in an Oxford League (the preliminary Oxford B-Line League). The games were still 'friendlies', although the twenty teams in the league had a proper fixture list, with ties home and away every week.

Their opposition included teams from Oxford, Kidlington, Highfield, Bicester and Witney – they were guaranteed to be playing the best teams in the area. Abingdon had also joined, as well as Oxford United Social Club, so all the town teams were competing too.

The first game, with the slightly re-organised team, saw them thrash Rose Hill (Oxford), 12-7. John wasn't unhappy with this. Although there were 7 goals conceded, Rose Hill were no mugs, and they had some fiery young players including young Paddy Malone, the manager's son, who scored four goals and was involved in everything. But Grove's counter attacking was awesome, and Sean Revell had a superb match, with Ollie Gomm and Billy supporting the work-rate. Ritchie and Sparkie were well set up and finished brilliantly, putting their chances away with style. With a bit of tightening-up, the team would come on well.

There followed another home game the next week, this time against a slightly less well-organised Quarry Rovers (Oxford). Yet again, and without too much to worry about in the defence department, the team flowed beautifully and chalked up a convincing 13-0 demolition. Again, John noted the metamorphosis that had occurred in general play in the year and a half that he had been in charge. The full backs were now encouraged to support the attack. They pushed on as the central defenders kept back. John let Webby and Wellsy come up for corners; they were good headers. They started scoring from free-kicks and corners.

The front two, superbly backed by an improving team, raised riot with their pace. Sparkie and Sean Revell also had good long-range shooting boots, and Ritchie's guile bought countless goals and, often, penalties or free-kicks around the box, as the opposition's defenders struggled to contain his pace and skill on the break.

The following match was against Radley, which was unfortunately cancelled due to lack of fit Radley players.

The team then got the chance to have another go at Witney Vikings, whom they had easily beaten 7-2 in last season's under-

8s friendly league. This encounter turned out to be a better fought contest, with Grove running out winners by 4 goals to 2, after being 2-1 down at half-time, following a stunning, spirited fight-back. A cool finish by Ollie Gomm equalised early in the second-half, a superb, long-range effort from Wellsy grabbed the lead, and a last-minute Webby header secured a fine victory.

Following this, they played another Abingdon team – St. Edmunds. This resulted in another drubbing for the opposition, this time 12-0, where John had the luxury of giving his substitutes a second-half airing – all of whom performed really well.

After another trip to Witney – this time to Tower Hill, a very strong and physical side where the boys played out a very creditable 2-2 draw – Grove had the opportunity again to host their main rivals Abingdon, at home. As they welcomed their visitors, having been allocated one of the smaller back pitches, John noticed how the boys were ready for the challenge. Once John had cleaned a suitable changing area for both teams, he pulled the team back for a quiet talk. He now had a good squad of boys, with the main nucleus of the team supported by five reserves.

Grove now represented a reasonably sturdy team. They still had a few smaller players, who would give their all when called upon. With the reliable Olly Dimblow in goal and a stronger defence, the loss of Dwight had gelled them together, and they were looking strong in all departments.

'Now, listen up, lads. Oy! Colin, pipe down!' He began, with a few minutes to kick off, 'Jamie, squat in at the end, right. Sit down and listen up!

He stood at the window end of the changing room, looking

down at the two rows of boys jammed onto the benches on either side.

'Most of you know how crap we were when we first started.' (Cheers) 'Alright! Now, we've been together for nearly two years, right? You are all from Grove or Wantage, and you are playing in the Oxford league.' (More cheers and a few boos) 'You should be proud of yourselves!'

'I am, John,' piped up Colin. 'And we all…'

'Shut it a minute, Colin, just listen – this is important.'

'In this league, this league of twenty teams, you, the boys from Grove, a little village out in the country, the first Grove team ever to play in the Oxford League,' (raucous cheers) 'seem…seem…' he hesitated for effect, '…to be holding your own.'

'So far you have played 5, won 4 and drawn 1, and that draw was against a *very* organised team.'

'Tossers!' shouted Sean Revell.

'Not tossers, Sean. Far from it! Anyway, so far you have scored 44 goals and conceded just 12 – ahem – that's seven too many in my opinion!' He looked at Olly Dimblow in fun. Olly smiled, but blushed and looked embarrassingly at the floor.

'No, seriously,' he continued. 'This means that – provided you continue to work for each other, play for each other, go the extra yard and enjoy what you are doing – there is no-one and no team we can't beat, or have a go at beating!' (Whooping cheers)!

Just then Tim Butler, the Abingdon manager, stopped and looked in from the doorway. John didn't care whether he had heard. This wasn't for his benefit.

'Uh, excuse me, John,' said Tim, casting his eyes around the room. 'Have you got a spare sponge for our bucket? We seem to have left ours at home.'

'Yeah, Tim, I'll find one,' replied John, as the Abingdon boys started to troop past their manager.

Some took a quick glance, others filed past.

'I'll bring it out when we come. See you in a few minutes.'

'Cheers – good luck boys,' said Tim earnestly to the Grove players.

'Boys, boys,' continued John when they had left, 'what I'm saying is that we have got a good little team here. What we do in training, how we defend and how we support the attack is how we are going to keep winning.' (More whooping cheers)!

'How many of you played in the first game when we played Abingdon away?' Most of the hands went up.

'They thrashed us, didn't they? They were cocky, they were nasty, and they gave us offside so many times. Their linesman had to have a month off work to rest his right arm.' (Hoots) 'What I want you to do is to be polite. Don't rise to them. Get out there and be calm. Play your game. Revs, don't get wound up – whatever happens.'

'Ritchie, Sparkie, you will have to time your runs from deep. Ollie, Billy, the two Jamies – *fair* bone-crunching tackles. Centre backs – tight – all the time on Pitson and Wilson. Plus, we're on the smaller pitch, which will suit us. Reserves, when you come on, you know your jobs. I want you to go out there and demoralise Abingdon. Outplay them. Snuff them out in attack, then take your chances. Remember, we still would have beaten them last season if we'd taken our chances! Boys, this is our time. We've lost Dwight since that game. But since then, we've got a proper keeper, defence, midfield and attack. So I can't see any reason why we can't go out there and beat them, can you?'

The boys half-heartedly cheered, looking a little sheepish.

'Can you? Come on! You can slaughter them!' (Cheers)!

'Now, get out there and play your hearts out!' (Raucous cheers)!

'In style!'

'Now, come on, Grove! Let's go to it – there's a battle to be won!'

'Come on, Grove!' echoed the boys as they clattered out onto the tarmac.

'And remember, be polite!'

After walking to the back pitch, John was quite pleased. His dads (unlike those of most other age-groups) had erected the goals, secured the netting, found and installed all the corner-flags and even nominated a linesman.

His education and warning to them early on let them know that their help was needed and appreciated. On a bad day, they would have to set up and take down the pitch. But more often than not, especially with an early kick-off, the pitch was left set-up for the next teams' games in the afternoon. So, the parents could drift home to lunch or have a drink in the clubhouse after the game.

Abingdon went through their usual exercise and routines, and John now took Grove through theirs, although it wasn't a patch on Abingdon's. Never mind. He had something in mind that would sort that issue out fairly soon. The immediate point was to beat Abingdon and beat them well.

This would be the test of how well the new full backs had integrated into the side, how they were performing, and how they had tightened up the defence after getting hammered by Abingdon just a few months ago. Technically, it should work perfectly; everyone in the team from defence to attack was also briefed to support the two Jamies. So apart from being stronger on the flanks, they were also well supported and looked after.

The match started gloriously when the midfield, after a sustained period of hacking about in the centre-circle, and with the ball bouncing around from player to player, was wrested from the Abingdon midfield. Sparkie broke right, and Ritchie set off left.

Ollie Gomm stepped out of the tackle and laid the ball back to Johnny Wells, who saw Ritchie's run and arrowed a diagonal pass inside the Abingdon right back. Coming from his own half, Ritchie raced outside him, stripped him for pace and, with two touches, bore into the half, leaving the defenders trailing behind.

As he approached the area, he side-stepped the centre-half and whipped in a cross to Mark Brind. Sparkie took a brief touch and got a stinging shot away, which rebounded off the keeper's gloves and knees as he tried to smother it. Sean Revell, following up at the edge of the area, watched the ball loop towards him and hit an arching half-volley into the vacant net for a great goal inside 5 minutes.

Abingdon were shell shocked, and John kept pushing from the side-lines to keep them focused. They controlled the game, winning everything in the 50/50's, time and again thwarting

Abingdon and counter-attacking superbly. Ollie and Sean dominated the midfield; the tackling was crisp, and they ran in at half time – 2-0 up – following a Billy McDonald tap in, after good work on the left from Jamie Skelton.

John brought the lads into the centre-circle at the break.

'Gather round,' he beckoned. 'Close up!'

'Right, lads…lads! Listen up. We're only half way through. It was a great performance, but we need to score again early on, we want to kill it. But don't stop playing. You've got them on the run.'

The boys were listening, hands on hips and puffing. The conditions were perfect. It was a clear, bright October day. The dads were on the touchlines, cheerily discussing the game.

'Okay, and when I'm happy that we've won it, I'll make some substitutions. Anyone got a problem?' Johnny Well's hand went up. A dead leg.

'Okay, Johnny, you come off now. Danny, jump into centre-half with Webby and listen to him, okay?'

Danny nodded happily.

'Webby, keep talking to your back-four,' John continued, nodding to his centre-half. 'Keep it tight.'

'Dan, stay tight on Pitson. Okay? Don't give him the chance to turn. Col, Charlie, I'll get you on when we get the chance. Okay? Now get back out there and win it. Well done, come on!'

The second half saw a determined assault from Abingdon, but after toiling for 15 minutes and coming up with a fizzled-out attack – which resulted in an easy catch for Olly Dimblow and a long-range effort from Abingdon's Richard Wilson that clipped the post – they simply faded away.

Ritchie was scorching down the left in the later second-half – and his pace bought a deserved 3rd goal – when Sparkie turned in his low cross at the second attempt, after his first shot was hacked off the line by a defender.

By now, Grove were soaring and full of confidence.

Another counter attack, on this occasion from a well-timed Elliott tackle on Abingdon's danger-man, Pitson; Gomm fed the ball forward to Mark Brind. Sparkie, looking up, played in Claydon who floated a first-time, out-swinging shot into the top corner, leaving the keeper watching. The subs came on and after re-establishing their superiority, Grove took control again.

In the 70th minute, Webby was the first to a Brind flick-on, rising at the far post to head a glorious fifth goal – that was it! The game was over as far as Abingdon went. Their boys looked deflated, and the last ten minutes were simply Grove holding off what challenge the dispirited Abingdon lads had left. When the final whistle blew, the Grove lads raised their arms and whooped in salute. It was their greatest victory over their most challenging opponents. Grove 5, Abingdon 0. Glorious!

A complete turn-around.

John looked for, and then spotted, Alan Elliott on the touchline with the other Grove parents. Alan was now stationed at Portsmouth, so he was around most weekends.

He was grinning and gesticulating enthusiastically at the performance and result.

John casually sauntered over.

'Hi, Alan. Could I have a word?' John asked as he approached Elliott, Jamie's dad, who was home on leave. He was a fit, well-built man, who had taken quite an interest in his son's footballing and the team in general. He had a fairly crisp manner, and was always keen to help, run the line, etc.

'What's up, John? Great team effort and result by the way,' said Alan, offering a handshake and still grinning.

'They had it coming, mate, cocky little shits,' snarled John with mock humour. 'We've been saving that up for them!'

'Well, it was a great performance,' Elliott agreed.

'Thanks, Alan.' John was beaming. 'Got time for a beer?' He motioned towards the clubhouse as the Grove boys whooped back to the changing rooms. 'There's something I want to run by you.'

Chapter 11
Villa v. Derby County Trip

Patrick Briggs stood on the north-bound platform at Oxford station just before 10 am on a drizzling Saturday morning in February. As he stood in the rain, 'Paddy' wore a scowl, looking up the line to his right for their train.

'Why ain't they ever on fucking time?' he grimaced, spinning on his heel and addressing his mates.

Paddy worked with Boily at MPC in John's Abingdon butchery unit. He was a solid and dependable worker and mate, slightly younger than Boily, and was a pretty interesting character in the workplace.

His college tutor had once approached him in the absence of his completed paperwork when he was working at the block in the butchery unit. Paddy was nonchalantly cutting pork chops for an order.

Frustrated by his attitude and response, the tutor had asked Paddy, 'Do you really want to be on this block all your life?'

Paddy had looked up and simply answered, 'Yes.' To which, the bemused tutor had no answer!

'Here you go, bud, have a can of *Stella*.' Boily held out a swinging pack of cold beers for Paddy.

'No thanks, mate. It's only 10 o'clock. I'll wait till we get to the pub.' Paddy shook his head with a shudder at the thought of a beer so early and turned back to grimace down the line again.

Standing on the platform at the Oxford Rail station with John, Marc, Boily and Derby in the light drizzle, the last thing

Paddy wanted was a beer. Marc also declined, but Derby and Boily were well on it, and it looked like they would be on it all day.

Derby was also wolfing down a hotdog and was dressed pretty ordinarily; he didn't have on all his football hooligan regalia, except for his Derby shirt under a denim jacket. So, apart from his gross eating and drinking habits, his skinhead haircut, the scar on his head and his bizarre, one-toothed grin, he looked not too out of place. The only other person wearing colours was Boily, who proudly sported his Villa home shirt over a sweater and wasn't wearing a jacket.

The rest were casual in jeans, with jackets and trainers and were dressed fairly respectfully. The train pulled in, and they all jumped on and found seats as the train rumbled out of the station towards New Street, Birmingham.

Derby had joined the lads again for Aston Villa v. Derby County in the first division, hoping for a County win. It was a Saturday and a league match; both teams were doing quite well, and they had decided to make a trip of it.

They were, despite the drinking, relaxed and quiet on the way up for the short journey, alighting at New Street still too early for opening hours – but they were following Boily's plan.

'Right, so Me, Neil and Rob came here a few weeks ago, and it was fucking brilliant,' began Boily, imparting his pub knowledge on the group.

'So, we were in the pub, having a few beers, and the landlady walked in with a fuckin' great pile of sandwiches. It was brilliant – apparently she always does it for the football, so let's get there and fill our boots.'

'I'll believe it when I see it!' scoffed Derby as they jumped into a taxi. 'I've heard these plans before! Free food? Don't fucking believe you!'

After a short taxi ride, they alighted and walked up the slope, somewhat happy and somewhat pissed, until they came upon their destination.

The New Inn at Saltgate was just off the ring road, but right on a main road. This pub, like so many in Birmingham, had seen much better days. It was a large stone building, imposing but faded with signs of decay, misuse and age. The windows were high, guarded and lined with red bricks. And the pub stood proud, and several steps led up to the main door.

It was obviously shut; it was still only ten to twelve.

'Right, boys, listen. We've never been here as a group before, but me and Neil have – and it's ok,' Boily regarded the group earnestly. 'Let me handle it. I'll get us in. I'll get the landlord to open up, so keep quiet, and I'll get us in in a minute. Don't worry and don't say anything – leave the talking to me.' He nodded to the group sagely.

The guys didn't want any trouble before the match, and they didn't want to get turned away either, so they let Boily approach the pub. He reached the top of the three steps and turned around with a knowing wink at his companions, who stood still and watched.

Resplendent in the weak sun, belly hanging over his jeans, he swayed, grinning and winking in his loud Villa home shirt. He put his finger to his lips as he surveyed his mates.

Boily hesitated, then smartly rapped on the locked front door thrice.

Moments later it opened, at first a crack, then swinging wider. Out stepped the landlord, rubbing his eyes and taking in the scene. He was a big old boy and was obviously quite adept at handling situations.

'Oright mate,' Boily started his plea.

The landlord gave him a once-over, looked down at the group and said, 'Right, you lot can come in, but you ain't coming in here dressed like that. We don't want no trouble. So, you lads come in, but you,' he pointed at Boily, 'get yerself off and change that fucking shirt. You ain't comin' in here with that on! Get rid of it! No bloody colours!'

The boys couldn't believe it. They were beside themselves with joy!

It was like Boily had been hit with a sledgehammer!

'What a dick,' laughed Marc as they left him outside.

Derby, quite rightly, had kept his Derby shirt carefully concealed beneath his jacket and stepped quietly behind the rest into the pub.

John, Marc and Derby filed into the pub as Boily made off down the steps cursing.

He had to go around the corner, whip his shirt off and put it back on inside out and back to front! As the lads settled in the lounge, he re-knocked at the door, gliding past the unconvinced landlord in his inside-out, backward Villa shirt, like a twit.

The boys were shaking with laughter by the time Boily entered the lounge.

Great! They were the first to arrive. There were plenty of seats and a pool table.

They were still laughing when their great protector eventually arrived.

'Yeah, well done, Steve. We would never have got in without you,' Marc sniggered.

'Fuck off, Giggly! We're in now, ain't we?'

'Yeah, no fuckin' thanks to you though, Boil,' Derby.

'Anyway, beer,'

The bitter was stunning, the decor slightly jaded. The last paint job would have been from the sixties, the paintwork was a jaundiced and smoke-stained blackened cream. The wallpapered lounge was over-painted (once scarlet, now faded).

The carpet was also a veteran, probably from the 70s; its greying flowers choked under decades of smoke and grime. The bar stools were also circa 1970 – stressed cotton with frayed edges and black, shiny tops testament to the hours of use they had taken throughout the pub's history.

The bar was solid and, again like so many of those old Birmingham pubs, Victorian, with stained-glass partitions, large brewery mirrors and gas-lamp style lighting. It was dimly lit, with a jukebox and a couple of fruit machines; a thing of the past really, and of different times.

But ostensibly, it was still, as it always had been, despite the changes in fashion and habits, a boozer. The landlady and the bar staff were helpful and personable, living within their small world in this part of the city.

The beer flowed, and the pool table was stacked up with 50p pieces, as they made themselves at home. Being the characters that they were, each with his own brand of humour and madness, they were always laughing and there was generally severe piss-taking and practical jokes going on.

The same bitter rules applied. A stunning pint of *Ansells* disappeared without a trace because it's so good that you don't even know you're drinking it! The *Ansells* kept flowing, and the pool got exciting as they laughed and messed about in the lounge.

After about half an hour, the landlady appeared: a stern but pleasant woman of about 50. She wore a white blouse with frilly cuffs and neck under a black sweater and black jeans with trainers. But what a beauty! What she was carrying into the bar on a silver platter adequately countered her appearance! She floated into the lounge unannounced with a great laden tray of freshly-cut sandwiches of all varieties: tuna, ham and mustard, cheese and onion, egg mayonnaise. She smiled at the group as she approached, acknowledging their appreciation.

'Here you go lads,' she bubbled, placing the tray down in the middle of their drinks. 'Enjoy.' She headed back towards the kitchen.

'Thanks, love,' they muttered as a group.

The lads were completely astonished!

It was exactly as Boily had described!

And amazingly welcome!

'Thank you very much, love. Much appreciated,' called Boily as she walked off.

'Jesus – stunning!' said John, happily filling up.

'I can't believe it!' Derby was grinning.

'Brilliant!' agreed Marc, grabbing a handful.

'Bloody Boily's outdone himself today. This is great!' said Deby, helping himself.

Marc sat down and started tucking into the sandwiches. After a while, a puzzled look appeared on his face, and he slowly stood up, feeling down to his rear.

As he turned round, the guys witnessed a great wet patch on his bottom.

He patted at his arse and burst out, 'Fuck! This fucking seat's soaked!'

Sure enough, there, on his bar stool, was a puddle of beer, which he'd just sat in.

'Shit!' Paddy exclaimed from the other side of the pool table. He stood up examining his bottom.

They were still laughing as Derby checked his arse.

Boily had spilt beer onto the bar stools as a joke.

This new Boily 'joke' was a new one; childish, but also stupid and really funny!

'Bloody hell! That's not funny!' shouted Derby, dabbing the seat of his jeans with an Ansell's bar towel.

As Derby went out to the gents to check upon his dampness, Boily grabbed his half-empty glass, dropped it under the table and applied his old piss-in-the-pint trick!

Derby came back, still cursing, and checked the bar stools for a dry one before grumbling into his freshly topped-up pint, taking a big swig.

'Hey, Derby! Are you taking the piss?' laughed Boily.

He had no idea.

'Fuck off, Westwood! You childish twat!'

The rest of the guys, now on stool and beer guard, roared with laughter while Derby eyed them incredulously.

'You lot are fucking mad, ain't you?'

'Right, who's up next? Is it you, Paddy?' Derby had just slaughtered John at pool.

Derby had won three frames on the trot, but Paddy was quite a useful player, representing the George and Dragon, Sutton Courtenay in the local pub league.

'Come on then, let's make it interesting and play for a fiver?' suggested Paddy, chalking up his cue.

'You're on, get your money on the table,' Derby ordered, pointing a chubby finger at the pool table.

Boily lounged against a pillar, with a wide sardonic grin, observing; Marc and John still guarding their seats and drinks, and they all watched as Paddy split the balls from the first break. Well, they were good players and there was a lot of cautious play, bearing in mind that most of the guys were getting quite pissed. The jukebox sputtered out ZZ Top's *Gimme All Your Lovin'*, the sun began to slant through the grimy windows and the battle commenced.

Derby had potted a few but announced, rubbing his crotch, 'Jesus, I need a piss.'

'So do I,' agreed Paddy, eyeing up Boily with a knowing glance and deliberately downing the remains of his pint.

'Well, I ain't going and leaving this table to you!' Derby announced, holding the cue across his chest.

'Jesus, don't you trust me?' asked Paddy.

'Not for a fuckin' fiver I don't, no! You'll have to come with me.'

The guys laughed at this, but Derby was adamant.

Paddy looked him in the eye.

'Come on then, Derby, we'll go together.'

They staggered off to the gent's. Paddy's arm around Derby's shoulders.

'Don't forget, it's my shot next,' said Derby.

'Okay!'

Off they went to the gent's, and Derby's glass dropped under the table again, and Boily quietly re-filled Derby's pint with another pissy top-up!

John and Marc, as one, jumped up to the table and swiftly manipulated Paddy's yellow balls to the edge of every pocket; they moved Derby's red balls away and into the central areas of the table. The two crumpled fivers sat under the chalk on the table. When they came out, instead of a finely balanced game, there would be a yellow ball hovering over every pocket.

As they emerged from the toilet, they both eyed the table, checking out the beer, the company and then the game. They grabbed their cues.

John and Marc were shaking with laughter as they watched the events unfold.

'My shot, mate,' said Derby.

'Bloody hell, not much choice here.'

Neither player seemed to have noticed the difference in the table.

Derby tried to play his first shot as a safety. He kissed the black and gave away two free shots. The knowing audience were stifling their laughter.

'Fuckin' 'ell! I thought I was in control of this game!'

Paddy stepped up and carefully cleared the table by tapping in each yellow ball with ease; he had two shots left to easily pot the black and win in less than two minutes.

'Well, Jesus, Paddy, that was incredible,' grimaced Derby, as he handed over the cash.

'Yeah, well done, Paddy. Hard luck, Derby!' shouted Boily, as they continued to piss themselves laughing.

'Great win. Must be you're round, Briggsy?'

'No worries,' answered Paddy, stuffing the money into his pocket. 'Same again?'

'Shiiit!' screamed Derby, as he seated himself on a newly wetted and particularly sodden bar stool.

'Twat!' he spat at Boily as he downed the last of his beery/piss cocktail!

The lads were by now falling off their chairs.

They left the pub and got to Villa Park for the match – all of them completely pissed and in great spirits. They made their way up into the Holte End. At this time, there were no seats, just a vast area of steep terracing. They stood and watched the game together, still laughing and joking. There was a big crowd and a great atmosphere.

John and Marc would be still talking about that day weeks later in the pub. But they could barely remember the match at all, or the final score!

They passed on the usual 'Shires' chicken Balti pies and Bovril at half-time, preferring to wait for a chicken Balti with green chillies at Azim's in the Lozells' Road afterwards. Azim's was worse than basic, but dead cheap and served a fantastic balti.

The decor was horrible and there was no alcohol licence, so you bought your own from the local shop across the road. If you had driven up, you tried to park your car outside so that you could keep an eye on it. And in the winter, once you had taken your seat, the waiters would roll the old *Calor Gas* heaters over to your table to give you a fighting chance of staying warm!

There were worn chairs and faded, peeling wallpaper, dim lighting and the most basic of starters, which were stored in an open butchers-style fridge in the main window. When you chose your starters, the grubby waiter simply grabbed the pakoras, samosas and shami-kebabs from the window and zapped them through the microwave on a plate!

But the actual *Balti* was stunning – a piece of culinary art in an oasis of culture. The guys all ordered chicken balti with green chillies and naan, and that was stunning and simply enough! No rice, no plates, just a bowl of heaven and delightful fluffy naans to dip in and mop up the divinely flavoured sauce – there was something almost religious about the food after the pub!

'Best fuckin' curry in Brum, Paddy,' mused Boily, dipping and swirling his naan in the delicious curry.

'No doubt about it,' agreed Paddy, looking up over his *Balti*.

'And the cheapest!' said John, who still couldn't believe what the meal had cost.

In those days, the *Balti* main course was just £2.50!

They greedily gobbled up the *Balti* and ordered takeaway in foil trays.

John had laughed all day and his ribs were sore, but the laughter didn't end there. They took a taxi down to New Street and boarded the train home.

While they were sitting in the stationary train, waiting to depart Birmingham, John was reading the sporting pink. Derby was snoring away, leaning his head against the window.

'I wonder which game will be on *Star Soccer* tomorrow,' mused John, scanning the pink for the afternoon's results.

In those days, pre-Sky, the only footy on a Sunday was *Star Soccer* on Midland or regional soccer – 'The Big Match' for London.

Hugh Johns had presented *Star Soccer* for donkey's years, and this would always feature the most prominent Midlands Derby.

They simply replayed extended highlights, so it could easily be Villa v. Derby, Wolves v. Leicester…that sort of thing.

The guys had had a great blast all day, and they hadn't stopped laughing all day long.

Marc's guess was somewhat random. As he scanned down the list of fixtures, he stopped at his preferred choice. 'Probably Newcastle v. Charlton?' he ventured.

There was a moment of silence in the train carriage, as the guys all pondered this guess.

Then, in his golden, Brummie tone, Boily questioned, 'Interesting decision, Marc.'

All eyes turned to Boily.

'As neither of those teams are anywhere near the Midlands,' he continued. 'In fact, Newcastle come from the North East and Charlton from South London. Hardly the most prominent Midlands derby, is it?' His comic timing was brilliant.

The eruption of laughter jolted the snoring Derby awake.

'Fucking hell, I'm bloody soaked!' cried Derby, touching his crotch. Boily had drizzled a stream of beer into his lap as he slept.

John was getting a headache and was making himself ill from laughing.

Derby jumped up. 'Fuck you, Boily!' he screamed. 'You are so fucking childish. I'm going to go and sit somewhere else!' He lumbered down the carriage to find some peace.

The train journey was uneventful; the boys all dropped off and dozed or slept all the way back.

Later, Lyn picked the lads up from Oxford station, dropping Paddy and Boily off in Wantage, then dropping Marc home in Grove.

'Had a good day then?' she sarcastically asked John as they arrived home, looking at him pityingly. He did look rough and was absolutely freaking exhausted.

'Just let me get to bed, love?' he pleaded. 'I just need to get to bed.'

'Jesus!' she exclaimed, watching him as he disappeared up the stairs, head in hands.

'Bloody football trips!' She was exasperated.

She just didn't see the point of them.

Chapter 12
Sixes

The annual six-a-side tournament was Grove's biggest fundraiser. At the sixes meetings, John had gladly put himself forward to assist in the event and agreed to run it, taking responsibility for the arrangement of the whole shenanigans at the end of the under-9s season. He wasn't fazed by it and had arranged, with the committee's help, the advertising, sponsorship, catering and organisation of the tournament, which was held over two days. 48 teams were to be playing – under-10s to under-16s on Saturday, and under-9s to under-15s on Sunday.

The fundraiser had been a very successful affair, as it had been well and consistently organised by hard-working local man, and ex-Challengers manager, Paul Archer for several years; after his untimely death, it was supported and staunchly carried on by his wife, Pat – who simultaneously ran the food at that time – and their two daughters, Tina and Steph. Paul had run and organised the Grove sixes, assisted by his lovely daughters who learned the ropes under their dad and had decided to carry on their roles in his name. John had met Pat and the girls at the first sixes meeting, and it was immediately clear they knew the event like the back of their hands. John warmed up to them from the outset and was really grateful for their help.

Tina and Steph weren't too involved in the general planning and didn't really get involved until Saturday morning, when they would arrive before the sixes started. Then they meticulously organised the boards, routines, refs and matches, all of which worked like clockwork.

They would stay all day Saturday and Sunday, until the clapping finally died down following the presentations to the winners and runners-up. At the meeting, John had offered his *Scholler Movenpick* freezer – an attractive deep blue ice-cream scooping cabinet – supported by another freezer from work stuffed with ice lollies and *Cornettos*. He charged the ices to himself at cost price, got Corine and her good mate, Becky (Elliott – Trigger's sister), to scoop and serve the ice-creams and lollies, paid the girls for the day and made a huge profit for the club.

The work involved in the organisational run-up for him was mainly phone calls from registering clubs. The sixes were always held on the first weekend of July and were always regarded as one of the best six-a-sides in the area. The first one that John had attended was the most traditional, whereby half a dozen teams from Northern Ireland would be hosted by Grove families and would socially interact through events outside the sixes. Then the various age groups would participate in the football game. In John's first participating year, the Northern Irish lads attended, but Joe had had real problems finding people to host them.

They were good lads, but some of them were a little over boisterous for the Grove folk, and those who had hosted previously were not always keen on them returning with their harsh accents and city ways. They were a real handful even to keep in the house, and those who had reached puberty were little womanisers to boot. Because their targets were often the daughters of the hosting families, this did not get a great response from those mothers and fathers. Many of the boys smoked, and the older ones (14 plus) also drank and were never to be found. And they could eat you out of house and home. Unfortunately, for those reasons, after several years of the visit, the village ran out of people willing to feed and bed them for three days, and the liaison ended.

The other thing, at that time, was that the under-8s weren't allowed to participate in the competition. They were deemed to be too young. There was a game, normally towards the end of Sunday, where the under-8s got a game; John's team had participated in their first year, playing and receiving a trophy for 'The Baby Mixers'. This purely enabled the youngsters to be involved, take in the atmosphere of the tournament and get a little trophy. Things were very traditional back then, and that was just the way it was.

The Rugby Club would be given over to the Challengers for the two days. There were three car parks to accommodate all the visitors, the charges for which were included in the 50p entrance fee programme that John had printed along with the sponsorship advertising inside. The car parks were manned by volunteers from the various age groups. Inside the car parks, along the front of the Rugby Club, would be stalls, bric-a-brac, a sports stall, selling replica kits and goalies gloves, caps, scarves etc. There was the barbeque, under a colourful put-me-up awning, sending a continuous ribbon of blue smoke over the trees.

Teams would arrive and set up camp around the perimeter of the field. Parents, who would possibly be there till six in the evening (if their boys were lucky enough to reach the finals), would bring tents, lean-to's and folding chairs. The green, blue and orange tents, some with banners or flags of recognition, made a colourful spectacle. The montage was completed with a myriad of different coloured shirts from the dozens of competing teams. Boys in yellows, reds, hoops and stripes darted from pitch to pitch, or raced to get a drink, a burger or ice-cream. They flew about, sweating happily, chasing wildly about between the penalty shoot-out competition, the scoring tent – where Tina and Steff studiously recorded the results – and the various pitches to watch other teams or support their mates. The whole site was commandeered, with pitches on the front, side and rear of the clubhouse.

All of this overlooked the lush pitches, mown by arrangement with the Parish Council on the Monday before the event. After which, teams of volunteers and managers spent every night after work on the playing fields, welding, grinding and painting the tatty goalposts, and mending, attaching and darning nets. The pitches all had to be marked out, mainly by Tony Keen, who was meticulous in his preparations; measuring, double-checking and carefully establishing, with the white-lining machine, the first marks. The white lines were re-done twice or thrice to ensure they lasted the weekend. The newly painted and restored white goals and their newly darned and repaired nets were numbered. The penalty spots were stencilled in lime. Then the pitches were staked and roped off, so that a walkway and spectator area separated the players and supporters.

On the eve of the sixes — when the newly rolled pitches had been crisply marked in virgin white lime, the sparkling new goals had been set up with their new-looking nets and the pitch areas staked — there was always the immense satisfaction of a job well done. The managers downed a well-earned pint on the clubhouse's terrace, admiring their work, along with the helpful parents and friends who had loaned their trucks, skills, welding tools and time to help the fundraiser.

By the morning of the event, the ice-cream stands, freezers and advertising, along with a few wooden benches, were located in front of the main entrance, up the terrace, atop the steps leading to the front door. Through the door, the bar was to the left, and the changing rooms (unused) and toilets were found to the right. Linda Keen, Tony's wife, used the kitchen to make sandwiches and tea for the substantial number of volunteer refs.

The bar opened early, and it was always Wimbledon Finals weekend: ladies' final on Saturday and the men's on Sunday.

As the first cars began to trundle through the gates, the stalls began to come to life; people milled about and took their stations, and the tournament began to take shape.

The girls arrived at about 8:30. John was already waiting in the scoring tent to welcome them.

'Hi Tina, hi Steph. How you doing?'

'Ooh, struggling just a little bit!' grimaced Tina.

'Yes, 'twas a little too late going to bed, given the wake-up time!' joined Steph.

'Ah, ladies, have I not warned you before about the demon drink?' he laughed, as they busied themselves.

'I am sure you have,' Tina laughed, 'but you know us – we never did take much notice.'

'Right, where's the cards?'

John pointed out the cards, and, to a large degree, that was him finished. His role had been roping in the 48 teams and making sure they were all booked and paid, no double bookings, no age groups in the wrong slot and so on. His time was taken up in the months before, with phone calls any time of the night and day, last minute pleadings, and enduring long, overstretched conversations with managers who wanted their teams to play in the tournament. He didn't really mind. But the deadline for the printed programmes – where all the fixtures were set out and printed – had to be completed and into the printer a month before the event. Old Gordon at 'B&G Print' in Challow always got the job done.

His rates were good, Marc worked there, and you couldn't resist the old fellow. He was the one who called everybody 'chap'. 'Chap' was a little general greeting by Gordon. He called everyone 'chap' because he wasn't good at all with names. So 'chap' had stuck with the lads and others, and still does to this day. They set the programme up, and, once the first proof was accepted, John would wait for cancellations and additions of reserves etc. so that Gordon could make last-minute adjustments.

Once the programme was printed, the monies were gathered in, and the teams just had to turn up on the day.

So, when Saturday morning arrived, John simply let the girls run the whole thing. They had been helping with it for four years, so they could do it with their eyes shut anyway. They certainly didn't need John's help. They organised the referees, whom they both knew well, bullying them light-heartedly and making sure the matches kicked off on time, and that the results were handed in by the refs. They kept the results board up to the minute and answered any questions, which were many and often. And they both thrived on it.

He stayed and oversaw, willing to assist or tackle problems, should any arise, along with the chairman and various committee members, who often popped in and out of the tent. It was a great social thing, and it normally went off without a problem. He mainly stayed in or around the tent, but he knew lots of the other teams and their managers, parents and Challengers colleagues, who were all over the event; he could go and watch a match, go to the bar and generally wander around at will. He also still had time, with the help of Graham Brind, to run two six-a-side teams of his own.

The under-9s had two teams (A and B) in the competition. John liked to try and get them relatively equal, so they both could progress, so he and Graham had picked the teams. He gave one of the teams, the one with Sparkie in it, to Graham.

They ran the teams separately, but in tandem. They supported each other, camped all together with the other Grove parents and had a good time.

There was plenty of time between games, so they all mixed and played and laughed together. This was the first time they had run teams in their own sixes, so the boys were quite excited and looked forward to their first games.

John had been a bit short of players, so he had asked Johnny Ashford (who lived next door to Ritchie), Skelton and Dwight if they wanted to play, all of whom had shown an interest and were around the tournament with their mates anyway.

The team had played in a few sixes already – away in Radley, St. Joseph's, near Swindon, Bicester and Kidlington – and they had had a great time. They got to the semis with one team on three occasions and were beaten in the final at St. Josephs on sudden-death penalties, which was hard on the losers, but at least they had their runners-up trophies. They had played some good and some bad football in those tournaments, but they enjoyed themselves, making some new friends along the way. The sixes were always a really good day out. On those warm summer days, as the managers and parents watched from the side-lines, John couldn't help but reflect on his views about the size of the pitches for the eleven-a-side games at this age. On a sixes pitch, you could be up and down the pitch in seconds, everyone was always involved in each game and if you possessed a bit of skill, as most of his lads did, you could play some marvellous football. On the large pitches, these little lads had to knock themselves out to get over the half-way line. It was so different, and the smaller pitches made it so easy.

There were definitely players, particularly defenders, who had not got enough touches, match after match, and inevitably dropped out of football altogether. Small pitches encouraged play and move; anyone could attack, anyone could defend, and you would be in the game, involved right to the final whistle.

John didn't know what to expect from the boys on the day of his Grove tournament, but both teams performed well, reaching the knockout stages, before the A team went out in the quarters, and then the B side – having brushed aside Swindon Robins in the second quarter-final – narrowly lost to Kidlington on corners! The game ended 1-1, but Kidlington had had three corners to Grove's two, a rule that seemed a very harsh way to lose a game, especially a semi-final. But rules are rules.

All through the day, the bar and barbeque had been busy. The hot weather meant the girls had been rushed off their feet with the ice creams, the bouncy castle, penalty competition and the various stalls had all been brisk. So, it looked like a good fundraiser all round. He checked with Becky and Corine at the freezers and noted that, in the morning, he would have to drive over to Faringdon – to work – and re-stock.

The last two teams, Kidlington and Abingdon, were slugging out the final as the sun crept behind the swaying trees and the last excited gaggle of onlookers and parents cheered them on. Kidlington eventually won the final 2-2, on corners again, and the teams of exhausted lads queued in panting, haphazard lines to collect their trophies from Bill Nelson.

Most of the refs had drifted off, but John, the girls and some Grove and Abingdon parents hung around for a beer, looking out over the deserted pitches as the last of the cars limped around the field in the lengthening shadows on their way home.

The next morning, having replenished his ice-cream stock and set up the girls in the tent, he gave himself the day. John had entered one team 'a year up', so he had under-9s playing in the under-10s tournament. He had picked a strong side, with Billy McDonald in goal, Sean Webb, Ollie Gomm, Johnny Wells, Revell, Dwight and Ritchie. The boys were excited, and they had nothing to lose, so they were really up for it. John thought they would do quite well, simply because the team was so strong, although quite small.

They proved to be phenomenal. Their footballing skills were outstanding from the outset, and they proceeded to beat the older boys from Donnington and Carterton 3-0 and 4-2, before drawing 0-0 with the team from Larkin (Ireland), to qualify top of their group. As they gathered for their ice-cream treats following the Larkin result, they all thought they were capable of going all the way and winning it.

Quite a few Grove parents had gathered round the patio area, enjoying the hot weather and a couple of beers in the casual atmosphere. The place was packed and in full swing. The boys were sweaty from their excursions.

'Go and see who we've got in the quarters, Revs,' John asked Revell, who had been brilliant.

Paul McDonald, Billy's dad, brought out another round of drinks as Sean, Billy and Webby scooted off to see the draw.

They came breathlessly back. 'Quarry Rovers!' Sean shouted.

'Have we seen them play?' asked Andy Wells.

'I watched them in their last game; they beat Radley 2-1 and looked quite useful,' said Jeb. 'Quite a big side, but beatable.' He nodded.

John didn't need to motivate the players. He told them to enjoy it.

The kick-off was scheduled for 1:30 pm.

As they kicked off, with a large local crowd watching, a few spots of rain drifted in on the breeze. The humidity had definitely increased, and as the game progressed, the rain became steady. Colourful umbrellas of all shapes and sizes were erected behind the goals and ropes that kept the spectators off the pitch. John left Ritchie up as the sole striker, and the team looked confident as they kicked off.

Dwight immediately selected the biggest player in the Quarry side and clattered him in the first minute as a statement of his presence.

Their opponents tried to use their height and strength to batter away at the smaller team, but the Grove team were like lightning round the pitch.

Billy McDonald made two great saves, Dwight headed a corner off the line, and Quarry led at the break by three corners to nil. But the boys had survived the onslaught. 0-0 at half-time, and there was grim determination from the Grove boys as Quarry kicked off the second.

Again, they came out on the attack and had an immediate long-shot skidding off the bar in the first minute.

The games went five minutes each way in the group stages, and seven-and-a-half minutes each way in the final stages. As the Oxford team continued to attack, they won another corner, meaning they were well ahead on corners even though it was still 0-0.

But with a minute left on the clock and Quarry committed in attack, Dwight made a superb, intercepting tackle, sliding in on the greasy surface; Johnny swept the loose ball out to Ritchie on the left. His pace beat his man, and he cut inside the ponderous defender, leaving him for dead. Looking up, he had Ollie racing into the box, and he slipped the ball right into his path. The Grove mothers screamed in anticipation. Here was the chance. Ollie took the ball first time, and as the huge keeper spread himself in front of the goal, Ollie dummied his shot, sending the keeper to his left, then sent a reverse pass straight back to the unmarked Ritchie for a tap-in and the lead. There was an immediate mass huddle, the boys emerging, punching the air and grinning madly.

The parents were hysterical and vociferous, shouting their praise and encouragement. The boys battled away for the last minute and nearly scored a second when Ritchie was sent away down the middle, only for the Quarry keeper to race off his line and smother at his feet. There was still some defending to do, and the Grove lads tackled for their life, but the Quarry Rovers were beaten. As the ref blew for full time, the boys and spectators whooped in the mild warm rain and wandered, delighted, back to the cover of the base tent or the bar. The dripping entourage of wet, sweaty boys and beaming, wet, bedraggled parents and grandparents lurched back towards the Rugby Club, ecstatic.

The result was unprecedented: for a younger age group to progress through the group rounds, then win through to the finals was a rare achievement. A fact not lost on both the winning and losing teams.

'Christ! We could win it, Dave,' John beamed to Dave Claydon, as they made their way back to the bar.

'Brilliant,' replied Dave. 'Even if we don't, we've given an amazing account of ourselves. But we look like we're good enough to win it, don't we? Ha ha!' He grinned madly. Then he pointed over the trees towards the north. 'Don't like the look of the weather though, it looks grim over there. And it's coming in!'

The next quarter final kicked off soon afterwards and with it, the rain worsened. A streak of lightning forked earth-wards followed by a rumble of thunder. Without hesitation, the ref blew his whistle, calling the players off and back towards the clubhouse. By now it was pouring, the sky was black, and the few remaining cars were beginning to crawl towards the exits. The players were soaked to their skins, and spectators limped back to the bar for shelter.

Back in the tent, Grove's new chairman Bill Nelson watched the mounting storm escalate. Within fifteen minutes, with the sky cobalt blue, rain roaring and soaking the water-logged pitches, thunder rolling and lightning flashing, he made an easy decision. Picking up the tannoy, he announced to the remaining parents and boys,

'Ladies and gentlemen, boys and girls, in the interest of safety, I regret to say the sixes have to be abandoned. There will be no more games tonight, and the tournament is over. I am very sorry to those teams that have reached the finals, but we cannot take any risks. So, thanks for coming, and could you please pack up and make your way to the exits as soon as possible?'

He shrugged to John, Steph and Tina. 'Sorry guys, there's nothing we can do.'

John made his way to the bar, where the remains of his team and their parents were looking up in expectation. 'No, sorry guys, we've just reached the semi-final, and it's all been called off.'

Gary Revell wasn't happy and muttered something about the chairman under his breath.

The boys were disappointed, but they were still high from the recent quarter-final victory, and they accepted it for the great achievement that it had been.

But a great moment and opportunity was lost as the rains teemed down, only leaving them to wonder whether the youngsters could have pulled it off.

'Never mind, we were great – well done, everybody! Now, is there anyone who fancies a pint?'

They grabbed the seats nearest to the windows and watched in awe as the storm and rain gathered momentum. On the telly in the corner, Pete Samprass had just won the Wimbledon final, and there were a few other players and parents around the club, which by now was gathering little puddles, in and around the bar area. This was populated by laughing parents and boys with hair plastered to their wet heads, in black and white stripes, bony knees with protruding shin-pads and jumpers or track-suits. Brothers and sisters of all ages were present too, all happy to be with their families and friends in the familiar surroundings of the club.

That storm, which had not been forecast and seemed to come from nowhere, raged on for another few hours. As they drove home, the pouring rain had sent rivers down the roadsides, sweeping debris and branches before it. When John and his family arrived home later that evening, the normally placid stream in their garden had become a swirling torrent and had moved up three feet onto his lawn, so there was no way they could have carried on. But they were all proud of the day and took it as a moral victory. Luckily, they had stocked up at *Jade*

Palace on the way home, and soon they were busy watching the rain through the patio windows while eating a lovely Chinese meal.

There were a few other sixes as the summer wore on, and the teams had mixed success without winning one. But they were such great social events that nobody seemed to mind, and with the sun, food, wine and company, the mothers got to know each other well. The team had gelled, plus there was now a nice vibe within the group, where it was well supported and easy going. Nobody minded putting themselves out, and there was always lots of silly chatter and laughter coming from the group, especially from the women, and especially after a glass or two of wine.

The sixes teams that John put out also played great football and were attracting more spectators as they progressed. It was great to watch the sixes, as the action went on non-stop. The ball was whisked from one end to another, and the skill levels and intensity were always on the edge. Everybody loved them. It helped that they were always in the middle of summer.

At the August meeting nearly a month later, when Brenda ran over the sixes profits, they were surprised by the successes. The ice-creams alone had raised a beautiful, clear profit of £459.30, despite the late storm and rainfall on Sunday. With the entrance fees, stalls, teas, competitions and stalls, the overall profit was over £1200.00.

John even joined the sixes committee for the following year and promised to do the same deal on the ice-creams.

In that meeting, during 'Any Other Business', the next Belgian visit was mentioned. Unusually, the 'hosting' was proving to be a problem. Billy Mulcock, whose upcoming under-11s were due to host next Easter, was struggling to get parents involved.

Grove and a delightful Belgian village, Sint-Niklaas, had been exchanging visits for a number of years. It was a simple arrangement – Grove hosted one year, Belgium the next, with two age groups participating, normally two years apart, so that both older and younger brothers could be involved.

There was an outdoor eleven-a-side men's game, an eleven-a-side ladies' game (for women and girls) and the boys' games, featuring the two age groups. There were also indoor six-a-side competitions for both boy's age groups, men's and women's. The games were competitive as both countries were playing to win, but it was also incredible fun and true-spirited.

All this was partaken in over the Easter weekend, starting when the visitors arrived by coach on Good Friday evening and were dispatched to their host families, before becoming involved in dinner and disco on Friday night. Football was indoors on Saturday, outdoors on Sunday. Saturday was sight-seeing day, normally with the host families, followed by dinner at their house and a quiet Saturday night. A big farewell party was held on Sunday after the football. It was a good thing to be involved in. By the time the guests left to catch the bus home on Monday morning, it was often a tearful farewell, because the weekend had been so good, and people had made new friends, young and old alike.

'None of my people seem to want to host,' Billy was saying. 'They want to go to Belgium next year, but even then, some of them want to stay in a hotel!'

'Over my dead body!' fumed Clare Parry. 'The hosting is what the visit is *all* about!' She shot him a sneer. 'Tell them they have to host.'

'Well, I've got three parents, including myself, who will do it.' Billy shrugged resignedly. 'None of the others are interested.'

Newly installed chairman, Bill Nelson, took centre stage, quietly removing his glasses and in his concentration, tweaking the hinge.

'Billy, man. We cannot have this!' cried Nelson sternly. 'The under-13s are also struggling with their host families, and we have to start raising funds as a matter of urgency. The hosting must be in place first. And we need them to commit. Otherwise, the whole bloody trip could be off.' He absently removed his glasses and placed them on the table.

'And if it fails next year, it will finish,' said Clare.

'Well, I wish I could be more helpful,' Billy uttered in response, very unhelpfully.

'Yeah, well, you've gotta be, otherwise it's dead in the water.' Nelson was agitated.

'What's the problem with the under-13s?' asked Pete Whareham.

'Same thing, Pete. Collective lethargy, I'd say,' commented Dave Gressham, the current under-12s manager.

'And if we can't get enough people to host, the whole trip is off?' returned Pete, quizzically.

'It better not be.' Clare was also beginning to get very agitated. 'This Belgian exchange has gone on year in-year out for nearly seven years now. People like Herman, the chairman, and his family host *every* year.'

'How come we can't get ten families from one age group to

host for one year? Especially since their reward is to be on the bus next Easter for a weekend of football with their families! I find the whole thing uncommitted from the whole team and their parents!' Clare was on a roll.

'Clare's right,' agreed Bill, re-attaching his glasses and flicking his hair back in a nervous gesture.

'We must have the commitment.'

'What about if we ask around *some* of the other ages?' Billy was now creeping around the issue.

The debate swung on.

After listening intently to the debate and some very deliberate thinking, John stood up.

His hatred of meetings and rhetoric had led him to a measured response.

'Please, please, ladies and gentlemen.' John gestured for a break in the proceedings.

'The problem, as I understand it, is that the two age groups parents cannot get enough response to host a reciprocal visit?' He looked around the ensemble for response. 'The answer is obvious and quite simple, surely, isn't it?'

Blank looks from the table.

'Change the age groups!' He threw his hands up for effect!

'What d'you mean, John?' asked Bill Nelson. 'It's their turn to go.'

'But Bill, you haven't got enough hosting for twenty people yet, and you need what? Sixty?'

Mulcock dropped into serious thought.

John turned to him for an answer.

Nelson looked perturbed. 'What are you thinking then, John?' he asked.

'Drop the age groups to under-10s and under-12s, and Me and Pete will take our teams. I'll bloody insist our parents' host, but I know they'll be up for it already, without even talking to them.' John looked on earnestly at the group.

Billy went to say something but changed his mind.

'Pete?' queried John.

Pete Whareham looked at John with his mouth open. 'Uhh…'

'Well, Pete, do you think you can get your parents to host next Easter?'

Pete looked confused but confident.

'Well, yeah, but…'

'Provided we get to go to Belgium on exchange the year after, Mr Chairman,' said John, looking squarely at Bill Nelson.

Clare Parry had become all sweetness and light.

'Well, that's a great idea!' She was practically glowing.

'But if I can get the parents?' Billy stuttered.

'If you and the under-13s can host the best part of fifty people, given that some Belgian friends will be staying with friends,' continued Bill Nelson. 'Then the under-11s and 13s will host and return to Belgium on the tour the following year.'

'But if you can't?' grinned Clare.

'Then we'll hand over the hosting to the younger age groups!' cried Bill with finality.

'A show of hands?' His gaze swept the table. 'Carried.'

Pete was looking decidedly worried.

John winked and nudged him in the ribs.

The meeting finished, and people started to get their coats.

'Well, boy?' asked John, while leaning on the bar facing Pete after the majority had drifted away.

'I reckon that we'd better get cracking!'

Pete and John both had great sets of parents and solid teams and team spirit. They were also close socially, both sets mixing and enjoying each other's company. John knew his parents would be mad for the Belgian experience; they would host, without any pushing, for the team.

Pete's parents just needed to drop in line – then they had a tour!

Belgians next year!

Bring it on.

Bill Nelson closed the meeting.

He looked absolutely exhausted!

Chapter 13
Under-9s – Playing and Improved Training

The performances up to this point were definitely benefitting from better training. John was very happy to have the usual small fifteen-minute game when training was over, and his love of first-touch often had five or ten minutes of 'one-touch only', encouraging players to pass and move. He got immediate results from many of the players, whose confidence grew as they aspired to improve and cement their places as first-teamers. He was also really keen for the boys to be two-footed, so he continued in those sessions to have five or ten minutes of 'the weaker foot only'. This could be painfully funny to watch, but it did encourage very one-footed players to have a go with their weaker foot. He was also sure they took this idea away as 'homework', so they could practice at home against a wall, or in the playground.

In the summer, he drove over to Haddenham to pick up some new footballs. He also picked up a copy of Trevor Spindler's *Soccer Techniques: A Guide for Teachers and Coaches* from Mr Spindler himself. Someone had recommended it, and it was a very interesting book. He found the book riveting. He followed the basics from the start of Chapter One: 'The Basics of Coaching'. A lot of it was so obvious and so simple. There were tips so basic – know the players, know their abilities, know who can come on and how, plan (planning a training session up to then had been pretty much a hit and miss) and so on.

He had never really thought of such obvious things (up until reading about it), running with the ball for example – to set off on a sprint with the ball, into space, to knock it forward six yards, and concentrate on the running. Although obvious, things like this had never been taught to him (or his old teammates). They had simply played football, and this type of thing came naturally.

But this was invaluable in training for the boys who had the basics. After all, training was just that, and he learnt and passed on many of the tips from Mr Spindler and tried to find something new to work on every session. He was particularly interested in the first few pages; Mr Spindler had a section on small-sided games. He endorsed what John had thought from day one.

Small-sided games would benefit all the boys who had received more contact with the ball and therefore had better game and skill practice, making the most of the training session. He also read that 'Indeed, there are strong arguments that all matches below the age of eleven should consist of small-sided games.' This was where he had always thought all boys would benefit. In the early years of the team, the size of the pitches and goals had always been a bone of contention for John. And he could clearly begin to see the benefits of small-sided training games to many of his players, who had begun to blossom and progress with some rapidity. Funnily enough, the other Grove managers who he talked to didn't seem bothered about it or were downright against small-sided pitches and games.

So, the training manual soon began to bring the players on apace. Before each small-sided game, which now came to be looked on as a 'bonus after training', a bit of fun, there were specific, planned practices, carefully set out in the prescribed area with the correct equipment, organisation and delivery.

This was followed by assessment, following the observations by John, Marc or Boily, all of whom contributed. Boily, as an ex-goalkeeper, also often took Olly and Billy aside in these periods for keeper training, also featured in the manual. All showed impressive signs of development in many areas.

So, when he thought they were ready, he would start to teach the progressing boys the turns, the inside hook, the drag-back and the Cruyff turn.

He also tried to harden the boys up, although this wasn't as easy, as the boys were all still happy-go-lucky, enjoyed training and playing, and really close and not that way. Organising a defensive wall was something that John found funny. He would organise free-kick positions to attack and defend on the training pitch. He taught keepers Olly and Billy to position the wall so they had a view, making sure the keeper held up fingers for the number of defenders immediately. Then he would encourage the keeper to have the wall facing the free-kick-taker, while Sean or Johnny Wells faced the keeper in the wall, arms linked, and moved it to the keeper's required position. All this worked like a charm. John wanted it trained, so they could organise it like clockwork, which they did.

The problem was the bravery of the boys in the wall. It is not easy standing ten yards away from someone who is going to smash the ball towards you, but some of the guys were as useless as chocolate fire-guards. When Sparkie, Revell, or John himself, shaped to take a free-kick – after all the meticulous and speedy defensive preparations to erect the wall –the defenders in the wall *ducked!* John tried everything to try and sort this problem, but he had real difficulty with it.

Stephen Casey, Danny O'Sullivan, Mark Brind, and Johnny Wells were often nominated for the wall, as they were amongst the biggest players. But each run-up from an attacker would result in a mad ducking scramble to get away from the ball to avoid being hit.

'Boys, boys,' John would call, laughing, 'Do not duck! The reason for you being in the wall is to be hit!'

208

But duck they did, closed eyes, turned backs. It was actually funny. You would probably get arrested for it now, but his light-hearted solution to the problem was to line a wall up, with four or five boys in it, then pretend to run up and blast a free kick at them. It worked! After the first few – when he would try and get them to stand their ground or even jump as the kick was taken, when they were almost diving to get out of the way – the wall realised its collective job and stood up. A few of the boys caught a stinging kick straight in the face, but as John pointed out, 'Look, this is the worst that can happen; anyway, they're not aiming at you like I am.

'They are trying to get a shot on target. If it hits you, you have done your job, and if it comes towards your face, just try to head the ball away!'

Of course, he had to demonstrate this so that the boys also had a chance to have a pop at him. And bloody hell, if you did cop it in the face, well, that could *really* sting. And that bloody Sean Revell got quite practised at aiming his ferocious free-kicks at John's head in these practices.

'But you are probably only going to have to face about one free-kick a game on goal, and more often than not, the ball will be sailing over your heads! There will be four or five of you in the wall, so the chances of you being hit are not very high. So stand and defend it – it's your job.'

Stephen Casey turned out to be the bravest in the end, and for years afterwards – when John saw professional teams breaking the wall or ducking, which they did – he often had a laugh about it and thought of old Casey from the first day of practice.

Following the Abingdon result, Grove went on to six straight victories over Berinsfield (2-0), Botley (8-1), Bullingdon (5-1),

Chesterton (9-0), Garden City (4-0) and Florence Park away (4-0). So, the team was now doing well. These teams were all okay, but Grove seemed to be able to get the better of most. On many occasions, the pitches were smaller, or as small as they had been, but the boys were getting bigger and stronger, and could kick the ball good distances. And they loved to counter attack. They were playing some nice football and attracting some good comments from opposition managers and parents. They were also making friends in that capacity.

It was also a very innocent time. The boys were still little kids and they would still play on climbing frames in the park when they got to grounds that had park facilities. They listened and liked to win, but they were still able to get away with cheeky comments to John, who was really happy with them, the team, training and parents.

As the season rolled on, they met a strong Highfield (Bicester) team on a late November day. The ground was hard and frosty, the pitch was a full-sized affair, with full-sized goals, and the Highfield boys had obviously heard of the Grove team's successes so far. They out-muscled, out-thought and out-played the Grove lads, who battled in vain, coming away with a Sean Revell consolation goal and a 3-1 reverse. Still, every team had to lose sometimes, and John was philosophical about it. After all, the boys had enjoyed a great run, and one defeat in thirteen games was table-topping form.

They had three games in December, beating Littlemore 4-1 at home, then Launton away and Barton at home both by 7 goals to 1. The football flowed, and in January 1994, the four fixtures brought four more straight victories – Kidlington, Rose Hill, Quarry Rovers and Radley, all away, by 3-1, 3-0, 7-1 and 11-0 respectively.

The quality of some of the football was sometimes very pleasing. The third goal at Quarry was a move that had started from the Grove penalty area, involving seven passes and sweeping through the opposition as if they weren't there. Sean Webb, picking up a loose ball, fed Billy, who side-stepped his marker, pushing the ball through to Mark Brind, with his back to goal on the half-way line. He held the ball up, then flicked it to Revell. Sean lifted his head, seeing Ritchie and Ollie Gomm set off on runs. He rolled the ball under his studs and floated a diagonal pass directly into Ritchie's path on the left wing.

Ritchie latched onto the ball, dropped his left shoulder, pushed the ball forward past his defender and swung in a delectable cross to the near post that was met with a stunning left-footed volley from Gomm, who had continued his run, smashing the ball into the net and leaving the keeper riveted. At this age and level, it was a scintillating goal, which bought forth a warm round of applause from everyone watching – and delirious celebrations by the ecstatic Grove parents.

The team was largely the same each week, and all the boys got games, as parents were often away, sisters were getting baptised or other commitments took precedence. John was lucky, he always had enough players, even though sometimes he could only take one sub. The boys stuck together, played their football and managed to get results. Looking at the fixture list, he noticed that the next two fixtures were also away, to Oxford United Social Club – who were improving – and St. Edmunds.

The two results were outstanding – 5-0 at OUFC and 5-1 at St. Edmunds, giving a run of six consecutive away wins! People were beginning to talk. The managers of other clubs would say nice things, and still, by and large, every player came from Grove. There were a few players like John Monery, Charlie Harris and

Casey who didn't play as often as they may have wanted, but still the morale was good, and they turned up every week. John was getting a little bit miffed with Jamie Skelton, although it wasn't particularly the player's fault. Home or away games, although he was one of the nearest to the Rugby Club's playing fields, John would still have to drive around to Skelton's house to pick him up.

Often, John would be driving off – no-one answered the phone or the door, and regularly, John would be knocking or ringing the doorbell for ten minutes – only for Jamie to appear at the last minute, tousle-headed and wiping the sleep from his eyes. John hadn't been able to rouse him for the match against Radley, so Jamie missed it.

The following week, against League-leaders Highfield, he was actually down to one sub, so he warned Jamie to be ready on time. John didn't mind picking him up. So long as he was there.

'Just get out of bed, Jamie. Be ready on time.'

His last conversation had been along the lines;

'Jamie, you're going to have to try harder mate, or you'll be letting the team down, especially for these away matches.' John had tried everything to motivate him.

Jamie had looked nonplussed. John thought that maybe the lad had not got much parental support. He seemed interested and always gave 100% on the pitch. But sometimes, he looked very puffy-eyed, like he'd been up all night, and John thought this was a big part of his reliability problem. Too many late nights watching telly until the small hours and sleeping in on match days.

'Come on son, you can do it. I don't want to lose you,' he had said. 'Will you make more effort? Your football is brilliant, we really want you in the team!'

Skelton seemed to be mulling over the question.

'Okay, John, I will,' the lad had replied, unconvincingly.

But he suspected that the kid's circumstances were not ideal. He was a nice lad and great once he got going, but it was hard to get him up and out of bed and into the action. However, John didn't have the time or inclination to mollycoddle individual boys on match days.

It was a crying shame, as he was a really good footballer.

John was not happy.

On the day of the match, John watched from the open changing room door as the Highfield team arrived, observing them drifting towards the changing rooms. They looked confident and strong, and they seemed to have plenty of substitutes.

But with the pitch set up and things ready for kick-off, John counted in his players but saw no Jamie Skelton. The kick-off was 11AM, so he had plenty of time to get there. John drove around and banged on the door. He looked at his watch. He phoned. He banged again. And finally, he cursed and drove back to the ground. Still no Skelton.

He drafted John Monery in at left-back and had just the one substitute, Charlie Harris. He watched in anger as the makeshift team got stuffed 3-1. Jamie never came back, and John never questioned it. But he made a conscious decision not to pursue him again.

***

Anyhow, with over half the season gone, the team had lost just two, drawn one and won 20. Amazing.

When he next arrived home in the week, Alan Elliott appeared for training on Wednesday and immediately jumped in amongst the players, who were milling around, fairly casually and non-disciplined. John knew he was now much more available. Here was the start of John's new plan.

Alan stepped forward, kitted up for a run.

'Right boys,' he announced, with considerable authority. 'John has invited me to become your physical fitness trainer! We will make this good fun. It will be hard work, but it will be to your benefit and will improve your fitness!'

'Okay?' He was pretty excited. The boys looked interested.

'We will be doing a bit more fitness work before training – we will be warming you up before training and before matches. This will improve your fitness and stop you from being injured during matches, so it will all be good; like I say, fun at the same time. Any questions?'

No answer, just bemused and interested looks.

'No? Okay! Follow me!'

He jogged off, and the boys gaggled along behind. He ran them round Wasborough field for about a quarter of a mile. Then they stopped and went through a succession of star-jumps, push-ups, running games, piggy backs, etc, finally bringing the bedraggled group back around the perimeter of the rec – Johnny Wells bringing up the rear, red-faced and panting.

Thus, began the new enhanced training. The team was actually in need of it. Some of the team were definitely putting on weight and some were slacking. John's idea was to get the team as fit as they possibly could. He also was desperate to get the warm-ups before the match sorted, so that they were in prime condition, well prepared and *looked like* a football team. Truthfully, this regime was a bit overdue, necessary and timed just right, making the team physically on par with other teams and ready to compete on every level.

He was happy with the football training and its progression. But now he had someone to share the responsibility with, who controlled the physical side of things; it was something that Alan was very happy and also competent to take on – his Royal Navy training definitely didn't do any harm. It was also something John did not have much experience with. So, the regime was nearly complete.

By now, though, the team was down to fourteen players – it was simply not enough. There was talk that Charlie Harris was thinking of quitting because there was a Grove B-team in formation, bizarrely with the intention of joining the old Vale League at next seasons' under-10s. This was not good news. John knew he had to strengthen his squad, ideally with another two or three players. He would have ideally liked sixteen in total, but sixteen strong players, so he could give them all a fair shout in the team.

He knew he had a few weaknesses, but those boys had been loyal and kept turning up, even as substitutes, week after week, rain or shine.

Olly Dimblow

Jamie Elliott   Sean Webb   Johnny Wells   Danny
O'Sullivan

Sean Revell   Billy McDonald   Oliver Gomm
Charlie Harris

Richard Claydon   Mark Brind

Subs: Colin Mercer, Steven Casey, John Monery.

He needed another full back – since Skelton had quit or
disappeared – as stronger cover for Col and Danny, and another
strong defender and midfielder or defensive midfielder. There
was plenty of creativity in the side, but they were still a bit
lightweight in some departments.

Therefore, this team needed to be strengthened, because,
inevitably, if the B-team did get going, the players on the
periphery would be tempted to move on – and straight into the
first team of the B-team every week, which would make sense for
them as they would get a game every Sunday. John was a bit
annoyed because the guy who was starting the B-team had done
it very quietly without any discussion. It was going to put a strain
on the available players and potential developers, although it
would prove to be an outlet for some of the not-so-gifted players
in his squad. He didn't know the chap who was allegedly starting
the team except that his name was Billy Bullstrode.

He was quite a nice bloke, quiet and slightly built, with a dark
beard. Apparently, he had introduced himself to the new
chairman, Bill Nelson, the amiable Sunderland-mad Geordie,
who had given him the green-light. They were introduced at the
March Monday meeting.

John was at a loss when Billy was introduced, because he really didn't have much of an idea this was actually going to happen. All he had heard of this was based upon rumour.

'And, finally, we come to "Any Other Business",' announced Nelson towards the conclusion of the meeting.

'I would like to introduce Mr Billy Bullstrode.' He waved as Bullstrode stood, colouring slightly.

'Billy is aiming to set up and run a second under-10's team next season,' announced Nelson.

Mild interest.

John sat up, suddenly alert.

'A "second" under-10s team?' he enquired.

'That's right, John. Billy is registering another under-10s team to play in the Vale League next season.'

The plot was thickening. There had been a lot of opposition to his team being the first from the club to join the Oxford League. This smacked of collusion, a little sub-plot to ensure that Grove still had an interest in the Vale League. As if to echo his thoughts, Nelson spoke again.

'Yes, according to Billy,' he went on, 'there are enough players around at this age group to easily support two under-10s next year.'

'I doubt that!' John couldn't restrain himself.

'Oh y-yes, there are, er…John,' responded Bullstrode. 'I have eight players interested by word of mouth, and we haven't started advertising yet.'

'But you'll need at least sixteen!' demanded John. 'That's 32 boys if we have two teams. That'll make us both struggle, and I'm struggling now.'

'Well, we may be able to help each other out,' Bullstrode continued. 'If you get anyone who wants to leave, for any reason…'

'What, and you may have a player or two who wants to move up?' John countered with sarcasm.

Bill Nelson stood, looking uncomfortable.

'Ah, not up, John,' said Nelson, nodding sagely. '*Across.*'

'Across, Bill?' questioned John, sticking his chin out at the chairman.

'This won't be a B-team.' Nelson fiddled with the hinge of his glasses, as he did when he was under pressure.

'Of course, it will be a B-team. I already have a team with the best players in Grove, one that I have been building for three years,' snorted John, beginning to fume.

'I can already sense, by the way this was kept quiet, and the suggestions so far, that there will be more to this than meets the eye!' John was trying to keep his calm.

'Not true, John. This is purely to give the boys of Grove the chance to play football,' replied Nelson, shuffling his papers nervously.

'The boys of Grove are already playing football!' countered John. 'If they're good enough, they're playing for their school primary team. They are playing in the playground.' John had the bit between his teeth now.

'Are they going to be good enough to play against properly organised teams, week by week?' John aimed this question straight at Bullstrode.

Bullstrode looked up contemptuously. 'We have already got some very good players.' He added, 'And they do want to play in a league, and they are good enough!'

John wondered who they were. His lads didn't appear to have known anything about the formation, or they would have said something.

'*Good enough*' he wondered. Who are they then? If they were '*good enough*'?

And why hadn't they been up with their mates for a trial with our team? Interesting!

'And where will they train?' queried John.

'On different days than you,' suggested Nelson.

'And how will the fixtures be arranged?' John countered again.

'A different league, John. Different days, different times. Look, we've worked it out and it's all viable.'

Fucking sounds like you have sorted it out – between you!

John didn't disagree one hundred per cent. Besides, here was a potential opportunity to strengthen the team, and perhaps there could be some two-way traffic!

He took a sip of his beer.

'Well, Bill, if you are happy with it, and you are sure they will have enough players, as long as they don't interfere with me. Because I am happy with my setup and I won't be getting involved. So long as it doesn't force our lads out of the changing rooms, or impact my refs, and they don't start poaching my players!'

'Fine, John. Fine, man. I think you'll all get along,' drawled Bill in Geordie.

Bullstrode and Nelson sat down simultaneously.

Bizarrely, this was yet another first – the first time the club had had two teams competing in the same age-group.

John looked squarely at Bullstrode. He didn't like him.

Bullstrode nervously stared at the floor.

'So, where are we going with the name, Mr Chairman?' John asked, straight out staring right at Nelson.

'Grove Challengers under-10s, I suppose,' said Nelson.

'We're Grove Challengers under-10s,' retorted John, his voice dripping with venom.

'Well, any other suggestions?' asked Nelson.

Pete Wareham, Billy Mulcock and the other managers, the two ladies of the committee, all shook their heads, looking at each other in vain.

Tony Keen stood up. 'Only one thing they can be called, en't there?'

Tony took a long swig to finish his pint. He stood up, brushed his lips and, once he had swept his twinkling eyes around everyone assembled there, announced through a mischievous smile, 'Grove B!'

Tony didn't like Bullstrode either.

'Goodnight all!' Tony grinned, pushing his chair back.

***

The training continued to improve. The book was becoming the bible. They all loved it. Everyone turned up for every training session if they could. John went over dribbling, shooting, crossing, tackling and setting out the exercises in accordance with the instructions.

The boys used to even help him drag out and erect a proper goal, so they could really practice shooting across the keeper, corners, free-kicks and other routines. John continued to be amazed by the books' direct simplicity. Even heading the ball could be taken to pieces, analysed and used to vastly improve techniques. He was learning so much himself!

The physical side, under Alan Elliott, was coming along really well; the boys largely loved the extra demands from the runs, and the little physical games along the way were great fun. As Alan had suggested at the outset, they were, as a group, beginning to improve their fitness; they loved it and at this age, needed it.

The next full training session was on a Wednesday night in late February. John was astonished and amazingly irritated to see Bullstrode casually walking over as the boys laid out the cones, accompanied by a lad that turned out to be his son, Brian. Ah! So Bullstrode was starting the B-team so his son could get a game. It was all news to John, as he had never seen or heard of either father or son up till now.

'Hi. John. I wonder whether we might be able to get a few tips, whether we might stay and watch?' he asked in all innocence.

John was taken aback. He couldn't believe the cheek of the man, standing there in Dun slacks and sandals, at an awkward angle and peering away.

'Uh, sorry, Billy. No, not really. You know we have our own way, and truthfully, I want to keep it that way.'

'Oh, that's okay, I understand. It's just…Well, I didn't really know how to start.'

'Oh man, that's easy,' quipped John. 'Just put the word out with your dads. You're bound to find one of them is a footballer – just start from there. I had no experience when I started and just sort of…made it up as I went along, really. You'll be fine.'

'Alright, well, thanks anyway. We're going to be training on a Thursday anyway, so we won't be interfering.'

He went to move off, seemed to be about to say something and then said, 'Come on Brian.' And they moved on past the goals compound.

John was annoyed. The boys were full of it. 'Was that Billy Bullshit?' howled Sean Revell.

'Sean!' cried John.

'Well, they've got a crap team, and they're always slagging us off!'

'I'm not bothered,' he told Sean. 'We just need to concentrate on ourselves and not get distracted.' He looked around.

'Where's Charlie?'

Charlie Harris was not at training, which was not at all like him.

That evening's exercises were 'secondary scoring chances' and 'heading in defence' for the benefit of all the players. Once again, Olly Dimblow was positioned in goal as he was a vital component in the secondary scoring chances, designed to make any supporting player aware that if an attacker's shot was parried, fluffed, hit the post or bar, or was drifting wide, they should be in a good position to score.

Again, thought John, so basic. If you were a natural footballer, you would have worked this out for yourself and been there to ram home any rebound. But the exercise was well received, particularly later when two defenders were introduced, both as a deterrent and as support for the keeper, and also for their benefit, as they also had the chance to block, or sweep up and clear any loose rebounds or parries.

The heading in defence wasn't as spectacular, but again, it gave the boys the basic principles and would be followed up on in the next session by 'heading in attack'.

As the second exercise came to its conclusion, and the players were almost ready for the fifteen-minute small-sided game, Colin Mercer squeaked, 'Hoy! There's Bullshit – he's been watching us!' pointing towards the clubhouse.

Sure enough, the father and son who had supposedly left over twenty minutes ago could just be seen legging it past the goals shed.

'Bloody hell!' said Sean. 'They've been spying on us!'

The pair could be glimpsed as they made their way down the pitch side, keeping close and ducking down behind the hedge for shelter.

'Ha, ha!' laughed John. 'They must be absolutely desperate to watch you shower!'

The boys joined in the laughter.

'Right, get into your teams. First five minutes, one touch football. Remember, give and go! Pass and move! Always moving into space!'

The little Grove team were now playing as a close knit unit, and following the Highfield defeat went on to win their next nine matches, scoring 53 and conceding just 6 goals.

Tower Hill then inflicted a 1-3 reverse in a close match against very able opponents.

On February 26th, almost a year since their lesson at Abingdon, the team returned to the scene of their most devastating defeat. There were just twelve players, so Grove again only had the one substitute. But by now, they were used to playing with – and for – one another.

John loved to see that – even though now Grove seemed to able to match Abingdon for skill – Alan was now running them through their warm-up, as professionally as any of their opponents, resplendent in their track-suits and presenting like a team that really meant business. John and Alan were also happy with the boys' improved fitness – the package was nearly complete! He also noted the looks and glances from the Abingdon boys; twelve months earlier, this Grove team had looked like a little team of ragamuffins and had been well beaten. The tables were turning.

Grove ran out comfortable 6-2 winners – an outstanding turn around in a year and without Dwight. John was full of praise for the boys afterwards. He gave Danny O'Sullivan Man of the

Match, because Dan had been a real rock, tackling and marking his opponent out of the game.

The defence, superbly marshalled by Sean Webb, had been terrific, repulsing waves of early attacks; but Grove had been blinding on the counter, scoring four second-half goals without reply. It had been a great game and fiercely fought, but Grove had had too much class in midfield with Billy and Ollie winning everything and setting up Sean, Ritchie and Sparkie, who shared the second-half goals. The cheering in the dressing room and the cries of 'We did the double!' were the come-back for the ribbing they had got a year ago after that loss.

Following the Abingdon result were wins against Berinsfield (home – 7-0) and Botley (away – 5-0) and a 2-2 home draw against Bullingdon when the team just couldn't get going. This was followed by the only goal-less encounter of the season, a 0-0 draw at home to Garden City, albeit a game Grove could have lost to a very organised side that seemed determined not to be beaten at all costs.

The team then had, as the weather and pitches improved, a cracking defeat of Horspath, by 5 goals to 2, away, a 2-0 home win over Florence Park (an improved Ali was still in goal, and he even saved a Mark Brind penalty!). There was sweet revenge against a superb Highfield side, reversing the 3-1 defeat, in probably the best game of the season. Then, after thumping Littlemore 5-1 on their own pitch, the following week's game – against Launton, away – was called off due to a waterlogged pitch after two days and nights' downpour.

John got the phone call on Thursday night.

'Hi, John?'

'Who's this?' asked John, not recognising the voice.

'It's me, Billy. Billy Bullstrode.'

'Oh, alright Billy, what's up?'

'Is that right, your match is off on the weekend?'

Now how the hell did he know that? John wondered. He had only found out that it was off last night, and there was a remote chance – just remote, but still an outside chance –that it could still be on. John had told the Launton manager to definitely cancel; he thought it might be nice to have a day off for everyone.

'Uh, yeah, that's right. Launton are waterlogged. We're having a weekend off.

How are you getting on, Billy?'

'Well, that's what I was phoning about…'

'Yes?' *Fuck me*, thought John, *I know what's coming!*

'Well, we've been getting together and playing friendlies, but we haven't got a game this weekend. Do you fancy playing us in a friendly?'

John thought. He looked at the mouthpiece of the phone for a minute.

'Well, really, our parents are already looking forward to doing something other than football…'

'I've got a pitch and a ref at 9:30, Saturday. You could use it as a training match,' suggested Bullstrode.

'Billy, if we play you, it won't cause any trouble – friction – will it? I don't want to ruin or disorientate any of the local lads.'

'John, we need a game. We know we'll probably get beat. We've seen you play, but we could use the experience. We have to be ready for the new league next season – You really would be doing us a massive favour.' He was pretty desperate for a game.

What the hell!

'Alright, I'll phone round now, if I can get 12, we'll give you a game. Half-nine, you say? And you've got a ref?'

'Who's that? Chris Rowes?

'Yeah, Chris is alright.'

It was a bizarre sight those two Grove teams lining up against each other. Bullstrode's team were wearing a light-blue kit, some sort of second-hand kit they had somehow acquired. Grove 'A' sported the normal black and white stripes. John didn't really know much about the opposition, he didn't really know who the players were. But they didn't look like pushovers. They had a massive centre-forward, Michael James, with long blond wavy hair who looked useful and a tall centre-back, who looked for all the world like a professional footballer. They had Jamie Skelton – *Jamie Skelton!* Richard Maurice and Will Roberts, all ex-A team players.

John was down to a bare eleven. One of his players hadn't turned up – Charlie Harris. Not like Charlie, although he hadn't been to training a couple of times. Still, it was only a friendly. Mind you, Marc and he had talked about the game and its importance. Not just to the managers, or the players, but the parents and the club.

'Jesus, what if we lose?' he'd asked in the Bay Tree the previous night.

'We won't lose. You have a strong squad, and they're nearly all proper footballers now.' Don't worry, we'll give them a good hiding!' Marc was confident.

'Well, we'd better, or we'll never live it down – The A-team getting beat by the B-team.'

'And a bloody strong squad of eleven or twelve tomorrow?' John spun a beermat absent-mindedly.

'Christ, it's only like the probables v. the possibles?' suggested Marc.

'If we get beat, so what, who's proved anything? We're both going our own way next season. It may even be a chance to get on, and maybe utilise the best from each other. Bridge-building!'

'Bridge-building? Bridge-building? Imminent sonic destruction more like!' John was a bit nervous.

'Come on, gloomy! It's only a game.' Marc laughed, finishing his *Old Speckled Hen*.

But inside, John felt this wasn't 'only a game'. He felt that points – scoring and undermining – was the name of the game.

A fact cemented by the fact that none other than Bill Nelson, the club chairman, was on the touchline as a spectator the next morning, along with some other club officials and managers. Plenty of parents were there too. Oh well – Only a game!

Within five minutes, it was clear the boys were battling for pride. The A-team because they were there to win, the B-team because they didn't want to lose. John hadn't bothered eavesdropping the managers' team chat. He had quietly spoken with his boys on the pitch and told them here was a chance to play in front of some different spectators – people who had never seen them play – and show them just how good they could be.

So, the match was hard-fought, Grove B were gutsy but lacking in defence, although the big centre-forward, supported by a wily blond lad called Roger Sevier and a burly, busy and bustling Adam Tampling knew their way to goal. The midfield battle didn't go all the way of the A-team, there were some well-built lads in the B-side too.

Richard Claydon hit the bar after ten minutes, after a sprawling dribble left three defenders on the ground. Mark Brind slammed the ball just over the bar, minutes later after Revell had wriggled into the box. But on thirteen minutes, disaster struck. The B-team counter-attacked, and when a long ball over the top found Sevier, he skipped outside Colin, and hit a powerful cross-shot that cannoned into the corner off Michael James' shins and put the B-team one up. They celebrated wildly, and the A-team looked downcast.

'Webby, Webby!' shouted John from the touchline. 'Get the lads up! Get your heads up! It's early yet. Keep 'em going.'

Sean gave a thumbs up and shouted, 'Come on, Grove' to the lads, clapping his hands together and gee-ing them up.

The parents responded with a little whooping cheer of encouragement from the side-lines.

The A-team then started to bombard the opponents, playing some great football, setting off the forwards left and right. Revell, McDonald, then even Trigger, who had found his way into the area, all had chances to equalise. But the keeper saved well, and the finishing was wayward. Grove A should have scored four or five times in the first half, but as the chances went begging, and the half ticked away, the first half ended with them 1-0 down.

John pulled the team to one side, off the pitch. Some of the parents closed in on the half-time huddle.

'You're doing fine,' John said, earnestly. 'Look, I've got no advice, because you're playing so well, I know you're gonna score. And once you score, that'll be it. But don't see them as inferior. You can see they have got some good players. Get through midfield. Ritchie, you and Sparkie switch wings now and again.' He looked for a reaction.

'Mix it up a bit, use the wings.

'They are weakest down their left. Ollie, push up more. Put Skelton under pressure. Get in behind their centre-backs. They have five good players, we have eleven. We will win!' cried John, patting their backs. 'Come on, let's do it!'

The boys bristled and looked grimly determined.

'Come on, Grove' the team responded, trotting back out, led by Webby.

The A-team parents applauded the lads as they took up their positions.

For five minutes, the B-team had a real go. Tackles from their five main players were winning the ball and pushing their cause. But it was never going to be enough.

The whole A-team seemed to be enlightened, and gradually, they began to wear the 'B' defence down. Time and again,

Ritchie, Sparkie, Ollie, Revs and Billy danced through, creating panic and desperate measures in the opponents' box.

Ten minutes into the second-half, Ollie Gomm received a ball to feet on the right edge of the box. His control and spin produced a superb pass behind Skelton, to the speeding Claydon. Ritchie's first-touch and pace left the full back for dead. The hapless defender's only option, as Ritchie accelerated into the area, was to lunge in with a tackle from behind, clattering the diminutive winger down heavily and clumsily.

It could easily have been a penalty. Right on the edge of the box. 50/50. But the ref awarded a free-kick just outside the box.

'This is mine,' stated Revell, as he placed the ball carefully for the resulting free kick.

It was just outside the penalty area right on the corner angle. The B-team weren't sure whether to erect a wall, so two defenders were milling about twelve yards away. The ref blew the whistle to signal the free-kick, Revell took his five strides and smashed the ball right into the top left-hand corner, like a rocket. Their goalkeeper hadn't even moved as the ball bounced around in the back of the net.

Now the A-team moved up a gear. Every 'B' weakness was exploited. Two minutes later, Mark Brind held the ball up on the half-way line, marked by the big centre-half, took a touch, laid it off to Billy, spun expertly and sprinted away to gather the measured return pass. As the keeper came out to narrow the angle, Sparkie slipped the ball perfectly into the right-hand corner to give the A-team the lead, amid wild celebrations.

Now the B-team began pointing and arguing with each other, and their concentration dropped. Heads dropped. Ritchie switched wings and beat two defenders with ease, before taking off and curling a left-footer over and around the stranded keeper on the run.

Johnny Wells smashed a ferocious free kick, laid back by Gomm from 25 yards. It was struck with such venom, straight at the keeper, that he could only parry it high into the net. That B-team keeper, Stephen Vaux, to his credit, made several good saves following all the pressure, but his defence was really struggling to control the flood of attacks from every direction.

In the final minutes, in a move straight off the training ground, a series of delightful, one-touch passing between Trigger, Webby, Revs and Ritchie saw Ollie walk the ball into the net with players strewn all over the pitch only able to watch. Grove A added insult to injury, right at the death, when Sean Webb thudded a header from a Trigger cross in off the bar, to make the final score – an emphatic 6-1.

The spectators applauded both teams at the end, and Bullstrode congratulated John on the performance. John wished him well and assured him they would be fine, as he did have the bones of a good side. He had been very impressed with Stephen Vaux, the keeper, Ben Higham, centre-back, Roger Sevier, Johnny Ashford and Adam Tampling in midfield and Michael James, who was the massive, well-built, quick and skilful centre-forward. Skelton had played well, but he wouldn't be re-visiting that player.

Although the others were mainly Grove boys, the team possessed some good and reasonable footballers, mates of his boys.

Jesus,' he said to Marc afterwards, 'There's a bit of talent there we didn't know about!'

'Yeah, I loved that Ashford lad, like Trevor Hebberd on the ball – Nijinsky! Silky skills, unfazed.'

'I like the front three. Chap, imagine having those four in your squad. Christ, then you would have a decent sixteen! Maybe it was worth having a game with them!' chortled Marc.

'Food for thought,' laughed John.

'Let's go and have a pint. Ollie, get the balls!'

As the season-end drew near, there was a straightforward away win the following week at Barton by 5 goals to 2. The last game of the season was a hard-fought 1-0 victory over a strong Kidlington side, who were very hard to break down, bringing the season to a very satisfactory end. Had this been an official league, John calculated, they would have won the league by 3 points from Highfield, the top four looking like this:

Final Table

(Top)

	P	W	D	L	F	A	Pts
Highfield	34	30	3	1	186	49	63
Grove	**35**	**28**	**3**	**2**	**196**	**37**	**59**
Tower Hill	36	25	4	7	122	63	54
Garden City	36	24	5	7	123	73	53

Unfortunately, at this level, this delightfully organised league was still unofficial, so it didn't count. John reconciled himself to the fact that the Grove campaign had been crackingly successful. And they still had the sixes to come!

However, he did receive an acceptance letter in the pre-season from the B-Line Oxford League, inviting his Grove Challengers team into the new Oxford League, which he was really happy about. The first Grove team to play in an Oxford (City) league.

The committee probably wouldn't like it.

Ah well!

Chapter 14
The Faintest of Touches...

So the rags-to-riches story continued, and after their Milk Cup triumph of 1986 and three seasons at the top level in the old First Division, soon to become the Premiership, Oxford United continued to slide down the leagues; in the 1993–94 season, they were eventually relegated to the third-flight, despite their best efforts.

Just a few days into that season, the manager, Brian Horton, left the club to take up his new position as the manager of Manchester City. The beloved and genial Maurice Evans, of course, stood up as caretaker manager, to be eventually replaced by the new man, Denis Smith.

John Durnin had left to join Portsmouth for £200,000, along with their amazingly talented centre-back, Andy Melville, to Sunderland (£500,000) in an exchange deal that also brought the talented left-back, Anton Rogan, to the Manor.

The form dipped as the team under Denis tried to regroup, but the fact remains that despite the manager's key signings of the gifted Johnny Byrne (from Millwall for £50,000), Keeper Phil Whitehead (Barnsley, £75,000) and the talented defender Matt Elliott (from Scunthorpe at £150,000) the gelling wasn't sufficient to stem indifferent form. Elliott was an outstanding footballer. Good in the air, he had a real presence. He was a great tackler, distributor, and weighed in with many goals from the back. He always had so much time on the ball and was an outstanding figure and leader in the new league.

Also signed was striker Paul Moody from Southampton. Moody was amazing to watch. He was really built like a superhero, and when he started off on a run, you never quite knew what was going to happen. He would often get twisted up comically in his own feet and crash to the ground, leaving the crowd laughing. But he was also capable and did, many times, bear down and beat two or three defenders with his skill and pace, before launching an unstoppable net-bursting shot into the roof of the net. He was a real dangerous weapon to have in your team for this reason because he could make something out of nothing. And he did it so often.

Paul Moody scored 25 goals in all competitions that season, despite an injury mid-season that made him miss a number of games between December and February, with Byrne contributing 10 league goals.

Despite all this activity, United only won eight league matches – following the 3-2 success at Leicester City in November – for the remainder of the season, succumbing to relegation even after winning two of their last three games, and they went down second bottom with Peterborough.

There was, however, a glimmer of hope in the middle of the season, after drawing Leeds United in round four of the FA Cup and credibly holding the top-tier team to a 2-2 draw at the Manor in January, despite being two-one up with a few minutes to go, with Dyer and Elliott on the scoresheet. Hard luck, but a replay at Premiership Leeds, at Elland Road, was a little money-spinner for Oxford United and an experience not to be missed for their fans.

So, another football trip was planned with John, Marc and another mate – an ex-colleague of Marc's and occasional ex-works five-a-side member – Tommy Cannon. The plan was to drive up to Leeds, have a few beers then meet up with Charlie, a mate who was now in Barnsley, and stay with him the night.

John decided to drive so the group finished work early, picked up Tommy from Didcot Town Centre and set off to the dales in search of a real pub and some proper *Tetley's* bitter.

Tommy's usual big smile was plastered across his face, and his hair was tousled and scruffy-looking. He was dressed comfortably in an open-neck, checked shirt and slightly baggy, faded jeans. He was swinging a can of *Stella* from a four pack as the boys drove up to the Prince of Wales, and he already looked like he'd had a few. Fair enough, he was a big Oxford United fan and was always looking forward to a day out.

'Alright, boys? Looking forward to this,' he grinned, as he snapped a tin open and took a swig. 'Want some?'

'No, you joker,' chided Marc, 'We've got all day and a long drive.'

'Well, don't mind if I do,' he said, still grinning

'Looks like we're a bit late for that mate!'

John negotiated the A43, A34 and M1, steering the BMW into the car park of a likely looking pub. Cannon had polished off the *Stellas* and was already swaying as he walked across the car park.

After they walked into the pub, John rang Charlie, who was going to meet them near the ground. Once in the pub – a warm and welcoming chain-type just outside of Leeds – the guys relaxed and had a few beers. Tom continued drinking in the lounge, having polished off the *Stellas*, and was now quite drunk and lairy, but they were all having a laugh and enjoying themselves in the ample time before the match.

'Oi, don't forget, I'm meeting Mark outside the ground, Marc,' Cannon bawled.

'Yeah, we know, we're meeting Charlie at the same time.'

John parked in a massive car park near the ground, and Marc and John met up with Charlie – an old mate and committed Birmingham City fan – outside the ground. He had got the bus there from his house in Barnsley.

Tommy found his friend Mark, who had his own transport and ticket nearby, also slightly the worse for drink.

They stumbled up the road, and just before they disappeared, Tommy turned and waved back, grinning madly.

'See you in there!' he bellowed.

'Twat!' muttered Marc, shaking his head. 'If he drinks much more, he'll never get in!'

They had a pint with Charlie in the *Drysalters*, taking the piss out of their errant companion and reminiscing about the old days in Oxford and their legendary sessions in the Prince of Wales, Iffley.

After the pub, the group walked to the ground and entered via the away end. The three found the away-fans entrance and entered Elland Road, locating the Oxford United fans who were occupying a large corner section, high up and opposite the home end.

Elland Road was a tricky place to visit, and the Leeds team was full of famous and talented international players, including top scorer Rod Wallace, Brian Deane, Gary Speed, Gary McCallister and Gordon Strachan.

Leeds were having a good season, eventually finishing fifth in the Premiership behind the winners Manchester United, Blackburn Rovers, Newcastle United and Arsenal. So, the

Oxford fans, although in good spirits, were not expecting much from the trip – just a good night out and a bit of a game and atmosphere. Around a thousand die-hard Oxford fans had made the tricky, mid-week trip to support their team.

It was a great, clear night, slightly frosty, and the floodlights highlighted the big stadium and enhanced the atmosphere. The dark night and the lights and green of the pitch made a pretty picture. It had a typical 'night-time game' feel about the place – a buzz.

'Quite a lot of Oxford, but not that many home fans, eh?' noted Marc, surveying the ground.

'No, there's lots of spaces, maybe they're not up for it?' John re-joined.

Before the game kicked-off, Tommy and Mark careered up the steps into the heart of the Oxford fans, drunkenly fighting with up-turned seats and pushing past seated spectators on the way to their seats. Mark was holding a dripping, half-eaten hotdog.

'Did you get any bets on, boy?' John asked Marc.

'Magilton and 1-0 to us, mate. May get a penalty. What d'you reckon?'

'Mate, not sure about this one. Fancy Byrne or Matty from a corner? Got Byrne and 2-1!' replied John, as they made their way up the steps.

As they found their seats, which had commanding views of the ground, the Oxford fans were already in song and good voice.

'Come on, you Yellows, come on, you Yellows!'

The game got off to a lively start, and Leeds pressed for the opening as Oxford defended stoutly. The game was evenly balanced in the first half as the Premiership side tried to press home their home advantage, and Oxford were happy to go in at half-time still in the game at 0-0.

In the second half, inspired by a quiet Leeds crowd and some great backing from the Yellow fans, United began to play with more freedom and confidence. The pressure eventually told when Oxford took the lead with the 'faintest of touches' from John Byrne. A free-kick from Magilton was headed on by Elliott, and Byrne was on the edge of the six-yard box as the ball dropped among the startled Leeds defenders. As he swung his boot, appearing to miss the ball completely, the ball by-passed the defender and keeper, nestling into the corner of the net.

When interviewed after the game about the goal, he was asked,

'Well Johnny, a great start. But was the first goal yours?'

'Well, yeah!' grinned Oxford's blond striker. 'I got the faintest of touches!'

From their distant position, high up in the away end, John and Marc hadn't seen that faintest of touches! But it was good enough to take the lead! Who cared? 1-0.

Then the man on the tannoy announced the 1st goal-scorer – 'John Byrne.' Marc turned to John. 'You spawny bastard, he never even touched it.'

'Never you mind! He's got the goal and me bet's on mate. Ha! Ha! Byrne and 2-1, at a very generous 28-1.'

As Leeds rallied in an attempt to snatch an equaliser, Oxford caught them on the break. Chrissie Allen drilled in a stunning cross-shot for the second goal after a great one-two with Joey Beauchamp. 0-2! Wild and delirious joy for the travelling Oxford fans.

By this time, Tommy Cannon was really pissed and beginning to be vile (along with his mate, Mark, and some other fans) towards the Leeds stewards. The Oxford fans were really buzzing, so a lot of goading and language was raining from the stand. The stewards approached, trying to keep them in order, but Tommy, dishevelled and unruly, was doing his gobby best to wind them up. He was really lucky not to get kicked out.

'Now, take it easy, son. Take your seat and watch your language.'

Unbelievably, it didn't stop him from going out of the ground at half time, already drunk, but still looking for more beer at the pub across the road. Of course, he took his mate Mark, and they had a couple in the pub and were somehow readmitted twenty minutes after the start of the second half. How they were readmitted in their state, the boys never knew; apparently, they had begged and pleaded to be let in, and were soon back up with the Oxford fans.

Oxford continued to hold, despite Leeds pressure, the fans rejoicing in the score-line and inevitable victory. Tom and his mate reached their seats, joining the singing and celebrating Oxford's two goal lead and upcoming giant – killing result.

At 0-2, with just three minutes of normal time left, the game was nearly done. Oxford had almost completed a stunning away giant-killing and just had to hold on…

Leeds were not looking dangerous and had not had clear chances, when Gordon Strachan, picking up a loose pass and out of absolutely nothing, hammered in from an angle and 25 yards a devastating effort. The ball flew into the top of the net past the helpless keeper for a wonder goal. It was late, and Oxford had controlled the game, though now, they had got a consolation…

'Ah well,' cried John over the crowd. 'Every cloud has a silver lining – there is my bet!'

And they continued to attack. The Oxford fans began to be jumpy, bearing in mind the late equaliser at the Manor. And Tommy Cannon was getting really aggressive, trying to rip out a plastic seat in front of the increasingly agitated stewards. The atmosphere in the away end changed from euphoria to panic, and the fans tried to rally the team, but Tommy went berserk, jumping up onto his seat and, yet again, attracting the now rattled stewards.

'Ey, mate! Stop what you're doing, or we'll take action!'

'Fuck off, you Northern bastards. We're only a little club and we're having a night out – AND beating you lot on your own muck-heap!' Cannon spat back.

The stewards mobbed up and were uneasy about him – he was a big bloke and obviously drunk, and they formed a little half circle around him and watched him like a hawk.

Another senior steward appeared, this time with a copper. The policeman was young, but onto Tommy straight away, the latter still jumping on his seat and hurling abuses.

'Come on, son, get off the chair and take a seat.'

'Fuck off, copper! I'm not doing anything wrong!' shouted back Tommy.

'What's your name?'

'Cannon.'

'What do you do?' The policeman was trying to placate him.

'What do I do?' asked Cannon sarcastically.

'What's your job?' pressed the officer, leaning in to hear above the din.

'Fuck me. I'm a printer – so what?' Now aggressive, Tommy spat back his reply.

'How old are you?' asked the policeman politely, stepping back.

'What?'

'How old are you?' he asked again.

'Jesus, eighteen!' Cannon hurled back.

'What's your date of birth?'

Tommy floundered, the worse for wear...

'I can't remember. What d'you want that for?' he asked, now looking bemused and agitated.

'Have you got any ID?' The policeman was beginning to become annoyed with Tommy's attitude.

Leeds continued to press, and the Oxford fans were warily watching the game go on and, at the same time, the action with the policeman.

'I'll ask you again. Get down, son,' said the constable.

Tommy looked him over. 'Fucking make me! I ain't doing nothing wrong!'

Leeds were now strongly pressing and buzzing around the visitor's box. The ninety minutes were up, the game was almost over. A minute into injury time, and they managed to force a corner on the right.

Oxford had defended well and stood by for the last assault as the ball dropped into the penalty area.

'Let's smash this into the stands' they were thinking, but the ball wasn't cleared, and it boggled around in the penalty area until it fell to White, who hit it goal-wards from twelve yards. Almost in slow-motion, the shot hopelessly deflected into the net past the wrong-footed keeper Whitehead for a dreary and depressing last-gasp equaliser.

Tommy was red, big, pissed and, now, menacing. In his anger, he had pulled and pulled until he'd ripped the seat from its mounting, taunting the stewards with it by flipping it about, then eventually he'd thrown it down the stand like a giant frisbee.

Now the stewards went mental, storming in riot-style behind the policeman.

'Right, we've warned you!' They swamped him and grappled him to the ground, handcuffing him and rolling him to his feet. He was in the aisle and had scraped his knees on the steps. Tommy just looked like a sad, red, pissed and lost mess. It was a shame, but they walked him away without too much care.

The stewards escorted their now meek and giant cargo down to the touchline where he began his walk of shame, muttering drunkenly, 'I ain't done nothing!'

His mate, Mark, had scuttled off in the other direction. The other lads were away from this action and concentrating on the game.

In their away corner, the Oxford fans were now gutted, crestfallen and despondent. They had all but won and were now on the back foot with extra-time looming. A perfectly played and virtually won away cup tie was now in danger of being lost.

Extra time, and with Carter ejected. Denis Smith had his work cut out on the half-way line, trying to gee up his players. The Oxford body language didn't look good. They had had the game won – all for those last few seconds…

Denis Smith, as a player and a manager, was fiercely competitive, and he rallied his weary and crestfallen troops as he prepared to wage war for another half-hour.

'Come on, lads, you know you can do it.'

'You've scored against them and led three or four times over two games,' he continued, a blue vein visibly pulsating on his forehead. 'They will be attacking and confident!' he barked. 'We'll catch them on the break. Just defend, keep your heads and discipline. Get back out there and beat them. Release early and catch them on the break,' he repeated, waiting for a response. 'You've got nothing to lose and everything to gain! Okay?'

Extra time was quite tight. The Oxford fans found their voices, and the team rallied once more.

They held their own, and after some time, Mike Ford hit a peach of a ball over the Leeds defence, which curled deliciously into the path of the scuttling run of Jimmy Magilton. The skilful midfielder looked up, before lobbing the keeper Lukic. The ball hung as the fans waited to see whether it would drop. And drop it did into the Leeds net, for a devastating and brilliant winner. 3-2. Oxford held on for the last few minutes. Leeds were out of the cup. Oxford were through to the next round! The Oxford fans were now jubilant.

Woah! Talk about deflation. Queuing in the muddy car in that muddy car park after the game was a miserable hour of trying to creep and crawl along, a foot at a time, towards the one exit gate. Cannon was nowhere to be found, Marc dropped off to sleep and eventually, the car popped out into the now virtually deserted Yorkshire town, as they managed to negotiate the drive up to Barnsley.

Unfortunately, Oxford couldn't quite get through the next round, a plum home draw to Chelsea, where despite dominating and leading through an early Joey Beauchamp goal, they conceded a couple of soft goals. In the last minute, United earned a penalty – which would have secured a worthy 2-2 draw – but Mike Ford's blinding strike cannoned off the top of the bar to end the cup run in a miserable and frustrating fashion.

Between these matches – and immediately following the Leeds win – Oxford were forced to accept an offer, which they couldn't turn down, for their star Jimmy Magilton, who moved to Southampton for £600,000 to the chagrin of the Oxford fans.

United also failed to capitalise in the league from their excellent cup form, and as both Birmingham City and West Bromwich Albion won on the last day of the season, Oxford were relegated to Division Two – despite a cracking 2-1 win at home to Notts County. Alas! That proved to not be enough to keep them up.

It was a shame as their recent form had not been that bad – they had just had a really grim period between late December and late February when they lost 6 and drew 3; in that period, they had won just three points from a possible twenty-seven! Relegation form despite their best and belated efforts.

On the positive side, the signatures of Byrne and Moody had resulted in a late run that had *almost* saved them, with the pair scoring 80% of United's goals in the run-in.

On the negative side, again desperate for money and inevitable survival, Oxford were soon forced to sell local legend Joey Beauchamp to West Ham for £1m to the bitter desperation of the Oxford supporters. But more of that later!

Chapter 15
Under-10s
Preliminary Oxford League

Following the successful under-9s season, sixes and not unreasonable summer, the training resumed in August. Charlie Harris, Jamie Skelton and Richard Maurice and others had moved on and were playing for the B-team with Bullstrode. John had signed Peter Wiggins, a big, skilful lad from Hanney, a nearby village, from where he had heard some good reports of Wiggins' skill. Also signed on was Johnny Ashford, who had so impressed him in the 'B' match. Johnny was easy to persuade, as he was Ritchie's mate and next-door neighbour. John really admired his calm and time on the ball, and he had silky skills. John had also flirted with the services of Roger Sevier, who had been around the team during the sixes; however, the player and his father were unsure of whether he wanted to commit to the A team, the B team, or, indeed, rugby. John, his father, was a big rugby man, and Roger was a pretty handy fly-half – slight but strong, with good skills and a rasping kick. Roger therefore remained an enigma. But anyway, he didn't immediately sign.

Dimblow

Elliott   Webb   Wells   O'Sullivan

Revell   Gomm   McDonald   Ashford

Brind   Claydon

Subs: Mercer, Casey, Monery, Wiggins

Training kicked off right where it had left off – on the Wasborough fields to the left of the Rugby Club. The boys turned up every Wednesday to get out the goal, run through the routines and have a ball while getting some lessons and keeping up to date with the tactics and football fundamentals. The atmosphere on the first day back for training was relaxed and informal, with the boys looking fit and happy. John looked on with pride at the group, now growing a little and mixing into what was beginning to look like a real football team.

The newly instigated Alan Elliott warm-up routine to start training off was begrudgingly appreciated and looked forward to. This helped keep the boys in order, keep them gelled and also introduced some proper warm-up routines into their pre-match. It was great for John, as he could concentrate on skills, techniques and the player management. Alan would then push the boys through this work on the training ground and also give them a proper, professional-looking warm up pre-match, something they needed and definitely benefitted from.

The season began with the first true season in the 'Oxford Boys B-Line League', with eighteen teams in total. Of the old enemies were Abingdon, OUSC, Garden City and Kidlington. Tower Hill had moved off to join the Witney League. From the remaining fourteen teams, nine were from Oxford itself and the rest made up from local villages. The very strong Highfield team had also joined the Oxford League in a different qualifying group.

To make up the teams, two leagues were to be formed, A and B. They started with four preliminary leagues, and in the Grove league were Horspath, Rose Hill, Florence Park, OUSC and Bullingdon. These five Oxford teams were all strong and represented good-quality opposition for Grove. Each team was played just once, with the top two from each group going into the A league, the remainder starting life in the B league.

Grove started their campaign well and had a really tough encounter at home to Horspath as their opening fixture. On a bright September day, in their latest team track-tops, the new under-10 side ran out, looking the part entirely against their Oxford opponents. The team ran out with the bag of balls and kicked around for five minutes. Then Elliott called them over, and they went through a pre-planned warm-up routine for the first time ever. They jogged, stretched, sprinted and jumped, following Alan's instruction, finally finishing it off just before kick-off. Webby had retained the captaincy, and the subs collected the track-suit tops as they prepared for the ref's starting whistle.

Horspath were a strong outfit, with eight or nine decent players; they came on strong to Grove, pinning them back with a succession of quick breaks and some dangerous crosses from the wings and the resultant corners. Olly Dimblow was kept busy, and his defence creaked a bit without being able to set up many of their famous counter-attacks. Ritchie had his one early chance and should have scored after a long cross-field pass from Sparkie. The little winger went outside his man but scuffed his shot just wide after drawing the keeper.

It was no surprise when Grove eventually conceded an opener. Elliott O'Brien, their star player – and a big handful for Wells and Webb – had relentlessly tormented the central defence in the middle of the park. He was sent away with a ball over the top and shrugged off Wellsy, sprinting past the remaining defenders and beating keeper Olly Dimblow, as he lolloped out of his area in the race for the ball. O'Brien's shot from the edge of the area lifted gracefully into the top corner for the opener. It was a first-class goal and a superb finish. But it was also the sign for Grove to start playing, and they began to knock the ball around.

Having gained the advantage, Horspath seemed to lose their edge, and Grove equalised just before half-time. After a sustained period of attack – which desperate defending, great goalkeeping and the woodwork had kept Grove at bay – Sean Revell finally fired a loose ball past the keeper, high into the net. The Grove lads celebrated and, as the ball bounced back into play, they ran back, celebrating past three beaten and forlorn Horspath defenders and the keeper.

The team talk was easy, and the boys came off for the half-time break buzzing and full of themselves. When the second half began, so did the Sean Revell Show. Suddenly, Revell was on fire on the right wing, and he cracked three more goals in the second half, capping a blistering performance to rightly earn the Man of the Match trophy, along with all the glory and points. Sean took the plaudits, which were well deserved, but the team performance had been very workmanlike, stemming the early pressure and coming in from behind. Although Grove conceded a late consolation, they ran out convincing 4-2 winners.

Next, they were away to Rose Hill. This was a challenging place, where the convoy was careful to park close together, just off the 'Oval', an elliptical on-road, car-parking area near the community centre. Rose Hill was a barren, bleak place even in September, when the grass on the community pitch was thin and the paint on the crooked, fixed goalposts was grey and flaking. Neither the parents nor the boys were particularly at ease.

The Spartan, pot-holed pitch was clinging to a 1950s council estate that had seen much better days, and the atmosphere was unwelcoming. Although, the manager, Mick McGuire – a bouncy, crop-haired Oxford United fan – was very accommodating to John and his team. Despite all the possession and effort they applied, Grove could not break through.

Indifferent refereeing and linesman-ship from the home team didn't help their cause, and the team now knew what it really meant to be in the Oxford league. The dirty, pitted dried-up pitch – full of potholes and littered with bricks and cycle parts – along with the bristly attitude of the few home spectators, conspired to help inflict a poor 1-0 reverse.

Danny O'Sullivan had caught a finger in the eye, and Peter Wiggins just didn't work at Rose Hill. He needed to work and apply himself, and despite his size – which John thought might be beneficial to the team – he wasn't competing. Ollie Gomm had been suffering from a chronic migraine and probably shouldn't have started the game. He was pale and never got into the game. So, John bought on all three substitutes, but it was not their day. Paddy McGuire – the diminutive, skin-headed, cross-eyed manager's son – tormented the full backs until he waltzed through three tackles and slid home a shot just after half time. Game over.

Grove created a handful of chances, but truthfully, they never really looked like scoring.

'Bloody hell, chap! That was rubbish!' John told Alan as they left the changing room.

'Best of luck, mate,' nodded the Rose Hill manager, as he sprang past with a bag of balls over his shoulder.

'Thanks, Mick.'

'Good luck in your next one. Who've you got?'

'Florence Park at home, Mick.'

'Well, good luck! You played well today and deserved something out of the game.'

'Don't think so!' muttered John under his breath, as they strolled down towards the Oval.

The next game came the following week, with perfect conditions: a sunny afternoon, and a full complement at home to Florence Park. Carlo and his boys had won their last game, so John warned his players not to take them lightly. Wiggins was dropped to the bench, and Johnny Ashford lined up in midfield. From early on, Grove assumed control. They let their opponents attack, and on the breakdown, they mercilessly counter-attacked. Sean Webb volleyed them into the lead on fifteen minutes, following a series of corners. Ollie Gomm finished a nice move involving Revell and Ashford. Mark Brind added the third goal, following a quick break and a rasping finish from outside the box. Finally, Ritchie dribbled through the defence before teasing the keeper off his line and sliding the ball home for 4-0 at half time.

Grove dominated the second half and could have scored four more goals, before Billy McDonald controlled a ball in midfield and sent a superb angled pass at Claydon again. This time, the tricky winger caught the ball sweet on the half-volley, lashing it over the keeper to complete the rout.

The only sour note was that despite all their attacking, Trigger never really got forward in support from right back. This infuriated his dad, who was by now on the touchline with John. Trigger was a good full back, the only criticism being he went to ground a bit early, something John had mentioned and gone through with him a few times. He had a biting tackle, and after a couple of those hits, the wingers were not perhaps the players they had been to start with.

So, he was a useful footballer. John noticed, though, that Alan had got on his case quite early in the game. This hadn't helped, and as the game progressed, if anything, Trigger went quieter and wasn't even going as far forward as he had been. This wasn't a problem, and John hadn't felt it necessary to talk to Alan about it. But Alan had got increasingly frustrated and vociferous as the game progressed, where Jamie seemed to shrink back. John put it down to a father-son thing and let it go.

However, in the bar after the game, Graham Brind and the others brought it to John's attention. Yes, he had gone on a bit. John thought they were exaggerating, as he had been wrapped up in the action of the game and hadn't really considered it to be a big deal. He made a mental note to have a chat with Alan and one separately with Trigger, so the problem didn't get out of control.

As the season progressed, and Alan's training and pre-match routines became the norm, it was natural that Alan should become John's assistant. Nothing was ever discussed, but as they were becoming friends, the talk over a beer or food became about the boys, training, opposition and the Belgian trip. Alan was good and always helpful, but John noticed he wasn't the most popular presence within the setup.

He seemed to have favourites and was often short if things didn't go right. Still, John appreciated his help as it made his life easier and the team more professional. Boily and Marc were not so involved any more, although they still came over to some training sessions, Boily still occasionally coaching goalkeeping to Olly Dimblow and Billy.

Their next game in the preliminary league was possibly their toughest – Oxford United Social Club, away. Peter Wiggins, John Monery and Billy McDonald were either away or not fit, meaning that John only had eleven players and no substitutes. They knew they were short, but only when they parked up did they realise that Peter was missing. OUSC was situated in Glanville Road, Headington, off the main London Road, about a mile from Oxford United's Manor Ground. The car parking was on the street; the pitch was on a small recreational site to the right, bordered by a small coppice and included a play area with swings and a slide.

On the other side of the road, by the disused cricket pitch, was the faded, wooden cricket pavilion, surrounded by tall, link-wire fencing, now covered in rust and bindweed. The cricket area was long overgrown and neglected. The football pitch was well-used, in good condition, with worn and already muddying goal mouths and a centre circle. It was a big pitch, as several age groups regularly used it. The Grove contingent trooped into the changing rooms, feeling a little anxious with a hint of doubt. The game had just got tougher.

After a chat with Alan, they decided to move Trigger to left back (despite the fact that he was so obviously right-footed) and Stephen Casey at right back (because he was even more one-footed)! It was a bit of a risk, but OUSC had Josias Carbon, the manager's nephew. He was a skilful, quick and strong forward, who used to roam about, but more often came in from the right. He was hard to contain, difficult to knock off the ball and had a fearsome shot. They hoped Trigger, being a bit quicker, would get a couple of hits on him early on, supported by the two centre-backs. But it was a big ask.

Missing two influential midfielders, Grove were torn into from the start, with Carbon and his mates dominating the early exchanges. They had a tricky winger too, Rickey Lambert, who saw a lot of the ball early on. John paced the line of the right touchline, sticking close to Casey.

'Case, Case, start closer to him mate.' He pointed at Lambert. 'Don't give him a head start. As soon as the ball comes at him, you get with him and breathe down his neck. Make him hate you!' John gave Casey a thumbs up and a wink.

Casey looked up and nodded. 'Then get your tackle in early.' Another nod. 'Time it, and get the ball away – otherwise, he'll leave you for dead,' John instructed. 'Okay?'

Sure enough, Casey got close. Trigger pushed up on Carbon. Grove soaked up the pressure. OUFC lost their way, and Grove started to have more possession. After the third Casey tackle, the lad just grew in confidence. The winger dropped further and further back, looking for the ball. Casey dominated the right flank. He won the ball and distributed it back with style, his confidence brimming.

At half-time, they were 0-0, and Grove, despite their lack of players, were still in the game.

'Right, lads, listen up! Amazing! Just amazing!' John enthused, slapping a few backs. 'They've got all these townies and three substitutes, and we are still in the game. We're going to win it!'

The Oxford Club's manager, Jason Carbon, Josias's uncle – a big black lad, and a fairly young, muscular footballer – was giving his boys the once-over in the background. John waved a dismissive hand in their direction.

'Trigger, you're doing a great job. Case, you were fantastic. You're all defending really well. So, keep defending. Get there first, and don't let them play. Get your tackles in hard and fair, but BE FIRST.'

'If you do this, you'll win it,' John continued, enthusiastically. 'And if you win it, we'll be in the A League. So, come on, Grove, let's win it!'

The second-half was still pressure, and the home team valiantly tried to break down the defence, but it remained resolute and rock-solid. After five minutes of pressure, Ritchie Claydon hared off down the left wing, skinning his marker and placing a cross onto the head of the arriving Mark Brind, who stooped to smash a downward header past the helpless keeper.

Ten minutes later, as OUSC attacked down the left, Casey slid in to win the ball from the rushing Lambert, sending Sean Revell scampering down the right. Sean advanced into the opposition half and dropped his shoulder to lose his defender, spinning a low cross into the area. Sparkie was there again and took a touch to control the pass before lifting the ball over the goalie for his second goal.

The celebrations were cut short by John, who warned his team to think and concentrate.

'Come on boys, remember what we talked about, don't lose your concentration,' John cried, clapping his hands for effect. 'And Stephen, look!' He pointed to the side-line. Ricky Lambert was being substituted. 'Look what you've done!'

Casey, after grasping the situation, started to smile, soon beaming from ear to ear. He spent the rest of the match hounding the new man, with a steely look of determination and wearing the pride of a job well done.

The hosts battled and pressured, looking for a reply, but with the defence on top – and Olly Dimblow dealing with a tip-over near the end from a long shot – they never really looked like scoring.

Jason congratulated John after the game. But with Jason, there was always a haughty attitude. He really had expected to win. John shook his head on the way back across the road to the changing rooms in the cricket hut and smiled. A cracking result!

'Gentlemen,' he cried, above the din of the changing room, while standing on the slatted bench, supporting himself from two hooks and looking down on his players. 'Gentlemen, congratulations to you all. That was a stunning effort and remarkable result. I would like to thank you all for your individual and team performances.'

'I would like to give special praise to Trigger and the defence for wrapping up Carbon.' The boys cheered wildly. 'But I give hearty congratulations for a superb Man of the Match performance, undeniably deserved by…Stephen Casey!' John presented the trophy to Casey amid wild applause.

It had been a funny old day for Casey. He had worked hard, been so focused, and he had picked up his first Man of the Match trophy. As the cheers roared and hands slapped him on the back, the last part of his role was to blush a deep scarlet.

The final game in the preliminary league was at home to Bullingdon. In a game with light wind and fitful gusty showers, Grove attacked from the outset and brushed their Oxford opponents aside with two goals in each half from Revell, Gomm, Brind and Claydon. They ran out very comfortable 4-0 winners.

The managers and parents celebrated on the touchline as the referee blew the full-time whistle. A great little run from a great little team, and they had really deserved it!

This result secured the teams' future in the 'A' League;

Joining them would be Littlemore, Bullingdon, Botley from the city, with Abingdon, and the two Kidlington teams (Kidlington and Garden City).

And Grove had successfully negotiated the first challenge, winning four out of five and therefore qualifying for the Under-10s 'A' League with the other qualifiers from the group; OUFCSC, Horspath and Bullingdon.

Florence Park and Rose Hill never made it and started in the 'B' division.

Brilliant. The new Oxford 'A' League was formed and Grove were in it!

***

The season was socially very good. All of John's parents were keen to become hosts for the Belgians' Easter visit, so there was fund raising, with skittles nights, race nights, raffles, sponsored bike-rides and so on, which started after the sixes and went on throughout the season.

Training was held on a Wednesday evening, and John and Alan ran an informal training session on a Saturday morning, when boys could turn up if they wanted. Most did, so there was plenty of training, football, preparation and fitness, and plenty of laughs.

After the Friday night ritual of going down to the pub after work, with the early training session on a Saturday, and the fact that John and Ollie were also season ticket holders at this time at Oxford United, there was an abundance of activity every weekend.

John's daughter Corine was a keen horse rider and was also kept busy at least one night a week and on Saturdays, riding, exercising and mucking out her mate and mentor's horse (Marc's sister, Laura). She was also involved in local gymkhanas, where she and her trusty steed, Bramble (a very brave, small, rescued Exmoor pony, grey and dappled), won several jump-offs, cups and rosettes.

So, the weekends were busy. And after Saturday, there was a game on Sunday, usually followed by lunch out on the way home or a Sunday lunch and a few pints after the home games.

Corine would have to come to the away games, where she would bring a book or magazine and her Walkman.

She had absolutely no interest in football; if she wasn't riding, she would stubbornly sit in the car wrapped up in her music and books until the game was over. During this period, she used her negotiating tactics to try and wangle a trip to TGI Friday's after the match as compensation. And it often worked!

***

Jimmy Magilton had left Oxford United immediately after scoring the winner at Leeds, prompted by his class and quality, and the fact that the club were desperately short of cash. Amongst the most remarkable departures was that of Joey Beauchamp, United's son and star player. Joey was a local lad from Didcot, who could terrorise defences wide right or left and shoot from a distance. He was a real loss. But West Ham rightly came in for him and Oxford sold him pre-season for a million pounds.

It was an offer that the cash-strapped club couldn't refuse. Remarkably, Joey played only once for the Hammers, in a friendly at Oxford City. The commute from his newly purchased house in Oxford to East London was murderous and monotonous. He wasn't happy, never settled, and was eventually snapped up by – of all teams, local rivals and deadly enemies – Swindon Town who had always had an interest, for £800,000.

Oxford started the new season brightly, winning their first four matches, with Byrne and Moody both getting hat-tricks in the opening two matches, which they won 4-0, 3-1, 1-0 and 2-0. The two strikers scored all those goals, Moody with seven and Byrne with three.

However, the Moody-Byrne partnership was broken up when John Byrne became the next controversial departure, unexpectedly and without any prior warning, deciding to return to Brighton on a free transfer. The Oxford fans were devastated, as there wasn't a hint of any movement. Just an announcement one day in February that he had gone.

On Boxing Day, Oxford went three points clear at the top of the table, following a stunning demolition of Peterborough with two goals from another new striker – the busy and prolific David Rush, another Denis Smith signing from Sunderland.

Just prior to this period, John, Marc and Ollie had bought tickets for the first round of the FA Cup, away to tiny Marlow Town. Ironically, the little Bucks outfit were managed by ex-Oxford United striker and local hero Peter Foley. What a day it had promised to be! An easy car ride down, a nice pub lunch in the Catherine Wheel and a little trip up to the ground to watch the boys stomp lowly Marlow into the dust.

The group had gone for seats in the main stand; a quaint, old wooden structure along one side of the ground. John sat next to the striker's mum and dad – according to Peter Foley, after the match, the striker wasn't even going to be in the Marlow starting line-up due to poor form.

Typically, he was in the right place twice to score both goals to the unsuppressed joy of his parents and the chagrin of John, Marc and Ollie.

A Marlow full-house of 3,050 witnessed an Oxford side – that included Byrne, Moody, Elliott and Whitehead, along with a full Oxford United team – embarrassingly and deservedly beaten 2-0 by their tiny neighbours.

The Marlow performance was as good as the Oxford one was inept. There was a horrible encounter between the hostile jeering away fans and the players as they left the field.

The pitch was separated by a huge galvanised gate behind the goal, and the Oxford players had to wait for the gate to be opened before they could exit and reach the sanctuary of the dressing rooms. The angry Oxford fans had to pass behind the gate on their way out.

As the players patiently waited, looking nervously about, there had amassed over a thousand angry Oxford fans, bristling behind the gate, just yards from the players as they waited to be let through.

Lots of vile cursing and insults were hurled at the team as they sheepishly crept through the gap. As a player in that position, there is nothing you can do. But they really didn't need to be told how crap they'd been. They were just as, if not more, embarrassed and disappointed as the fans.

They simply hadn't performed, and this was the price they had to pay. John, Marc and Ollie winced as they stood in the crowd, listening to the roar of abuse and hoping the stewards would hurry up and put their misery to an end.

After the team's heroics at Leeds in the previous campaign, this was particularly hard to take; it coincided with the team's worst period, starting with a home defeat to neighbours Wycombe Wanderers, and just three points from the next nine games.

Oxford's title ambitions were ruined around this period, and despite a late season rally, they finished a disappointing seventh in the league, fourteen points behind the champions, Birmingham City.

Amazingly, in October 1995, Oxford boy, Beauchamp, returned to the Manor for an incredible cut-price £75,000 from Swindon Town. Joey had played just once for West Ham, in a friendly, bizarrely against Oxford City.

His commute to East London had not been ideal, and his interest and relationship with the Manager Harry Redknap had been challenging. Swindon (Glen Hoddle and John Gorman) were deeply impressed and interested in Joey's natural talent. Joey signed for them and enjoyed a good time at Swindon until Hoddle and Gorman left and went to Spurs. Joey immediately realised that he would never figure in the new Swindon manager, Steve McMahon's plans, and he never played for him.

Incredibly, for the Yellows, he had initially been sold to make money for the club – but his relationships with the management of West Ham or Swindon Town gave his home-town club the chance to re-sign him for that amazing price with a fantastic net profit in the period for the club!

Joey's run of late season goals from March 1996 – starting
with the winner against Bournemouth – sparked a remarkable
run the following season 1995–96, which helped Oxford United
get promotion that season along with the old enemy, Swindon.
And despite later bids from Nottingham Forest and
Southampton, which were agreed at £800,000, the stalwart
remained an Oxford player for the rest of his league career.

His stunning pace, ability to turn defenders inside-out, his
delivery of quality crosses and consistently score-blistering goals,
while continuing to dazzle opposition defences for years to
come, truly made him one of Oxfords' all-time greats.

"There's only one Joey Beauchamp!"

Chapter 16
Oxford Till I Die

John could not clearly remember his first ever game at the Manor, but he could easily recall his early memories, sights, smells and events from the age of ten, when his father had taken him out to watch the Us in his early days as a schoolboy supporter.

His dad, Don, was a pretty ordinary man. He was in his mid-thirties at that time, a father of three and a factory worker at the trim-shop at Morris', where most of Cowley's working population were employed. He and his wife Pat spent their leisure time drinking and often taking their young children to the numerous local country pubs (where the kids were reasonably happy, not knowing any different, to sit inside the car in the car-park, eating crisps and sipping bottles of Coca-Cola through a straw, waiting patiently, until the adults emerged near closing-time).

John's early memories were of a pretty happy childhood. His very early memories were of his dad's flat cap hanging over the coat-stand in the hall. His dad's fading, work jacket would always be draped over the bannisters at the bottom of the stairs, making available easy shillings, and sometimes even a two-bob bit, for the picking, jangling loose in the pocket, which occasionally helped supplement John's pocket-money.

Don was an easy-going, hard-working and reasonable dad. When Oxford weren't playing at home on a Saturday afternoon, he would take John up to *Morris Motors* social club to watch the Morris Motors football team play.

But what he did do was introduce John to Oxford United when the team were just promoted and still on the rise. Don enjoyed football, followed Oxford United and enjoyed going up to the Manor with his friends, whilst introducing young John to the club. At the time, he couldn't have known what an impact this introduction would have on his ten-year-old son. He couldn't have known that it would influence young John, who was hooked from day one, and for his entire lifetime.

The atmosphere at the Manor was always great, but at night it was amazing; the smell of wintergreen as the players trotted out onto the pitch, the steel-cold grip on the exposed crush-barriers, the white jets of breath from the supporters as they stamped their feet to keep warm, the mesmerising movement of the fans as they cascaded down the London Road End, and the guttural, rhythmic, humorous and raucous songs – It was love at first sight!

Any *true* football fan will know that despite other loftier clubs and the temptation to latch onto a winning side, your home club is the one with which you are smitten. You will go to watch them every week, come rain or shine, promotion, indifference or relegation threats.

John was, therefore, *smitten* with Oxford United from that age. Years later – in bad or adverse games or conditions, standing freezing on ice-cold concrete terracing and 3-0 down – he often cursed that first day his dad had dragged him along to his first Oxford match. But he couldn't help it. He had to go and watch his team. He couldn't stop himself.

When Oxford were playing at home, they used to drive up to Headington with his dad's mates in their Vauxhall Cresta, have a few drinks in the social club (then located under the Beech Road

Stand) and stand to the left of the Cuckoo Lane End, about six steps up.

The adults joshed and joked about the team and players, whilst John gazed on in awe, praying for goals scored – and *please*, none against!

The first match he actually recalled being at was really clear in his memory. It was a midweek night match against Doncaster Rovers. It was just John and his dad. Because they had got there late, father and son stood at the most convenient vantage-point – at the foot of the London Road, just by the Osler Road entrance, under the corner floodlight.

John noted his dad's excitement as he gazed across the pitch.

'Now, have a look at this, son,' his dad said, pointing to the emerging players. 'The goalie is Harry Fearnley. Remember him from last season?'

Don rested his hand on his son's head, eyes shining and reflecting the floodlights, his pale face and brown eyes surveying the illuminated pitch.

'Yes, I remember Harry,' replied the young John, having witnessed the goalie's antics close-up from the Cuckoo Lane last season.

'I bet you do!' cried his dad excitedly. 'He's a nutter!'

Young John regarded his happy father from the exit gate where he rested.

His dad wore his beige raincoat and was busy with a thermos flask full of tea, unscrewing the cap and offering a steaming cup to John with a nod.

His dad was grinning in his works cap, chuckling with mirth and anticipation as the two teams took the pitch.

'Come on, Harry!' he called, clapping the teams on with the rest of the crowd.

Oxford had signed the amazing Jimmy Barron, mid-season 1965–66, and the genial Fearnley had left Oxford and signed for Doncaster Rovers at the same time. Harry was a great servant of the club and a great character too.

The game was very memorable for John because Graham Atkinson started a 6-1 rout, and his dad was enjoying Fearnley picking the ball out of the net so often. His dad was chortling with joy, and even Harry seemed to be enjoying the game, despite the result. He waved madly to the Oxford fans as the team filed off, grinning away despite the thrashing. John remembered the whole thing as if it were yesterday for the rest of his life.

And following that game he became a regular. When he was old enough, he would even walk up to the Manor on his own, from home. Certainly, the times were different then. He left the house from Barns road in Cowley, walked past Cowley Center, and round the *Swan*. Then up the Slade and along Windmill road, through Headington to the Manor. He would do this on his own or with a mate.

When you reached the ground, you could still choose which entrance you went in and where in the ground you chose to stand. At this time, you could still, literally, walk all the way around the ground.

Then straight after the game, he would walk back again, picking up a *Sporting Green* from the paper-stand outside the

Original Swan, which gave a great report of the match (up to half-time)!

In those early days, he used to hang around the changing rooms, waiting for John Shuker, Maurice Kyle, Micky Bullock, or any of his other heroes, to get an autograph, before watching from the Beech Road terrace or the Cuckoo Lane behind the goal. He wasn't quite man enough, or big enough yet for the London Road. But that would happen soon.

John also did support Chelsea around this time, and in 1967–68 – aged 13 and influenced by his classmates at Cheney – he would also, along with his school pals, visit Stamford Bridge to watch Chelsea, usually when Oxford were away.

This involved taking a bus from Cowley Center to the Oxford train station, then a train from Oxford to Paddington. They got the tube from Paddington, made a change on the tube from the Circle line to the District line at High Street Kensington and then finally alighted at Fulham Broadway, followed by a short walk along the Kings Road to the ground.

In those days, again, you simply turned up at the ground, paid at the turnstile and walked in. Stamford Bridge was massive compared to the Manor. The boys used to stand on the right side of *The Shed* – the famous Chelsea end and stronghold of their most vociferous supporters – avoiding the hordes of incoming *Forest* or other opposing fans as they tried to storm *The Shed* from the left.

John did love this team, and it stuck with him all his life. But he particularly adored the three talents – Peter Osgood and Ian Hutchinson for their legendary goal-scoring talents and the amazing Charlie Cooke, the darling of the wings. John followed Chelsea, and they were his second team, fuelling rivalry and banter each Monday morning with Man. Utd, Leeds and Tottenham fans.

In a glorious FA Cup run, (they hadn't won a thing since the league in 1954–55) the Blues reached the final in 1970 vs their arch rivals, Leeds United.

The final was a big deal for John. His dad was a closet Tottenham Hotspur fan, and they had their own little personal rivalry between these two teams. Chelsea reaching the Cup final was his dream, although Leeds had a much stronger, workmanlike and clinical team. John hoped against hope that Chelsea won, but he was worried by the power of Leeds, with the likes of Allan Clarke, Billy Bremner, Johnny Giles and Eddie Gray to name a few of *their* stars.

John settled in front of the settee at home as the game kicked off, with a bottle of lime *Corona* and a couple of bags of *Wotsits* for company.

Leeds applied their power; early in the game, after acute pressure, Jack Charlton managed to leap the highest from a corner and head the ball in between the defending Chelsea full-backs McCreadie and Harris to give Leeds the lead. Chelsea survived more pressure and earned an equaliser when the stylish Peter Houseman steadied and turned in a knock-down on the edge of the box, beating Gary Sprake to his left corner.

Gray terrorised Ron Harris throughout the game. Leeds' Mick Jones and Peter Lorimer had good chances, but the Chelsea keeper, Peter Bonetti, was equal to anything Leeds threw at them.

Ian Hutchinson had a great chance to put Chelsea in the lead, with Sprake and his defence making good saves and blocks to deny the young Chelsea striker.

Following this double chance, Leeds pushed on – in front of the 100,000 fans – dominating their opponents on the heavy, sanded and badly cut-up pitch. After continued Leeds pressure, Gray hit the bar. Soon after, Clarke hit the woodwork again, this time the post. The ball rebounded and squirmed back into the path of centre-forward Mick Jones, who joyfully slotted the ball beyond Bonetti for a deserved 2-1 lead for Leeds.

As the match reached its conclusion, John was clutching a cushion – hardly daring to watch – hoping for anything else from his team and just praying they could hold on and perhaps get something from the game. The commentator – as Leeds United continued to push – described the pitch as 'like a sand pit'. But what a fantastic, end-to-end game of football it had been. An epic, entertaining and pulsating final.

With a few minutes remaining, Harris took a throw-in to John Hollins. Hollins looked up and saw Hutchinson on a run across the penalty area. He delivered a perfect, near-post cross that Ian Hutchinson met on the full, for a glorious and spectacularly headed Chelsea equaliser.

John leapt up screaming. The cushion inadvertently went flying sideways onto the top of the *Grundig* radiogram, knocking off and scattering the rack of vinyl singles that were stored thereon, and also decapitating an effeminate Capo de Monte hunting figure, which he believed (later) to be fairly valuable.

He stooped down to gather what he could, eyes still glued to the screen, where Leeds had kicked-off and were labouring with intent through the quagmire towards the Chelsea goal.

He subconsciously noted the *Parlophone* singles in one hand, the headless hunter in the other, and hoped he hadn't damaged any of his original Beatles singles.

Leeds had one last attack. Once again, Allan Clarke's chance thankfully came back off the bar. After extra time, the Cup final was a 2-2 draw.

There would need to be a replay!

And the replay took place eighteen days later – 29th April 1970 at Old Trafford. The place was packed with Leeds and Chelsea fans. The game turned out to be just as pulsating as the original final, and again, as expected, the Yorkshire outfit were soon in the ascendancy.

After several chances, Leeds' centre-forward Jones galloped off on a crushing run and beat the full-back, before unleashing an unstoppable drive into the top corner. Bonetti never even saw it.

Chelsea countered, and Leeds continued to be dangerous – Eddie Gray always instrumental in the Leeds attacks.

Leeds' attacking full-back Terry Cooper had a great run in the second half, his fierce shot parried by Bonetti.

As Leeds began to run out of ideas in midfield, Charlie Cooke worked his way through the middle and picked out a sublime pass for Osgood, who steamed into the penalty area behind the Leeds defence to equalise spectacularly, with an unstoppable diving header.

Alone on the settee again, John leapt up and ran around the room in ecstasy as his team had come from behind again. Could they go on and win it?

Yes, they could – Against all odds. Ian Hutchinson was preparing a long-throw. 'Hutch' had a monstrous long throw in his repertoire. Chelsea fans hoped and prayed. Hutchinson took a run-up, and then he launched the throw 'like a free-kick' into the area. Someone's head, attacker or defender, knocked the ball on. The ball sailed to the far-post. Chelsea thunderously attacked it. Centre-half David Webb rose highest, heading powerfully into the net for 2-1.

John hugged and kissed the telly.

Chelsea had just won the cup!

Later, John's son Ollie would briefly support Norwich City, after simply watching Jeremy Goss' stunning volley in Europe versus Bayern Munich. He even got John to get him a Norwich shirt with 'Goss' emblazoned on the back.

John loved Brian Clough, so he followed that legend through his amazing Nottingham Forest days – including that astonishing Liverpool rivalry – becoming a Forest fan for a while.

During that time, Ollie had latched on to Liverpool, inspired by their quality on the pitch, and influenced by his school mates – who had dominated Europe – and who he continued to support whilst quietly *following* Oxford.

But John's interest in other clubs, including Chelsea, waned over the years. Whatever happened in the world of football, he eventually returned to his first love – Oxford United FC. It took him a while to realise this, but he had to admit that whenever he was asked the question 'Who do you support?'

His reply, practiced and profound, was short and sweet;

'I'm an Oxford United fan!'

Dave Gomm

And he was proud of it.

'Oxford till I die!

I'm Oxford till I die!

I know I am,

I'm sure I am –

…I'm Oxford till I die!'

Chapter 17
Under-10s 'A' League

Having progressed through the preliminary league and qualified for the newly formed 'A' league, Grove Challenger's under-10s – the first Grove team to play in the newly formed B-Line League – now found themselves competing with the best teams in the area.

The first match was away at Littlemore, where they ran out comfortable winners by four goals to nil, with a brace each for Mark Brind and Ritchie Claydon. Grove dominated, were in complete command and scored a routine victory without breaking a sweat.

Their first home match looked like a routine affair, but they went down by five goals to four, despite leading twice; possibly because they underestimated their opponents. Bullingdon simply never gave up, and they kept on pressing throughout the match, eventually securing the points with a well-taken goal with five minutes left. Grove were shell-shocked, and at the final hearing, they simply did not deserve to win.

The Bullingdon team, however, were ecstatic!

There followed another away Abingdon encounter, this time much harder-fought; again, although the double-act of Claydon and Brind equalised a 2-0 deficit, Richard Wilson, once again, clinched the points near the end for a 3-2 win for their oldest adversaries.

The team was looking strong and still gelling; the new boys were fitting in, but also exposing some weaknesses within the team.

When they hosted Garden City next, it turned out to be a bitter scrap, where both teams were battling away. Neither team created that many chances as both cancelled the other out. Peter Wiggins, in spite of his size and ability, seemed to be detached from his teammates. Some of the boys were simply out of their depth at this level, and there was still work to be done. 0-0.

The atmosphere within the group was still as good as ever, with the boys enjoying their footballing experience. But, yet again, they went down by 3-4 in the next home encounter to a spirited Kidlington side, despite a Ritchie Claydon hat-trick.

Grove had light relief when they went away to Botley. Claydon, Revell and Gomm all got on the scoresheet, but Mark Brind took all the plaudits, with a double-brace of well-taken goals to comfortably win 8-2.

After these five results (two wins, two defeats and a draw), Grove went off to 'B' League Florence Park for the first round of the cup. The team were high after the Botley win and expected an easy victory, playing at Florence Park for the first time. Florence Park played at the Marsh in Cowley, a mile from where John had lived his early life, two miles from where he had been born and half a mile from his first house in Ridgefield road.

He knew the Marsh well. As a kid, he had played football there, biked to the top and passed it many times throughout the years.

It was right on the edge of the Cowley Road, and there were two pubs, *The Marsh Harrier* and *The Exeter Hall*, right by the side of it, both of which he had frequented in his adolescence.

The Grove convoy parked up for a 10 o'clock kick off on a chilly October morning. There was some car parking inside the main gates, and the boys and parents walked across to the changing rooms in the big council-run complex. There was plenty of room, and they received a warm welcome from their old friend and adversary, the genial manager of Florence Park, Carlo. As John and Alan led the boys past the hockey pitches, grey mist lingered on the pitches. A light rain came and went, but it was a cold early morning. Some dog-walkers strolled about, huddled against the elements, but the vista was of cold, open space. The pitch was five or six hundred yards away, having been properly prepared, but it seemed to lie in the middle of nowhere.

It was not the fault of John, the boys, the support, the conditions or their efforts that they lost that morning. They didn't take Florence Park lightly. They battered them for eighty minutes. They hit the woodwork five times, had two goals disallowed and missed a penalty (which hit the bar). They must have had thirty shots and headers, fourteen corners and almost the entire possession. Their improved keeper, Ali Tamsam, was the Man of the Match, and they defended like their lives depended on it. Grove were awesome, dominating their opponents from start to finish. Florence Park were simply not in the game. Carlo had obviously set out to defend, but in all his wildest dreams, he couldn't have imagined the outcome following the barrage they received right from the kick off.

At the start of the second-half, the Oxford side launched one of their few attacks and somehow let in the lively Kiri Bieleczi, who fired a shot into the net, having made some space for himself. Billy was in goal, but couldn't do anything about it, and the Florence Park boys clung tenaciously to the lead until the minutes ticked away. At the final whistle, the Florence Park team celebrated with their manager as if they had won the cup.

Grove trooped off, shaking their heads; the boys were muddied, wet and sweating from their efforts. The rain had begun to sweep across, and the day was grey as the mist clung to the edge of the field.

The truth is that the team, at this level, was missing a Dwight, someone who could stamp his authority on the game, put himself about and drill fear into the opponent. They were still a team in transition, but Dwight would have made that subtle difference between success, dominance and defeat. Grove were a nice little village team, who played some good football, but they were lacking a dominant edge in midfield, where they competed admirably, but on a similar level to their opponents – at this level.

Well, the parents liked to win, and they certainly didn't like to lose. But they also wanted their boys to play every week, which was only somewhat possible. Fielding a weakened team to keep the lesser players happy would certainly have not gone down well with the camp if they had taken a beating.

John had even begun to be glad of Bullstrode's B-team, as he really wished he *could* fit every player in *every* week. But it was not practical. He wanted the team to be successful, and, indeed, he wanted to attract new and better players. But he didn't think he was alone in this. Surely even Billy Bullstrode had the same principles. After all, who likes to lose?

The larking around days, of Andrew Dawson's, Colin Mercer's and Richard Maurice's light-hearted antics, were no longer acceptable. Their opponents wanted to beat them and, given half a chance, would – hence the closeness of the match and unlucky defeat by Kidlington. Truthfully, that match could have gone either way, but Kidlington had the edge and therefore ran out winners.

Florence Park was a bit different. We have all seen teams dominate, not score and lose. It's football. It happens. It was still good, clean fun and still brilliant; it was still boys' football. But there's a fine line between mercilessly slaughtering teams, competing and holding the boys together, and getting beat every week!

They had wanted a bigger challenge, and in this league, they had found it. The competition was inviting them to step up another level and progress up the league.

'What d'ya reckon then, chap?' John asked Alan, as they headed back to the changing room. 'Unluckiest team on earth?'

Alan was downcast, looking down at the ground as they walked.

'I don't know. It's fucking shite, John. They've got no commitment, and they don't give a shit about winning.' Alan was bordering on being depressed.

John wondered what game he had been watching!

'Jesus, mate. We're still competing, and they are giving their best – we could have scored six.' John tried to inject some light-heartedness. 'We were just bloody unlucky.'

'No, no. They aren't – they've got to have a killer-instinct. This is how the other teams see it.' Elliott continued, still downcast, 'They've got to see teams like this off.'

'Fuck, I'm not sure that's right – blimey, we all need to be enjoying it,' John interjected, giving his right-hand man a sideways glance – and the benefit of the doubt.

Death look…Alan looked suicidal!

'Well, I think,' he returned, 'that there were a few out there who just weren't bloody interested, mate.'

'Christ, Al. Who are you talking about?' John asked. Some of the Grove parents were already there, trying to get some shelter from the drifting rain. 'I thought they gave 100 percent.' John was actually beginning to get pissed off with Alan's attitude. *Fuck me, they're only ten-year-old kids!*

'Some didn't take it seriously. Revell should have scored three, Sparkie missed the penalty, and Ritchie was on half-speed!' blundered Alan. 'They didn't give them any respect.'

Graham Brind caught part of the conversation as they entered the changing rooms and raised an eyebrow at John. 'Well, unlucky chap!' he beamed, winking and holding the door open.

'Cheers, Graham. Well done, Carlo.' John offered his hand to the beaming Florence Park manager who had just walked in behind them.

John looked up, and Alan had grabbed Trigger, hurrying him out with a curt 'See you.'

'What a moody fucker!' John shook his head. 'Jesus!'

'I think some people take this a little too seriously,' quipped Graham, grinning.

'You're not kidding, Graham. I thought we gave everything. I reckon we could have played 180 minutes and still not scored!' He looked around the changing room at the remaining players, nine and ten-year-olds. Colin Mercer was flicking away with his towel, Ollie and Ritchie were talking about *Transformers*, so the boys were still quite happy – despite the defeat! So they had just played and lost a football match.

Fuck me, even Liverpool do that!

Killer instincts. Jesus? Did they need killer instincts at this level? Boys under-10 football!

***

Their next League encounter went to show how tough this new League was. Despite playing brilliantly, and a featuring a stunning hat-trick from Ritchie Claydon, Grove went down 3-4 against a very strong and improved Kidlington.

So, when they went over to Horspath the next drizzly November Sunday afternoon, the message was to beat this decent team at all costs. Colin was dropped, and John only took one substitute, John Monery. Horspath were flying at the top of the League and had had some good results in the league with the deadly Elliott O'Brien scoring for fun!

The team performed heroics, supported well by the Grove parents; after a goalless draw in the first-half, they took the lead when Gomm poached a goal on 65 minutes, and Billy McDonald rattled in a header from a Claydon free-kick four minutes later.

The team then dug in, as Horspath, led by the inspirational O'Brien, continued to pound away, eventually getting a goal back with eight minutes left. Great organisation, resilience and bloody-minded defending kept Grove ahead. The team were solid, and John took the decision of leaving Monery on the bench to take the win. Grove withstood the pressure. The final whistle blew, and the Grove boys, staff and parents were whooping it up on the touchlines with a brilliant win and points.

It was a great result and proved that they could dig in when necessary, and that some of the players they had did have the bottle to compete at this level. John thanked all the boys for their heroic efforts, including John Monery, whom he pulled to one side and explained the reasons for not bringing him on.

'Sorry John, I didn't want to risk those last few minutes, so I didn't call you on,' John explained, feeling a little guilty.

'Hope you understand – we needed the win.'

'Thanks for being there.'

John was looking up at the manager dolefully, nodding.

'Next time.' etc…

Saying all the parents were ecstatic wasn't strictly true either.

Monery's dad, Brian, caught John in the car park afterwards and gave him a piece of his mind.

'John, can I have a word?' Brian was not happy. He was a gentle man, but he was almost shaking with anger.

'You can't bring a kid all the way out here for a match and not bring him on,' he fumed. 'It's just not right.' Brian was really pissed off. 'Don't you see? The boy is distraught!'

John could see that little John wasn't happy at all. But he *had* taken the decision to not bring him on, to get the result for the team. And he stood by it, despite the repercussions.

'Brian, sorry mate, we wanted to win. I always try to bring on the subs – I did explain to little John,' he apologised, knowing deep down the parent had a point. Brian was right.

'I know, but they're kids, playing football. You could have bought him on – even for the last few minutes,' Brian said angrily, confronting the coach.

The two men stood facing one another for a moment.

John was lost for words, but finally Monery angrily broke the silence;

'Who do you think you are?' He glared. 'Alex fucking Ferguson?'

Another boys' football issue. John knew, but what could he do?

Another bloody case of *'you can't please everyone'.'*

Alex Ferguson!

Despite the outburst and his concern, he couldn't help a little smile on the way back to the car. A bloody great result!

Oxford United Social Club were next at home and the honours were even this time in a 2-2 draw, Claydon and Brind again the scorers, with a full team and three subs, all used.

The same two players netted again, away at Garden City in another good away win by two goals to nil. Another good performance, with a strong midfield and defence dominating, giving the platform for the win.

In the middle of the season, the team were also involved in the Supplementary Cup winning 4-1 at Rose Hill, 6-0 against St. Edmunds, and drawing 1-1 at home to Bullingdon, to qualify for the semi-final against Abingdon.

John had now moved Johnny Wells back alongside Sean Webb in the centre of defence, Colin and John Monery had lost their places and were now more periphery players and reserves. Danny O'Sullivan was sound at left back, with Revell, Gomm and McDonald the key midfielders, backed up by Wiggins and

Ashford, who could both be sublime on their day; although, they possibly lacked the bite and vigour of the regulars.

Brind and Claydon terrorised defences and scored the majority of the goals for the team with staunch regularity.

So, Grove, again in metamorphosis, were developing and learning to cope with their opposition – against a growing number of ever-improving teams.

After the Rose Hill win, followed a 4-4 draw at Kidlington, another Claydon hat-trick, a 3-0 home win v. Botley, and a cracking return against Horspath at Grove. This time, it was Sean Revell who rescued a point, following a vicious drive that flew into the top of the net after a fine run had seen him sprint past two defenders, creating the chance for himself.

The last four league games saw two wins, 6-0 v. Littlemore and 3-2 at home to Abingdon, and two defeats, 1-2 away to OUFCSC and another defeat by Bullingdon 1-3.

There were also two friendlies, 2-1 at home to Abingdon and a 3-4 away loss to Garden City.

All in all, the season had had mixed success.

League results

Played	Won	Drawn	Lost	Goals For	Goals Against	Pts
16	7	4	5	46	29	25

Grove finished fifth in the league, behind the winners Abingdon, OUSC, Garden City and Horspath. It had been a serious challenge after the easy run-outs in the Under-9's. But that's what John had been looking for.

Littlemore and Botley were relegated to the 'B' League, from where Florence Park (champions) and runners-up Apollo (Abingdon) were promoted.

So not a stunning success, but not a disaster either; the boys (mainly) were still enjoying the experience, becoming hardened to the demands of a 'town' league and continuing in winning new friends along the way.

But the balancing-act of keeping boys and parents interested (especially if they were nearly always substitutes) had taken a toll. John had already lost Charlie Harris, Skelton, Dawson, Maurice, Howe and Ciampioli for various reasons. Now there were questions over whether Mercer, Casey and Monery would even be back next season.

This was beginning to present quite a challenge!

The semi-final at Abingdon was a complete disaster in that Grove could have won it 10-0. Such was their dominance. Unbelievably though, they had to fight back from two goals down, drawing level at 2-2 with ten minutes to go.

In a replication of their earlier defeat to the same opponents earlier in the season, the Grove parents sensed a little deja vu as Mark Brind fired over the bar just after, and from the resulting goal-kick, Abingdon, to their credit, swept the ball up the field and scored a classy goal, deserving to go through to the final. Grove were just not meant to win on the day!

The team had played and performed well with great performances against all the good sides. With a little more luck, and a player or two more, this successful season could have included silverware.

Generally, the team more or less picked itself and was on the up!

It just desperately needed to find a few more decent players.

Chapter 18
The Vale of the White Horse

The second season of the B-Line Oxford boys League as under-11s had developed the teams from the under 10 preliminary and proper leagues; The 'A' League now contained the group winners from the other divisions;

Grove A

Highfield

Abindgon A

OUFCSC

Kidlington

Radley

Garden City

Crowmarsh

Carterton

Florence Park

Robins

Bullingdon

Donnington

And Horspath

This league truly represented the very strongest teams in the area, and each match, every week, would be a challenge.

Also, in year 3, at the under-11s level, there came the trials for the Grove boys, to join the Vale of the White Horse district team. There was a lot of excitement, as many of the boys from the Grove schools were selected for the initial trials.

The first trial was held at the Radley sports ground in Abingdon, on a sunny Monday afternoon after school. From the Grove first team's schools were Olly Dimblow, Ollie Gomm, Ritchie Claydon, Sean Webb, Mark Brind, Stephen Casey, Billy McDonald, Charlie Harris, Jamie Elliott and Johnnie Wells.

From the newly formed 'B-team', Jonathon Ashford, Roger Sevier, Stephen Vaux, Josh Rowe and the lanky forward, Michael James.

The trials were well organised, giving the boys the chance to show off what they could do. As always, Ritchie and Ollie played out of their skins, as they always seemed to do at any trial. There followed a thinning-out process at the next trial at Newbury, following another test in front of the Vale's manager, Dave Stemp. Happily selected for the final 24, a few weeks later at home to Swindon, were Dimblow, Casey, Sevier, Claydon, Gomm, Brind, Webb, Rowe and Vaux.

The match at Westminster college was a two-team affair; the boys were split into an 'A' and a 'B' team, playing Swindon 'A' and 'B', to determine, as trial games, who was to make the final squad.

After somewhat disjointed performances, including some outstanding individual ones, there followed a similar match at Burford, vs. Mid Oxon, involving the same players. The final 15 were selected from the two strong teams. From strong competition, Grove only finished with two representative players, Ritchie and Ollie Gomm, who went on to proudly play for the Vale for the following matches in the 'County League'.

In many ways, unfortunately, here was the process that was to inevitably begin the demise of the Grove team, which was built on scraps, from nothing, with ordinary boys from walking distance of the rec. As the reps circled for talent, Ritchie was inevitably scouted and approached by Oxford United and Ollie by Wycombe Wanderers.

However, the Vale games were great for John and Ollie, and they gave forth a pretty intense sporting weekend, consisting of the Vale game on Saturday morning, plus Oxford United home games every other week (they were season-ticket holders then); on Sunday, the normal Grove league and cup matches.

So, the boys trained twice a week in the evenings and played their league matches on Sundays; now, the Vale Boys also played on Saturday mornings at home at Westminster College, or away at opponents within the County League.

The dads soon got to know each other and met up before the games to talk football and clubs, before walking across the pitches to watch the match.

Westminster College's pitches were up on top of a plateau in Botley, and the facilities and pitches were top-rate. Dave Stemp liked to play football, and the final fifteen were all good footballers, who were mainly on the small side; the two Grove players, along with *Oggy* (James Organ), Liam Barson and the goalkeeper Tom Butler, were amongst the smallest.

But the blend of the team was good, and they had some strong, bigger lads too, who could also play a bit.

The team quickly integrated and began to play well as a unit, and John, as a dad, enjoyed the luxury of fixed goals, pre-arranged fixtures, marked-out pitches and proper refs and linesmen. As a manager, it was a joy to just turn up and watch the match, without the hassle of worrying about whether everyone had turned up, what subs he may use, who was to be found for running the line and all the decision-making associated with keeping everyone happy and getting a result.

The Vale games were somewhat of a luxury for him, and Ollie survived on his own merits. He was proud of Ollie, his boy, from where he had started to where he was now, holding his place in the starting line-up of the representative side. He was becoming a tidy little part of the engine room of the Vale, and he worked well with Ritchie as well as with the other lads who had been sourced from other schools and teams.

The team started a bit nervously in their first Cotswold League game, securing a 2-2 draw at home to Reading, gradually easing into the ascendency and having a perfectly good last-minute winner disallowed for offside to rob them of the victory.

Their first away game was to arch-rivals and title contenders, Oxford City, where they eventually lost out by 3 goals to 1 in a fiercely fought contest.

The football was a joy to watch, and the results kept coming with a home win versus Chiltern & South Bucks 4-0, an away victory at South Oxon by five goals to nil, and then another home success v. High Wycombe 5-3.

That day, Saturday 16th December 1995, after defeating High Wycome in a pulsating Cotswold League match at Westminster, the parents were requested to remain after the match and told they would be given a letter. Despite them knowing what was coming, the final nine Vale players, selected by Dave Stemp and Paul Kearns, were to be selected as representatives in the upcoming ESDA/ADIDAS PREDATOR Premier 7s competition.

This was a really important annual seven-a-side competition, on a national basis. There were regional games and the finalists would battle out for the final at Wembley in May after the regional finals against all the local winners, the Vale's finals would be held in Devon.

As they milled around awaiting the decision, John resigned himself to the fact that, despite Ollie's performances for the Vale to date, there were other, better, stronger, bigger players who would surely be in front of him. He was acutely aware that the team had always been on the small side, and the need for stamina and robustness would probably edge Ollie out.

He had no doubt that Ritchie and Jack (Vale captain and midfield dynamo) would be the first names on the sheet. As a striker, Ritchie was skilful, quick and deadly, but in midfield, they had not only outstanding talents like Jack, but other good players like Kevin Hussey, Paul Hayes, Chris Kershaw, Joe Brewerton and Liam Barson in the squad, and all except Liam were bigger and more robust.

He kept his thoughts to himself, but deep down, he knew that if *he* had been the manager of the Vale team, Ollie probably would have made way. So, he accepted that, as Ollie came skipping down the steps, this was one competition Ollie would not be selected for.

'Awright, mate? Well played,' he grinned at his son.

'Yeah alright, Dad.' Ollie was beaming back at his dad. 'Did you see that through ball to Liam with me left foot?'

John grinned down at his lad.

'Are you going for a pint before we go to football?' he asked in all innocence.

United were away at Bristol Rovers that day.

'No, mate, you know we are away today,' John replied, 'and it wasn't a bad ball!'

Oxford were in the middle of a winning frenzy in the old Division 2; they had had five consecutive victories largely thanks to the Moody-Byrne-Rush striking combination that was tearing defences to pieces that season.

He ruffled Ollie's blond hair as they walked up to the changing rooms. 'We're taking Mum and Corine out to lunch.'

Dave Claydon and Colin Barson sidled over with Ritchie and Liam.

The three diminutive players, awash with excitement and enthusiasm, mingled at their feet – three small blond lads with oodles of skill between them. They did make a sight, all three tiny and grinning, pure blond hair shining from the shower and radiating real energy as they punted an empty can about absently in the dust outside the changing rooms.

Tony King looked over at John gave him a little wink and thumbs up.

'What d'you reckon then, John?' mused Colin, looking sideways. 'Think all three of 'em will get in?'

'Not sure, Col – I think Ritchie will be in. Jack, Joe, Reynolds? Don't know about the rest – it's a tough one to call.' The players were all of such a high standard, it would be difficult to choose.

'When the going gets tough, the tough get going,' piped up Ollie, paraphrasing the legendary Jim Smith!

'Liam's been playing well. Hope he gets the chance,' said John politely.

Liam was looking hopefully up at his dad.

'Not long to wait – here's Stempy!' Colin waved towards the tarpaulin huts that served as changing facilities.

Dave Stemp's gangly frame entered the space with his long dark hair tossed to the back of his head. His piercing dark eyes wandered kindly around the assembled hopefuls, and he began to speak;

'Parents, boys, players…Thanks for waiting, and well played today. Your dads will all have letters, and they will all know what a tough decision it's been picking nine players from this squad. You've all been great and reliable, and it has been a difficult task to leave some of you out. Good luck, and we'll see you all next week.'

He passed around the assembled parents, handing out a letter to each.

'Dads, if you could take the boys home, and let them know when you are ready. And congratulations to the nine, commiserations if you didn't make it. Good luck.' Stemp nodded sternly, then spun on his heel with a wave as he strode back to the dressing rooms.

Dave Stemp, having delivered his notices, left the crowd of boys looking up at their dads. Most of the dads had the envelope in their hands, loosely hanging. They exchanged knowing glances and made their goodbyes.

John led Ollie back to the car, bidding goodbye to everyone, and settled into the front seat of the BMW, with Ollie in the passenger seat. He was going to get it over with, win or lose.

'Right son, let's open it here, shall we?' John looked kindly at his little muddied son, dwarfed by the padded passenger seat. 'Is that okay?'

A nod of agreement.

'What do you reckon?' he threw at Ollie.

Ollie looked up innocently and shrugged.

John opened the letter and read it. Then he re-read it. He thought he had made a mistake... 'I have selected your son to play in the inter-association seven-a-side competition.'

He had, against all odds, made it!

Woohoo!

They drove away, euphoric. John couldn't believe it.

What a result for Ollie and his dad.

That tiny lad had made it through the best players in the South of Oxford, to win a place in a select seven-a-side team on the cusp of a nationwide competition.

What an achievement for the lad! Brilliant!

***

Oxford United were to lose 0-2 away to Bristol Rovers that afternoon in the league – so there was no home game at the Manor.

They made their way home to a sandwich place in Grove, where Lyn had just delivered Corine from riding. John announced the amazing news and Corine asked, 'Brilliant! Let's go and celebrate at Old Orleans, Dad! Can we? Please?'

It was always a family favourite, in Oxford's centre, especially after the main course. When you had devoured your stack of smoky pork ribs and licked your fingers, they would always share the 'Outrageous' – a great, big sharing bowl of chocolate and vanilla ice-creams, warm chocolate brownie, chocolate fudge sauce, Maltesers and chocolate flakes with marshmallows!

'Well done, Ollie! You keep getting into these teams, and we'll keep coming down here,' said Corine, grinning from ear to ear as she finished off the pot!

Ollie grinned and replied, 'Well, we can come here after the final if you like?' winking at his dad.

The rest of the Vale season had been a runaway success. A Southern Counties Cup defeat at home to Southampton 1-3 in November was followed by a brilliant run in the Witney Cup Competition, where they progressed following a 5-1 demolition of Woking in round two and a comprehensive drubbing of St. Albans in the third round.

The semi-final was a tough, tough game against a very talented passing team at Gloucester, who out-passed and outplayed the Vale for large periods of the game. Once again, the deadlock was broken on a swift Vale counter-attack, when

Dave Gomm

Gomm freed Ritchie Claydon, who sprinted clear and earned a 1-0 win with a tidy finish to break the Gloucester hearts.

Once again, Vale were rewarded with a final tie against the other stand-out team, their nearest and bitterest rivals – Oxford City.

In the league, still neck to neck with Oxford City, Vale continued their fine form, winning at Chiltern & South Bucks 2-1 then away victory over South Oxon 3-1.

Vale produced a stunning away victory at Reading 4-3, coming from 2-0 down to secure the points as the season drew to a close in March.

The run culminated in a tetchy encounter with their old adversary, Oxford City, a team that included many of their Oxford playing opponents from Kidlington, Oxford Blackbirds, Rose Hill, Barton and their old enemy Oxford United Social Club.

Vale needed to win this match to have any chance of pipping Oxford City, and they heroically mustered a 2-1 victory after an end-to-end match of high quality and some tension.

This left an away trip to High Wycombe in mid-April, which, quite simply, the team had to win to pip OC to the league title.

It proved a bridge too treacherous to cross, despite putting on a gallant display. Vale lost the title by a point in a disappointing 1-1 draw against good opponents that matched them on the day. The boys trooped off at the final whistle, reminding themselves that this lost point, and the point dropped against Reading in their first game (with that last-minute disallowed goal), would be the points by which they just failed to pip Oxford City to the League title.

Two weeks later – in the Witney Cup Final at Abingdon Town FC – Vale lost 0-2 to a strong Oxford City side to end an incredible season, where their flair, skill and enterprise would, in another season, have possibly landed them the double, losing both league and cup to the Oxford City side that had dominated.

It was a brilliant little team!

Final League Table

The County League 95–96	P	W	D	L	F	A	Pts
Oxford City	10	8	1	1	36	11	17
Vale of the White Horse	10	7	2	1	29	15	16
Reading	10	5	1	4	24	20	11
High Wycombe	10	2	3	5	17	20	7
Chiltern & South Bucks	10	2	1	7	13	32	5
South Oxon	10	2	0	8	11	32	4

Before all this had panned out, the Vale seven-a-side had had an astonishing run in the English Schools Football Association 'Predator' Premier Cup Competition.

The final nine, including Ollie, had been selected as

1) **Tom Butler (Thomas Reade)**
2) **Jack King (Harwell)**
3) **Joe Brewerton (St Nicholas)**

4) **Richard Claydon (Charlton)**
5) **Oliver Gomm (Millbrook)**
6) **James Organ (Rush Common)**
7) **Marc Reynolds (Botley)**
8) **James Reynoldson (Rush Common)**
9) **Nick Tate (Sutton Courtenay)**

This group was a classy, nifty little unit, some might say five-a-side specialists; Joe, Marc, James and Nick Tate (the latter playing up a year) were the only ones of any size. The rest were pretty small boys, but all bundles of fired-up determination.

They didn't like getting beaten. So, they attacked their opponents with vigour, sweeping them aside with their skilful attacking, clinical control and vicious finishing. Tom was amazing in goal, being the same size as the majority. They really were a devastating force.

The preliminary 7's Cup match, again v. Oxford City at Temple Cowley, resulted in a hard-fought 0-0 draw, a result that was good for both teams, but which Vale were unlucky not to win.

But following an outstanding display in the next match, against Mid-Oxon, Vale comfortably ran out 2-0 winners, courtesy of a brace from Ritchie Claydon, to win the section and book themselves a place in the South-West regional finals at Paignton; scenes of joyous delight followed the match!

The trip to Devon on Saturday 9th March was therefore greatly anticipated. As coaches, Dave Stemp and Malcolm had got the boys playing well, efficiently and dangerously; as long as they defended as a unit, they were unstoppable when they swept forward.

When they arrived at the beautiful Paignton complex, on a crisp spring day, they were met with a colourful and exciting scene amongst the hills and rolling Devon countryside.

Qualifying teams from all over the South East were participating and had been split into two groups: Group one containing Plymouth, Poole & East Dorset, Bristol, Southampton and Reading.

Grove were facing stiff opposition from West Cornwall, Gloucester, Jersey and – brilliantly for John, Ollie and the Oxford fans – Swindon.

The boys looked bright and ready on the day of the match. John and Lyn had brought Becky Elliott with them as company for Corine. There was a carnival atmosphere, with people, parents, flags, sponsors, players and teams cutting a real spectacle of colour and movement in the valley where they were camped.

There were food stalls, football gear stalls and a stand sponsored by the new 'Predator' company, which had developed a 'new' boot, with deep ridges on the meat of the boot (for more spin/backspin and control)!

The ten teams, entourages, players, families and dogs milled around and waited for the action to begin. John got a program as Ollie and Ritchie met Jack, and the three players made their way over to Stemp and the rest of the squad.

Dave and Paul gave the boys a little light routine, followed by some ball work and light running and stretching as John returned to the car with coffee for Lyn.

The whole squad and parents were able to afford the time to watch the first match in Group 1; Plymouth narrowly defeating Poole & East Dorset by two goals to one.

For a finals competition, the standard was inevitably very high.

As Bristol lined up against Southampton for the next match in that group, the Vale entourage moved to their pitch to finalise their last-minute training and stretching routines. Looking a little nervous, they watched from behind the ropes as a strong Gloucester side beat West Cornwall 1-0, looking impressive.

As the final whistle blew, they took their place on the pitch, bursting on dribbling balls and racing towards the goal for their first group game v. Swindon. This proved to be very nip and tuck, where both teams looked comfortable on the ball, with only last-ditch defending and exceptional goalkeeping from both sides, resulting in a lively 0-0 draw.

The boys came off puffing, and Stemp congratulated them on the result.

'Well done lads.' He looked down at his little group. 'That may have been your hardest game!'

'Yeah, they were good,' panted Jack, red-faced from his exertions.

'Really good defenders,' said Ritchie.

'So were you guys,' returned the proud manager. 'Take a break?'

'It's Jersey v. West Cornwall, then Gloucester-Swindon before we play. Let's go and watch before our next game,' announced Stemp, turning away.

'Who've we got next, Dave?' asked Joe.

'Jersey. Boys, let's go and suss them out!' cried Stemp, moving towards the game.

Jersey proved to look steady but unspectacular. Grove were confident when the Jersey game kicked off, and soon they assumed control.

Marc Reynolds finished a typically sweeping Vale attack with a clinical finish, before Jack King sealed the points against the Jersey team that frankly, looked almost beaten before they started. Good work for the Vale; a win and a draw in the first two games and smiles all round for the performances.

As it turned out, Jersey beat West Cornwall 1-0, then lost by the same score to Swindon, followed by a tough 1-0 result v. Gloucester.

Following their Jersey win, as a wonderful touch, all the finalists lined up to accept their qualification certificate for their achievement on reaching the finals. The boys, resplendently smart in their track suits of many colours, were all also presented with a new pair of *Predators*.

As they lined up, they all looked ecstatic and yet dreadfully nervous, as the competition was only half-way through.

John and Lyn walked Sally around the perimeter, then grabbed a hot pasty and a coffee. Corine and Becky, *absolutely* disinterested in any of the football (given the players were all about two years younger than themselves), were happily sitting away from the pitches on railings, and as John approached them with his camera, Corine managed a very nice one-fingered salute, which John managed to catch on camera as a souvenir!

Fair play. It was a long way to come if you weren't interested in football at all – so it was a long day for the girls, although they were chatting and making the most of the cold Devon day.

'Are we there yet?' joked Corine as they approached, smiling.

Rebecca launched into a massive yawn.

'Won't be long, love. Do you girls want something to eat?'

Before their next game, Vale happily watched Swindon in another 0-0 v. West Cornwall – a great result for them, and a disappointing one for Swindon – before dispatching Gloucester 1-0 (Marc Reynolds again) and West Cornwall (again 1-0, and again the goal from Claydon), meaning that whatever the outcome in the final match, Vale had won the group outright.

They, the team, management and parents, were ecstatic. The Vale topped the group and had deservedly earned a semi-final place against Reading.

They now had the bit between their teeth and tore into Reading, with a brilliant attacking display and goals in each half from Claydon and Reynolds, brilliantly supported by King, Gomm and Brewerton in midfield. The 2-0 result left the Reading boys trooping off the pitch dejectedly as the Vale boys whooped off back to their HQ tent.

They were also in time to watch a ding-dong semi on the adjacent pitch, as Swindon eventually triumphed over Bristol, following a 5-4 penalty shoot-out win after a 0-0 draw in the West-country derby.

'Swindon in the final!' shouted John in disbelief, holding his head in his hands.

'Swindon in the final! Unbelievable!' echoed Graham Brewerton. 'A free pass!'

Truthfully though, the best two teams at the event had made it to the final.

John was in two minds as he marched back from the porta-loos.

Bloody Swindon always caused trouble for him and his Oxford United team.

'We can beat anybody!' beamed Stempy, as he noted John's worried look.

'Don't worry about them. We've already played them, and we have them sussed!'

'Let's hope so, Dave.' John was still quietly confident in the team and the way they were playing.

'No problem!' Stemp was also confident in his tiny charges. By Christ! They were the smallest side there by miles.

He called the boys over and stooped to address them in their huddle.

He talked for over two minutes, and not one of the parents could hear what he was saying, but at the end of the huddle, the team whooped it up with a monstrous 'Come on Vale!', as they scattered again, booting footballs away in front of them.

Vale of the White Horse v. Swindon

English Schools Football Association

Predator Cup Seven-a-side South-West Final

Of course, they all knew it – the managers, parents, and most of all the boys – but this meant they were on the edge of a *National Final* at Wembley Stadium.

'One game from Wembley,' smiled Tony King, as he approached John and Lyn before the match.

'Yeah, against bloody Swindon,' retorted John, now getting nervous.

'They'll be fine, Gommy. Look how they are up for it.' Tony pointed out the confident-looking group.

Dave Stemp had taken note of the first meeting in the group stages and made a subtle change to the line-up, leaving the free-scoring Marc Reynolds on the bench, and starting with young Nick Tate with a free role in midfield. He asked Ollie and Jack to tuck in to the middle to keep the midfield tight, and he dropped Joe into defence, leaving Ritchie as the lone striker.

This plan worked quite well, as Vale pushed Swindon and won the ball back through the tenacious tackling of Gomm and King in midfield and Joe Brewerton at the back. Nevertheless, Swindon wanted to win just as badly, and they swept forward. But only to be thwarted time and again.

Nick Tate was a good outlet for Vale, as he was such a lovely ball-carrier. His inclusion gave the Vale good possession. Ritchie tried to dent the defence in vain, and Nick created some good chances. It was end-to-end stuff, and both teams were flat out. 0-0 at half time, and the teams remained the same.

Again, the work-rate was great, and Tate supplied the outlet as the teams battled for a breakthrough.

Jack King hit the bar after a cross by Claydon, then Tom Butler raced out of his goal to smother a one-on-one when Swindon's Ross Adams looked certain to score.

Joe Brewerton headed a goal-bound half volley off the line; then Tate, after a mazy dribble, saw his shot graze the outside of the post with the keeper beaten.

In the last two minutes, Stemp introduced his two subs – Marc Reynolds for the flagging Tate, and James Reynolds for Joe Brewerton, who had picked up a knock. The substitution almost had an immediate effect, as Reynolds, fresh and full of running, raced onto a Jack King pass. Racing into the box, he controlled the ball first time, then lashed a ferocious shot, agonising inches over the bar!

Extra time. 0-0.

Sudden death.

Huddle.

The parents could clearly see how the Vale boys were wired. They were bursting to get back out there and finish the job. But Swindon would not lie down. The first three minutes came and went, and as the boys turned around for the second-half, the final 3 minutes – should they not be decided by a goal – would mean the tie would go to penalties.

Sudden death is a cruel way to end such an epic contest, but in the last minute of the match, it brought its result when, again – this time put through by Gomm – the tiring Swindon defender Wallace, knackered and struggling for pace, brought down Marc Reynolds from behind as the Vale forward galloped into the area.

'Penalty!' screamed Dave Claydon.

'Penalty!' cried Brewerton.

'It's a penalty!' John was jumping up and down on the spot.

It was a clear and undisputed penalty to the Vale.

The poor Swindon players were forlorn.

And the gangly ref was pointing to the spot!

Last kick of the game!

Maybe.

'We have to score,' said John to Tony, knuckles bleached.

'What happens if we don't?' asked Lyn.

'This is it! If he misses, the game is over, then it will go to a penalty competition,' he wheezed. 'But believe me,' He winked at his wife with confidence, 'Jack won't miss. This is it!'

The ladies from the Vale support squirmed, the men gazed on.

For a small boys football game, the stakes simply could not have been higher.

In the middle of the pitch, the diminutive number 2, Jack King, quietly strode up to the edge of the box. Freckled, ginger, unsmiling and composed in his muddied black-and-white stripes and red socks. He looked much more mature than his years. He took the ball and placed it on the penalty spot. The goal looked massive, and the keeper looked tiny. Jack composed himself, hands on hips. A whistle from the ref. Jack stepped up.

Yes, Jack didn't miss penalties. He kept his nerve and smashed the ball high to the keeper's right, leaving him helpless and unmoving. The ball hit the back of the net and dropped down behind him in slow-motion to the delirious delight of the Vale players and parents – the deed was done!

The Vale players and mums and dads and dogs and everyone else spewed onto the pitch in scenes of wild jubilation, and the boys hugged and the mums cried; they all grabbed each other and whirled around in ecstasy in the muddy centre-circle, singing and patting and hugging and picking up, crying, grinning, laughing, punching the air and Wow! Wow! Celebrating!

We've done it! We've done it! We're going to Wembley! Wembully! Wembully!

The whole entourage was stung with emotion and were singing, dancing and hugging. Those boys had only gone and fucking done it!

Come on, Vale! We're all going to Wembley for the finals!

Amazing!

Chapter 19
The Butchers Arms

During the run-in to the end of the 1995-96 season, as Oxford harboured faint promotion hopes from Division 2, they hosted high-flying Blackpool, themselves a decent team who were top of the league then.

John had parked up near 'The Butchers Arms', and himself, Marc, Cannon and the Jimmies made themselves comfortable in the mahogany-coloured lounge. John ordered a jug of *London Pride* and a mixture of cheese & onion and ham & mustard rolls, as the lads seated themselves under the Sky Sports screen. A match from the top flight was playing, and they parked themselves around the table, pulling off Oxford scarves and their coats, which they draped over the back of the chairs.

The atmosphere in the pub was building, with fans nursing pints of foaming ale, grinning, laughing and chatting, in the build up to the match at the Manor.

'Eh!' barked John, looking away from the screen. 'Did you see that Liverpool/Newcastle match on Wednesday?'

'Jesus! It was amazing!' agreed Mark, through a mouthful of cheese & onion.

'Yeah, that Robbie Fowler is amazing,' joined Tommy Cannon, 'reminds me a bit of myself. Quite a useful striker.' Cannon grinned, picking up his *London Pride*.

'Twat!' offered Mark in response.

'What about Collymore, though, what a finish!' cried John.

Arguably (and later voted to be) the greatest ever Premier League game ever played, the match had had absolutely everything. Collymore had set up Robbie Fowler to put the reds up inside two minutes, only for Les Ferdinand to equalise with a crisp finish eight minutes later. Newcastle then took the lead on fourteen minutes through the stylish David Ginola.

The match swept from end to end with numerous chances, and after half-time, Fowler grabbed another equaliser to set the scores at 2-2. Liverpool had been playing wonderful football, but were knocked back once more two minutes later. The gangly Ecuadorian, Faustino Asprilla, capitalised on a long pass and used his pace to outstrip the Liverpool defence before toe-poking a long-range goal past the out-rushing keeper for the Toon, once more putting Newcastle back in the lead.

In a pulsating match, the effervescent Stan Collymore then steered a delightful Jason McAteer cross in for another Liverpool equaliser on 68 minutes. The Geordie fans were seen to be in some distress, wondering what exactly they had to do to actually win this match.

After relentless Liverpool pressure, in the second minute of injury time, and after a succession of Liverpool one-twos and some desperate defending on the edge of the Newcastle box, John Barnes switched a pass out on the left to the oncoming Collymore.

Stan took one touch and slammed a shot goalwards. The ball flew in at the near post to the absolute rapture of the Liverpool fans and team.

The cameras focused on the benches, where Kevin Keegan could be seen visibly deflated and slumped over the advertising hoardings, completely distraught, as the match wound down to end with Liverpool victorious at the last-gasp.

The result more or less killed Keegan's title hopes, and his Newcastle team that had been twelve points clear at the top of the table in January, were now virtually out of it.

Later Keegan described the match as 'a classic'. But despite their amazing attacking prowess, Newcastle United were also shipping goals. The consensus was that they were never going to win a title playing this gung-ho football, however attractive. And so, it was to be proved.

Nevertheless, it was a cracking, pulsating and incredible game of football.

Marc looked around the pub.

'D' you know how fuckin' lucky are we?' He raised his glass, grinning.

'Life doesn't get much better than this.'

'Eh?' Cannon looked bemused. 'What d'ya mean, Marc?'

'Well, it's a lovely pub, with great beer, good food, a live, promotion battle football match to watch, football on the telly, and good company! Life couldn't get much better!' Marc was beaming, holding up and waving his pint.

'Yeah!' agreed Jimmy Oram.

'Right!' John also consented.

'Unless you were Stan Collymore?' Tommy now looked far-off and thoughtful.

Everyone looked round at Tommy.

'What do you mean, Tom?' John raised an eyebrow at the group.

'I mean life as Stan Collymore!' continued Cannon sipping his beer.

'Yeah. Fit as a fiddle,' he went on, abstractedly, 'good looking, earning thousands a week, probably driving a Ferrarri, shagging Ulrika Jonson, playing up front for Liverpool, adored by fans and women alike, and playing alongside the likes of Robbie Fowler!'

The lads joined him in thought as they pondered the information.

He continued his ramble. 'With a big house in Cheshire, probably a villa in Spain, anything he wants, designer clothes, football and celebrity mates, probably free food in nice restaurants, a personal trainer and assistant, *and* still only in his twenties!'

'Fucking hell!' exclaimed the two Jimmies simultaneously.

John scratched his chin.

'You're right, Tommy! Life *could* get loads better than this.'

'You tosser!' cried Marc, laughing out loud.

They all joined in the laughter and threw the rolled-up plastic from their rolls at the grinning idiot Tommy.

'Shut up and get another jug of *Pride!*' John flicked a beer mat at their daft mate.

Following their discussions on the 'best premier league game of all time', the friends were witness to the 'greatest goal ever scored at the manor', the very same afternoon, scored by the amazing Joey Beauchamp. The brilliant winger hit a thunderous, dipping, 35-yard volley for a 1-0 win against League leaders Blackpool to keep Oxford's promotion challenge very much alive.

Back in The Butchers Arms after the game, buoyed by the goal and the Oxford result, they were still chuckling about Stan Collymore and how good life was – and how much better it could be!

If you were Stan.

Or Joey!

Chapter 20
1996
More Sixes and a Wembley Performance

Grove Challengers under-10s had had a reasonable season and brilliant sixes.

These were the six-a-side tournaments of the summer where Grove had now become an amazing and deadly force. They had won or become runners-up in six of the eight tournaments that they had entered –amazing considering they generally took an A and B team (which John mixed up). But when they had the little guys playing (Keeper, Elliott, McDonald, Revell, Brind, Gomm and Claydon), they were unstoppable and played the most amazing football, which blew most of their opponents away.

These sixes were the teams' little crowd-pleasers. The pressure was off. They knew that they had an awesome team, and the mums and dads brought wine, sandwiches, scotch eggs and homemade sausage rolls, blankets and lean-tos, newspapers, beer and music. It was a great social time for all the kids and their young parents to have a few minutes off and see the team playing with skill and style. The adults sought out a space under a tree and spread themselves out, tying up the dogs and bonneting the babes. All was well. This was always a Saturday or Sunday well-spent.

The team entered eight sixes competitions, winning at Radley, Eynsham and Wickham, finishing as runners-up at Westside, Cholsey and Garden City.

In the Cholsey tournament, a makeshift Grove B-team beat a makeshift Grove A-team (they were short of players and had to draft in three 'casual' local lads who were hanging around for a game) in an astonishing semi-final.

The match went on and ended 1-1. There followed three minutes each way of extra time. No more goals were scored as John and Alan madly consulted the rules in the program.

'In the event of a drawn game there shall be three minutes each way of extra-time.'

'In the event of no winner, after the extra three minutes each way, there will be further play until a golden goal is scored. The Golden Goal will decide the match.'

'Bloody hell,' said Alan, 'I hope it doesn't go on too long then. They're knackered!'

'What d'ya mean? How long does this go on for?' John was slightly puzzled.

'There's no limit, mate,' Alan observed. 'It's to the death!'

John looked incredulously at the boys, who were playing their hearts out and absolutely tired, labouring from one end to the other with ever decreasing stamina.

The three minutes each way soon ended, continuing the stalemate; the next period started. Due to the small teams and the bit of borrowing that had gone on, neither team had a sub – so the same boys toiled on in the heat, bashing away at each other as the minutes ticked by.

On and on they went, attack, defence, tackle, save, attack, tackle, run, save, tackle, goal kick, corner!

Five more minutes went by, six, eight, ten.

Some of the parents started complaining to John and Alan, then started targeting the ref and officials. But rules were rules, and after an extra fourteen minutes, Billy McDonald turned the ball in from close range under his best mate, Olly Dimblow, to eventually win the epic semi-final.

The biggest cheers came from the Cholsey boys, who were to be their opponents in the final (due to kick off eleven minutes ago)!

The two knackered Grove teams trooped off, some limping, some crying, but all exhausted.

The winners had to kick off five minutes later and, unsurprisingly, got thumped 3-0 by a Cholsey team buoyed up by the fact that they had a distinct physical and emotional advantage.

The picture that John took of the two Grove teams as they limped off was a treasure. It had every emotion ingrained that you could imagine!

Shit rules! Good fun!

Each tournament had different rules. But these had been the worst!

It couldn't detract from a great season of sixes.

The best success was at Radley; perhaps not the best win, but the style in which they delivered. The football, from the first kick-off, was exemplary, stunning and irresistible.

That day, the team attracted friends and admirers, because they played so well in each match that the whole of the crowd gathered to watch them.

They won their group, quarters and semis, playing superb, one-touch passing football, hardly conceding a goal, as they tore into their opponents. They were a fine sight in their black-and-white stripes, all still on the small side, but deadly on the ball.

The opposition hardly got a kick that day, and Horspath, St. Edmunds and Robins were swept aside in the group, then Abingdon 3-0 in the quarter-final; the semi was another one-sided affair against Carterton, who were easily dispatched before they faced their old rivals, Kidlington, in the final.

They kicked off and swept up-field, passing and sprinting away from the opposition and imposing all their attacking flair, enough to frighten any team, to take a 2-0 half-time lead through Claydon and Brind. The Grove parents, eager on the touchline, watched and cheered in support and in awe of the display of attacking football. Kidlington, as with all their other opposition that day, had nothing to offer in defence, and Grove split them open at will. Total football!

Ollie Gomm got the third goal, and then dissected the defence for Mark Brind to head down to the onrushing Claydon to make it four with a tap in. A brilliant success that won them the tournament.

'Bloody hell! It's like watching *Brazil 1970*, Gommy!' said the on-looking Graham Brewerton, here as a dad to watch his son, Joe, play for St. Edmunds.

'No, I know. They are absolutely on fire,' replied John proudly.

'Absolutely amazing, mate. Well done!'

'Brilliant mate!' added a passing Tim Butler, patting John on the back. 'Thank fuck we didn't meet you in the final!'

'Frightening!' Colin Barson also appreciated the display, grinning at John.

As the final whistle blew, the red-faced and puffing young team raced around hugging and whooping away like they had just won the World Cup, the parents almost as excited. And this wasn't just winning a final. This was the pinnacle. The boys had played exhibition football all through the tournament. Everyone who was at the event watched the final and was astonished by every game's performance.

John could hardly believe it, and he and Alan embraced on the touchline. The boys were grinning like fat Cheshire cats! They knew what they had done and that they had blown any opposition away as if they didn't exist.

The managers walked back to the control tent, shaking their heads in disbelief.

They got some great pictures, had the presentations – the boys still red-faced, puffing and buoyant – and they wandered away with their winner's trophy sticking up in the air as the crowd applauded wildly, and they made their way back to the Grove camp.

Some days stick in the memory, and this was the greatest sixes day of all. Perfect weather, perfect company, and ideal surroundings topped by a totally amazing level of performance. The brilliant winners' picture also made the *Oxford Mail!*

***

Now at Under-11, the Vale seven-a-side team, which had reached Wembley following the success at Paignton, were minor celebrities. They had won through to the Wembley finals to play as the curtain-raisers to the England v. Spain under-18s international.

John got a phone call at work from Lyn, as he read the back page of the *Oxford Mail* with a grinning Vale team being kitted out by a local sports shop.

'Guess what?' Lyn sounded pretty excited.

'No idea.' He was still in work mode. 'What?'

'Dave Stemp has just rung. He wants three of our players to go down to Wembley this week to do a promotional shoot with Sharon Davies and "Cobra" (one of the famous TV Gladiators)!'

'You're kidding!' cried John, wide-eyed. 'Who does he want?'

'Jack, Ritchie and…Ollie!' expostulated Lyn, now barely able to contain her excitement.

'You're fucking joking!'

'Straight up – I'm not kidding!' she continued. 'Amazing, eh?'

Well, the season had just got blooming madder!

Following the photoshoot and subsequent photos in the local press, there followed articles in the *Oxford Mail* and *Times*, all the local papers and a big spread in the *Wantage Herald*.

There was a personal letter of congratulations from the Oxford United manager Denis Smith, and a sponsorship for shirts from 'Touchwood Sports' – again featured in the local papers. There was a full page spread in the Oxford v. Brighton program by Youth Development manager, Malcolm Elias, also congratulating the team on their achievement.

In short, it was a little roller-coaster of support and congratulations from all angles. What a great result this had been for local schoolboy football with the finals around the corner at Wembley on 9th March 1996.

What a great occasion this turned out to be. The boys were whisked up to London on Friday morning, given a tour of Wembley and checked into the Wembley Hilton Hotel prior to the finals the next day. Their excitement was immense, and it actually got the better of some of the squad; Ollie in particular got a severe migraine and fell ill during the evening meal.

But the day arrived, and John, Lyn and Corine spewed off the coach when it eventually arrived in the Wembley car park. There had been some delays in getting there, and Lyn had hammered the driver into letting them out before he had parked so as not to be late.

'My son's playing at 1 o'clock, let us out! Quick! Or we'll miss the kick-off!'

'Calm down, love,' said John gently, 'we've got plenty of time.'

Nevertheless, they sprinted up the steps in front of the twin towers and raced up into the seats reserved for the parents, grabbing a beer on the way.

They proudly bought programs and settled down in the Wembley seats on the half-way line, up above the royal box and presentation area, high in the stands, awaiting a glimpse of their team and their boys.

The England v. Spain Under-18s International was the main highlight of the day, and it was due to kick off at 3 pm. But the Vale parents, along with all the rest of the semi-finalists, were sitting on tenterhooks, fraught with emotion and desperate to see their boys perform on the lush green grass of Wembley.

As the tension grew and the minutes ticked away, the parents were at last rewarded as the four teams of finalists emerged from the tunnel and ran up and down the touchline, looking up and waving madly, but unable to pick out their relatives who were sitting so high up.

The pitches were marked up as two, small-sided sevens pitches marked by cones, with smaller goals; as the teams took their place on the field, following Dave Stemp, they looked swamped by the hugeness of their surroundings.

Although Wembley was looking quite empty, there were over 18,000 fans there to watch the Youth International, and the noise generated was pretty awesome. Deafening when you consider these teams would normally have played their matches in front of a dozen and a half mums and dads!

Vale's first opponents were East Riding, a gritty Humberside outfit, who matched Vale for work and effort in the semi-final. But a goal either side of half-time, from the prolific Marc Reynolds, took the southern side into the final. The Vale of the White Horse team hung on to their advantage and finished two-nil victors.

The Vale boys looked comfortable on the ball and came off worthy winners, booking themselves a place in the final against Sutton – a very strong Surrey team. They also came out as 2-0 winners in their semi against the North finalists, Wakefield.

As they lined up for the final, the Sutton boys seemed to have the physical advantage. They were all big lads. This had never been an issue for the Vale boys – they had always managed to be competitive, plus normally more skilful and adept.

The match was very evenly contested until the stroke of half-time, when Sutton struck a great header from a poorly-defended corner to take the lead. The Vale hit back, and counter attacked through King, Claydon and Reynolds. With two minutes left, Gomm hit the bar with a dipping drive from outside the area. From the ensuing attack, Sutton swept into a two-goal lead when their big forward muscled his way through to slide the ball past the out-rushing Butler, to finally end the most amazing run of the Vale boys.

Unbelievably, these were the first goals they had conceded in the whole tournament! However, this was not to be their final, and Sutton hung on and went through as worthy winners by two goals to nil.

Now the Vale boys' heads did not go down. They were briefed by Stempy that win, lose or draw, they were to enjoy and remember the day in front of the fans, their parents, friends and siblings, and they all marched off smiling and joshing with each other.

Amassed on the running-track at the bottom of the steps, the boys were now able to see their families, waving deliriously and grinning up at them in their white *Predator* track suits!

And then it was time – time to climb those Wembley steps, up to the Royal Box, where they had all, dozens of times, seen the cup winners collect their League and FA Cups!

They were climbing these stairs, staring wide-eyed around at the crowd, stadium, parents, event, and it was them who were collecting their medals!

Dave Gomm

Arsenal and England's legendary coach, Don Howe, shook every boy by the hand and hung a medal around each boy's neck as they shuffled along the Royal Box, shyly taking in the applause and the moment.

There was wild and enthusiastic applause from the Wembley crowd as they made their way down through the supporters, medals swinging and grinning like maniacs. Not an actual win but a proper and amazing result.

Runners-up in a national final. Things couldn't have got *much* better!

And what a run! Everyone was proud, excited and elated – the boys, the coaches-and especially the parents!

Well done, the Vale.

Well done, Stempy.

And well done, boys!

Chapter 21
England v Spain Euro '96

It was 1996, and England were hosting *Euro '96*. After the disappointments in the last World Cup finals, the country was in a buoyant mood and looking forward to a major tournament with a strong team, which had a good mixture of top-class and also several world-class players. England had progressed through to the quarter finals quite smoothly, starting with a 1-1 draw against Switzerland.

They followed this with a very ordinary performance against Scotland, which started with a second-half, diving header from Shearer; they survived an equaliser when Gary McAllister's penalty was pushed away to his right by David Seaman. As England rallied, Paul Gascoigne burst through after 79 minutes. Receiving a pass from the left, with a great first-touch, he found space in the Scottish rear-guard and drifted towards the area. As he received the ball, with a quick look, his vision somehow enabled him to loft the ball over the hapless last defender, Colin Hendry. He whipped around Hendry, and as the ball dropped, he sublimely volleyed home a right-footer into the left corner of the net.

Wild celebrations ensued from the England players, and the Scots were beaten. The team was obviously in tune, and the result further united the England fans in the stadium and throughout the country.

If this game and result had lifted English spirits, the following game against the fancied Dutch – one of the tournament favourites – was truly incredible. The English gave the masters a lesson in football. On a wonderful and oh-so-rare-night, the third goal – started by Steve McManaman – found Gascoigne, who slinked past a defender on the left before finding Sheringham in space in the box. Everyone thought Teddy was going to shoot – he had a clear sight of the goal with plenty of space. But Sheringham unselfishly continued the move, sliding a first-time pass into Shearer's path, who had the simplest job of blasting the ball home unchallenged. Wembley erupted.

Even better things were to come when Teddy Sheringham stroked home an Anderson effort that came back to him off the keeper. 4-0 against the Dutch! Holland were fortunate to even get a consolation. The goal that made it 4-1 actually had them qualify on goals scored. Their goal difference was equal to Scotland's, but it was enough to send them through and Scotland home. England qualified top of their group!

Marc, John and Boily were staunch England fans. They watched the Swiss game in a packed Boars Head in Wantage, the Scotland game in the Bay Tree and the Holland game at John's house (having been to the Bay Tree who had the usual two bar staff on – or so it seemed). Anyway, having eventually forced their way in through the packed bar, they couldn't get served, and so they watched the game at home with ice-cold *Stella*, *Oranjeboom* and nibbles.

The quarter finals against Spain were held the following Saturday. Spain had won one and drawn two to qualify second behind France. They hadn't been too impressive, having drawn against France in their last group game after beating Romania 2-1 and drawing with Bulgaria 1-1. The mood in the country was beginning to boil, and the summer was good. The lads decided to watch the match at the Bay Tree again. There was the promise of proper seating in the lounge, and a flat-screen TV had been brought in to show the game. A barbeque had also been set up in the garden, so the Euro 96 Tournament – with England poised to reach the semi-finals – was really heating up.

John had a bit of work to do in the morning, but he met up with Lyn in the early afternoon as a sports day of sorts was being held down at Millbrook School. Ollie and some of the boys were taking part in it, as was Corine.

The community was good. Everybody knew everybody, so it was quite a social event. A scorching sun burst through the white, fluffy clouds as they entered the gates of the little, village-like primary school. The Brinds, Elliotts, Caseys and Harrises, amongst others, were there with their various offspring. There was also a barbeque set up, along with a few scattered craft, bric-a-brac and tombola stalls.

John bumped into Graham Brind, Sparkie's dad, and Alan Elliott.

'Oright boy?' asked Graham, coming over, eyes sparkling and head cocked. 'You going to enter the fifty meters?'

'You're having a laugh, Graham!' laughed John. 'I didn't even know there was one.'

'Oh yeah, chap! Got a few tasty rivals too!' said Ian Wilkins, Jamie's dad, motioning surreptitiously to Alan.

'How many adult races are there then?' John had little knowledge of the proceedings.

'Oh, just two or three. But the main ones are the parents' sprint, men and ladies – I won it last year, chap!'

Graham was beaming at the memory of his winning.

'Yeah, but I wasn't here last year,' said Elliott, with mock grandeur.

Graham stared at him for a few moments before saying, 'Let's have a fiver, Al?'

Graham continued to stare with feigned menace.

'I'm not a betting man, Graham.' Alan smiled, looking mildly annoyed. 'But go on then!'

John always knew he had some competitive parents, but normally they were on the same side. Fair enough. He had seen them galvanised against Abingdon when the away parents and linesman had been belligerent and partisan, but he gave a quick smile at the antics of these two. Alan had returned from the Navy and been to a couple of the boys' games and training sessions. And John had put the fracas of his first meeting with Sharon behind him. John and Lyn knew both couples socially but had been friends with Graham and Karen for years.

John was sensing an increase of hostility in the air between the two. But anyway, he wasn't even planning to stay for the sports. He was meeting Marc in the Bay Tree. So Lyn and he made their excuses, got the kids a burger each, and John left Lyn with the kids and the rest of the parents. The Bay Tree was virtually next door.

After the disappointing state of the pub for the Holland game, John was impressed. The Bay Tree manager must have had complaints and other walk-outs. The lounge had been transformed into a cinema. The manager had pulled all the curtains shut, removed all the tables and installed the flat-screen (a revelation in those days. It was literally a small, cinema screen with a projected image). It was like watching football at the movies. Only the sunlight streaming through the curtains made the images on the screen a bit pasty, grey and somewhat difficult to see.

The chairs were arranged in fifteen rows of eight. It took up the entire lounge, with access down the window side and lots of room at the bar to get a drink. At least six bar staff were bustling about, including the manager, and people were already milling about and taking their seats for the afternoon kick off.

As usual, John had to hunt for Marc in the bar, who he found wasn't there yet. Just as he had ordered a drink, Marc sauntered in the back way.

'*Morland's*?' asked John.

'Go on then.' Marc winced. 'What's it like?'

'Well, haven't tasted it yet, but you can see through it at least,' John quipped, taking a sip.

'Yes, very acceptable. What d'you think then? Same team, Fowler and Ferdinand on the bench, a great result against the Dutch on Tuesday and everything looking cushdie.' Marc waved his arm around in a grand gesture.

John turned to the seating with his foaming ale.

'Beautiful surroundings, amicable bar staff and plenty of them. A nice pint of *Morland's*, and a fine sunny day. Come and see the theatre, my friend – there's seating and everything.'

'I can't see us playing like that again, chap,' Marc countered with a grimace. 'That was a once in a lifetime performance. But we can always hope.'

'Well, Spain will be up for it,' said John. 'But I see us rolling them over in style.' Always the optimist!

Marc looked sceptical. 'Done any bets?' he asked.

John liked a football bet, but he usually went for long-shot-doubles, which very occasionally came in.

'No, too nervous. I don't want to tempt fate.' John smacked his lips, appreciating the great bitter.

Marc looked sideways and grinned.

As the pub filled, the national anthems were sung. Kick off had arrived. With 120 punters sitting and plenty standing, the pub was really buzzing. There were sporadic bursts of 'Enger-land, Enger-land', as boys and men – clad in identical England tops and shorts – downed pints in hope and desperation. Greene King, the landlord, had supplied plenty of mini St. Georges' plastic flags. The bar was adorned with them, and lots of them were strewn across the seats.

They had also supplied freebies: Union Jack plastic bowler hats, which you wouldn't normally be caught dead in, but these were also much in abundance. The atmosphere was tense, with a tingle in the air. The sun through the scarlet curtains was creating a different scene from the normal football days in the pub. And this was England. Football, they all knew, was 'Coming Home'. The song said so.

Kick off.

England started where they had left off against the Dutch, with three early chances from Gary Neville first, then from Gascoigne and Shearer, as they laid siege to the Spanish goal. As historically, though, the Spanish proved to be tough. They were organised opponents and managed to swing the game back their way. Salinas and Kiko were wreaking havoc in the English defence, and the Bay Tree crowd swore and then roared when Kiko had the ball in the net after 22 minutes.

'Offside!'

Ten minutes later, they scored again; this time, with Salinas also ruled offside. Worryingly, on both occasions, the English defenders had quietly let the Spaniards slip through the defence at will. The second decision – had the goal counted – would have been the defence's fault for not closing down, then standing appealing with their arms outstretched. It could have been embarrassing.

As the ref blew the whistle, the crowd bit their fingernails. This goal had looked distinctly on-side. The relief flowed through the watching supporters, who were increasingly becoming nervous, agitated, loud and critical the more they drank. 0-0 at half time, and the England boys considered themselves lucky to not be behind.

'Jesus, what was that all about?' shouted Marc at the bar. 'We were bloody lucky with that second one!'

'Only half-way boy!' countered John, although he was hardly convinced himself.

They settled back into their seats for the second half. Almost immediately, the substitute Alonso was brought down in the area by Gascoigne. Once again, the pub held its breath and erupted into the biggest cheer of the day as the referee awarded a free kick to England and booked Alonso for diving! Amazing!

'Good grief! Is this our lucky day?' shouted Smithy – a local, mate, electrician and ex-MPC five-a-side player – over their heads, following the latest decision.

'Lucky – We have been so, so lucky! Our name is on this trophy!' gleamed Marc.

'Come on, England!' John watched on with his mates, hoping for more luck.

The game continued to flow, as did the beer, and the pub atmosphere was beginning to throb. The animated, reddened faces became more intense and excited as they prayed for the result. The noise from the crowd was now deafening and littered with expletives; people leapt up from their seats and screamed at the ref and players with every incident.

By now, the floor was damp with spilt beer, swimming in some places, chairs had fallen over, and ashtrays were upturned; the air was thick and blue with cigarette smoke. People kicked chairs or dribbled little trails of beer as they tried to regain their seats. The Union Jack hats lay trampled and forgotten on the floor.

The game continued apace, and both sides continued to attack – Anderton and Shearer both missing chances for England. Spain had another penalty appeal turned down when Tony Adams launched an inelegant tackle on substitute Caminero. From the clearance, England swept up-field; after a flowing move, Shearer amazingly blasted the ball over the bar from a yard out, with the keeper a mere spectator, beaten. With the minutes ticking away and the levels at fever pitch, Kiko's shot was well saved by Seaman to keep England in the competition. The crowd was getting more boisterous and worried as time ticked on. They were desperate for England to score – and desperate for Spain not to!

Ninety minutes came, and still no score.

After 120 minutes, as Mr Batta blew the final whistle, the deadlock had not ended. Extra time had produced no 'Golden Goal', with Gascoigne coming the closest for the home team.

And so, it moved on to penalties.

Penalties.

England weren't good at penalties. The pub atmosphere, fuelled throughout the afternoon – and now swelled by the noise, the occasion and the fact that sports day at Millbrook had finished – was vibrant. Noisy, smoky, loud and tense. The England team re-grouped in the centre of the pitch. How did they look? Worried? Defiant? Confident? They were certainly exhausted, their hands were on their hips and they were squatting, panting and relieving each other from cramps.

What were the 76,000 in the stadium thinking? Awash with excitement, expectation and dread. All over England, men, women, and children who had been absorbed in this journey felt the same. All over the world in bars and front rooms, Englishmen – starved so often of success in the latter stages of major competitions – looked on and prayed. Could we do it? Or would it be another penalty shoot-out disaster and an early exit? Surely the Spaniards would be more nervous, faced with this huge partisan crowd. Would they keep their nerve?

The Grove parents from the sports day were now in the crowd, and mostly those who had started with seats had retained them. Many of the original occupants were seven parts drunk by now and ready to go to heaven – or hell. John tried to speak to Graham but couldn't hear or be heard. Their sons had followed them in; the place was filled, pulsating and swaying to the rafters. They greeted each other with a thumbs-up.

The television image closed in on Stuart Pearce, who was wheeling around, waving his arms and shouting at his team mates with a massively contorted face. 'Come on!'

The penalty competition was ready to go. Both teams were huddled in their groups. The atmosphere was electric, and the minutes ticked by.

Alan Shearer walked up to the area with a grim look of determination etched onto his face.

Here we go.

Shearer deliberately placed the ball on the penalty spot. He took a pointedly, lingering look at the keeper.

As the referee blew, he started his run-up. Top left-hand corner. 1-0! He wheeled away, grinning broadly with his trademark, one-arm salute.

The stadium erupted with a deafening roar. The pub went wild!

Hierro stepped up for Spain. The Spaniard hit his penalty well, but it smashed against the bar. Another roar. Drinks were spilt, glass was broken.

David Platt for number two. 'Yes!' Pandemonium. Mayhem.

Amor for Spain. Gets one back. Slips into the far left-hand corner. 2-1

Then Pearce.

Pearce. Stuart Pearce. The Stuart Pearce who had carried the weight of the nation for six years since his infamous penalty miss against Germany in the 1990 World Cup semi-finals. Another close-up, and Stuart Pearce shouted, for the nation to see-crystal clear 'I'm taking one. I'm taking one!' He's grabbed the ball. Stormed off down the pitch. Looking stern, ashen-faced and determined. Fans everywhere stood open-mouthed, not quite prepared for this astonishing bottle. Pearcy. Pearcy!

Pearce looked at the goal then at the keeper. Deliberately placed the ball. Paced to the edge of the area. Turns on his heel. A short run-up. The whole set up is Pearce.

Exactly the same set up as it was at the World Cup, Italia 90, six years earlier in Turin, when England drew 1-1 with Germany in the semi-final. In that penalty shoot-out, Pearce smashed his penalty too close to the keeper, who saved it with his legs, devastatingly sending England home one hurdle short again.

Six years of hurt.

Back to the present.

But now Pearce looked full of confidence.

The nation held its breath.

His run-up was only four steps. His left foot struck the ball, and the crowd watched as the ball was smashed like an arrow into the top corner, past the helpless goalkeeper.

The huge guttural roar from the crowd in the pub was aided by the fact that the crowd had stood and flooded forward. Boys who had been in the garden outside rushed in, swelling the mayhem. From the rear, chairs, bodies, beer, hats and the lot surged forward.

The back rows cascaded to the front as boisterous fans jumped, leapt, swung, cried, rolled, screamed and met. The seating arrangement crumpled and collapsed in the surging torrent, as fans leapt to the side for fear of being swept away.

'We've done it! We're there!' The pub was in disarray.

The image of Stuart Pearce lasted on the screen for a long, long time. His moment had arrived, and he was released. He looked like a cross between an axe-murderer and a Viking warrior as he saluted and roared at the berserk Wembley crowd. In the replay, he actually looked like a madman. A spontaneous burst of 'Football's coming home' roared throughout the pub. Mums from the garden had followed their sons to see what all the commotion was about.

But it wasn't over yet. The seats were pushed aside, and the fans surged closer to the screen.

Another penalty.

Belsu for Spain. Calmly sent Seaman the wrong way for 3-2.

More calm. Now the crowd, anticipating a victory, watched as Paul Gascoigne stepped up.

Surely Gazza?

Sure enough. Relief. Gazza kept his nerve for 4-2.

Now Nadal. Nadal to keep Spain in the match and in the competition.

Steps up. Places the ball. Another short run-up.

Seaman dives to his left. A great save. Another great save from the Man of the Match!

Euphoria. England have won!

We're in the semis! Drunkenly hugging, making deafening noise and drowning out the remaining commentary, the crowd spills out into the sun. Mad looks came from the mums left in the garden. A mini-rush of sheer delight. 'Enger-land, Enger-land!'

Boys, men and mates were running and hugging, punching the air.

The landlord stood by the bar, scratching his chin and trying to calculate whether his extra outgoings and expenditure had made a fortune, minus the obvious damages. He surveyed the carnage to his lounge and ruefully hoped for much more drinking as the evening went on. He needn't have worried. This was the beginning of a big celebration.

Marc and John had drunk seven pints. But they were still euphoric as they took their eighth one out to the garden twenty minutes after the game had ended.

Spain had been unlucky. And England had had their fair share of good luck for a change. But England were in the semis!

They went and sat with the Graham and some of the Grove mothers.

'How did the fifty meters go, Graham?' John queried, raising an eyebrow.

Graham looked daggers.

'Fuckin' Elliott beat me!' he hissed, glowering and gesticulating towards his adversary.

Alan, sitting on a facing wall caught the drift and raised his glass at the group with a sardonic smile.

'Fucking short head!' he glowered. 'Lucky twat!'

He had definitely lost his edge.

But England are in the semis!

Football's coming home!

Dave Gomm

Chapter 22
Belgian Visitors

So it was that the parents, boys and families of the under-11s and under-13s, along with the chairman and various old acquaintances, were in the lounge of The Bay Tree at 4 pm on Good Friday, when the visitors from Sint-Niklaas arrived in their coach.

The Belgian party had been exchanging visits every year for about twelve years, so there were many old friends among the older boys and parents. Some, whose sons and daughters had grown up, drove over in their cars for the weekend to 'unofficially' stay with their old friends. The Grove people would do the same by visiting their Belgian mates on home turf the following year. But to John's party, this was an exciting visitation. He and Lyn were hosting three boys, one of whom was the son of the Sint-Niklaas chairman, Herman.

As the coach unloaded its Belgian visitors into the pub car park, Dave and Pete's parents hovered in anticipation of meeting their new lodgers for the first time. The grinning Belgians met and shook hands as they were announced and introduced to their allotted host families. The Grove contingent ushered them into The Bay Tree and bought drinks for their visitors, bustling round the tables in the lounge amid rucksacks and spare anoraks.

Without wasting too much time, Bill Nelson welcomed them all, and after the welcoming speeches and a quick review of the itinerary, families and guests began to filter out through the back of the pub to walk or get a car ride back home.

John and Lyn stayed on with Pete, Alan and a few others, but weren't long, conscious of the fact the families had left Belgium early in the morning and had been travelling all day. Their boys, Martin, Thomas and Nicki, were three quite different characters, who started off being very quiet and demure, becoming more jaunty and cheeky after a short while with the family.

Martin was the eldest. He was a blond-haired, blue-eyed, Nordish-looking lad, who was quiet, with good English. He soon became the unofficial spokesman for the three boys. Thomas was right in the middle with the temperament, stature and alacrity about half-way between the other two boys.

Nicki, the chairman's son, quickly came to be the cheekiest, with a heavily accented voice and long locks of dark flowing hair, resembling a brown-eyed Mowgli from *The Jungle Book*.

Once they had established the boys in their rooms, with some sulky and sarcastic comments from Corine – who gave up her room for them – the family and the Belgian boys wolfed down their homemade burgers; after a little introduction, the lads all went off to bed, dog-tired after a hard day's travel.

The Belgian itinerary was pretty robust. After the meeting, troop dispersal, Skittles and disco, the Saturday morning was free, followed by indoor football at Faringdon Leisure Centre. The Wantage Town Centre, Abingdon and the White Horse monument were busy visitors attractions, with the parties of mixed families bumping into each other as they tried to entertain their guests.

The Saturday morning was cold and clear, and after breakfast, the Gomms took all the kids and Sally up to The White Horse Hill, as the morning was free. As they walked up to the ruined castle site, the Vale of the White Horse spread below them in all its glory on that beautiful, frosty morning. Corine and Ollie and the three boys were getting on well. They smiled when they saw that a vast number of Belgian visitors with their hosts were also following the same path! Martin and the boys loved Sally and were throwing sticks for her as she dashed about the hills.

After lunch at the White Horse, Woolstone, the party went back to Grove and got their kit for the afternoon at Faringdon. The agenda was – under-11s, under-13s, mens', followed by the ladies' five-a-side. Grove won the under-11s but lost the under-13s, unremarkably lost the ladies' match with a really inexperienced (clueless) ladies team, including Corine, Becky Elliott and Lyn Gomm in goal (who remarkably saved a penalty – if you class 'saved' as the ball hitting you on the back of the head!).

In the ladies' match, the Belgian ladies had brought over a very strong, experienced ensemble. Helen Casey, Jill Claydon, Lyn, Jane Dimblow, Karen Brind and several others, including many of their daughters supporting, nervously took to the five-a-side court. They had a real good go for a few minutes, but they were ladies and girls rather than women footballers.

Grove did win the shrieking though, by miles, as the girls mis-kicked, fell, crashed and tripped the opposition. It was a very funny sight. The Belgian women took it all in stride, and they ended up winning both games convincingly, 7-2 and 5-2 (with the help of some dodgy, helpful home refereeing and three generous Grove penalties)!

So, first blood was to the Belgians, and then it was the boys' turn. John and Pete both had two five-a-side teams, and after the women's game, the atmosphere changed to something a little more competitive.

The Leisure Centre at Faringdon was good, as there were viewing galleries on either side of the main court, and the entire party squeezed in to watch as John's younger age group came up against their Sint-Niklaas opposition.

The teams he had picked were quite equal, although John did like Ollie and Ritchie on the same side. Even though they were both quite slight, their interaction and passing made them very difficult to play against. They notched up a 3-1 win in good fashion. This was followed by a 2-0 win against the 'B'-team – Mark Brind cracking in a brace, to go through to the final.

Pete's first team also went through, but his 'B'-team were not as strong and went out 0-3 to much stronger opponents. In the finals, Grove 'B' under-11s narrowly beat Grove 'A' 3-2. It was a great little five-a-side match with plenty of good skill and movement, the Grove boys fighting hard to overcome each other. Pete's 'A'-team also won their final, on penalties, with Paul Rose blasting the winner high into the small goal to seal it.

Then came the men's matches, which were interesting as Grove had quite a number of proper footballers including Jeb Ciampioli, Graham Brind, Pete Rowes and Alan Elliott. John put himself in the 'B'-team and picked a strong 'A'-team.

To be fair, the Belgian contingent were footballers through the age-groups. You had young men in the early throes of puberty to Herman the chairman, probably in his late 50s.

The Grove 'B'-team put up a good fight, eventually losing 1-2 to a stronger team, played in good spirit. The teams played a bit of football, Grove just losing out.

The 'A'-team final was a bit different. It got competitive – tackles were fierce, and it was a real scrap. Mike Rowes led the attack with Graham, and they had a real go at the (slightly older) Belgians. The whole group – English and Belgian parents, their children, wives, parents, friends and relatives – watched in horror as, half-way through and for no apparent reason, Mike and Graham were suddenly locked in stalemate, grappling each other with intent in the middle of the floor.

'Yeah, what the fuck?' Graham was trying to get his arms around the squirming figure of Mike. 'C'mon asshole, I'll fucking do ya!' cried Rowes in retaliation.

They crashed to the floor, entwined.

'Whoa, whoa, lads, calm down.' Alan Elliott came between them to calm the situation.

Mike had his fist drawn back as if to smash Graham, who glowered back at him, both still locked in the tussle. Graham's left hand was locked around Mike's neck!

'Get the fuck off me, Graham!' Mike hissed from his pinned-down stance.

The Belgians looked on at the spectacle in astonishment.

The Grove spectators were mortified.

'Let him go, I'll finish him!' Jesus, Graham was beside himself.

'Jesus, lads! For fuck's sake,' Elliott held them apart as well as he could manage, 'calm down and get on with the match!'

Which, thankfully, they did. And they were best mates afterwards!

There was absolutely no idea of what went on or why the handbags. Twats!

John stood on the touchline shaking his head and feeling embarrassed for the Belgian visitors.

And Grove, despite the in-fighting, won 2-0!

After the matches, the crowd moved on to Grove, to the Rugby Club. As they assembled in the chilly air, the hosts and their families emerged with drinks to the front of the clubhouse. Directly in front of the clubhouse, there was arranged a skittles tournament for the guests and their visitors. The pitches had been marked out with white lining; five pitches, all framed by the planked 'ends' to catch the wooden balls as they hurtled down. The weather was still okay, if a little chilly, and Christine Barguss had her little hot dog stand running, so the delicious aroma of fried onions wafted across the front of the club.

The Belgians took to the skittles, and some had played on previous meetings, but everyone, including the kids had a go and enjoyed the night. The various teams of four were invariably a mix of Challengers' players and parents, and their Belgian visitors. There followed a disco in the Rugby Club to round the night off.

The disco that followed was good, with lots of cranked-up, cheesy music blasting out and a good deal of meeting, singing and drinking. John and Lyn had been there all evening, so they had a pretty crooked walk home, much to the amusement of the boys. Lyn had uncharacteristically walked along the small single-bricked wall in the Rugby Club car park, achieving legendary status amongst the Belgian lads, and to the chagrin of Ollie, who, quite rightly, accused his mother of being 'pissed'.

When they got home, John put on a Ghostbusters mask and chased them about a bit, and they shrieked and ran about screaming, 'Drunkie! Drunkie!' Corine had got the video camera out and videoed the meal and the antics.

It was all good fun, and the family and boys became good friends that night. Lyn had cooked a beef stew and dumplings, but she wasn't sure whether the foreign visitors would be up for it. It went down like a house on fire! They ate the lot and wiped out the crockpot with bread to finish it off.

By the end of the evening, the three Belgian lads were already part of the family, hooting and shrieking with laughter until everyone's sides hurt. They were, after the long day, severely ready for their beds, which they happily tumbled into, knackered.

All in all, a bloody good experience.

Sunday bought a similar clutch of games: under-11s, under-13s, men's and ladies' games. All of them went off really well, with a great deal of laughter, camaraderie and silliness. Pennants were exchanged, teams were mixed with ages and abilities, and a jolly good time was had by all.

Again, the ladies' game was really good fun, with the Belgian ladies, better prepared and seasoned campaigners, coming to the fore to win comfortably. But not without some mass-hysteria and side-splitting laughter throughout.

The evening do was the pre-filmed horse racing with much drinking, merriment and more raucous laughter, which both nationalities, young and old, enjoyed without restraint.

When it came to Monday morning, seeing the group off became a painful affair. As the coach pulled out on the way to the Tower of London, their entertainment on the return journey, there were many tears, fond goodbyes and 'until next times'.

Martin, Nicki, and Thomas had, in a very short span of time, endeared themselves to the Gomm family, who had all had a marvellously and, somewhat unexpectedly, brilliant experience. As had everybody else that had hosted.

John, Lyn and the kids, along with the other Grove parents, friends and associates were so sad to see them go! Blimey, they hadn't known these people three days ago, and now they were heartbroken at their leaving.

They couldn't wait for the return trip to Belgium next year to renew their friendships.

The family wiped a tear away as their three boys, having made their way to the back seat of the coach, now smiled and waved madly to their adopted English family.

The coach cruised silently down the car park, turned left and onto Cane Lane, where all the Sint-Niklaas people on the left side presented themselves through the coach windows to the watching Grove crowd, waving and blowing kisses.

The Grove delegation – parents, players and siblings – waved weakly as the coach drove out of sight, heavy-hearted at their departing friends, new and old.

Bring on Belgium next year!

Chapter 23
Promotion and another Germany Semi-Final

Following the defeat at Bristol Rovers in December, Oxford United went on to become a major force in the Football League Division 2 (Then the old Third Division). With Phil Gilchrist and Matt Elliott dominating their back four as a rock-solid centrepiece, and Aldridge, Beauchamp, Rush and the irrepressible Moody rampant in attack, things went from ordinary to wonderful.

Unbelievably in that season, 1995–96, United hadn't yet won away. That was until they defeated Burnley by two goals to nil at Turf Moor on January 30th, with goals from Chrissy Allen and Stuart Massey. The cut-price re-signing of Joey Beauchamp for just £75,000 was massive to the team, who then went on in the league to win sixteen, draw four and lose just five in the last four months of the season.

The Manor had become a fortress again, where the Us had won eleven and drawn three since the Rovers game, including a 3-0 midweek drubbing of enemies Swindon (Aldridge, Elliott and brilliantly Joey Beauchamp – back in the side and mesmeric form after his West Ham and Swindon episodes – scoring in that demolition).

Another notable home result in this period was a 5-0 win against Burnley, including an astonishing fifteen-minute cameo from Moody, who managed to smash a hat-trick in those fifteen minutes and a massive 6-0 destruction of Shrewsbury Town. The club had also managed the £100,000 signing of David Rush from Sunderland; he was, in this period, a very willing, busy and creative worker, normally introduced as a substitute in the latter part of the season.

At this time, John and Ollie had season tickets to the Manor Club, the 'relatively' luxurious, former dressing rooms and stand, where you could get a pint easily. It was comfortable, uncrowded surroundings, and they had very easy access to their season-ticketed seating, which was comfortably situated right at the junction of the Beech Road and Cuckoo Lane End, at right angles (i.e. facing the pitch from that corner).

It was a great day when on Saturday 4th May 1996, they took their place in the club with Marc for the last game of the season – a match that they needed to win – against Peterborough United.

As they took their seats, everyone in the ground was well aware that a win would automatically promote Oxford from the second position and up to Division 1. Peterborough at home? In their current form? Absolutely no problem.

Truthfully, given the occasion, a *reasonable* crowd – 7,535 attended to watch the slaughter and potential promotion party. Peterborough, however, were in no mood to be scapegoats. They matched Oxford in every department, marking Matty Elliott in numbers when he ventured forward for set pieces, and pressurising the midfield and wingers to deny Oxford chances.

The chances did come, but the home team failed to look impressive; Joey Beauchamp spurned a couple of gilt-edged chances alongside misses from good opportunities from Massey, Elliott, Rush and Moody.

They were playing okay, but without the vim and swagger of the previous home-match demolitions. Such was the resolve of the Posh that day, that Oxford couldn't muster a single corner in the first-half.

Marc, Ollie and John watched on in frustration, eventually climbing down the stairs of the Manor Club at half-time for a frustrated beer as the teams trooped off 0-0.

'Bloody hell, we're shocking!' groaned John, as another pass went wayward.

'We look so frightened,' noted Ollie in disbelief.

'We'll be ok when we score.' Marc didn't sound too convincing.

'Jesus, we haven't even had a bloody corner.' John sprang from his seat as the ref blew for half-time.

'Rushy'll sort it, Dad!' checked Ollie from his seat and diving into bag of cheese and onion crisps.

'Let's bloody hope so, son!' He motioned for Ollie to join them, but the young man declined.

With the start of the second half, there was much more urgency from the home team and much more pressing.

'Come on, Oxford!' willed the crowd.

Pressure.

Pressure.

Push on.

Attack.

Attack.

Pressure, push on, attack – and shoot – blocked-wide, cross-out, back in. Header, keeper up…It's a corner!

Most of the Peterborough defence were trying to mark the gloriously deadly Matt Elliott as the deep cross swung in from Joey Beauchamp.

Elliott, menacing as ever, from set pieces, attracted three defenders who tussled and leapt for the in-swinging ball.

One of the desperate defenders managed to get a touch on the ball, flicking it away from the danger of Elliott – but also sending it over the floundering keeper and onto the hapless, defending, full-back Grazioli.

The Oxford crowd rise in anticipation. Grazioli has nowhere to go – he's under pressure from the burly and oncoming Paul Moody, and he's facing the wrong way…

Nothing he can do except swing a foot at the ball – The net bulges. An own goal.

The breakthrough!

1-0 the Us!

The touch-paper was ignited, and Oxford started to play. All of a sudden, the shackles were off and the swaggering, irresistible tide had turned; wave after wave of United attacks swept forward as the Posh crumbled.

The Manor, not packed but swelled with impetus, started to rock, the London Road creating a pulsating backing with their songs, yellow and blue everywhere. All sides of the Manor – as it did on these occasions – became a bear-pit of noise and intimidation. Each stand was so close to the pitch that it seemed to weigh down on the opposition and give the home team an extra man.

On 66 minutes; Rush, Massey – MOODY!! 2-0!

And just two minutes later, the hard-working Massey combined with Gray and Gilchrist, whose cross was flicked-on by Rush. A beaming Matt Elliott steamed in to head the third goal and surely the winner.

The visitors' defence creaked under the onslaught; in another four minutes, it really was all over. Mike Ford slotted a delightful through-ball that split Peterborough wide open. The ever-industrious David Rush ran in to finish with a sublime chip over the on-rushing keeper Jon Sheffield.

'Waaagghh!' screamed the crowd, and Oxford had done it in style.

'Come on, you Yellows!'

'Told you Rushy would do it, Dad!' Ollie grinned, as John swung his son round in celebration.

Mickey Lewis came on for Rush as Oxford – then strutting about, playing exhibition football and after ten years of decline – was halted in half a season and one half of football in one afternoon. The game finished with grinning Oxford players applauding the noisy and delighted crowd.

Manager Denis Smith – almost sacked near the start of the season – was the new messiah and was seen cavorting around the pitch with David Rush in a ridiculous tartan cap and ginger-haired Scotch wig at the final whistle. But ba-jesus! He had done it. And truthfully, in dynamic style. The crowd stayed and swayed and chanted and bellowed in a sea of yellow and blue.

Promotion. Oxford were up! And back where they belonged!

Down in the bowels of the Manor Club – as Massey and Ford and Elliott mixed with the remaining Oxford fans – the chanting and atmosphere was charged with success and promotion. Couldn't get much better!

And second in the league to Swindon! In the same league again next season.

Come on, you Yellows!

'U's are going up, I say U's are going up!'

'U's are going up, I say U's are going up!'

***

On the way to the Bay Tree, just before the Euro '96 semi-finals v. Germany in June 1996, John's (or rather Lyn's) 'pig', their second car, their old VW Jetta, spluttered out of life on the Denchworth Road, 150 yards from the pub. God knows what happened. John was already late for the second Euro semi-final, and so he pulled over and casually parked up on the street.

'I can deal with that tomorrow morning' he thought to himself, stepping along the pavement towards the already booming pub.

Bedecked and awash, the pub was covered in England flags and banners, with red and white flower arrangements and fans milling around out front.

It was a balmy evening, balmy and light, and all the doors were open to allow access and air. The sound system was up full blast, and the crowd of fans inside and out were raucous already.

He muscled his way into the overcrowded public bar and found that Marc, Boily and the rest of the gang were already well into it. The beer was flowing, and the place was so packed that you could barely stand or see the screens.

'Where you fucking been?' screamed Marc over the din.

'Fuckin' pig's broken down!' John returned, pushing towards the bar.

'Ha ha! Where is she?' Marc screamed over the noise again.

'Left it down the road.' John responded, looking at the telly. 'What's the news?'

'No news.' Marc nodded optimistically. 'Fowler's on the bench, all fit, looking good!' 'What d'ya want? *Morland's*?'

'Yeah.' John studied the beer pumps. 'No, I'll tell you what. The day I've had, I'll have a *Stella*!'

Marc passed the gloriously cold, frothing *Stella* over as the match started.

John swept the ice-cold *Stella* to his lips and gasped in exhilaration at the cold!

'Come on, England!' he cried. 'Got any bets on?'

The prelude and punters were already reporting from a packed Wembley. This was on the same pitch just three months after Ollie and the Vale boys had lost their final at the same venue! The game kicked off, and England swept into the attack and had an immediate shot from Paul Ince that the keeper struggled to push over the bar.

Three minutes in, and from the resulting corner, Alan Shearer – who else? – stooped to head home and give the hosts the perfect start.

The lead was short-lived, and Germany equalised thirteen minutes later when Helmer turned in the area and crossed for

Kuntz to smash the ball past David Seaman. England continued to push, and Sheringham had an effort cleared of the line; then Shearer, again, could have grabbed the lead with a bullet header from an Anderton cross that flew inches wide.

'Oooohhh!' screamed the crowd. 'Aaarghhh!'

'Fuck!' John and Marc shouted at the screen together.

More beers were passed over, and the pub's temperature began to climb. Surely, we would win this. Bloody Germans.

They escaped outside at half-time, desperate that it was still level, and got some welcome respite from the heat and pulsating sweatiness of the bar. John got another *Stella* and another round in as they swore, cursed and dissected the first half between them.

'We should be two up by now,' groaned Boily. 'Gotta take our chances!'

'We'll be alright, we're all over 'em!' Marc's optimism had not abated.

'Yeah, they're bloody Germans though, ain't they?' observed Boily on his way to the bar. 'You got to bloody bury them!'

The second half resumed, and things started to get tighter.

Nobody wants to lose a semi-final. Thomas Helmer had a great chance, which he steered just over the bar. England attacked down the right, and the ball fell perfectly for Darren Anderton, twelve yards out. He struck it perfectly and watched in disbelief as the ball came back off the post with the German keeper, Kopke, beaten. The crowd in the pub roared in disbelief!

By now, the atmosphere in the pub was dripping. The crowd groaned as the chances went begging with extra-time, and the Golden Goal time started looming.

People were starting to get edgy, wild and pissed; the noise level soared as they roared the team on in a desperate search for that elusive winner.

Moments later, from a similar move, Shearer found space. His cross-shot beat all the German defence with the goal gaping and unguarded. Gascoigne, racing in unmarked, flailed and failed by inches to poke in the Golden Goal. A stud, a lace, a breath – any touch and England were in the final. He crashed in and was somehow beaten by the pace on the cross. The touch never came. This game was going to penalties.

'Fucking wanker!' yelled Boily.

'Just unlucky,' countered Marc.

'It's gonna be penalties!' John cried, resigning to the outcome.

'Wankers! Fucking wankers!' Boily was seething with rage. The truth is that either team could have won this encounter since it was really close between two great teams.

'Just like Euro 90?' he drunkenly spluttered, cracking his empty pint glass down on the table, then turning off towards the loo. 'We're going to lose on fucking penalties again!'

By now, the atmosphere in the Bay Tree had moved to hopeful/malevolent.

People stared, glassy-eyed. The noise was now more rumbling gloom, with a foreboding of impending doom.

Germany didn't lose penalty shoot-outs. England did. That's the way it was. Inevitably, after successful penalties, and at 5-5, Gareth Southgate – looking as nervous as a kitten in front of 100,000 nail-biting fans – stroked his penalty to Kopke's right, soft and easy for the keeper to smother.

Southgate disintegrated. Such responsibility died with failure.

'Shitting fuck!' screamed Boily.

All eyes, prayers, hopes and fears silently wishing as the German captain, Andreas Moller, strode up looking completely nonplussed.

The hopes of a million Englishmen and 100,000 in the ground, wished, pleaded and hoped beyond hope that this would sail into the stand.

Two steps and Moller lashed his penalty high into Seaman's net, giving the keeper and England absolutely no chance.

Desperation. The pub dropped into almost complete silence.

'Fucking shit!' screamed Boily, drunkenly racing out of the pub and into the street.

'Shite, shite, shite!'

By now, the lads were all pretty well oiled.

But John was hammered. Not used to drinking *Stella* on a session, he was past the coherent stage; the shutters were down, and the whole pub seemed the same. Everyone was walking round in a daze, the German team were hugging each other on the pitch and…

England, again, were out of the competition.

Another semi. Another one against the Germans. And another loss.

Cigarette smoke, betting slips, glasses, hats, sodden beer mats, half-finished pints and pools of stale beer, piss, discarded flags, banners, fag-ends, ashtrays, roll-ups, hot-dog boxes and all the shite you could think of were left littering the pub as the disgruntled England fans streamed out, gutted.

'Jesus Christ, we're out to the Germans again?' John couldn't hide his despair.

'Fuck it, I'm off home,' said Marc. 'Where's that idiot gone?' The pub was emptying quickly. Boily was already halfway to Wantage – on foot.

The two friends blankly took one last look towards the screen.

The dancing Germans were still there…

'See you…laterrr,' slurred John. They staggered out the front door, right and left.

The fans melted into the summer night as the pub cooled down and the cleaners moved in to clean up the mess. Another occasion where they should all be celebrating and yet again, England fans were in mourning.

Could things get any worse?

Mind you, how often have England reached the semi-finals?

For England, that's almost a result!

With these thoughts cannoning around his befuddled head, John reached home.

He stood swaying for a good while, fumbling and trying unsuccessfully to find a key that fitted the lock in the front door.

'Good game?' Lyn opened up the door that John was still struggling to open.

Her drunken husband dejectedly shook his head.

She despaired as he blankly stared back, key in hand.

Lyn watched as the retreating frame of her drunken husband made steady, swaying progress up the stairs, muttering something that she couldn't clearly make out, but that sounded a bit like 'Bloody Germans!'

The *Stella* had been a massive mistake, which he realised with a vengeance the next morning.

He was so ill he had to leave work early, but instead of going off to fix the abandoned 'pig', he went straight to go home to bed with a raging head and the mother of all hangovers.

Chapter 24
Under-11s
We've Got There!

By the start of the under-11 season in 1995–96, John and his Grove team had reached a new level. The boys were fit, confident, determined and used to winning. The improved training and match-practice had helped them reach this level, and they thought they could take on, match and beat any opponent in the area.

With the likes of OUFSC, Abingdon, Highworth and Kidlington in the 'A' League, they could be sure of a game every week.

They had the sponsored kit, training kit, club tracksuits and all the support within the club they needed; after a few training sessions, they were ready for the forthcoming action and campaign within the Oxford B-Line League. They had a proper trainer and warm-up, pre-match routines. Short of nothing but a couple of players in reserve.

By now, everything was busting! – The Vale trials, schools football, and the new league was all going on at the same time. And the boys were dying to play. Johnny Ashford was beginning to demand a regular place in the team, and Danny O'Sullivan became the regular left back. John managed to re-secure the signing of Sevier, but Steven Casey and John Monery had stepped off into the B-team, joining Charlie Harris and Colin Mercer.

The moody Wiggins was still in the mix and brilliant on his day. Though the nucleus of the team was strong, the cover was definitely sparse.

Dimblow

Elliott   Webb   Wells   O'Sullivan

Revell   Gomm   McDonald   Ashford

Brind   Claydon

Subs: Wiggins, Sevier

The boys had also, quite naturally, grown; half the team were beginning to sprout up, especially the keeper Olly Dimblow, Johnny Wells and Peter Wiggins. As the stature of the team increased, the massive pitches began to become increasingly manageable. The boys were able to make it up and down the pitch with much greater ease. No more defenders not allowed over the half-way line!

The convoy pulled out of the Gomm-by and twenty minutes later, filtered into Radley, where they were met convivially by their hosts. It was a fine September morning in the country. John watched as the boys went through their pre-match training regime with Alan. Sean O'Sullivan was already holding the orange linesman's flag in preparation for running the line. The boys looked great in their new training tops: black and gold with the *Challengers* logo emblazoned across the back.

'Blimey, look at the team,' John murmured to Lyn proudly. 'Don't they look great?'

'Like a proper football team,' his wife admitted, smiling. 'Yes, love, they do look the part,' she continued. 'Let's hope they play as good as they look.'

'Yep, we really have come a long way.' John walked her towards the pitch. 'They're fit, happy, and raring to go. A bit different from our start at the under-7s at Didcot.'

She smiled reflectively.

'Well, they are up for it,' joined Alan, as he sauntered up to the group.

'Come on!'

The pitch was perfect, with the green, dewy grass, the white lines and goalposts and the blue sky creating a beautiful scene – a perfect one on which to play some sport.

When the pitch was still being set up – with the corner flags being prised into the clay and the clanking of the hammer on the goal post joints – the Radley parents busied themselves in preparation for the game.

John walked with Sally on the lead around the pitch, on the far side, to deposit his bucket and sponge near the half-way line. He approached two Radley parents, walking back towards the clubhouse and caught a bit of their conversation.

'Ere – this is that team that's got them two nutters on the touchline, e'nt it?'

'Oh, them two gob-shites that never stop screaming at the boys?'

'Yeah, that's them. They never bloody stop!'

'Ah well! To each his own. Noisy buggers though, let's hope we stuff them!'

Bloody hell! They were talking about John and Alan! Blimey. He had never realised they were that bad! Sure, the boys (at least their boys) needed constant reminding about keeping their positions, playing attackers onside, moving off the ball, etc.

Maybe other teams didn't need so much work in this department, but this Grove team did.

Certainly, John and Alan had found it necessary to be involved. But, to their knowledge, they had never been labelled 'nutters' before. John smiled and shook his head as he passed the men, then chuckled as he thought of telling Alan. He was also niggled and had a mind to not get so vocal in the future. Assholes!

If the opposition had noticed, surely the Grove parents had? What were they thinking? Nobody had ever said anything, and they all seemed pretty happy – maybe that was down to results. Fuck. Who knew? But he wasn't going to lose any sleep over it.

He did mention it to Alan before the kick-off, and the two mates had a laugh over it. But to be fair, they were both not noticeably so noisy, vocal or animated throughout the game!

With a wink from Alan and a rousing 'Come on, Grove' from the huddle, the team took up their customary starting positions. Nods and thumbs up from Sean O'Sullivan and the Radley linesman to the ref and the managers. The referee put the whistle to his lips, and the new under-11 Oxford B-Line League was under way.

These boys had now been playing together for four years, and as they grew, so did their knowledge, know-how and skill. They knew how John wanted them to play, and they knocked the ball around with purpose, little one-twos here, safe, short passes there – a bit of skill when it was needed – carefully probing and holding possession.

McDonald held the ball and slipped it ahead to Gomm. A little turn and a feint – Jamie Elliott overlapped. The ball slipped back to Revell – a clever step-over, a dummy and a flick up to Brind; Sparkie holds it up, holding off the defender; Back to Wells, galloping forward from the half-way line; a look up; Claydon makes a run inside his defender; Wellsy's pass dissects the defence, and he's away; Ritchie beats the on-rushing full back – looks inside – a pass to Gomm – one touch to Brind. A first-time pass back to Claydon, inside the area; square to Revell and…GOAL!!

Ritchie Claydon was instrumental all day in terrorising the poor Radley right back to create both goals. The performance also echoed the work and bonding that the unit had built. Everyone knew their jobs, the passes and flicks, the running off the ball into space, the awareness, touches and lay-offs, the through ball and the anticipating of a run off the ball.

Ritchie had been outstanding and was a constant threat, but the work-rate and guile of the other team members made a difficult opponent for any team. This team had become a unit – fit, confident and smart.

This made the team a joy to watch. The marking, the jockeying, the crunching tackles, the sweeping of the ball forward on the counter attack – it all meant this group had arrived as a *team*. These boys would work, defend, attack and celebrate their footballing skills as an arrival and something that was very difficult to defend and play against. Success breeding success.

The defence, marshalled by Captain Sean Webb and Dimblow, was tight and hard to beat; if Grove got the chance to re-cycle the ball, they swept into attack again through midfield!

This was all directly related to the training, growing and the relative size of the pitches and goals.

It was a great start to the new league, sweeping aside a spirited Radley by two goals to nil, with goals in each half and Johnny Ashford sealing the win after Revell's opener.

By now, the Elliotts were good friends of the Gomms. John and Alan got on really well, as did Sharon and Lyn, while both Rebecca and Corine, and Trigger and Ollie were best mates, in and out of school. They all went off to the Barley Mow, Clifton Hampden, for some drinks and lunch to chew the fat, dissect the game, celebrate, and talk about the boys or the latest video game!

'Well, chap, that wasn't too shabby, was it?' John arrived at the table, menus under his arm.

'Outstanding! We were great,' agreed Alan. 'I reckon we'll be ok in this league.'

'Well, I hope so,' replied John. 'Radley were no mugs. Mind you, they have some really good players.'

'Yeah, and they had a good keeper, that little right back and that tall lad in midfield.'

'See what happens next week against Robins.' He smiled over the menu. 'But we were good!'

'Cheers!'

'Salute!'

***

A visit to Robins (Swindon), which were newly appointed to the Oxford League, was where Roger Sevier made his debut. John played him up front, and he looked really lively, although everyone could see he was very nervous. Just before half-time – as Claydon squirmed past a defender, drew the keeper and slotted a delightful curler towards the corner of the net – Roger, like a good striker, was on hand to follow up.

He patiently allowed Ritchie's shot to score. He was a yard away from the empty net and could easily have stabbed the ball in, but he didn't want to steal Ritchie's glory; when the ball narrowly missed the target, struck the post and rebounded to his feet, Roger was so shocked and nervous to impress that he completely miss-kicked the rebound, almost making an air-shot and scuffing the ball wide. Poor lad looked like his world had just ended as he trotted away, head in hands! He couldn't believe he'd missed the sitter! Too polite! Not greedy enough!

Order was restored in the second half, and the half-time substitute Mark Brind scored a brace, supported by another Revell screamer for a convincing 3-0 success.

In the same month came similar home wins, as Grove, in dominant form, slaughtered Berinsfield 8-0, with a first Sevier goal and a hat-trick from Gomm; then a stirring defeat of old enemies Abingdon, following a ding-dong, bad-tempered affair where Grove won 3-1, Claydon (2) and Brind scoring again.

So, the team finished September with four straight wins, scoring 16 and conceding just once (Richard Wilson of Abingdon! – who else?).

While all this league action was going on – on a Sunday morning of course –Ritchie and Ollie were in action at Westminster College or across the county playing for the Vale each Saturday. Their football and results had been good, and the atmosphere amongst the players, staff and parents was second to none; despite the players' excursions, the lads were still able to give it all on a Sunday for their local club, grinding out performances and results:

Grove's good league run came to an abrupt end on the first day of October, at home again to Oxford United Social Club.

This team had become much stronger. The Oxford City catchment area submitted no end of big, tough, footballing boys who were only too keen to prove themselves to Mr Jason Carbon. Jason had run an Oxfordshire rep side for Oxford city, for which previously at under-10 level, Ritchie Claydon and Oliver Gomm were previously selected and had played.

Jason knew everybody, and he knew all the key players from Oxford and the surrounds.

He brought his team to Grove on October 1st.

John knew something was wrong when he was confronted by the road jammed with parked cars leading up to the Rugby Club, and a full car park as he drove up that morning.

There turned out to be an event taking place on the same morning as their match with OUFCSC. Not only an event, this was the massive Grove annual boys' rugby tournament.

And it was huge.

There was literally nowhere to park!

Everywhere was packed, and John was massively surprised. He kicked himself for not paying attention! He should have known.

It got worse as he approached the clubhouse. None of the changing rooms were available as they were already full of rugby boys, so they had to share the poor strip of the muddy, cold, wet, dirty half room with OUFC!

Dave Gomm

A freezing, wet gale was blowing in from the north – you could barely stand!

Just one pitch (the front/biggest) for the football. And it was pouring!

He kicked himself again for not taking any notice. He should have known all about this and (probably) cancelled – there was simply no room for the football teams.

Everything was wrong for Grove that day. The kick-off was delayed because so many people couldn't get parking nearby. Grove had Wiggins and Sean Webb missing, so they had a makeshift defence with Billy McDonald dropping into the back four.

And they had no substitutes, whilst playing in these torrential conditions, surrounded by raucous rugby movement and distractions, noises, parents, players and their families.

Grove kicked off with the storm behind them and had a go. The Oxford boys, big as they were, struggled to clear their lines in the conditions.

To be fair, Grove made a good first of it. Ritchie scored a 1st goal from a Brind flick-on after ten minutes. Josias Carbon then bagged a brace in the 28th and 32nd minutes, only for Johnny Ashford to fire in an equaliser on half-time. Grove had had the benefit of the wind in the first half. John tried a rousing pep-talk outside the crowded changing rooms in the break.

But as the eleven Grove lads braced themselves against the elements and then the onslaught from the Oxford team, they were soon defending for their lives, conceding a third and fourth against the elements and a bigger team they simply couldn't hold. John was reminded of the under-7s days, when the boys couldn't

375

kick the ball out of the penalty area. Playing against the wind, you had to try to play the ball along the floor, anything else was just held up (and swept back), with the wind!

As they continued battling against the unnaturally strong wind, they did get a third with five minutes to go through Claydon. OUFC continued to press and finished with five as Carbon finished against a weary Grove to run out winners 5-3.

John was livid because the conditions off the pitch worsened as the teams continued to play. Both teams struggled to get back into the changing rooms, of which theirs was now also occupied with rugby boys; Clothes had been moved and dropped into heaps, and mud deposits were all over the floor – the place was an overcrowded pigsty.

He apologised to Jason, who to be fair, was buzzing from the win, so really not that bothered.

'No worries, John.' Carbon smiled. 'I can see you had exceptional circumstances today.'

'Yeah, but why didn't they call off the football, Jase?' John was still fuming. 'Making us look like pillocks with nowhere to change.' He offered his hand. 'Bloody rugby club – we're always second-class citizens.'

'Never mind, mate. Well played today anyway. Good game.' Jason wore his usual, affable grin.

'Snidey bastard,' snarled Alan as he walked off.

'We need more players, mate. On a different day, with some decent subs, we still could have won that.' John manoeuvred past a group of junior rugby players. 'Those boys were knackered today with the bare eleven.' John picked up his net of muddy balls and slung them over his shoulder.

'Hmm…'

The following week, John was standing on the touchline, having prepared the pitch with his dads. He was waiting with Alan for the kick off on the same pitch, albeit somewhat quieter than the previous week.

This was a second-round cup game against lower league opposition.

'They look a bit nervous, mate,' noted Alan, nudging John.

'No, they'll be okay. Blackbirds are "B" League,' John countered confidently. 'Although they are having a good season, our quality will get us through.'

'Dunno.' Alan wasn't convinced. 'They're top of their league and look pretty up for this!'

The Oxford Blackbirds, from Blackbird Leys in Oxford, did look like they meant business. They had a lot of smaller players but exuded an aura of competitiveness, which was clearly worrying the Grove boys.

In other words, Grove looked frightened of them!

And so it proved. Blackbirds played fierce football, and the Grove lads weren't up to the challenge. Despite the return of Webby and Wiggins, they were quicker to the 50/50s, more determined in the tackle and would never give anything up without trying desperately to get the ball back at all costs. Yes, they were dirty. Yes, they gave away free-kicks, but they could also play. The mild-mannered Grove lads were simply no match for their aggressive demeanour. The match finished 1-2 on the day to knock Grove out of the cup, at home, in the second round.

'Christ! Two home defeats on the trot – and one to a crap B-league team!' John looked bemused. 'They weren't any better than us, just tougher.'

'I know, we need to strengthen the team – we've got no cover,' suggested Alan. 'What we need is a bit of steel in the side.'

'Yep, I know,' mused John. 'And I know just the bloke! Let me have a word.'

Up until this point – with the exception of Wiggins from one of the local villages – the entire squad and every player they had had was from Grove.

Yes, it was a thriving, big village (second in population only to Kidlington in the whole country).

But the resources had clearly been stretched to breaking, especially with the advent of the 'Grove B' side forming.

'I'll ask Tony King about Jack!'

***

Jack King

Jack King was the captain of the under-11 Vale team. He was a classy, well-built, elegant player, who could tackle, lead and win. He was in the same midfield as Ollie and Ritchie, and he was a smooth midfielder who always had time on the ball, with great awareness and skill.

His dad, Tony, had so far kept Jack out of any local team, so that he was fit and ready 'for the protection of his knees, mate' and so he could have a football career.

John had approached Tony about Jack becoming involved with Grove on a few tentative occasions, but Tony had always declined for that reason. However, they were quite close (Tony and Jack were also keen Oxford United fans), and they followed the next four Grove games (two massive wins – 9-0 against Bullingdon away, then 11-0 at home to Carterton, followed by a brilliantly fought 4-5 loss at home to the dangerous Highfield and another reverse this time, away 0-3 at the improving Kidlington).

John caught Tony at the Vale games and invited them both to come and watch Grove.

'Yeah, come along, mate,' he suggested, as they walked towards the dressing room following the Vale's demolition of South Oxfordshire, where Ritchie, Ollie and Jack had all been dominating the midfield.

'What d'ya reckon, son?' asked Tony, as Jack looked eagerly up at the pair.

'Yeah, let's go and see 'em play!' beamed Jack. 'Can't be that bad, can they?'

So, Tony and Jack watched the next two games for Grove – typical Grove performances, with two clean sheets: 5-0 away at Florence Park and 3-0 at home to Garden City.

In the Rugby Club bar, following the Garden City win, John was curious to know whether they had any interest in Jack joining.

Truthfully, he already knew that Jack was very keen to join his new mates, but John was cautious about approaching Tony, who had, after all, made a conscious decision to 'rest' Jack from team football.

'Here you go, mate,' he said, placing a foaming pint of *Morland's* down in front of Tony. 'What did you think?'

'Well, Gommy, I'm quite impressed!' He grinned, taking his first sip.

'I like the work-rate and was impressed with young Revell,' continued Tony. 'Played some very good football as well.'

Jack sat around the table, watching and listening to the men, with Ollie and Ritchie.

'Well, Tone, we just need a bit of help...bit of cover. If Jack was up for it now and again?' He wasn't begging but wasn't far off!

'Don't bullshit me, Gommy!' Tony retorted good naturedly. 'You can see the lad is dying to join Grove!'

'Especially after today's slaughter!' joked Jack, with a huge grin.

'But seriously, Tony, if you don't want him to play often, we can cope with that.'

John took a sip of his pint and looked at the three boys, who were still in rapt concentration, sipping their cokes and nibbling at their crisps.

'We are short of players, and someone like Jack's going to make a massive difference to this team. We'll just rotate the team.' John looked Tony in the eye, taking a sip of his beer.

Dave Gomm

'Well, son?' Tony beamed at Jack. 'Are we in?'

'Yeeessssss!' screamed the three mates together.

'Hey what about asking Joe, Gommy?' Tony asked earnestly. 'If you are short?'

Joe Brewerton was another good player who could defend, head, shoot and tackle, and he had made his place as an outstanding defender in the Vale team.

'All in good time, mate. All in good time.' John raised his pint to Tony, winking.

The signing of Jack was exactly the strengthening that the side needed. Resolute, commanding and resilient, the midfield trio of McDonald, King and Gomm hassled, bit and dominated teams, freeing up the attack and bolstering the defence, and making the team strong and complete.

Now Grove had good players in all positions, and although there were still only fourteen in the squad, they had cover in each department. They became immediately more consistent and harder to beat and were playing decent football.

In this period, and with this settled team, Grove won fifteen of their next sixteen games, losing none; the only points dropped were away to OUFCSC in a 1-1 draw. The best result was a fantastic 5-4 win away at Highfield.

This was a match on a grim, grey day, away on a freezing Saturday morning. The usual parents had travelled, and Grove knew they were in for a test against the strong and unbeaten Highfield boys.

They had lost at home to 0-2 to Highfield in late November, and the Bicester outfit were scoring for fun. The match kicked off, and the hosts scored an early goal, followed by another midway through the first-half. John and Alan shouted the team on from the touchline, and Grove's perseverance paid off when Ollie Gomm turned in a Revell cross on the stroke of half-time.

Normally, John would keep the team on the pitch at the break, but it was so cold, and the changing rooms were so close that he called the boys in as the whistle went off and took them indoors.

He was excited, and so were they – they had been 2-0 down, and now they were back in it! Another goal and we're level. Keep tackling, keep pushing, don't give up and get in their faces. Show them we can score goals too! The boys responded to the team talk and came bursting from the changing rooms ready to fight!

They played, passed, tackled and battled for everything. They began to control the game and swept forward. Revell equalised with a ferocious strike.

Highfield began to jitter and make mistakes. Grove stopped the Highfield attacks in midfield and continued to push forward. Another mazy run into the area and Ritchie Claydon struck goal number three – 3-2 to Grove!

The whole team battled and kept attacking, with Gomm getting the fourth goal, before Highfield rallied and came back to 3-4.

Sean Webb and Johnny Wells had had a very busy morning in the centre of defence. And as Grove won a corner with five minutes to go, both centre-backs went forward for the set-piece.

Revell's corner was headed on by Johnnie Wells, and Sean Webb planted the ball with a bullet of a header straight into the top of the net to lead five goals to three!

Highfield sagged but still re-rallied, battling away at Grove for the last few minutes, and eventually they found a way through Olly Dimblow for a last-minute consolation. But that was it, Grove had come back from the dead against a top team. They had beaten Highfield on their own pitch in a stunning, all-round display of guts and grit.

Highfield 4, Grove 5!

Happy days! Then began the start of a run of eleven straight wins, scoring 42, conceding just six, and keeping seven clean sheets in the process.

So the final league table, including cancellations, finished as

(Top four)

Team	P	W	D	L	F	A	Pts
Highfield	23	22	0	1	170	39	66
Grove	24	20	1	3	97	26	61
OUSC	25	15	1	4	90	26	46
Abingdon	23	15	1	7	71	45	46

Donnington and Horspath were relegated to Division B.

Ritchie Claydon (30) and Mark Brind (27) scored 57 of the Grove Goals, with nine other players contributing.

Highfield had been absolutely dominant, scoring an amazing 170 goals!

In a different season, Grove could have won the league, but even then, in this league, second place/runner-up was a great result.

Overall, it had been a very satisfactory and eventful season.

And they were still improving!

Chapter 25
Under 12s
A Shot at the League

What a brilliant year 1995–96 had been all round. England had reached the semi-finals of the brilliant Euro '96 tournament, bringing hope, glory and solidarity to a whole nation that had been starved of quality and had agonisingly missed out on the final.

Following a devastating season and with a rampant new attack, Oxford United had won promotion; they were once again looking like a quality side and exuding much promise for the following season.

And after all the drama and excitement of the under-11s season, the Vale successes and the Belgium visit, the team swept forward in the B-Line Oxford Boys League (under-12 A).

The atmosphere amongst the squad and parents was now really solid, and training continued to improve. Added to Jack King's signing in the previous season were the talented Nicky Tate, from Sutton Courtenay, and the immense and efficient Joe Brewerton from Radley.

Where Joe would add stability, height and strength – to support the back four and defensive midfield – Nick was a gifted, silky midfielder capable of taking on and beating opponents with his fluid and balanced attacking style. He was stylish – that's how he was on the pitch – a fluid, attacking version of Bobby Moore. They were both acquisitions from John's Vale-side contacts of last season. Nick was actually playing a year up. He was a great addition to the midfield but, as agreed with his dad, was to be used sparingly – which suited everyone (except Nick, who was often frustrated with this arrangement).

The squad was now up to a very decent fifteen, all very strong players, giving John the opportunity to rest and change the defence, attack and midfield every week if he desired. Any side he put out was a match for any of the teams in the 'A' League; mainly because Ollie, Ritchie, Jack, Joe and Nick also represented the Vale rep side. Most of these boys were also attached to their Football League clubs.

The strengthening definitely gave the team a strong backbone, and they thundered into the season, scoring goals for fun. Grove immediately hit the top of the league by securing straight wins over Radley and Littlemore (both 4-0), a 5-2 demolition of Abingdon and another away, trouncing the Swindon Robins by 7 goals to 2. As usual, the deadly Claydon–Brind combination netted the majority of the goals, but with a strong midfield – alternately containing Ashford, King, Gomm, Tate, McDonald, Wiggins and Revell – they were getting some excellent service, supported by the closely knit, mean defence.

The league worked well, and the team progressed excellently.

Within the Vale trials, all the boys who participated in the previous season's brilliant under-11s' successes were joined by Mark Brind, while the new under-12s Vale side lost Nick Tate (who re-joined his correct age-group a year down in the new under-11s).

Unfortunately, the Vale 12s did not have the same groove as the previous year; something was missing here – perhaps the spark between Dave Stemp, Paul Kearns and the boys? The following Vale season turned into a fairly mundane Cotswold

League, and of course, it would never have lived up to the amazing achievements of the previous season.

But in the B-Line League, Grove were striving forward, shoulder to shoulder with the other two contenders, Oxford United Social Club and Kidlington.

After nine games, Grove were still on top on goal difference, unbeaten and ahead of OUSC, having won seven and drawn two. They had scored forty goals and conceded just twelve. Garden City, Highfield and a much improving Oxford Blackbirds were also taking points from anyone, so the league was strong and competitive.

The joy of playing was still very obvious – the boys were still confident and grinning whilst playing some great football. The pitches now evened out the boys' size and stamina.

Added to this, Ritchie, Jack and Nick were now training with Oxford United FC, as was Ollie at Wycombe Wanderers FC. They were getting extra, better training and were only attached to the clubs at this age for their weekly skills and training. No club matches, so they were still able to play for their local teams.

As the season rolled on, the team really began to click, and again, the season's result was the visit to last years' double-winners, Highfield. Again, Grove took all the points, this time not by the odd goal but in a stunning goal-fest and by six goals to one.

Highfield 1 Grove 'A' 6!

They were now a team to be reckoned with: hard to stop, hard to score against and strong in all departments. Following this game, the top four in the league read as

	P	W	D	L	F	A	PTS
OUFCSC	16	12	2	2	76	26	38
Grove	15	11	4	0	71	17	37
Kidlington	15	12	1	2	72	34	37
Highfield	17	11	3	3	90	49	36

So, it was a pretty close league, and Highfield were still top-scoring but were now also conceding goals and losing matches. These top four teams were battling it out all season, all taking points off each other and staying in a close-knit group at the top of the league.

When the Grove party trundled out of the Gomm-by on the road to Kidlington the following week, they were a team still unbeaten.

By now, all the teams knew each other, so John and Alan were greeted by a broadly grinning Roy Evans as they approached the changing rooms.

'Jesus, what happened at Highfield last week, Gommy? Were they shite or were you on fire?'

'Got a bit of luck I think, Roy.' John winked.

'6-1? Thrashed 'em didn't ya?' Well done – Hey, none of that shit here today, mind? Ha ha!' Roy slapped John good-naturedly on the back.

'Cheers, mate. How are you playing?' asked John. 'A six-pointer today, with us on the same points?'

'Yeah, we're playing okay, especially at home! Should be a good 'un!' retorted Roy, moving on.

'Best of luck, mate!' John called, as Roy approached the home dressing room.

'Same to you guys! Beer after?' asked Roy, tipping an imaginary pint.

'Does a bear shit in the woods?' laughed John. 'Good luck!'

'Cheers!'

The team talk was much the same – Keep your concentration. Watch out for Danny Evans and Billy Kershaw. Keep pressing and win the ball. Catch them on the counter-attack. Get the ball to Ritchie on the left. Battle for every ball. And never give up!

'Come on, Grove!'

Most of the top teams in the A League had also added better quality players from their districts. They were, at that under-12 level, pretty good representations of very decent footballing sides.

John was still really proud of his side, who were still mostly Grove lads. The one boy who was in the team but still on the periphery was Peter Wiggins. He was really skilful, comfortable with both feet and massive compared to most of the boys around him. He was literally twice the size of Ritchie and Ollie.

'Come on, Peter! You are starting today, so use your size and strength to dominate them.'

John patted Wiggins on the head as they walked from the changing rooms. 'We are going to win, so we need to win the midfield, and I want you to outmuscle them in the middle of the park.'

A moody nod in reply. Eyes to the ground.

John wasn't sure about this kid at all. He was big, and he had great ball control.

Problem was that he just wasn't part of the team. He just didn't fit.

'Okay?' John wanted a reaction.

Wiggins stared at the ground and nodded.

For fuck's sake!

'Okay, come on.' He wanted to move on. 'Let's go and get 'em!'

Clad in their black and white stripes, Grove kicked off, ripping into Kidlington. Ollie, Billy and Jack launched into their tackles, asserting a dominance in the midfield. Wiggins was obviously a worry for the Kidlington boys because of his size – he could have booted them one by one over the moon. But he was more frightened of them, and his obvious advantages were not used as the other midfielders began to arrest control.

With fifteen minutes gone, Jack King sent Sean Revell off down the right, and his high, looping cross evaded the Kidlington defence and the on-rushing Sparkie, but it wasn't missed on Ritchie Claydon, who finished with aplomb into the far corner on the half-volley.

'Right. Come on, hold it!' screamed John from the touchline.

'Keep it tight!' he cried, as he wandered towards the half-way line, squeezing his hands together for effect.

Two minutes later, Claydon could have sealed it when he was put through by Gomm, but his shot was flicked away by the keeper. Grove continued to dominate and could have scored twice more through Brind and Wells – one was shot straight at the keeper and the other, a ferocious, long-range effort, narrowly missed the angle of post and bar.

Shit! On a different day, it would have been 0-4 by now!

Inevitably, and after all the pressure, Kidlington launched an attack that resulted in Danny Evans squirming through to plant an exquisite drive beyond Olly Dimblow for the equaliser on the stroke of half-time.

'Fucking hell! Who's marking who?!' screamed Alan. 'Christ! You're all shit! Come on! What was that?'

John looked at him in astonishment. Bloody hell, you'd think the world had ended!

'Jesus, mate! Cool down, it's an equaliser. That's all.'

'Fucking rubbish. We've been all over them – it's every fucking time!'

Christ, John thought. *Where did that come from? Every time?*

He didn't get it.

'Who was supposed to be marking?' He turned away as Olly Dimblow and a couple of the defenders looked dejectedly across at John for some support. Jamie looked particularly forlorn.

Dave Gomm

Alan had reddened and was looking daggers at the team as they trooped back to kick off.

John was really pissed off with Alan's attitude. Bloody hell. Boys football!

It wasn't as if they were Brazil!

John turned to have a quiet word with Alan as the half-time whistle blew.

But he wasn't there.

John watched in astonishment, but his assistant was already off, stomping past the Grove goal and flinging an arm towards the pitch. 'Fucking rubbish!' He shouted back over his shoulder with a derisory glance at the general defence.

Jamie shrunk into his frame in embarrassment.

And John shook his head as he watched his assistant manager wander off behind the Grove goalposts. It was so comical that he thought of the '*Who do you think you are? Alex fucking Ferguson?*' quote from earlier in the season.

He had to chuckle as he mock shouted after Alan, now well out of earshot;

'Who do you think you are? Brian fucking Kidd?'

(Alex Ferguson's assistant at Man Utd)

But he was really pissed off with the behaviour that came out of nowhere, and for virtually no reason!

The boys had clearly heard the outburst, and normally, they would muster on the pitch for a few minutes at half-time, with an orange and a drink. On this occasion, John decided to take them back to the changing rooms for a motivational chat.

He was still fuming with Alan.

On reaching the changing rooms, and with no sign of Alan, John calmly sat the lads down – just him and the team.

'Right. First of all, WELL DONE! You are playing a top team, and you have just DOMINATED them! We could easily be 4-0 up, and you have played really well. They are scared of us, and they can't defend against us.' He surveyed the faces.

'So, I don't want you to do anything different than what you have been doing,' he went on. 'Just get out there with the same attitude and WE WILL WIN!' he finished, raising a clenched fist. 'Okay?'

'Don't take any notice of what anyone has said. Just get out there and prove to me, and yourselves, that we are Grove and we will win.'

'Peter, believe in yourself. They are SHIT SCARED of you, so kick some arse!'

'Play like your lives depend on it,' he continued. 'Come on!'

'Questions?' John looked around.

Silence reigned in the Kidlington changing room.

Positive looks and smiles from the troops.

'Let's do it.' He patted each of the boys on the back as they clomped their way out.

Second half kick-off and still no sign of Alan.

More domination, and more bite in midfield. A stunning solo goal by Wiggins, where he dummied a left-wing pass and waltzed through two tackles before rounding the keeper and planting the winner crisply into the net.

'Well done, Peter! I told you, you could do it!' shouted John to Wiggins as he was mobbed by his teammates.

There followed heroic defending from the Challengers.

And another win.

John was so chuffed with the response from the boys but still really, really pissed off with his 'assistant'.

He never got an apology or explanation. Someone dropped Jamie off, so no one knew where Alan had gone off to. What bizarre behaviour.

This wouldn't do. At all.

John – admittedly chuffed that he had shown the faith and got the result – was not at all happy with the response and wondered whether their footballing relationship would ever quite be the same – not for the first time.

But he was pleased that the team – despite their assistant manager's petulant behaviour – had responded, recovered and come back to win the match.

What character from the manager and the players!

***

Oxford United, newly promoted, lost four of their first five games in Division 1. Still led by Denis Smith, they did rally and finished mid table with games against old rivals Swindon and

Reading (with a win and a loss against each one). This was the season when building began on the Minchery Farm Stadium and was halted because of lack of funding.

Grove continued to steamroller their way through the Cup, and it very likely looked like a double-winning season.

Unbelievably, they were drawn against Grove B in the first round (from the Oxford B League now and mid-table). The gulf in class was now palpable, with the A team playing astonishing, quick-passing football that their opponents couldn't compete with, and they ran in at half-time five goals to nil up.

It was so comfortable that John brought on his subs to start the second half, which wasn't all that clever for the B team because Nicky Tate sliced through the defence again and again, scoring twice (once after a sublime run, dummy and drag-back on the edge of the area, before chipping the hapless keeper, Vaux).

Jack King also scored twice, one free-kick curled over the wall and into the top corner, and a last-minute penalty when Tate was upended by the over-enthusiastic Adam Tampling.

John was complimentary to the losing manager, but truthfully, this was a lesson and a barometer of the great heights his team had reached. The B team trooped off, dejected and exhausted, beaten 9-0 (and effectively at home)!

Grove then dispatched Bullingdon away – 9-0, with hat tricks for Revell and Brind and with Claydon (2) and Gomm completing the rout.

Following this, they won at Berinsfield, 4-0, in a competent display, where John fielded a slightly weakened side (Tate, Ashford, King and Wells scoring two in each half).

The Cup semi-final was held on neutral ground on the Horspath fields versus Donnington – an improving Oxford team who were top of the B League with a 100% record in their division: played fifteen, won fifteen.

The lads were confident as they trotted across the field to meet their opposition on a cold, frosty morning; the spectators consisted quite a few parents from both sides, plus a sprinkling of other interested managers and football families on the touchline.

The match was fairly tight, with both high-scoring teams, as you would expect, attacking and counter-attacking. Olly Dimblow kept their lively attack at bay with two good saves, diving to his right to tip a fierce cross-shot away for a corner. Moments later, he had to scamper out of his area and slide in with a good tackle to thwart the lively winger Osibadou.

Jack King smashed a shot against the bar from outside the area, then Ritchie Claydon, clean through, and uncharacteristically found the side netting with Mark Brind unmarked in the box.

The Donnington boys were street savvy and tough opponents, verging on being dirty, although they shielded this well from the ref. Grove were encouraged here by the Oxford crowd on the touchline, who hassled and heckled the ref as the half progressed.

At half-time, John and Alan got the boys into a huddle and basically told them to produce more of the same and not get drawn into the bickering or retaliate, ensuring their football would be the winner.

Peter Wiggins hadn't the appetite for such a scrap, so John invited Nicky Tate to start the second-half in his place. Immediately, Nick began to stretch away in his mazy dribbles, being bought down twice and setting up two free kicks, one of which the keeper parried away, again from King.

With ten minutes left, Tate outpaced the flat Donnington defence again, playing a one-two with Ritchie before escaping into the area at pace only to be hacked down from behind by the beaten centre-half.

Penalty.

Stonewall.

And a sending-off for their defender.

It was a desperate lunging tackle from behind, which left Nicky writhing. The offending right-back had to go, and Grove would surely score the penalty. Nick, maddened by the challenge, jumped up and gave the defender a piece of his mind, rubbing his grazed thigh.

The referee ambled across and was reaching into his pocket. The skinny, gangly, slicked-up, greasy ref produced a red card. But not at the Donnington player. At Nick! Poor Nick couldn't believe it. He started to complain, but the ref just waved him away.

He gave a free-kick to Grove *outside* the area.

The Grove boys looked on in amazement. Gary Revell and the Grove parents were absolutely fuming. It had been so blatant and was nothing short of a massive cheat. Everyone was screaming and waving.

The childish Oxford dads cheered and jeered young Nick off as he left the field in tears.

The atmosphere turned nasty, and Grove continued to press. In the last minute – down to ten men and still bombarding the Donnington goal – the Oxford team, inevitably, made a surging counter-attack against the weakened defence, and their centre-forward slipped the ball under the advancing Dimblow to win it.

This time, the boys were visibly gutted. Their heads went down, and bodies slumped as the Oxford boys leapt about like madmen, celebrating a historic and wonderful semi-final victory.

There wasn't much to say on the way back to the changing room. Alan queried the ref as to why he had sent Nick off and not the hacker who had bought him down – IN the penalty area. He only replied, 'Dissent!'

John couldn't speak to the cheat. Gary called him a 'cheating, fucking wanker!' as he walked off flanked by his two linesmen.

But it was all to no avail. They were out of the cup. This was the only time (apart from desperate dads running the line) that John had ever encountered blatant cheating amounting to match-fixing.

He was disgusted and calmed the boys down in the changing room, even though, for twelve-year-olds, their language was pretty fruity.

The Grove party got into their cars and drove away, firmly determined to put this behind them and win the league. As they left, they couldn't help noticing the ref, who was propped up at the back of the changing rooms, having a well-deserved fag with some of the Donnington dads. Unbelievable!

Grove continued their impressive march towards the league title, having a couple of glitches (Carterton at home 2-3 and Blackbirds at home 1-1 and away a 0-1 loss) – which meant they had to play out the last few matches to secure top status – and other silly dropped points, leading to home draws against Garden City and Crowmarsh.

This culminated in the last match away to OUFCSC in May – a match they had to win.

The two high-flying teams were locked at the top of the league, going into this last and fitting match of the season.

	P	W	D	L	F	A	Pts
OUFCSC	23	16	3	4	109	44	51
Grove Challengers	23	15	5	2	95	33	50

Grove were just a point behind, and the Social Club had a superior goal difference of only three goals. Therefore, a point would not be enough, and the draw would mean the Oxford club would win the league.

Jason welcomed them, fair play, with his big grin and bigger handshake – he had always striven to outdo Grove, and truthfully, they were very well-matched teams. OUFCSC had the build, Grove the skill. They had had some real ding-dong battles over the last three years as the Oxford team had continued to strengthen and improve. And there were always lots of goals! Grove had already beaten them 5-2 at home earlier in the season.

This was a match in which John was able to field his strongest team;

Dave Gomm

Dimblow

Elliott   Webb   Wells   O'Sullivan

Revell   Gomm   King   McDonald

Brind   Claydon

Subs: Tate, Ashford, Brewerton, Wiggins

Brilliantly, ten of the starting eleven and eleven of the fifteen were all original Grove players, all from the rec and all of whom (more or less) had been with the team since under-7s.

The Challengers team went through their warm up, looking happy and confident. As they lined up, John was really proud of what he and his mates, his helpers, his parents, and the boys, had achieved up to this moment. As captain Sean Webb called 'heads' prior to kick off to choose ends, he trotted back to his position with a broad smile, and looked, like his team-mates, more than ready for this, their biggest challenge so far.

The boys looked fit and smart in their black and white stripes, happy and up for anything that the Oxford team could throw at them.

'Right, come on boys' urged Jack King, clapping his hands together for effect as OUFCSC kicked off. 'Let's get right at them?'

The game was fast and furious from the start, both teams knew what rested on the result. Oxford attacked and were repelled. Grove's defence stood firm. The midfield tacklers stamped out the threat. Grove counter-attacked through Brind, Revell and Claydon.

Jason Carbon urged his boys on frantically. Grove competed and held their own. Every boy in the team was fighting with 100%. After 20 minutes, it was still goalless.

The Home team's pressure was rewarded when Grove eventually conceded the first goal during a massive Oxford bombardment. The Oxford players celebrated the goal wildly, running around the back of the goal like they had just won the League, in a big, grinning huddle.

Grove kicked off looking composed, and they equalised two minutes later through Jack King, with a crisp shot following a Grove corner. This equaliser buoyed their confidence and they took the lead before half-time, with a Johnny Wells pile-driver from twenty yards into the top corner.

Grove then moved up a gear, taking control of the game and outmuscling their opponents until the home team began to look deflated, seeming to be running out of ideas. Grove were now set up for their preferred counter-attacking style as they loved to, sweeping up the pitch with a series of telling passes.

John's half-time talk was easy. Keep going the way you are. Keep tackling. Keep passing. Keep thinking. Help each other out!

The teams took to the pitch for the second-half. The day was warm, the sun shone down, and the feeling within the Grove contingent was sunny. They were going to win!

After another early onslaught from the hosts, the attacking Ritchie Claydon, put through by Revell, beat his man, then delightfully curled in the third goal to make Grove comfortable.

John brought on Joe Brewerton to play in front of the back four, securing the threat from midfield, and then he brought on Nicky Tate to hold up the ball and have a run at Oxford.

With five minutes left, Mark Brind put the away side 4-1 up with a thunderous half-volley from the edge of the area following another break, after Joe had dispossessed their playmaker in midfield.

Challengers finished the game as they continued to tackle, pass, play and dominate with swaggering confidence.

The OUFCSC heads went down, and Grove had done it!

Jason was screaming at his troops to attack, and they did grab a consolation near the end, but Grove dominated the event and saw the game out beautifully. Their football and performance brought an instinctive round of applause from both sets of parents and the other spectators as the final whistle blew.

Then it was the turn of the Grove lads to go mental!

OUFCSC 2 Grove Challengers FC 4

League champions!

John hugged Alan and Marc, who had been with the little team of ragamuffins from the start, back when they were six-year-olds. To think that the higgledy-piggledy bunch of tiny little kids would reach these heights was remarkable, and he brushed away a tear as they whooped it up on the pitch.

After all the trials and tribulations, the training, the comings and goings, the fun, the work put in on those massive men's pitches, the fact these lads had made it to become a successful, League-winning side was amazing and overwhelming.

They had competed with the best that Oxford and the district could offer, and had won the League as a united village team.

John was nearly speechless.

This had been an amazing effort and he was so proud of the team and what they had become and achieved.

Challengers as Champions!

Life couldn't get…well you know..!

Chapter 26
Slippery Slope

Following their glorious promotion of 1996 into the old Division 1 (now the Championship), Oxford United eventually finished 17th the following season and a slightly improved 12th place in 1997–98 before starting with a new manager the next year.

Despite the guile and hard work that Denis Smith had cemented into the team – who were hard to beat and still played enthusiastic and attractive football – they struggled as a club to fight events off the pitch.

The construction of the new stadium at Minchery Farm had been started with a completion date of summer 1997. This exciting prospect took a nose-dive when the contractors walked off-site at Christmas due to unpaid bills.

The concrete and steel skeletons of the three incomplete stands loomed eerily over the landscape as work on the stadium came to a halt. The Oxford fans were amazed and perplexed by this development, especially since the football side had started to improve.

The unfinished stadium, resembling an abandoned ship, was gathering dust and growing weeds; it was beginning to look like an omen of gloom and impending disaster.

There were also significant departures, as mentioned, specifically that of the glorious Matt Elliott to Leicester City at £1.6m, which, until recently, remained as United's record sale.

Also leaving was the livewire winger and local boy Chrissie Alan, to Nottingham Forest at £450,000.

Still, Denis Smith continued to trade well, bringing in two masterstrokes with the brilliant young Leyton Orient as centre-back and Darren Purse, a classy, ball playing defender. He followed this by purchasing the laid-back, super-skilled Nigel Jemson – an amazing asset, goal-scorer and great entertainer – for a snip of £60,000 from Notts County.

This only went some way to alleviate the mounting financial burdens. In October 1997, Chairman Robin Herd resigned from the club, followed in December by the long-suffering manager, Denis Smith.

As the club recovered with a better second half of the season, it still had to withstand the further departure of the newly appointed manager, Smith's second in command, Malcolm Crosby. He had run the team for a month before resigning himself, following his ex-boss to West Bromwich Albion, again as his number two.

The anger and angst of the supporters swept former Captain, League and Cup winner and peoples' favourite, Malcolm Shotton, into the new manager's role. This led to a concerted campaign to try and establish some continuity for the team and more significantly, the club.

However, during this period of unrest and movement of personalities, the club accepted bids for both Purse and Jemson (£500,000 and £100,000 respectively).

Alas for OUFC, they also sold the colossus, brilliant Paul Moody (to Fulham for £200,000) and the classy midfielder, Bobby Ford (Sheffield United – £400,000).

At the beginning of the 1998–99 season, Shotton's first managerial campaign saw just six league wins from August to mid-January, a total of 10 for the entire season and two record defeats: a 7-0 thrashing at Sunderland and a horrible 1-7 home reverse to Birmingham City. Luckily, John and Ollie were away, and he had given his Manor Club season tickets to his mate Charlie, to the great delight of Charlie's nephew, Sean. So, they hadn't had to suffer the disaster first-hand. By this time, the club were in turmoil with consortiums, unpaid players, pressure groups and club staff.

In October, the PFA eventually stepped in to help get the unpaid players paid, but the staff remained unpaid; members of the public actually donated and delivered food-parcels to the club during this period.

The fans were astonished that after all the good work leading to the promotion to the second-tier, there had been so much trauma regarding ownership, the stadium and personnel, leading to things deteriorating so quickly. Despite all the efforts on the pitch, the disasters around the club inevitably brought relegation in May 1999; second bottom, with Bristol City.

This happened in a season when they had signed on the goal-scoring Dean Windass from Aberdeen for a club record £475,000. It was a sign of the times that after almost beating Chelsea in the FA Cup, (being robbed of a home win by a controversial penalty), Windass, despite his eighteen League and Cup goals in 38 appearances, had to be sold mid-season to balance the books.

There was controversy here too, because Aberdeen didn't receive a penny of their £475,000 from Oxford until the Windass transfer to Bradford City, in March 1999, for £950,000.

United dropped down into (the old) Division Two with the stadium plans in disarray, with an inexperienced manager in

Shotton, no money and mounting, crippling debts, problems with board resignations and the developers – Firoz Kassam, Oxford City Council – and now most of their best players were gone.

Managers had come and gone with alarming regularity, from Denis Smith in 1996–97 to Malcolm Crosby, Malcolm Shotton, Mickey Lewis (caretaker) and eventually Denis Smith, who returned in February 1999.

The changes in directors and ownership was far more fraught; there were constant changes at the top and power struggles, threatening to scupper the club with its internal bickering. Two groups – FOUL (Fighting for Oxford United's Life), a pressure group, and SOUS (Save Oxford United's Soccer), a fundraising group – were formed by supporters' groups and were instrumental in raising awareness and continuing to offer support and assistance.

When and where the disastrous demise had begun, and how it had reached such epic proportions, was anyone's guess. The transfer fees, comings and goings, purchase of the stadium, historical outstanding monies and all sorts of other complex issues had plunged the club to the very brink of administration. When Firoz Kassam appeared as the front-runner to take over, beating off rival bids and consortia, the Oxford United debt had risen to over £10m, with an additional £15m still outstanding for the uncompleted stadium.

After much negotiation, Mr Kassam eventually stepped in and purchased Oxford United Football Club for £1,000,000, taking on the debts as part of the deal.

He managed to secure a Company Voluntary Agreement (CVA) in July which agreed to slash United's unsecured debt to

£900,000. Larger creditors were to receive 10p to the pound, and smaller creditors were to be paid in full.

What a state of affairs! And within all this turbulence, there was a sporting football club that just wanted to go about its business.

In circumstances such as these – where the fans support the club, but where their resolve is challenged, particularly following a successful period in their history – the support can easily begin to dissipate; especially if the standard of the players, the quality of the football and the integrity of the management and owners are in question.

The following season, under two managers and two care-taker managers (Denis Smith, David Kemp and Mike Ford – twice as care-taker manager following both departures), the team won just seven league games all throughout the season.

After that disappointing season, and prior to the following season, a disillusioned John bought season tickets to Aston Villa for Ollie and himself so they could watch Premier League football. Being a season-ticket holder at Villa was okay, but not hugely satisfactory, as they found themselves happily situated in their lofty Trinity Road seats, often favouring the away teams, without anyone to 'support'. Same old spec, for despite watching top-level football and the best teams in the country week after week, and with the continuing and worsening problems at Oxford, they were still Oxford fans! Their meanderings to the Midlands twice a fortnight did not do them much good at all. Inevitably, they soon lost interest in the Aston Villa trips.

The home gates at the Manor in that last season would often drop below 4000, which was about as bad as the Oxford home support ever got (those faithful witnessed just five home wins in nine months). The team suffered greatly amongst all these movements and the political unrest, and they were relegated to rock-bottom and ten points behind their nearest rivals, Swansea, in May 2000. Oxford were down to Division 3.

From rags to riches.

And back to rags.

Chapter 27
The Beginning of the End

Inevitably, after the rigours and successes of the glorious under-12 season (following the epic under-11s) – and largely fuelled by the Football League Clubs interest in the boys as players – came the actual player losses from the local teams to the professional clubs.

Jack, Nick, Ollie and Ritchie had already spent a year in the under-12s season training with their new football league clubs, but those training sessions on Monday nights had not interfered with their club football, they had probably enhanced it. Now, those clubs wanted the boys exclusively, and they weren't allowed to continue playing for their local clubs – apparently, not even six-a-sides. John was obviously torn and in two camps about this – the boys were enjoying their progress, but the guts were being ripped out of the team piece by piece.

So, at the start of the under-13s season, Grove lost four lads from the original under-7s line up – Sean Revell (who went to play with Grove a year up), Billy McDonald (who was moving to Indonesia with his family), Ritchie Claydon (to Oxford United FC) and Oliver Gomm (Wycombe Wanderers FC).

The recent new-comers Jack King and Nick Tate were also lost (to OUFC).

John reconciled himself to the fact that Ollie would be full-time at Wycombe this year. Inevitably, this meant that the team had been worse than decimated by losing six really great players from last year's squad of fifteen. He had a meeting with his old, long-time adversary, and now good mate, Tim Butler and Alan; as Abingdon had suffered a similar fate, they agreed that Grove

'A' and Abingdon 'A' would merge as the new Grove 'A' Under-13s'.

So, after many successful and brilliant seasons, it came to be that the team was all but broken up. True, they knew the Abingdon boys. True, they would make a good side. But the team that had started six years ago, as tiny, goofy, clueless, little kids, was all but done.

The parents whose boys had been chosen for league clubs, including John, were all dead excited with the prospect. But if they had sat down and thought about it, and had had the benefit of hindsight, they probably would have had their lads stay where they were.

After all, they were breaking up a local, league-winning team that were all mates. The 'club' boys would still be their mates, go to school together and play in the school team together, but Grove would not really be Grove. John had built this beautiful, little team from scratch, learning as he went, nurturing, cajoling and teasing performances and results from these boys over six seasons.

Did he really want to leave? Not really. Did he want to hand it over to other people? No! Would he miss it? Bloody hell yes! And although he was glad to be relieved of the responsibility of arranging everything, making sure he had a team, happy subs, happy parents and dealing with all the hassles that occurred on a weekly basis, a part of him was desperate to keep it – keep it all together, keep the team, keep all the boys and take them to the next level.

The end of season presentation, held at the Old Mill Hall in June, was a poignant affair and one of great sadness. The team had recently returned from a successful eleven-a-side competition in Sussex Beach at a grotty, old Pontins, which was dilapidated and damp. They had had a great comp, and they came away as runners-up to Brimsgrove FC of Middlesex, along with the 'Fair Play' award (Not difficult in the week, as most other teams – namely Bromsgrove and the York-based Copmanthorpe FC – were involved in a massive scrap, which included a lot of the parents!).

Their sixes had been great, as usual, winning three (St. Josephs, then Radley and Grove, their home tournament, again), plus runners-up in three and semi-finalists in a higher age-group. The team were definitely going out on a high!

John thanked the boys, parents and supporters who had been together throughout the years. He named Karen and Graham Brind, who had helped organise and run the Sussex Beach tournament, and some of the parents who had turned up to put up and take down the goals, run the line, run lifts, etc. Special thanks went to Alan Elliott for his role in training and fitness.

And once again, he thanked everyone who had all supported and encouraged the success of the team one way or another.

John was delighted and surprised to receive gifts of pictures, mugs and coasters along with a brilliant picture of the squad, looking resplendent in their kit with the trophies alongside the managers. They made their speeches, had a few beers, saw out the rest of the evening, wished each other all the best and then quietly made their ways home – yes, the end of an era.

John, Lyn, Ollie and Corine trooped back along the lane past the Bay Tree, sad at what had been and may never be again…

'Well, I hope we don't lose our friends,' moped Lyn, as they headed across the green.

'Why should we?' John gave her a cynical frown. 'We are all local, you'll still see everyone.'

'Mmm…' She didn't look convinced.

***

When the new season started in August, John was instructed to temporarily report back to The Wycombe training ground, located off the M40, close to TGI Friday's and Waitrose. They both knew a few of the boys and parents there: Danny Evans and his dad Roy, Elliott O'Brien with his dad Paddy, Liam Barson with his father Colin, all from their area. There were a few others whom he knew to nod at.

Training was brisk and efficient, with quick, one-touch passing and moving on five-a-side, synthetic, pitches and small goals. The dads huddled to the side as the lads tried to impress.

Kidlington, Horspath, Radley, Abingdon, Grove and many other teams had lost their best players, who now paraded their skills on a different level. One of the first things John noticed on their return was the size of some of the new recruits. These boys were growing! Some of them were becoming men!

In truth, between thirteen and fifteen years of age, some of these boys were really becoming men. And as skilful as the Wycome team were, if some hulk who was twice as big as you decided to launch you, there wasn't really a lot you could do about it. Ollie, Jack, Ritchie, Tom, Liam and all the smaller boys had always been aggressive and able to handle themselves. But this was literally the start of a different ball-game.

Imagine starting a football game when your opponent is twice as big as you! You can only compete on a certain level, but technically, you will be out-jumped, out-muscled, out-run and therefore out-played for eighty minutes. In the early days, this height and weight advantage wasn't so frequent and was the same for every team, but as the boys hit thirteen/fourteen, it became significant. The clumsiest players at that age could simply mow through the smaller lads, and at Wycombe Wanderers FC, as at the other clubs, there were no clumsy players, but a lot of bigger ones! They were all good players, and the club wanted to progress their best boys through the academy and potentially into the first team at some point. So, the coaches were quite aware of this issue and were carefully monitoring it.

Fair play to Ollie, Liam, Danny and the smaller lads holding their own at Wycombe – they were still small, but really skilful. The dads hovered around the touchline, chattering and giving opinions from the side and watching the progress of their own kids. The standards, as you would expect, were high – the best footballers from the area were now together. The competition was quietly fierce.

Friendlies were arranged on Sunday mornings in Princess Risborough against similar academies – Watford, Southampton, QPR and so on; usually, the Wycombe boys were as good or better than their opponents. However, at this level, the trainers' eagle-eyes were on the boys' performance and progress.

The group started with more than forty boys, and Aidy, the trainer, would lose a couple of lads following certain matches. So, after Christmas, they were down to thirty. Some really skilful boys, mainly the smaller ones, were becoming casualties of the cull.

The drive to Wycombe was a trek, as training would start about 6:30 pm. John would have to leave work by 3 pm, pick Ollie up literally straight from school and whip down the M40 to get there at 6.

Ollie seemed to love this connection and his new club, and John was always querying him as to whether he was happy. To be truthful, it would have been a lot more convenient if he had been signed by Oxford United. But hey-ho, they continued happily week by week.

Ollie held his own in the team, and the coach really liked him. When the time came for ball skills in training, his two feet and balance shone through as one of the more skilful players. 'Because of the basketball-football training!' according to his dad. He was, and always had been, two footed; his right foot was obviously stronger than his left, but he was adept with both. He was quick, skilful and tricky could still offer a steely tackle, even with the size difference of the bigger players.

Following a Sunday match against Stevenage Borough – where Aidy decided to play the boys in all sorts of different positions and where the final score was 9-3 to Wycombe – Ollie scored two goals from playing up-front: one a glancing header from a corner, and the other was a right-footed plant beyond the advancing keeper. The keeper denied him a hat-trick with a blinding save from close range following a goalmouth scramble. Afterwards, an announcement was made – training was moving from Wycombe to Bisham Abbey near Marlow next week onwards.

'Bloody hell, John,' mused Paddy, as they walked to the car park.

'Well, we knew it was coming, Paddy,' John replied, opening the car from a distance with his remote key.

'Yeah, but Bisham's more tricky to get to, especially in the winter.' Paddy sighed.

'Well, mate, Wycombe is a mission. But with Bisham, at least you could come through Henley?' suggested John.

O'Brien raised his eyebrows. 'Not from bloody Horspath, mate!' He snorted. 'Easy from Wantage.' He laughed as he motioned Elliott along. 'Naw, we'll still come down the 40 and spur off.'

Ollie and Elliott were trailing alongside, swinging their boots.

'Well done, Ollie!' he smiled at his son, following a change of position, a great performance, and two goals! He grinned down at Ollie.

'Should have got the hat-trick, though.' He laughed, walking on.

'Hey Dad?' Ollie and his mate had been chatting on the way down to the car.

'Yes, mate?' John looked down at his beaming son.

'Isn't Bisham Abbey where England train?' He grinned.

'You know, I do believe it is!' said John, as they jumped into the BMW. 'I do believe it is!'

'Brilliant!'

So, the Monday night treks to Bisham Abbey began.

It was quite an impressive site and venue.

The old Abbey stood quietly and grandly over the floodlit AstroTurf of the playing areas, vast, green, shadowed and sheltered by tall, mature trees. There were several pre-marked pitches, and upon arrival, the boys made like maniacs straight to the bag of footballs so they could start kick-ups, tricks and skills.

To be fair, the set-up wasn't dissimilar to their previous arrangement at Wycombe. It was a bit grander and had more dedicated space (i.e. they weren't sharing it with anyone else); plus, there were other Wycombe age-groups involved on the same night, so they had obviously made some sort of deal. And then there were the inside facilities and, of course, the outside pitches.

Aidy preferred Ollie to start on the left-side of midfield in the training matches, where he was quite comfortable. Elliott, Danny and Liam were all holding their own and continued to impress on the Abbey's training pitches.

The Grove/Abingdon alliance was working fairly well. But as the season progressed and even though John and Ollie had committed to Monday training, Sunday matches and still went up regularly to watch Oxford, it was inevitable that both father and son were starting to lose touch with the old Grove team.

Alan and Tim, the new managers, were still struggling to get thirteen players a week and continued to moan about it. The boys left there were beginning to find other interests (girls and cigarettes). Since a lot of their mates had moved on, they were not so keen on turning up for training or on match-day.

They were still in the A League but now a fairly ordinary, mid-table team, winning as often as drawing or losing. The academy boys still saw each other at school and were still able to play for their school teams, but the academy and the parent club didn't really interact anymore, being separate entities.

So, John progressed with Ollie at Wycombe, still often enquiring of his son, 'Are you happy with this?'

To be fair, Ollie always answered that he loved it, and deep down, he was thinking of the day that he would make his debut for Wycombe Wanderers in the first team.

They played every week against quality opposition and were trained every week under good coaches on Bisham Abbey's AstroTurf. The team began to take shape, and the dads drove their kids to the venues, then met up on the touchlines to support and chatter amongst themselves, and the boys obviously did enjoy the experience.

The games were mainly of little significance, because at this stage they were only training games, there was no league and lots of substitutions and role-swapping.

All for the good of the football club.

And the development of the boys?

Chapter 28
Sint-Niklaas – The Belgium Return Trip

Around Easter, after the very successful season and a lot of arrangements by the Belgian Committee's teams and parents, it was time for the return trip for John's under-12s and Pete Whareham's under-14s. And so, on Good Friday 1996, a coach-load full of Grove families turned up from the Grove rugby club – destination Sint-Niklaas, Belgium.

The trip was full of incidents. At one point, the bus doors flew open, and Paul McDonald was just about able to save Billy from hurtling out onto the A34 at 70 mph!

Because John and Lyn had hosted the chairman's son, Nicki, and the two other lads the previous year, their invitation to stay was reciprocated by Herman, the chairman, and his wife, Ingrid. They were really nice people, but John and Lyn were disappointed, because they had met them previously and found them to be a very staid couple.

The Elliotts had hosted Frankie and Arlette Van Der Linden, a young and fun pair who loved to eat and drink (Frankie, being a chef, allegedly kept a large fridge full of drinks in their bedroom!). The lucky sods were going to stay with them, whilst John and his wife had reservations about what their stay would bring.

And so – after the journey to Belgium and the welcoming drinks at the VOS Rienaert clubhouse – the young family, including Ollie and Corine, arrived at the house of Herman and Ingrid at 8:30 pm on Good Friday.

Their house was nice, spacious, and European-looking, with a well-clipped garden of mainly shrubs (it was still a bit cold for any spring-time colour).

They had had a couple of drinks en route, plus a few at the club, but they were hungry. Now, they were no food snobs, but they ran a food company and were used to good food and eating out regularly – and John and Lyn both liked a drink. So, they were a little dismayed when Herman announced, 'We hope you like chicken and pineapple.'

Ingrid was nodding vigorously.

John slid Lyn a look, and his eyes widened.

Lyn returned the look and kicked her husband gently, smiling.

Anybody (especially a chef) knows that any food done simply and well is very acceptable, and that no frills are necessary if the dish is done well (take for example a humble shepherd's pie or gammon, egg and chips).

Well, prior to the meal, the Belgian hosts produced a chilled *Liebfraumilch* (John being a red-wine drinker, Lyn preferring dry white). Okay, okay, stop whinging! They exchanged looks again – *let's just make do!*

In the kitchen, when the large, standing freezer was opened, it displayed a tribute to 'Herman the German's' disciplined organisational skills – every product was neatly stacked in piles and labelled in military fashion. Lyn raised an eyebrow as they walked through to the dining room.

Then Ingrid bought out the chicken – a whole roast chicken with pineapple rings on the breast, with salad, vegetables and no potatoes or bread.

As she sliced the chicken apart, it became evident that these guys were no dinner-party specialists. The legs and breast were still bloody, and the chicken wasn't cooked. Ingrid cast a look of horror as she sliced it open but proceeded to launch it onto everyone's plates, who looked on in disbelief but had no choice but to politely accept.

They very quickly dispatched the four glasses of *Liebfraumilch* (one per person), and some canned peaches and cream completed the dismal meal, from which they all picked through the raw chicken with as much gusto as they could muster.

In short, it was an uncomfortable meal – one which should have been so welcoming – and the conversation with the clipped chairman was not easy. His wife was more gregarious, and of course, they all knew Nicki, so it was not a complete social disaster. They both were thinking of the time the Belgian lads had come to their house and demolished the crock-pot full of stew and dumplings, the kids' raucous behaviour and the fact that it had been a bloody good night at the club. This event could not have been any more different. The dreary meal ended around 9:45 pm in a flurry of nothingness.

John was desperate for another beer, and Lyn for another wine. To make things worse, they were both imagining how the Elliotts were getting on with Frankie and Arlette, with their beer and wine fridge in the bedroom and the Van Der Linden's gusty, boozy manner.

Just at that time, Herman announced, 'Well, we have all had busy days. I think it's time for bed!'

It was so disappointing compared to that brilliant evening they had had just a year ago, and they said their goodnights hoping tomorrow would bring much better things.

John and Lyn were saddened – and relieved at the same time – and the kids were ready, so they went to their room. Once they were inside, John, as quietly as he could, cracked open a bottle of *Pinot* and found his *Talisker* in the suitcase for a little deserved and much-appreciated nightcap.

It was just as well, as the bedroom was absolutely freezing, and the young couple had a laugh about the whole evening.

They awoke relieved to know they were not suffering from either *salmonella* or *staphylococcus* food poisoning, and they quickly got dressed in the freezing bedroom.

To be fair, their hosts couldn't have been nicer or more attentive, and the family could not have been more welcoming. Plus, Herman had organised most of the activities, so he had been, and still was, quite busy.

There were trips out, meetings with other families and social events. They were treated really well along with the rest of the Grove families, and things were great, especially since the sport was yet to come.

After the usual sight-seeing tours of the local area – where the Gomms constantly bumped into other Grove families and boys on similar excursions – and some Belgian coffees, pastries and chocolates, the whole group of English and Belgians descended upon the very well-equipped leisure centre.

The highlights here were the ladies' indoor five-a side, where the much superior VOS Reinaert ladies eventually lost on penalties to a loosely cobbled-together ladies team, which included Helen Casey, Kim Revell, Gill Claydon, Sharon and Becky Elliott, of course Corine, and more reluctantly (in goal) Lyn.

The Grove ladies were playing in their new 'Grove Calling' t-shirts, designed by John and printed by Marc at his newly established t-shirt printing company back home. These had been shipped to Sint-Niklaas in large numbers by John to sell!

The Grove women were far from being footballers in the loosest sense of the sport; however, the VOS Reinaert girls and ladies were very much footballers, so credit to the giggling, miss-kicking and panting English for even getting to penalties. At first, the Belgian women seemed to resent their opponents' jocularity and behaviour. But by the end, everyone was laughing, hugging and taking photos – so it was a great success!

Reinaert won the men's indoors in a scrap, Pete's under-14s narrowly lost and John's under-12s – devastatingly skilful, quick and adept at five-a-sides – thrashed their Belgian counterparts, as expected.

There was a lovely meal for everyone in a local tavern, and the two communities renewed their friendships and acquaintances. Following all these exertions, eating and drinking, the Grove families were glad to get to bed on Saturday night. John and Lyn didn't even have to grab a nightcap!

The main outdoor matches were held the next day. The ladies played first before a fine drizzle set in, and the Belgians won easily. As the men's match kicked-off, the rain started falling more heavily, making the pitches waterlogged. John and Alan started as two centre-backs, teaming up and thwarting the constant bombardment from the VR men, playing out their match in the continuous drizzle and on the increasingly challenging wet pitch. They ended up with a deserved, meritorious 2-2 draw.

As they broke for lunch, the heavens opened, and the Belgian landscape had become a sodden, miserable mass of mud.

By now, the English and Belgian boys were changed and ready for their 10/12 match (some younger brothers, such as Liam Revell, and some older ones made up the teams). They were shivering in their track suits and huddled underneath the awning of the clubhouse. But they all wanted to play.

'What do you think, John?' asked Herman. 'Is it playable, or shall we call it off?'

'Come on Herman.' John was really upbeat. 'We didn't come all the way over here for a postponement! Look at them.' He pointed to the boys.

'Well, we are ready and want to play the match.' Herman smiled. 'It's only a little rain after all.' He shrugged.

John shifted, motioning to the eager-looking Ollie and Ritchie. 'Get 'em on the pitch!'

'Hooray!' shouted the boys, noisily bursting out from under the shelter of the lean-to behind the changing rooms.

'Come on, Grove!'

When it came to the kick-off in this main under-11s match, the main pitch was just playable and very wet, with puddles and small ponds at the centre-circle and throughout the pitch and goalmouths.

Everyone spectating – the other teams, their siblings, mums, dads, aunties, uncles, grandparents and friends – was in raincoats and huddled under umbrellas as the two teams, quickly becoming a brown mass, kicked-off and began slogging away at each other.

Well, it wasn't ideal for any type of football, but the boys made a great effort. Through the rain, mud and gore, Grove managed to play a bit of football, ending up 3-0 winners. The atmosphere was great, and the players from both teams were completely bedraggled, splattered in mud and soaked from head to toe!

Richard Maurice and Liam Revell were so covered in mud that their tiny frames could barely be distinguished from the pitch. The rain continued to pour down, and the temperature dropped. To their credit, both teams slugged it out, enjoying the atrociously cold, wet and windy conditions.

At the final whistle, the Grove lads made a dash for the corner and proceeded to slide, belly-first, toward the parents in delighted celebration, completing the mud make-up. Now, they were virtually unrecognisable from anything other than grinning, plastered, brown boys!

The Reinaert boys thought this was a great idea, and soon they were sliding face-down in the mud with their opponents and friends. It was a great sight, and it warmed the hearts of the watching parents, once again cementing the bond between the groups.

As the boys trooped off – thick with mud, dripping and deliriously happy – the night began to set in, and the lit-up clubhouse bar started to feel warm, cosy and very welcoming.

The boys changed and showered in the steamy changing rooms, singing, laughing and flicking towels as the party started next door. They walked through the adjoining door and entered the clubhouse. This room was large and wooden, with a little bar in the corner, adorned with lots of famous Belgian beers and hundreds of dedicated glasses to match. The lights reflected off the glassware, further illuminating and adding to the sparkling atmosphere. There were also many colourful flags, banners and a large, well-stocked trophy cabinet hanging from the dark, wooden walls. The walls were further covered in pictures of previous VOS Reinaert and Grove teams, grinning and hugging in their team colours.

Large, colourful rugs covered most of the wooden floor, and dark ornate tables and chairs were already filling with the Belgians and their visitors.

Compared to the wintry conditions outside, it was snug and warm, and the candle-like electric lights cast a warm glow on the assembled parents and their families.

Many of the parents were now firm friends, even with each age-group and the Belgians, who were turning out to be exemplary hosts. Many were aware that this was the last night, and many had had a few drinks in the afternoon; so, the clubhouse was a most welcoming place to John, especially when he had turned off the changing-room lights and walked into the clubhouse to find everybody ensconced, happy and flushed.

Sometimes, out of the blue, there comes an event where the atmosphere becomes charged, thick, rich and so overwhelming that you wish it would last forever – this evening was one of those rare occasions.

Everyone was so happy and now warm and dry. The sport was over; the friendships were starting to click in, and the social side coming to the fore.

The drinks flowed, and the clubhouse became something of a whole, warm, glowing oneness with music and laughter. The ambience was something really very special.

Following the speeches came the awards, and John's team went up to collect their winner's medals, still madly grinning from ear to ear!

'Hey, come on, guys!' John shouted over to Alan and Mike Webb, Sean's dad.

'We haven't finished selling our t-shirts – We've got about 25 to go!'

John started up towards the corner of the clubhouse, where the 'Grove Calling' shirts were stored in a cupboard. The three of them went over and got an announcement made; soon, a few boys and parents, mainly the Belgians, began to come over to buy the t-shirts.

As the sizes started to go, John was left with a couple of extra-extra-larges and just one medium size. He was exhaustively handing out the last two big ones when he looked up into the sparkling, blue eyes of Frankie Van Der Linden, who was standing in front of the table with an inane grin and a bottle of ice-cold lager in his outstretched hand for John.

John gave Frankie a big hug, then happily gave his friend the last 'Grove Calling' t-shirt.

Brilliant. What a tour!

Chapter 29
A New Chairman and a Small-Sided Game Development

Ollie had been training and playing with Wycombe Wanderers FC for fifteen months. He was still holding his own, despite now being one of the three smallest boys remaining in the squad.

Every Sunday, down at the Princess Risborough pitch, Wycombe played similar league teams – Tottenham, Stevenage, Watford, QPR and so on, with mixed performances and results.

Training on Monday nights at the Bisham Abbey complex was more intense, as the coaches worked hard on the boys' ball-skills, fitness, attitude and desire. Several coaches assisted Aidy on those nights. These sessions would always end in a small-sided game on the AstroTurf under the floodlights.

In these games, Ollie was still preferred on the left-side of midfield, and he continued to play well in that position. Truthfully, the three smaller lads could be out-muscled by some of the bigger lads, many of whom were by now more man than boy.

But after training, Ollie continued to come off the pitch beaming, still really happy to be training, participating and involved with the group, trainers and experience.

'Can we go and get a Burger King, Dad?'

'Course, mate!' John would always agree, ruffling his son's blond hair.

They would nearly always stop at Reading Services for a Burger King on the M4 half-way home, where the burgers were okay, but the coffee was vile and expensive.

The trip took 7–8 hours, and John often shook his head at this commitment to simply 'train', but he justified the journey and the expense so long as Ollie continued to enjoy it. At least he could afford the time to do it, and Ollie was developing into a classy, little player.

In the close season, everyone got together at the Grove sixes. John was still running the event; although, because this was his fifth one, he had decided it would be his last. The event was still aided and abetted by the very willing Tina and Steph.

Tim and Alan ran the two Grove teams, with the Abingdon boys plus Dwight, Ritchie, Jack, Ollie, Sparkie and Webby all involved.

The 'A' team won the event on Saturday, beating Tower Hill in the finals, 2-0. It was good to see the boys playing together again and having the crack on and off the pitch as mates.

Jack and Ritchie, as well as the long-departed Dwight, were still at Oxford United FC and were doing well there.

The Grove/Abingdon liaison team had done okay, but John was sensing that all was far from perfect. The team had finished the Under-13s League fifth out of twelve, with mixed results. John by now realized that Alan could be bloody moody and wondered how the good-natured Tim was coping with that. Not great, he suspected.

The team had now lost Sean Revell (up an age), Liam Revell and Mark Brind (down), Billy McDonald (emigrated), Ollie

Gomm, Dwight, Ritchie, Peter Wiggins Charlie Harris, Jack King and Nick Tate– all key players, along with several other boys.

So the team really had been decimated from last years' championship-winning team. And, although the new team had been bolstered by the Abingdon signings and some very good players at that, the team was never going to be as strong or as gelled.

Socially, this also became a problem, because mates John, Alan, Graham and Dave Claydon (and their respective families), amongst others, watched their boys at different venues every week.

Still, there were get-togethers and occasional meet-ups for drinks at the Rugby Club, the Bay Tree or at house parties. There was also a strong meeting of the boys and dads from the early Grove team when they continued to meet up and participate at the annual Grove sixes, which they were always keen and happy to do.

After the Saturday sixes competition, still flushed from the A team's win, John turned up at 8 am the following Sunday morning almost before anyone else. The pitches were lush, and the goals just needed to be tipped up the right way. The pitches had held up well after the Saturday, and a few early-morning, dog-walkers mooched around the field edges as the volunteers began to straggle in.

As he unzipped the tent door, which served as the PA HQ for the event, he spotted Tina and Steph almost running across the fields towards him, loaded with charts, bags and clipboards.

'Morning, ladies.' John sensed their urgency. 'What's the rush?'

'You haven't heard then?' gushed Steph, as she threw her stuff behind her chair.

'Heard what? What's happened now?'

'Joe Moreland has resigned as chairman!' she gasped.

Joe had only been chairman for just over a year, elected when Bill Nelson has stepped down.

'Never! When? I don't believe it, we're in the middle of the bloody sixes!' 'What on earth happened?' John expostulated.

'Nobody knows, but it happened last night after the sixes, we think.' said Tina, with a questioning pout.

Well, I'm buggered!

Steph grinned wryly, joining her beaming sister. 'Coffee?'

Nobody appeared to know about Moreland's resignation at all. John found and spoke to Clare Parry, Tony Keen and other committee members, who all confirmed the news but were equally ignorant as to the reasons.

The committee seemed to have been really strong. Joe had lost the plot with some of the youngest age-groups at recent meetings, who were constantly barracking about the proposed new changes to one of John's long-time and deep-rooted boys football issues – small-sided football.

It appeared the FA had taken notice at last and were discussing bringing in significant changes to boys football – with a motion to split it into small-sided games, on smaller pitches, with smaller goals and timings, designed to bring the out best of the boys' abilities.

Eureka! Thought John, when he had heard the news. Something bloody close to his heart, principles and sanity! Everyone would benefit, especially the boys and their long-term development.

But, amazingly, the younger age-groups' managers were vehemently opposed to this. John and Joe as managers who had been through the big pitch syndrome and really struggled to achieve any successful football until their boys had physical grown and started to develop at ten and eleven. They cited this information to the younger age-groups, but they would not listen and those younger managers still preferred to keep things as they were.

Joe had been exasperated following a big verbal attack after the last meeting. John and Pete Whareham had fought Joe's corner. But the ongoing consensus was that Joe (and any other parent who was doing something for nothing, should do so in his own time) had simply had enough, and quit.

In any case, he wouldn't talk to anyone about it, so he must have been really pissed off. The upshot was that he had stepped down and left the club with immediate effect – leaving the club without a leader and chairman.

John spoke at length with Clare, and after a little consideration, he decided to offer his services. He was not going to be bullied by the younger groups' managers who knew little or nothing about the problems of tiny kids playing on eleven-a-side men's pitches.

'I'll step in, if I can help.' he volunteered to Clare in the clubhouse.

'What, as chairman, John?' she queried.

He nodded. '*Acting* chairman, Clare.'

'Will you be able to manage the other age-groups?' She looked at him doubtfully.

He shrugged.

Bring 'em on! He thought for a moment, wondering whether he should be getting involved at all. But he didn't need to think for too long.

'Course I can manage them!' he continued. 'I know all their arguments and have been there in the field.'

'If it will help the club in the short term, and I can do it, then I will be an interim chairman until you appoint a new one,' he suggested.

Clare took a little time in answering, mulling over the implications.

'Okay, John, fine in principle. So far as I'm concerned, you can take over straight away.'

'We can sort out the details later, until we get a proper elected chairman.'

'Will you be interested in that?' She looked him in the eyes.

John knew that he could easily handle the chairman's duties, but not every meeting's repetitive bullshit in the long-term.

'Not really, Clare,' John reasoned. 'I'll help out till you sort out a new face. After that, I'm just a parent.' She was nodding sagely. 'Is that okay?'

The committee agreed in principle, and shortly afterwards, John took up the responsibilities of the chairman temporarily in the interest of the Grove Challengers Football Club.

Jesus! As soon as he took on the post, his phone started ringing!

These younger managers were furious with the proposed changes, not understanding why the FA should be involved or how this was going to help anyone! They were really interested to know what the club was going to do about the changes!

At first, he tried to reason with them, explaining that the club had no power or influence over the FA's decision. He could not understand why they were so opposed to the changes, but he could not explain or convince them that this was a good move and that the boys and they, would benefit from the new FA rules.

After many calls, cussing and raised eyebrows from Lyn, he crashed back onto the settee. His astonishment knew no bounds as he tried to work out why none of the younger guys had a minute to see the good points. They were blinded and could not see.

He put it down to them simply being frightened of change.

So, whilst he researched and understood the exact FA proposals and timings, he told them to stop ringing. A meeting was scheduled at the Rugby Club, in two weeks.

The recent meetings still revolved around the (ongoing) issues of re-siting the football-club shed, floodlighting the rear field (to which the County Council were absolutely against and constantly refused) and then, the small-sided football proposals.

On the evenings of the meeting, all the managers were present and had come in force and with hostility. They patiently went through their minutes and achievements. Pete was now vice-chairman and in total support of John regarding the potential developments. The two braced themselves when the meeting reached 'Any Other Business'.

John Foyle shot up with the question, 'Is this club supporting the proposed new changes from the FA to bring in small-sided football from under-10s down?'

John, in his new role as stand-in chairman answered, motioning Foyle to sit.

He cleared his throat.

'The Football Association have conducted a three-year study which will possibly be implemented as early as the beginning of next season.'

Geoff Swinden and Foyle jumped up like two jack-in-the boxes.

'Gents, please sit and hear me out.'

'This could involve non-competitive, small-sided games for boys *and* girls, on small pitches, with small goals and limited game-times. All ultimately for the benefit and development of the children.'

'Boys *and* girls?' shrieked Doug McDougall.

'How come we're suddenly not allowed to play in competitive leagues?' Swinden shouted from his seat.

'Yeah! And why are they discriminating against us?' joined Tony Woolfson.

'What can the club do to fight it?' McDougall was scowling.

'We don't agree, and we don't want it!' shouted Swinden.

'Isn't the club going to oppose the idea?' Woolfson asked.

'Yeah! Why hasn't the club done anything to try and stop it from happening?' Geoff quipped. 'Because it doesn't care, that's why!' he cried, pointing at the committee.

John stood up, glowering, hands on the table and beginning to quietly fume.

'Guys, guys, calm down!' He tried to pour oil on the water. 'Believe me, I am actually *not* against the idea!'

'I actually *agree* with the proposals,' he continued. 'As do Pete *and* Clare *and* the other committee members.'

'Yeah, it's okay for you! You've played competitive football since you were under-7s!' Swinden cried vehemently.

'Jesus, I have been there, and I've experienced the ridiculous situation of tiny boys trying to play football on men's pitches!' John was almost shouting now, trying to stay cool. 'Believe me, it doesn't work!'

'I don't understand how none of you, not one, can see that this will benefit the players, yourselves and FOOTBALL.' He shook his head. 'These boys from under-7s are INFANTS.'

'What you'll get in the long-term,' he continued, as the noise died down, 'are stronger, more confident players, because the kids and their skills will develop quicker.'

'What you'll get is ball-playing centre-halves and full backs, with players able to take opponents on and accurately pass the ball because they have had so much small-side practice and game-time!' He was nodding, remembering all his small-sided, practice matches.

'Then, when your teams reach under-11s,' he went on, 'you will have young, fit and skilful players who can compete on the bigger pitches in a competitive league.' He waited for a response, but none came. 'They won't be knackered, have knee problems or be fed up with not touching the ball. They will be raring to go!'

John cleared his throat. 'Now guys, please listen.' he said, waving Woolfson down for the third time.

'Believe me, this is an FA proposal, and whatever happens, *if* it goes through, this club – and any other club – will have to abide by those rules.' He looked around at the quieting managers.

'Understand that this has *nothing* to do with Grove Challengers. But if it goes through, under-7s through under-10s *will* be playing small-sided footy next season.'

He paused, awaiting a response, just getting hostile looks in return.

'You should embrace the idea and believe this will benefit boys football!' John smiled, sitting and taking a deserved sip of his warming *Morland's*.

'And girls football,' added Clare, with an ironic smile.

John Foyle smashed his fist onto the table, shaking the drinks.

'We don't want it, and you can't or won't do anything about it.' His eyes were bulging.

Dave Gomm

'And who are you to be telling us about this anyway? You haven't even been democratically voted on by the committee as chairman!'

John rolled his eyes at Pete. *Told you so, Pete!*

Fucking hell! No wonder Joe had resigned.

Who needed this shit?

'Any more "Any Other Business"?' asked Brenda, glancing furtively around and secretly hoping for no response.

The goals shed and the proposed floodlighting were the last items on the agenda.

The floodlighting was still being declined.

The most talked-about shed in the world remained in its spot until it was eventually demolished years later, in about 2012.

The back field was floodlit around the same time, allowing football and rugby training on dark, winter evenings.

Small-sided soccer was introduced by the FA in September 1999.

Chapter 30
Euro 2000

In June 2000, England had qualified by the skin of their teeth and via the play-offs for the finals of Euro 2000, jointly hosted in Holland and Belgium (a first for co-hosting).

Boily, Marc and Paddy had planned the Euro 2000 trip well in advance and were going to Belgium straight after the Portugal game. John had declined the trip and was happy to watch the tournament on TV at home. Before long, the three friends, minus John, sauntered across over the channel in Boily's old Citroen.

They had watched the Portugal game at John's house as the Bay Tree had been so packed on arrival; having waited fifteen minutes to get served, they went to the comfort of John's home, where the match was on TV and there was plenty of beer in the fridge.

England had started brightly and opened up an early 2-0 lead against Portugal. However, the joy was not to last; the England fans had to endure a stunning comeback from the skilful Portuguese, who fought back and eventually won by three goals to two. Long-suffering England fans, home and abroad, were dismayed and devastated with this setback.

It was a bad result, as this group-match defeat meant a result was necessary in their next game. This scheduled England against the old rival – Germany. Germany had also had a poor result – a 1-1 draw with Romania – to make this encounter a bit more interesting.

The huge numbers of England fans flooding across the channel attracted lots of attention and plenty of trouble, as the

Dutch, Germans and local Turks prepared for the 'soft' English. Droves of English fans had assembled in Brussels in anticipation of the first England v. Portugal game. The English fans had gone, by and large, for the experience and the result, but they sold themselves out with huge drinking bouts in the sun, where – as the English culture demanded – they drank and drank all day until they were hammered.

They consequently made easy targets for any opposition, thugs, fans or police and were capable of being set off like tinder to very swiftly become a drunken, menacing mob.

That match against Germany was scheduled to take place in Charleroi in the ageing Stade du Pays de Charleroi, which was deemed by many – and given the massive significance and stature of the two participating teams and their prospective support – to be too small. This stadium held a maximum capacity of 30,000, which could have been filled three times over.

40,000 England fans had crossed the channel to support their national team, so there were thousands of English, German and neutral fans in the town without tickets or the remotest chance of getting a ticket for the game.

Marc, Boily and Paddy had arrived in the centre of Charleroi, departing from Brussels at 9:30 am, without tickets for the game but with big anticipations. An epic day on the piss, surrounded by England fans, the big screens, endless beer and, of course, the chance of a result.

They had started drinking right away but chose to move away from the town centre, towards the Old Town, drinking in several small, quiet bars, playing pool, chewing the fat, taking the piss, and generally having a good time.

The atmosphere had been carnival-like all day. There were giant screens around the square, thousands of jovial England fans and massive numbers of which were dressed in medieval St. Georges' costumes, wearing helmets, holding shields and brandishing plastic swords. The party atmosphere, fuelled by sunshine, good company and drink made it a party worth being at. And the England fans loved it.

The three friends continued drinking and were having the crack. They met and talked with a group of Germans and had a great banter with them, until they were accosted and met by the 'Burnley Suicide Squad'. They interrupted their patter with their remarks and opinions, embarrassingly sending the amicable Germans diving for cover.

Marc thought it would be a good idea at this point to move on too, to somewhere quieter. They finished their drinks and ended up in a quieter Irish pub in the Place de la Bourse, just off the town centre.

The bar, as they remembered, was nevertheless still 'full and very lively'.

By now, they had been drinking all day.

Marc and Paddy were happy pissed and approaching a state of near oblivion.

Marc felt his head clouded and spinning.

It inevitably happened that – in the midst of Charleroi's delightful and historical squares and avenues, full of bars and restaurants, and full of English fans – trouble kicked off.

The trouble flared as police took action, deciding to close that same Irish pub for safety reasons, because things had started to get too lively as it filled with large numbers of England fans. The decision was made by the police to close the bar to new customers. As the riot police closed in, some England fans decided to barricade themselves inside the bar, chanting and launching beer bottles and chairs at the approaching police.

The riot police reacted with tear-gas, trying to eke out the trouble-makers by force as they attempted to storm the bar. Officers grappled and wrestled innocent and guilty alike as they dashed out of the bar. Many of these England fans were not troublemakers at all, just fathers, sons and mates who had previously been having a drink in a foreign city amongst their kind and in anticipation of their team doing well.

Marc, Boily and Paddy were playing pool, and had been for some time, in that same bar. They had been drinking all day and had no idea of any problems or issues until a chair came flying in through the window and showered the group of drinkers with glass

As the trouble outside the bar ensued (the police had closed it to prevent more England fans from getting in), the three friends, perturbed by the chair incident and hostility outside, thought seriously about getting out.

Given the previous week's events, the lads had a little trepidation regarding the potential actions of the authorities.

'Fuck me!' Marc exclaimed, with some concern. 'What's fucking going on?'

Boily looked up, shrugged and took his next shot.

England fans crowded to the window.

'Hey, Marc,' Paddy whispered. 'I've got a bad feeling about this.'

'What d'ya mean, Paddy?' asked Marc, carefully balancing his beer on the edge of the table.

'I've got a feeling.' Paddy seemed nervous. 'This is all going to go tits-up!'

'Like last week?'

'C'mon, Paddy,' replied Marc, sympathetically. 'Chill out, everything will be okay.'

'No mate, it's not what I'm feeling.' Paddy really did look troubled by the events.

'Come on, boys?' he pleaded, pointing to the window.

'We haven't got a fucking clue what's going on out there!'

'Fuck all's going on!' Boily interjected, sinking the last of his lager.

Marc and Paddy were both nervously staring out at the window, through the crowd, into the square.

'What's up with you two?' Boily looked at them disdainfully. 'Have you gone fucking soft? I'm getting another beer.'

Paddy ignored his goading.

'Let's get to another bar?' he pleaded to Marc. 'Somewhere quieter?'

'No, we're sound staying here!' interrupted Boily.

'You're wrong, mate. I vote we get the fuck out of here now before any more trouble starts.' Paddy was now desperate to move on.

Outside, through the broken window, smoke and riot police could be seen across the square and close by to the bar.

'Hey, Boily! We're thinking of getting out. Paddy thinks there's more trouble coming.'

Marc was in two minds, fuddled with the drink. 'What d'you think?'

'Fuck off!' Boily wasn't interested in moving on. 'I'm happy here.'

'If you wanna move on, do it.' He waved them off towards the door. 'This'll blow over in a minute. I'll take me chances here. And I'll catch up with you later.'

Marc looked up at Paddy – who was usually not averse to danger – and sensed his worry.

Fuck.

He didn't want any shit.

Paddy missed his shot, handing the pool cue over to Boily with a curt nod.

'Come on, Steve,' implored Marc to the nonplussed Boily.

'We don't want to get caught up in any trouble.'

'Why should we?' retorted Boily, clearing the table with the black and a flourish.

'We're doing fuck all wrong!' He grinned. 'More beer!'

Fuck Boily, thought Paddy. He was not happy being there anymore.

The helmets, sticks, and shields of the riot police could be glimpsed in a line just outside the bar, like they were waiting to pounce.

'Well, fuck it, mate. I'm going,' hissed Paddy with heartfelt emotion.

Marc looked at Paddy long and hard. He was absolutely fucking serious.

'I think I'm gonna go with him!' shouted Marc to Boily.

'Take our fucking chances!' Paddy winced, moving away.

'Whatever, whatever.' Boily continued waving dismissively, grinning and tipping his glass in salute.

'See you losers in some time.' Boily stood there in his England shirt with his legs spread-eagled.

Marc followed Paddy to the door.

Evidently, there seemed to be no immediate trouble in the square, just a thin line of police half-way. The place was still semi-lit, and people thronged about. The floodlights had started to cast deep shadows on the architecture. The two friends, absolutely pissed up but as gentle as lambs, approached a Belgian riot police officer in the middle of the line.

'Fuck me, he's only eleven,' whispered Marc, as they approached.

'Guys, where are you going?' asked the fresh-faced officer, in perfect English, as they approached the line.

'Yeah, we're just going to another bar, then home, back to Brussels, our hotel, the train station,' blurted Paddy.

'No, you can't. You can't get through here,' the helmeted officer replied. 'Everything is closed.'

'Come on, mate,' Paddy pleaded. 'We just want to get home. We don't want any trouble.'

Instinctively, all three of them looked back at the line of bars as a great whooping sound came from that direction.

'No, guys, go back the way you came. We are securing this area.'

Marc and Paddy, sensing an issue, stopped and looked at each other.

The three men looked back towards the bar, where Boily was still knocking it back with oblivious abandon.

English, German and local Turks had set up the atmosphere throughout the day. The 300 Belgian riot police were not about to be compromised by a bunch of drunken thugs.

'Stand still.' He hesitated, but only briefly. He had his orders. 'Please remain where you are.'

He appraised them efficiently. 'You cannot go through here,' he announced, looking around at his colleagues for support.

Suddenly, something in the young officer's mind snapped to a decision.

He momentarily turned from Boy-Scout cadet to Gestapo officer.

'You are under arrest!' he barked, gesturing for help from a nearby colleague.

'Arrest them!'

'What?' Paddy was crestfallen. Marc looked astonished.

'Hands out!' demanded the Belgian policeman.

The handcuffs went on Marc and Paddy.

'Shit!' Marc couldn't believe what was happening.

Earlier, in similar circumstances, the police had jumped on England fans as they broke the cover, many gagging, holding their hands over their mouths and vomiting from the effect of tear-gas.

Paddy and Marc were relatively unscathed and quite lucky.

The snatch-squads eventually arrested 174 English fans and attempted to deport 139 of them, with 35 facing jail term on disorder, fighting and vandalism charges.

Marc spent a quiet night in the 'very comfortable' cells provided by the Belgian police in anticipation of trouble. He was given chocolate and a bottle of water and was able to get his head down and have a fitful night's rest.

Paddy didn't fare quite as well. He was taken off in a different direction (he looked a bit more alternative with dreadlocks, nose-rings and earrings). He was escorted to and deposited into a mobile cage, which housed hundreds of the 'worst-looking offenders', and he was treated like a criminal like all the others in the cage.

After a while, some of the ringleaders in the cage decided to 'have a go' at the police.

The response was alarming and clinical. Water cannons! The police attacked the mob in the cage with raging torrents of icy water, drenching them and smashing them backwards and off their feet, crashing them into one another and forcing them to the back of the cage.

Paddy saw it coming and dashed to the back of the cage to the shelter of the toilets. He tried to force the door open, but it was too late. The door was secured by many men with the same idea who had reached the latrine before him.

The jet of icy water hit him below the knees, smashing him and several others into the rear wall. They were freezing and in pain, disorientated and bruised, soaked, freezing, pissed, fucked and just about ready to die.

He was awake all night, worried about his fellow inmates, catching his death of cold and nursing a bitch of a hangover. His lips were swollen and cracked, his ribs ached, and his feet were blocks of ice.

Around 7: 30 am, the police simply opened up the gates and shouted, 'You can leave now!' The scowling fans shuffled out, disgruntled and dirty, but relieved.

As Marc gingerly crossed the now deserted square in the pale morning light, he remarkably bumped into Paddy, walking in from another direction.

'Fucking hell, Paddy! What happened to you?' he asked, grinning madly at the state of his mate.

'You don't want to know, mate.' Paddy smiled weakly, grabbing hold of Marc.

He was limping and had a big, red patch on his forehead.

'Where's Boily?' asked Paddy.

'Fuck knows.' Marc steadied his mate as they set off across the square. 'He would definitely have been arrested though!' He chortled in anticipation of the result. 'They were getting ready to storm that bar again.'

They walked back to the station and caught an early train back to Brussels.

They dozed off on the journey back, barely talking.

The train station was quiet with commuters beginning to come and go on the early morning trains as they stepped off the train, attracting some choice looks from the locals.

They walked back through the awakening Brussels to their hotel.

The hotel was quiet, almost serene, as the two exhausted friends entered and made their way up the staircase to their shared room.

Marc stopped at the door, winked at Paddy, knocked rapidly and jokingly shouted, 'Room Service!'

'Fuck off!' came the reply in the dulcet tones of Westwood.

'I didn't order any fucking room service!'

Paddy pushed the door open, and a tousle-headed Boily raised himself up on one elbow in his bed.

'Fuck me!' He burst out laughing. 'What a state! What happened to you, Paddy? You look like you're going to peg it! Ha ha!'

'I was going to save you a bit of pizza, but I wasn't sure who was coming back, so I ate it!' he said, rolling back over in bed.

'What happened to you, Steve?' Marc was really curious. 'How did you get out?'

'Just had a couple more pints, watched the football, and played another game of pool. Then, when we left, there was no one about – couple of gobbie Turks, but no coppers,' he explained. 'Just walked back to the station, got me pizza and came home to bed. Slept like a fuckin' log!'

'What and no trouble?' Marc and Paddy couldn't believe his luck!

'I told you there'd be no trouble.' He looked Paddy over again.

'Not so sure now though. You look like you've had a bit.' He laughed again. 'Cor, you do look fucking rough, Paddy!'

Paddy was shaking his head in disbelief

'How did England get on then?' He tentatively enquired of his lucky pal

'Did we win?'

Chapter 31
Bisham Abbey

Upon returning to training at Bisham in September, the boys were put through their paces. A few new lads of good ability had joined, bolstering the numbers again. All these under-14s were good footballers; they were, effectively, the best local players in their local teams and were now in the hands of this Football League set-up.

Wycombe Wanderers FC was probably typical of the way things worked. Dwight and Ritchie had been at OUFC for a couple of seasons and were doing quite well; although, John had learnt that Rich was now preferred at left-back, which was quite frankly a waste of his sublime attacking and goal-scoring talent.

Mark Brind, on John's recommendation, had spent the last half of the season with Ollie at Wycombe but had since dropped back to his age-group with Grove.

So, they continued to train and then play at Risborough on Sundays, much like last season.

The new boys were bigger, which left Ollie, Liam and Danny the smallest lads at the club. Some boys were actually built like men and so it was the most acute difference ever seen in an age group.

The winter months set in, and Wycombe continued to play home and away fixtures against well-organised league teams. After training one Monday night in March, Aidy approached the dads as the boys filtered off towards their parents.

'Risborough, Sunday, boys.'

Thumbs-up to the dads.

'10:30 kick-off. Be there by 9:30, please?'

'Watford,' said Colin Barson to John and Paddy, as they strolled towards the car park.

'Yeah, should be a good one!' said John, sauntering off. 'See you Sunday, Col!'

'See you, Paddy!' The three dads and their boys jumped into their cars.

'Bye guys!' Ollie waved them off as he took his seat next to John.

The match was held on Sunday, on a frosty, clear day over at Princess Risborough, and it was good – end to end, with the coaches watching intently. They swapped the boys around at will, changing positions, formations and personnel. The friendly match, fast-paced and skilful, was competitive and enjoyable. It ended in a 5-5 draw where both teams had played lots of good attacking football and ended up with some good moves and a couple of cracking goals. The boys were red-faced and panting by the time the game ended.

The score, as usual, was largely irrelevant – the scrutiny was focused mainly on the performers.

Afterwards, Aidy and his coaches gave a quick resume and thank you, as they always did.

The dads analysed the teams and then their boys' performances with their expert knowledge as usual! They agreed that it had been a good game and performance by the Wycombe boys.

John had taken his Canon EOS out before the game to see whether he could get a couple of action shots, as he sometimes did.

When the squad emerged from the changing rooms – all clad in Wycombe blue quarters – he politely asked Aidy if he could get a team photo.

Aidy had no problem with this, and John managed to get a great group shot with Aidy and Malcolm on either end of the photo.

The resulting photo was a good one with, yet again, an astonishing size difference between the biggest and the smallest. *Men against boys!*

As the boys finished off their sandwiches and made their way out to their dads, Aidy popped up again with a wave.

'See you at training on Monday, guys!'

Monday saw John and Ollie speeding down the M40 with Blur's *Country House* blaring from the BMW's sound system. They sang along in a good mood. The family had just had a cracking weekend – Oxford, bobbing along in Division 1 (now Championship), had thrashed Stoke City 5-1 on Saturday with goals from Beauchamp, Francis (2) and the affable and lovable Stuart Massey (2). This win was after a great away win the previous week at Manchester City by two goals to nil (Beauchamp and Cook).

As they pulled into the car park at Bisham Abbey, Colin and Liam walked over to join them, and the boys sprinted to the nets of footballs lying on the side of the pitch.

It was a cold, black night, with a touch of frost starting and a light, fine rain drifting in the beam of the floodlights. The lights brightly reflected on the silvery-wet playing surface, as the boys started their kick-ups, skills and ball-work in front of the coaches.

John looked on in admiration as the training game started. Ollie was still playing left-midfield despite his size and despite being mainly right-footed. He buzzed around like a hornet, playing as if his life depended on it. He played with skill, guts and determination.

The dads watched the training match in the drizzle, with their collars pulled up and hats pulled down to stave off the wet. Paddy O'Brien hopped from foot to foot, trying to stay warm. They were proud of their lads for being part of this set-up, and the boys were in good company – amongst the best footballers in the county. They were fit, skilful and savvy. All of that training was beginning to turn them into proper footballers. They lived and died for their football.

Malcolm eventually blew up to end the wind-swept training session at 9 am.

As the boys dispersed, Paddy nudged John in the ribs to get his attention. He pointed over to the far edge of the pitch. The thin rain continued to drizzle silver in the floodlights.

Aidy had beckoned a few of the lads over to him.

John, Paddy, Roy Evans and Colin looked on as the three boys singled out and made their way towards him at the far corner of the AstroTurf.

The boys were Danny, Liam and Ollie. The three smallest boys left in the set-up.

John looked on, not quite knowing what to expect.

Aidy talked, and the boys nodded.

Aidy waved his arms around. The boys continued to nod, listening intently.

They stood there for some time, with Aidy getting more animated.

Eventually, he shook them all by the hand, one by one.

As they turned away, he gave them the thumbs-up.

The trio turned and walked back towards their parents across the sparkling green pitches.

Aidy turned around and walked off in the other direction.

The boys shrugged in begrudging acceptance.

'What's going on, Liam?' Colin asked his son as the lads reached their parents.

'He says he's not happy with our development, Dad.'

'He says we are welcome to keep training with the group, but we won't be able to play for Wycombe again.' Ollie looked downcast.

'What, so you can train but can't play?' John gazed down questionably at his son.

'Development?' Colin was pissed. 'What does he mean "not happy with their development"?'

'Size!' John knew something like this had been coming.

'Eh?' Colin looked quizzical.

'It's their size, Col! Have a look.' John pointed out the bigger boys, some nearly as big as their dads now, as they filed off the pitch. 'That's what he means by "development"!' He continued, 'They're too small *now*!'

'But these are the only small boys left in the whole squad!' Now Roy was getting angry.

'I've been on about this "men against boys" thing for bloody ages,' John went on, looking at the three boys. 'Now they are not big enough to fit in with the competitiveness of the bigger lads. They've just got rid of their three smallest players!'

'Yeah, but they are some of the most skilful,' argued Roy.

'Doesn't matter. He's talking about their size.' John didn't agree, but he could see why. 'That's why he's said they can continue to train with the team.' He shrugged.

'Well I'm not fucking hanging around here to train and not get a game,' snorted Colin.

'Jesus, it's not your shout, Col.' John grabbed the retreating Colin's shoulder.

'Boys, what do you think? Do you want to train but not be involved in the games?' John looked at each of them for a response.

The boys looked up at the men, shrugging and unsure.

'Well, I reckon we ought to give them the chance to sleep on it and have a good think about it.' John was trying to be reasonable.

'What d'you reckon Ollie?' he asked, looking steadfastly at his young son.

Ollie shrugged, nonplussed.

'I dunno, Dad,' chirped Ollie. 'Right now, I don't really want to. But you're right, we probably need to think about it.'

'Well, I'm not going to think about it,' snarled the diminutive and feisty Liam.

'I'm fucked if I'm staying here just for the training.' Swearing in front of the parents was particularly unusual, but by now he was mad.

'I'll be off. Don't care what anyone thinks,' he snarled. 'I can go back to my club and play football with me mates every week!'

Ollie and Danny looked at each other, then instinctively, up at their dads.

'Well, it's not the end of the world. Come on, let's get off. We can chat in the week.'

Roy was seeing the coaches' reasoning.

Colin wasn't so convinced about the coach.

'What a sneaky little coward that fuckin' Aidy is!' he spat towards the retreating figure in the distance. 'Not man enough to tell us to our faces!'

'Okay, well, let's get back to the car.' John and the other dads turned on their heel and walked away.

The boys looked over their shoulders at the Bisham Abbey pitches for the last time, and throwing their boot-bags over their shoulders, they headed off into the drizzle, trailing behind their parents, blond hair streaked and greasy with the rain.

Chapter 32
Football Results

So, upon writing and finishing this story, a novel based largely on truth about the wonderful time we had with the kids. All the experiences, the winning and losing, the laughter and tears, challenges and heartaches, I suppose the moral is that these memoires and jottings are just the human ones.

The innocence of the set-up in those days is deteriorating with political correctness by the day, so I am privileged to have experienced the manufacture of a football team from a mere idea. The fact that I was completely clueless when we started the team, the incredible size of the pitches and the goals compared to those little fellows, all made a mockery of trying to begin a proper boys' football team.

That the boys were happy to start under these conditions and embrace them, is testament to their wish just to play football under any circumstances.

They really were great times; both the boys and their families were brilliant company. We had wonderful times, the weekly games, the trek and convoy to the away games, the tournaments, the sixes. Thanks to all of you who were involved – it was a great journey.

When the three lads were rejected by Wycombe, the coach could have come over to the parents and explained that the club were happy to retain, train and include them on a weekly basis- pending their development *physically*. After all, they all grew up into men, they were just late developers. Had this been explained, to us waiting parents, and had they told us they were very happy to continue with the lads, who knows, they may well have stayed?

We all know that small players can make it if they persevere, provided they are good enough. So, the end of a football career for those boys, and thousands of others, who were good enough, arrived prematurely – and the knock that they took at the end deflated them and many did not flourish in football after this.

Add to this the massive influx of foreign coaches and players that have flooded the game today, and you can see why tons of local talent has been squeezed out of the top-level.

The Grove and Abingdon players that didn't make it into club academies probably continued playing their local football unencumbered and enjoyed kicking around with their mates for years after. I am sure these lads were happier, playing week after week with and against their mates, whilst living their normal lives.

Skilful as they were at seven years of age, and despite years at Oxford United FC, Dwight and Ritchie never played for the Oxford United first team, or professionally. So far as I am aware, from our group, only Jack King went on to play League football, joining Preston in 2012 and helping the League One side achieve promotion to the Championship in 2014–15. Jack then had short spells with Scunthorpe and Stevenage.

Ollie played little football following his exit from Wycombe, later turning to skate-boarding with some of his mates. Most of the lads grew up to take sensible jobs. A few years later as adults, the nucleus of the early team, Mark Brind, Ritchie Claydon, Liam Revell, Sean Webb, and Billy McDonald, joined together at East Hendred Reserves, where they had a cracking little League and Cup-winning team as men.

Small-sided soccer was embraced and accepted, and it continues to grow. The players have much more of the ball and are able to grow as their skills are honed on pitches and goals that are playable and fun – ones where they can express themselves and contribute.

The larger pitches and goals, as discussed in the early chapters, were the norm back then. The small-sided FA changes were great for the development of boys and girls football.

I am sure that the adults reading this book and who have played football will remember those days with great nostalgia, and I am glad we experienced it and remember the games with a twinkle in our eyes and a lot of laughter.

Football will always be our glorious game and will always attract fans and players from an early age despite the expense and its shortcomings, with current players diving and rolling around as if they've been shot while trying to get their opponents red-carded!

Oxford United's slump has been arrested, and the climb back has been great and quite well supported recently with some great football being played.

Championship here we come!

(This comment is fluid and could be subject to change)!

Grove Challengers eventually got their own clubhouse which is, funnily enough, located near the site of the fabled old goals-shed. They continue to thrive and grow as a club with boys and girls football.

Boily and Marc still go off to their various Villa and England trips.

I stopped going because, I'm sorry, I just can't keep up.

My All-time Oxford United 11;

Jimmy Barron

Dave Langan   Maurice Kyle   Matt Elliott   Bobby McDonald

Kevin Brock Ray Houghton Trevor Hebberd Joey Beauchamp

John Aldridge   Dean Saunders

Subs; Roy Burton, Gary Smart, Colin Clarke, David Fogg, Gary Briggs, Jim Magilton, Les Phillips and Paul Moody.

Honorary mentions for amazing short-term contributions; John Byrne, Billy Hamilton, Dean Windass, Bobby Ford.

Sue me Ron!

Edited by PaperTrue.

Thanks to Martin Brodetsky for dates and records from *Oxford United: The Complete Record.*

Printed in Great Britain
by Amazon